the Truth is Out There

the Truth is Out There

X-FILES VOLUME TWO
EDITED BY JONATHAN MABERRY

PUBLISHING

Become our fan on Facebook **facebook.com/idwpublishing**
Follow us on Twitter **@idwpublishing**
Check us out on YouTube **youtube.com/idwpublishing**
Instagram **instagram.com/idwpublishing**
deviantART **idwpublishing.deviantart.com**
Pinterest **pinterest.com/idwpublishing/idw-staff-faves**

978-1-63140-526-6   19 18 17 16   1 2 3 4

COVER TREATMENT BY
WES DRIVER

EDITED BY
JUSTIN EISINGER

EDITORIAL ASSISTANCE BY
LESLIE MANES AND
SARAH DUFFY

COLLECTION DESIGN BY
RICHARD SHEINAUS/
GOTHAM

Ted Adams, CEO & Publisher
Greg Goldstein, President & COO
Robbie Robbins, EVP/Sr. Graphic Artist
Chris Ryall, Chief Creative Officer/Editor-in-Chief
Matthew Ruzicka, CPA, Chief Financial Officer
Alan Payne, VP of Sales
Dirk Wood, VP of Marketing
Lorelei Bunjes, VP of Digital Services
Jeff Webber, VP of Licensing, Digital and Subsidiary Rights
Jerry Bennington, VP of New Product Development

IDW founded by Ted Adams, Alex Garner, Kris Oprisko, and Robbie Robbins

For international rights, contact licensing@idwpublishing.com

TABLE OF CONTENTS

INTRODUCTION

By Dean Haglund

L et me explain how deadlines work. Editors often asks a writer *months* in advance if they would like to contribute a story to an anthology. Then the writer says yes and promptly forgets all about it 'til a crushing deadline suddenly pops up on their calendar and they work feverishly to complete their work. Flushed with coffee and inspiration and, if they are lucky, some notes, they plow through the night and lay out some brilliant prose.

Or, if you are like me, you get completely overwhelmed with so many projects, podcast invites, crazy convention appearances, and a successful Kickstarter project yet to be completed, all the while moving to a new country Down Under and getting used to funny colored money. (Also the spelling of "colour" is funny down here.) Then you lose your file that was perhaps shaping up to be a story, plus you try to find some 240 voltage electrical converters that can power up your old computers all the while making sure the dogs are fed.

Anyway, clearly the editors felt sorry for my predicament and asked if I could write an introduction for this anthology, with at least three emails asking when will I have *that* completed. Luckily, being on the other side of the International Date Line, my answer is always "tomorrow."

Welcome to the introduction!

And, it's an introduction to *The X-Files*.

As an actor on *The X-Files* for ten years, I still remember the thrill of a new script arriving on my doorstep. After counting how many lines I would have to learn, I would sit back and have another exciting episode unfold before me. It's because I love great writing. Writing is such a fundamental power in the growth of our civilization. Look at the following words and see if you can determine what I am trying to say. Of course you can, because somewhere you learned how to string all these symbols together to make the words that have agreed upon meaning, and these meanings can be arranged in such a way as to affect emotions. How powerful is that?

And I like reading. And I like reading stuff about writing, and then writing about reading stuff that was written. Hence this introduction.

If *The X-Files* stood out for anything it was about great writing. In fact, I owe my career to the great writing those creators slaved over episode after episode. *The X-Files* has been immeasurable in its ripple effect throughout all the arts and culture in general. Everyone knows about *The X-Files*, even the (few) people who never watched it. It's become part of our shared global culture.

The very essence of *The X-Files*, at its heart, is the enduring mystery of the void. Both the void of the ultimate "truth" and the void of an enduring relationship between two great-looking FBI agents that base their affection for each other on respect for each other's intelligence and morality. In fact, the phrase *The Truth is Out There* reflects this endless quest, that something as subjective and ambiguous as "truth" is forever "out there," removed from one's personal connection to one's own truth, and fighting through endless levels of government conspiracies and bureaucratic red tape to find the universal truth that is ultimately un-findable, forever just beyond grasp of a stoic agent, determined never to waver from his goal. And by his side, a partner, every bit his equal, as focused on her search as he is on his; the difference in their point of views only strengthen the bond between them.

And how about that world those writers created? A larger syndication of shadowy figures working in unison with (maybe) an alien invasion force opposed only by a few agents and a ragtag group that included my character, Langly, one of the Lone Gunmen. As one producer said to me, "The beauty of the structure is, even if you get to the bottom of this ring, there is very likely a larger circle of overlords controlling them, and so on, leading one to forever try to untangle the massive conspiracy." Imagine the depth of possibilities for any creator to come in at any level, any angle, and explore the nooks and crannies of undiscovered nuggets.

So let's go forward to the future of mythology. Of course, at the time of this writing I signed an NDA (nondisclosure agreement) and so cannot speak much to the future of *The X-Files* story arc, but I can raise my arms in celebration, my fist in defiance, my voice in good cheer for all those who are about to add their minds and talents to that world.

Come to it with spirit of fun and adventure, open minds and hearts aflutter. Charge in and tip toe through the following stories and find again, for the first time, the very thing that you loved about *The X-Files* in the first place.

It was personal to each of us, and universal to all.

We all still want to believe. We all still believe that the truth is out there. And it's in here. Turn the page and join the hunt…

— Dean Haglund, Actor
  Richard "Ringo" Langly

the
Truth
is Out
There

DEAD RINGER
By Kelley Armstrong

ELK STATE FOREST, PENNSYLVANIA
12th OCTOBER, 1993, 2:10 a.m.

Aubrey peered into the darkness. That was all she saw—darkness. She knew there were trees and other tents, but even the embers of last night's bonfire had gone out.

Never leave the tent without a buddy.

That was rule number one of Brownie camp. And it seemed so easy to obey, but here Aubrey was, leaving her tent alone, because, if she didn't, she was going to wet the sleeping bag, and that would be…. She shuddered to think how bad that would be, her first overnight camp, the little baby who peed her sleeping bag. It wouldn't matter if she'd tried—really tried—to wake up Leader Beth; no one would believe her. So, flashlight in hand, she slipped from the tent alone.

She didn't dare turn on her light yet, so she felt her way with her feet and hands, pretending she was playing Blind Man's Bluff. Just a game. That's all. Not walking into the deep, dark forest alone.

The cloud-covered moon lit her way just enough that she saw the trees before she bashed into them. She could hear the forest now, the wind rustling in the leaves and the twigs cracking underfoot and the burble of the nearby stream. That was all she heard—nothing scary, just nature, like in the forest behind her house. Leader Beth said there wasn't anything bigger than a fox out here, and if you saw a fox, you were lucky, because they almost always ran before you spotted them.

Once she seemed far enough from the tents, Aubrey turned on her flashlight. And that's when she saw something much bigger than a fox. It looked like one of the other girls, in her pajamas. Just standing there.

Aubrey flicked off the light quickly, before she got caught. Then, she listened for voices, presuming the girl was waiting for her buddy to pee. No voices came, and, as the clouds passed, Aubrey could see the figure in the moonlight. It wasn't a girl from camp. It was a boy.

He looked her age, seven or eight, and he was just standing there, kind of staring but not really, his gaze not seeming fixed on anything at all. He wore blue pajamas with some sports team design. He had dark hair, and she'd have thought she was too far to see the color of his eyes, but they were wide open and glowing faintly blue in the moonlight. His pale skin glowed, too, and she could see a bruise on his cheekbone. His nose was crooked, with a splotch of red under it, like dried blood.

Did people sleepwalk with their eyes open? She thought she'd heard that they did, but where could the boy have come from? They'd hiked almost a mile from the road before setting up camp, and the leaders said there was no one else around. No houses. No cabins. No other campers.

Aubrey stepped back, and a twig cracked under her bare foot. The boy's chin shot up, and his head turned her way. He squinted to see in the dark. He didn't move, though. Didn't say a word. Just looked in her direction.

"Who are you?" she called.

He blinked hard. She turned on the flashlight and shone it at him, but, weirdly, that *didn't* make him blink. He looked straight into the light. Standing as still as a statue. The hairs on her neck rose and something deep in her stomach told her to run. But that was silly. It was just a boy.

"Who are you?" she asked again.

"Who are you?" he repeated. Then his lips pursed, and his head tilted, and he said, "No… you mean who am I?" His nose wrinkled, and he seemed to think very hard. Then, he smiled suddenly, as if the answer just hit him. "I am Jason Kent. I live at 534 Peachtree Lane. In Comstock." A pause. Then, a frown, his eyes rolling up, as if searching for something. A grin as he found it. "Yes. You. What is your name?"

"Aubrey…" she said carefully. "Are you lost?"

"Lost?" He seemed to consider the word. "No. Not lost. Found." A bright smile. "You found me. Thank you." Another pause. Then, "What should we do now, Aubrey?"

She glanced over her shoulder, toward camp. "I think—"

"We could play a game," he said. "I know many games."

Those hairs prickled again.

Stop that. He's just confused. I'd be confused too if I got lost out here. Confused and scared.

"We could dance," he said.

"Dance?"

His eyes lit up, and he seemed to glow, his whole body illuminated in the flashlight beam. "Yes, can you hear the music? It's so beautiful. We can…"

The light around him ebbed as he frowned. "No, I do not hear the music anymore."

He dropped his head and made a strange noise, and she realized he was crying. She took a slow step toward him. He looked up, tears glistening on his pale and freckled cheeks, the glow getting stronger, as if the flashlight beam were reflecting off metal, blinding her. She reached down to turn the light off. She flicked the switch. Nothing happened. The boy just kept watching her, the light around him blinding, and she looked down to see her flashlight was off.

"The music is gone, Aubrey," he said, tears trickling down. "Gone forever now."

That's when she turned and ran, screaming, for camp.

"Are you sure this is a shortcut?" Scully said, peering out the window as the endless forest whizzed past.

Mulder turned the wheel sharply, narrowly avoiding a suicidal squirrel. "Mmm, not exactly a shortcut."

"You said—"

"I said I knew *another* way. One that avoided traffic." He waved at the empty two-lane road. "When's the last time we passed a car?"

"When's the last time we passed a *house*? Where the hell are we, Mulder?"

"Pennsylvania," he said.

"Are we even going to *get* to New York in time? The symposium starts at eight tomorrow."

"Thursday."

"What?"

"The symposium is Thursday. First, we have…" He pulled a folder from under the seat and flourished it. "…an X-File. Which just happens to be on the way." He looked out at the forest. "Relatively speaking."

She opened the file. "And you couldn't have just said so? Before we left?"

"Spontaneity, Scully. Your life needs more spontaneity. I am providing it. Along with a conveniently located X-File that I'm sure you'll find fascin—"

"No," she said, slapping the file shut. "Hell, no."

"All right, Comstock is a little out of our way, but—"

"I understand that you want to know what happened to your sister. I understand that you think you *do* know, and you want proof. But we cannot chase down every mildly unusual reappearance of a missing child."

"Mildly unusual? Jason Kent was found two hundred miles from his home wandering in the forest, two hours after his father kissed him goodnight. Short of hitching a ride on a passing jet, there's no way he could have traveled that far."

"Then someone is mistaken about the timeline."

"A seven-year-old Girl Scout Brownie found him. She said he was acting strangely."

"He would be, wouldn't he? If he'd been abducted from his bed and left in a forest?"

"She said he glowed with a bright light."

"She's *seven*, Mulder. Did she see Santa's sleigh drop him off, too?"

"No." He sounded disappointed. "There were no reports of unusual lights in the sky that night. However, young Jason reappeared with a few medical anomalies that you might find interesting."

"Such as…"

"Memory loss. While he can recall basic facts and skills, like the letters of the alphabet or how to tie his shoes, he has very little memory of his life before the abduction. He only vaguely remembers his parents, and he has no recollection of his grandparents, or his friends or his school teacher."

"Retrograde amnesia. Most commonly occurring after a severe trauma, like being abducted from his bed. By *humans*."

"He also has a birthmark on his cheek that wasn't there before. His nose appears to have been broken and long healed, despite no evidence of a previous injury in his medical records. He also shows a broken—and healed—arm, several healed ribs, and what appears to be a large birthmark under his hair, though one could argue that, given the location, that could have appeared previously and gone unnoticed." He glanced over at her. "I'm pointing that out before you do. As for the rest…"

She said nothing.

"At a loss for a rational explanation, Scully? Be still my heart."

"No, I'm thinking. I don't know what would cause the sudden appearance of long-healed injuries—"

"Alien abduction coupled with temporal disruption."

"—but I will need to examine the boy before I draw any conclusions."

"I would expect no less. I notice, however, that your wording suggests you do intend to examine him."

She said nothing.

He smiled. "Admit it. I've piqued your interest."

"No." She waved at the road sign ahead. "But, given that Comstock is only five miles away, there's no point turning back now. I'm humoring you. This time."

"That's all I ask."

"Agent Mulder, FBI." Mulder flashed his badge to the pleasant-looking brunette who'd answered the Kents' door. "This is my partner, Agent Scully. Are you Janice Kent?"

She nodded. "Is this about Jason?"

"It is. We'd like to ask a few questions—"

"Of course," she cut in, with an anxious glance over her shoulder. "Why don't we step out onto the porch?"

"Who is it?" called a man's voice.

Mrs. Kent said nothing, frozen there, clearly torn between answering and pretending she hadn't heard him. Footsteps sounded, and her shoulders sagged. A man appeared. Late thirties, balding, his beefy face lined with stress, his blue eyes bloodshot. Scully detected the faint whiff of alcohol as he approached but saw no signs of inebriation. From the look of his clothes, he'd slept in them, and they were likely permeated with boozy sweat from the night before.

Mulder repeated his introduction. Scully watched Mrs. Kent's face, noting the tension there and that she was braced for trouble but cringing, too, as if she feared embarrassment more.

"We were just about to speak to your wife," Scully said. "We can do that out here, and then we can talk to you. I'm sorry to intrude on what must be a difficult time."

"No intrusion at all," Kent said. "I'm glad someone's taking this mess seriously."

"I can assure you we're taking it very seriously," Scully said, earning her a raised eyebrow from Mulder. "Now, we'll speak to your wife first about your son's reappearance."

"It's not my son."

Mrs. Kent flinched. "John, please."

"All right," Scully said slowly, glancing down at the folder. "Then we were misinformed. Your stepson, I presume?"

"My son disappeared. This thing that came back is not him."

"John, please," Mrs. Kent whispered.

"I don't know what happened that night. But I know it wasn't natural. Neither is that thing that came back looking like my son."

"*John!*"

"Mrs. Kent?" Mulder said. "I hate to impose, but it was a long drive, and we didn't pass a restaurant in town. Is there any chance I could get a coffee?" He smiled. "Yawning during an interview is very unprofessional."

When she hesitated, Scully said, "What happened last week was extremely traumatic. Not just for Jason, but for both of you. The unusual circumstances make it even more difficult. Agent Mulder and I are accustomed to dealing with cases like this, and we fully understand the strain it puts on all involved."

Mrs. Kent nodded, her eyes closing in relief. "Yes, thank you. It does. I… I'll make that coffee. You can sit outside if you like."

They moved onto the porch as she disappeared into the house. Once they were seated, Kent said, "I know it sounds crazy, but that thing is not my son."

"Can you walk us through last Friday night?"

Kent did. His wife—a nurse—had been on night shift. Jason went to bed at eight. At twelve-thirty, Kent went in and gave his son a goodnight kiss. Four hours later, he awoke to a phone call saying Jason had been found in Elk State Forest. He'd thought it was a mistake. Then he found his son's bed empty.

"You say you kissed him goodnight at twelve-thirty?" Scully said. "Could you be mistaken on the time?"

"No. I watched Arsenio Hall, and then I went to bed, stopping in his room on my way past. There's no way he could have been in that forest a couple of hours later. That thing isn't my son."

"I understand Jason is experiencing amnesia," Scully said. "That will affect both his personality and his behavior toward you."

"It's not the damned amnesia. It's him. A parent knows his child, and that *thing* is not mine." He glanced back at the house and lowered his voice. "It stalks me."

Mulder frowned.

"That… thing. It follows me around. Janice says Jason's just studying me, trying to remember me better. But it's not studying. It's stalking. I fall asleep on the couch or in bed, and, when I wake up, it's right there, staring at me." He folded his hands, sank in his seat. "So, I don't sleep. I don't dare, because, one of these times, I'm going to wake up to a knife…"

He trailed off as he looked at them. "You think I'm crazy."

"No," Scully said. "I think—"

"I feel like I'm crazy. You know that? Like I'm losing my mind. Or I've already lost it. Can't quite decide which." A harsh laugh. "My son disappeared, and I never even realized he was gone. Then he turns up an impossibly far distance away, with impossible-to-explain marks, ones that should prove it's not Jason, and yet everyone acts like nothing's wrong. Like we should thank God for a miracle. It's not *God* behind this. If that's my son, then he's been possessed—"

"John!" Mrs. Kent said, nearly dropping the coffee tray as she stepped out.

Kent mumbled something and went inside. When Mrs. Kent turned back to them, her eyes glistened with tears. "I'm so sorry. I don't know what's gotten into him."

"I understand it's a traumatic situation," Scully said, taking the coffees from the tray. "With the amnesia, Jason's behavior will seem erratic and uncharacteristic. Your husband is coping with that as best he can. Counseling might help, if this continues."

"Have you observed the behavior your husband mentioned?" Mulder asked. "Jason following him about, watching him as he sleeps?"

"Watching him as he sleeps? John said that? No. Jason is sticking closer to us than usual, and at times he appears to be studying us, but the doctor said that's normal."

"As he struggles to remember you and form new memories," Scully said.

Mrs. Kent nodded.

"Would we be able to speak to Jason?" Mulder asked. "We have some questions for him."

"Of course. He's over at Heidi's place right now."

"Heidi…"

"Bannister." Mrs. Kent's face softened in a smile. "She's our local historian and gardener extraordinaire. She's been a godsend these last few days, helping Jason cope. As you might expect, no one understands what he's going through the way she does."

"Why's that?"

Mrs. Kent frowned, as if she expected them to know the answer. "Because the same thing happened to her when she was a little girl."

Mrs. Kent took them to Heidi Bannister's house, three blocks away. When no one answered the door, Mrs. Kent led them around back. There, they found the yard transformed into a massive garden.

"This is peppermint," a woman's voice said. "Notice the smell? It's used for calming upset stomachs. Now, over here, is catnip, which looks similar, but it's not going to help you feel better."

"Unless you're a cat," a boy piped up.

The woman's tinkling laugh answered. "That's right."

"Catnip is also called catmint. It's related to peppermint, which is why it looks like it."

"Excellent! See, you do remember. It's all about memory, Jason. The old and the new and sorting it out."

They walked past a greenhouse to see a blond woman in her forties, crouched beside a young boy as she pointed out plants in the garden. When the boy saw them, trepidation touched with anxiety crossed his face, as if he was frantically trying to place them, fearing they were yet more people he should recognize and didn't. Then, he saw Mrs. Kent, and his face lit up in a smile.

"Hey, Mom," he said. "Heidi's showing me the garden."

"So I see. And it's 'Ms. Bannister.'"

Heidi smiled. "That makes me feel old, and I feel quite old enough already."

"Don't we all," Mrs. Kent said with a laugh. "All right, then. If Ms. Bannister gave you permission to call her by her first name, then you may do that. Right now, though, we have guests. This is Agent Mulder and Agent Scully. They're from the FBI."

That same look, consternation and anxiety. Mulder hunkered down in front of the child. "You met the local police when you came back home, right?"

Jason nodded.

"Those were the Comstock police," Mulder said. "When you were found, that was the Pennsylvania force, which takes care of the state. The FBI is in charge of the whole country."

The boy's lips curved in a tentative smile. "That's a lot of police."

"It is. And they're all trying to figure out what happened to you. So they have a lot of questions. Is that okay?"

Jason nodded.

"Why don't we go inside," Heidi said. "It was almost time for a lemonade break anyway."

Questioning Jason didn't add anything to their file. He tried his best, but it was clear from his frustration that he wasn't holding anything back. He'd told the state and local PD everything he could, and his memory of the event showed no signs of improving.

As for his memory in general, the boy could, with prompting, recall significant people in his life, but he had no event-based memories to go with those recollections. He knew that Heidi had taught him to play the piano, and he could still play it, but he could not provide context for any of those lessons: where they took place or how old he'd been at the time. Likewise, he remembered nothing of the night of his abduction or the events before he was discovered in the forest. Even his recollection of being found was hazy. A forest? A girl? He remembered that he'd said something about dancing. He laughed as he said that.

"Weird, huh? Why would I talk to her about dancing? No wonder she ran away."

His mother assured him that he'd been confused and, as the doctor said, likely suffering from a blow to the head. A typical seven-year-old, Jason didn't seem too concerned. The dancing thing was weird, but nothing more.

Scully checked the birthmarks, which seemed exactly that: birthmarks. It also seemed as if his nose had been broken and healed. After that, Jason and his mother left, and Mulder turned his attention to Heidi.

"I hear the same thing happened to you as a girl," he said. "The sheriff seems to have left that out of his report."

She laughed. "Being a small town, that's not surprising. It was huge news at the time, and there's not a lot of that in Comstock. No need to remark on it when everyone here still remembers the story."

"Care to fill us in?"

"Of course."

At the age of twelve, Heidi Bannister—then Heidi Channing—had disappeared from her bed. In her case, though, her parents *did* realize she was gone… because she wasn't found by morning. For three days, the entire town searched for Heidi. Then, she appeared in a forest thirty miles away, wandering and confused. Like Jason, she could barely remember her own name and had forgotten most of her childhood memories.

"They never came back," she said. "I don't tell Janice that, because I'm hoping it'll be different for Jason. But I'm trying to prepare him, too. Help him focus on building new memories while asking those around him to talk about his past and fill it in for him."

Like Jason, she'd also returned with unusual marks on her body.

"May I ask what?" Scully said.

"Birthmarks mostly. On my torso and here."

She took a tissue from a box and tilted her head back. When the light hit Heidi's neck, Scully could make out dark splotches. Heidi rubbed at them with a tissue, taking off a thin layer of makeup, and they came clearer.

"I usually cover them," she said with a faint smile. "Part of my morning routine, like brushing my teeth. Otherwise, my poor husband gets funny looks when we go out."

Scully could see why. From a distance, the faint purple birthmarks looked like bruises, similar to those found with strangulation.

"I'm sure Sheriff Lyons has photos of the ones on my stomach," Heidi said. "You're welcome to examine me, but I'd prefer a little privacy for that."

"Understood. Did the doctor ever determine the cause of the marks?"

Heidi shook her head. "My parents took me to a dermatologist, who said they seemed to be normal birthmarks. It's a mystery. If you find an answer, I'd love to know."

"Do you otherwise have any idea what happened to you?"

"No more than Jason, I'm afraid."

Mulder leaned forward. "Were any theories circulated at the time?"

"Only alien abduction." She caught Scully's expression and laughed. "Sorry. I guess I'm not supposed to lead with that, am I? You have to remember it was the sixties. People were a lot quicker to jump to woo-woo theories." She grinned. "Especially out here, where herbs weren't the only thing people grew in their gardens. *Everyone* thought it was aliens." She sobered a little. "Mostly, I think, because it was better than the alternative."

"Which was?" Mulder asked.

She lifted her brows. "Twelve-year-old girl goes missing from her bed?"

"Sexual interference," Scully said. "They thought you'd been abducted by a predator."

Heidi nodded. "That was the prevailing theory when I disappeared. They had a suspect and everything. The local creepy guy who pays too much attention to little girls. My parents say people were about ready to lynch him. Then I turned up in the forest, showing no signs of assault, and people decided I'd been abducted by a less scary monster: little green men from outer space."

"Did she seem old to you?" Mulder asked Scully as they walked to the car.

"What?" Scully looked over startled by the question.

"How old would you guess Heidi Bannister is?"

"Well, if she went missing at twelve and that was twenty-five years ago, she'd be about thirty-seven. She might have joked about feeling old, but I'd say she looks just fine for her age."

"Hmm."

Scully paused and looked over the car roof at him. "What does that mean?"

"Something in her eyes. They seemed… older."

"Let me guess: that's a sign of alien abduction and temporal displacement?"

"No, just… an observation."

He climbed into the car before she could reply. She shook her head and got in with him.

The town sheriff—a past-retirement man named Lyons—made no apologies for leaving Heidi's story out of the official report.

"If anyone followed up, I'd have told them about it," he said. "You're following up, so I'm telling you."

"Wouldn't putting it in the report increase the *chances* of someone following up?" Scully asked.

"Yep," he said.

"Which you didn't want."

He shrugged. "Don't particularly want it. Don't particularly not want it. It's a local matter, and I'm not eager to have the Feds poking around my town, asking questions. You're here now, and if you come up with answers, I'll take them."

"Do *you* have any answers?" Mulder asked.

"Nope."

"Ms. Bannister seems to think the prevailing theory was alien abduction."

"Yep." Not so much as a flicker of dismay crossed the man's face.

"Any evidence to support that?" Mulder said.

"Besides the fact that two kids inexplicably disappeared twenty-five years apart? Under similar circumstances? Reappearing equally inexplicably? With inexplicable memory loss and physical marks? If you've got a better idea, I'm happy to hear it. I'm not set on aliens. Not going to dismiss the possibility either."

"I like how you think, Sheriff," Mulder said.

Lyons only shrugged, seeming neither flattered nor fearing mockery. "So, I'm guessing you want to see Heidi's case file?"

"Please."

That file added little to what Heidi had told them. The most interesting part for Scully was the photographs of the marks left on the girl's body: birthmarks around her neck and lines on her torso, almost like stretch marks, but running in random directions.

Scully held a photo at arm's length and studied it.

"It looks like she was attacked," Mulder said.

"It does, doesn't it?" Scully mused. "Strangled and stabbed in the abdomen. Yet the doctor's and dermatologist's reports make it clear they're just pigmentation irregularities. And on Jason, we have similar marks plus long-healed bones from fractures he never had."

"Ghosts," Mulder murmured.

"Hmm?"

He shook his head and passed her a sheaf of pages from the file. "Remember how Heidi said they had a suspect in her disappearance? Maurice Clark. Heidi called him 'The local creepy guy who pays too much attention to little girls.' That's exactly what he was. That local guy everyone knows is a pervert, but he has family in town, and he's never done anything, so they just keep an eye on him. There were multiple reports of him watching and approaching young girls. Including one from Heidi's parents."

"No one followed up?"

Mulder shrugged. "It was the sixties. As long as he didn't *do* anything, he was considered a harmless perv."

"Until Heidi disappeared."

"And then it was lynch mob time. Heidi wasn't exaggerating about that. The police had to take him into protective custody until Heidi was found."

"And afterwards Clark lived happily ever after?"

"You could say that. I'm sure they have him on enough meds that he's very happy." He pointed to a notation on the pages. "Maurice Clark has spent the last twenty-five years in a mental hospital. Where he was dragged, kicking and screaming and ranting that it was Heidi Bannister's fault. That she drove him to madness."

Maurice Clark was in a mental hospital. After claiming that Heidi drove him mad. Heidi, who'd suffered a trauma almost identical to Jason Kent's. Jason, whose father now claimed he felt as if he was going mad.

The similarities didn't stop there. John Kent said his son was following him, stalking him, watching him as he slept, hovering over him when he woke. Which was exactly what Maurice Clark claimed Heidi had done twenty-five years ago. She'd followed him whenever he left the house. She would watch him from his yard. She would be there, standing over him, when he woke.

In Clark's case, that was only the beginning. Soon, he said, Heidi wasn't content to watch him. She'd whisper to him when she walked behind him. Whisper to him as he slept. Whisper to him even when he couldn't see her.

"Whisper what?" Scully said, flipping through the file pages.

"He never said. Just 'malicious' whispering. *'Accusatory'* whispering."

"Accusing him of taking her?"

"Presumably. He refused to give details. Which is one reason the police ignored him. That and the fact that he could never prove she was in his yard or his house. In fact, friends and family confirmed she was with them once, at a birthday party, when he claimed he woke to see her looming over him."

"All right…"

"The only thing they could prove was that she *was* seen following him from his house a few times. When confronted, she admitted she was trying to figure out what had happened to her, that she knew he'd been accused of kidnapping her, and she was curious. She promised to stop and apparently did—though Clark says otherwise."

"And the sheriff's conclusion?"

"According to the doctor Lyons consulted, Heidi's interest in Clark was perfectly natural under the circumstances, and her behavior may have seemed odd, but was understandable, given the trauma and memory loss. The rest, the sheriff concluded, seemed more like the guilt of a man who has something to be guilty about. Lyons investigated him more thoroughly as a suspect, but could prove nothing, and, when Clark was committed, Lyons closed the file."

Scully flipped through the pages. "And *your* conclusion?"

"That I hope Mr. Clark likes visitors, because he's about to have two."

"Doesn't look very secure," Mulder said as the nurse led them through an unlocked door into the ward common room.

The nurse bristled. "This isn't a prison, Agent Mulder. Mr. Clark has never shown any signs of violence. He's here because he is unable to care for himself, not because he poses any danger to the public."

"Our apologies," Scully said. "We misunderstood the situation. Can you tell us the conditions of Mr. Clark's stay? Is he free to leave?"

"He is permitted day passes, under the accompaniment of an approved guardian. Unfortunately, no one has applied to do so since his mother died ten years ago."

"Is he otherwise able to leave?"

"Without permission?" Mulder added.

"What my partner is asking is whether there's a possibility he may have left last Friday night."

"He isn't allowed to leave the grounds without approval."

"'Allowed' being the key word," Mulder said. "In other words, he could have escaped."

Her lips tightened. "We have never had a patient—"

"Oh, I'm sure you have. Sneak off at night. Return before morning. They just haven't been caught."

Scully cut the nurse's protest short with a murmured apology and quickly changed the subject as they entered the common room. The nurse led them to a corner, where a cadaverously thin man sat fingering rosary beads.

"Maurice?" the nurse said. "These people would like to talk to you, if you feel up to receiving visitors."

Her tone said she was almost hoping he'd refuse, but he nodded, rose, and shuffled ahead of them to a small private room.

"About that security…?" Mulder said to the nurse as they walked. Scully shot him a look, but he didn't see her. Or pretended not to.

He continued, also ignoring the way the nurse stiffened. "You say no one ever leaves without permission…"

"They don't."

"I suppose if I ask to speak to someone in security about that, you'll tell me no one is available to answer my questions."

"Of course not," she snapped. "I'll go get the head of security for you. He'll be here when you're done with Maurice."

Mulder smiled as she stalked off. Then, he half closed the visiting room door and turned to Clark. "We're here to talk to you about Heidi Channing. Do you remember—?"

Clark cut him off with a noise like a hiss and fingered his rosary faster, muttering, "Heidi. Bad Heidi."

Mulder pulled a chair up across from the man and sat down, leaning forward, hands folded over his knees, almost as if in prayer. "I heard she wasn't very nice to you."

"Nice?" A ragged laugh, almost a cackle. "No, not nice. Bad. Very bad." He lifted his watery eyes to Mulder. "Evil."

Mulder nodded sympathetically. "Can you tell me what she did?"

That took a while, as Clark ranted, nearly indecipherable in his quiet rage. Scully started casting anxious looks toward the door, expecting the nurse to storm back, but Mulder patiently listened as Clark raved about how Heidi had driven him here.

"Bad girl," he said finally. "Bad, bad, bad."

"Very bad," Mulder agreed.

"Naughty, *naughty* girl."

Footsteps sounded in the hall, and Scully motioned for Mulder to get on with it, but, again, he just kept nodding while Clark went on about Heidi and how bad she was, how naughty.

"Was she always like that?" Mulder asked finally, as the footsteps passed the door and Scully relaxed.

Clark nodded. "She was mean. Very mean. I wanted to talk to her, and she said no, and if I kept asking, she'd tell her parents, and then she did, and I got in big trouble. The police came."

"She wasn't very nice to you."

"Not nice. Not nice at all. That's why I put her in the hole."

"The hole?"

"To teach her to be nice. I put her in the hole, and she was supposed to stay there, but she didn't."

"She got out of the hole?"

He shook his head. "I checked, and she was still in the hole, but she wasn't. She came back, *and* she was still there. Back and there. Back and there."

"That's not possible," Mulder said, leaning back now.

"No, it is. It is. I saw her. Saw her there and here. There and here."

"She must have escaped the hole, Maurice. You made a mistake."

"No. No, no, *no*. No mistake."

Mulder looked doubtful, a little disappointed, as if he'd wanted so much to trust Clark, and the man had let him down.

"She's *there*," Clark insisted. "Still there."

"In the hole?"

"Yes. Yes, yes, yes. You can look. Look in the hole. You'll see her."

Mulder sighed and took out a pad of paper and pen. "Fine. Tell me where I'll find this hole."

Scully was convinced Clark was completely mad and had sent them on a wild goose chase, following his twisted fantasies. Instead, his directions led to a small bomb shelter in a field that had once been owned by Clark's parents.

They had to hack through the undergrowth to get to the spot and then cut through more to find the hatch. And, when they went down inside? They found exactly what Clark claimed was there.

"Heidi Channing," Mulder said, as they looked down on the body of a girl, unwrapped from the blankets that had swaddled her.

"Hardly," Scully said as she knelt beside the corpse. "It appears to be a *young* woman, a girl roughly the age of Heidi when she was taken. Given the remarkably preserved condition of the body, I can confirm the victim also shares her hair color and body type. Beyond that, though, we are a very long way from drawing any conclusions. Particularly one that would attempt to claim this is the same woman we met earlier today. A woman who is twenty-five years older and, also"—she looked at Mulder—"alive."

"It's Heidi Channing, Scully. You know it is."

"Without extensive examination and laboratory results, I know nothing of the sort."

Mulder pulled out his notebook. "On the night she disappeared, Heidi Channing was wearing a Pink Panther nightgown. We both saw the Christmas morning photos of it. This body is wearing the same nightgown."

"Yes, it appears to be similar—"

"It's *exactly* the same, Scully. Right down to the old chocolate stain on the collar. Now, I'm sure you'll tell me it's another girl in the same nightgown. So note that Heidi had gone to bed wearing rag curlers for school photos the next day. We can see a few remaining rags in her hair, the color and length of which matches Heidi Channing's." He lifted his gaze. "Shall I go on?"

"It's circumstantial. We need—"

"We need proof. But, at this point, we need to agree that what we are looking at seems to be the remains of Heidi Channing."

Scully looked around. The blankets and the lined shelter had provided the right environment for the body to partially mummify rather than decay. In the dim light, it was almost as if the girl were sleeping, lying on her side… with her hands and feet bound.

Scully shone her flashlight on the corpse. She could make out the ring of bruises around the girl's neck. She appeared to have been strangled.

She remembered Heidi wiping away her makeup… to reveal the same pattern of birthmarks on her neck.

I usually cover them. Part of my morning routine, like brushing my teeth. Otherwise, my poor husband gets funny looks when we go out.

Because it looked as if someone had put his arms around her neck… and squeezed the life out of her.

Scully moved her flashlight to the front of the girl's nightgown, scored with bloody slashes.

"Exactly where Heidi has those marks on her stomach," Mulder said as Scully carefully prodded open one of the holes to see stab wounds below. "Clark brought her here. He did whatever he planned to do to her, and then he killed her. Stabbed her and, when that failed to kill her, he strangled her."

"That's—"

"Speculation requiring extensive forensics analysis," he said. "I know. But for the purposes of developing a theory, pending that analysis, I think, at the very least, I'm going to rule out alien abduction."

"In favor of what?" She rocked back on her heels. "You said something earlier about ghosts. Are you suggesting Heidi is a ghost?"

"I think her husband would have realized that by now. No, she's obviously a living, breathing creature."

"Creature?"

"Folklore is filled with beings that imitate humans. Sometimes completely taking their place. Doppelgängers, changelings, fetches, evil twins…"

"Doppelgängers are often a delusion associated with schizophrenia and epilepsy. Evil twins are a rationalization for our own violent impulses. Changelings are used to explain children with mental or physical disabilities, freeing their parents of responsibility for their conditions."

Mulder lifted his brows. "You've been hitting the books."

"I've been researching rational explanations for seemingly irrational occurrences."

He smiled. "Of course. But, if we have a walking, talking woman who has taken the life of a dead child for twenty-five years, I'm going to bet the explanation isn't rational. Unless you're going to tell me she's Heidi's twin, stolen at birth, returned at the exact moment of death. *That* would be irrational."

"No, that would be as unbelievably far-fetched as doppelgängers."

"The ancient Assyrians believed—"

Scully raised her hand. "We can debate folklore later. Right now, I want to get this body removed as quietly as possible and have a talk with Heidi Bannister."

They climbed the ladder to the surface. Scully had Mulder go first so she could take a last look around, committing the scene to memory in situ. Mulder barely got his head through the hatch when he called down, "If you want to talk to Heidi, I'd suggest you move. She's heading that way"—he pointed—"in a hurry."

Scully emerged from the bomb shelter to see twilight was falling fast, lighting the field in a sickly yellow that made her blink hard. When she spotted Mulder running for the forest, she yelled, "Hey!"

"She ran in there," he called back.

Who ran in there? That was the question, wasn't it? If the body in the hole seemed to be Heidi Chandler, then whom was Mulder chasing? Or, more importantly, *what*.

She started to shout for him to be careful but he was already gone, disappeared into the darkening forest. Chasing after his mysteries, determined never to let them outrun him, even when, perhaps, they should.

Scully shook her head and broke into a run. When she reached the forest, she swore it'd gone from twilight to total darkness in five minutes flat. She could hear the scuffle of leaves and crackle of branches, signaling pursuit. She raced into the dark woods after them and seemed only to get a few steps before the sounds stopped.

"Mulder?" she called.

Silence. She took another careful step as she strained to listen. The forest had gone silent. Eerily, unnaturally silent.

Stop that, Dana.

Scully had never been one to start at shadows or shiver at ghost stories. As a girl, when she'd gone to sleepovers and the others started scaring themselves over creaks and whispers and bumps, Scully would explain that they were hearing water pipes or the wind or the heating, which never made her a very popular guest. Even a few months with Mulder hadn't changed that. She still went for the logical explanation until proven wrong. So now, out here in the quiet, dark forest, she didn't jump to preternatural conclusions. Instead, she catalogued the actual possible dangers. Like bears. And hunters. And old rusty bear traps laid by hunters. Which made her feel so much safer.

She took another careful step and kept listening. Why couldn't she hear Mulder? Why couldn't she hear anything?

Then it came. A whisper. One that wasn't water in pipes or the whoosh of air in heating ducts. One that wasn't even the wind in the trees. It was, unmistakably, a whisper.

A child's whisper.

Scully rubbed down the hairs on her neck and turned toward the sound. As soon as she did, it stopped, but she continued on following her memory of it, that wordless whispering until her foot caught on something and her mind screamed "trap" and she stumbled back, her foot still caught and when she grabbed a tree to keep her balance, she looked to see the corner of a ripped blue blanket caught on her shoe. And wrapped in the other end, half fallen free of its shroud: the body of Jason Kent.

"That's what I wanted you to see," a voice said from the trees as Heidi stepped out.

"Step back," Scully said, lifting her gun. "Hands over your head."

"Yes, ma'am."

Mulder caught up then, slipping through the trees and stopping short when he saw Scully had the situation under control. Scully bent and looked into the face of Jason Kent, his nose broken and bloodied, a contusion at his temple. His skin was gray, the smell of decomposition already wafting up.

"He wanted to play a game with his dad," a voice said, and Scully looked up to see Heidi right there, beside Mulder. "That's how it started. Over a game. They'd lost their babysitter a few weeks ago, and John had to look after Jason on the evenings that Janice worked. He resented that. Looking after children is women's work."

Heidi crouched beside Jason, running her finger down his cheek. "He only wanted to play a video game with his dad. Such a simple thing. But it was past his bedtime, and his father was in a foul mood."

"So he killed Jason? Because he wouldn't go to bed?"

"They'd had problems before. With John hitting Janice. He drank, and he'd hit her, and she put up with it. One day, he hit Jason, and she *didn't* put up with that. She left. That was a year ago. He won her back—stopped drinking, promised to never hit either of them again. He didn't hit Janice. As for Jason…" Heidi shrugged. "There are ways of hitting a child and telling yourself you're just disciplining him, like your daddy disciplined you, and there's no need for your wife to know about that, is there? Just be careful how you do it. That night, he lost his temper and broke Jason's nose. The boy was crying and John was trying to convince him to tell his mother he'd fallen down the stairs, and Jason wouldn't lie. That's when his father snapped."

Heidi eased back. "John hit him hard, knocked him into the brick fireplace mantel. Jason hit his head. Here…" She pointed out the spot, covered in dried blood, where the living Jason had a new birthmark. "One could argue it was an accident. But the beating before that? No accident. John Kent killed his son as surely as Maurice Clark killed little Heidi."

"You admit you're not Heidi," Mulder said.

She passed him a wry smile. "I admit I am not *little* Heidi. For all intents and purposes, though, I'm Heidi Bannister. I have been for twenty-five years, longer than she was, sadly."

"And how do you explain that?"

The smile grew a little, still tinged with sadness. "Magic."

"What exactly are—?"

"Does it matter?" She pushed to her feet. "Heidi died. Horribly. I took her place. I was coming to the end of a very long life, and this is how I chose to end it. Being Heidi. I'm not a monster, Agent. I'm a devoted wife, daughter, and sister. I love my family. That's not an act. I came to them when they needed me, and I was Heidi for them, and they looked after me, and now I look after them and always will. This town took me in, and, in return, I've stayed and become an active member of the community. I pay my debts, this one gladly. As will Jason."

"And his mother?" Scully said. "Doesn't she deserve to know what happened to her son?"

"No, she does not. Janice Kent is a good woman, and she doesn't deserve to spend the rest of her life alone, knowing her husband killed their son, knowing she failed to see the signs, that she left Jason in that situation. What she deserves is what she will have: a good son who will love and care for her as much as, if not more than, her real one. She'll have a good life, which *is* what she deserves."

"You mean she *will* have a good life," Mulder said, "once Jason gets his father committed."

Heidi turned to him, and her eyes… for a moment, Scully saw what Mulder must have, in that first meeting. They were not human eyes. They were old and tired. Very old. Very tired.

"Does that bother you, Agent? Do you not think that's what *he* deserves?"

"He deserves a life in prison," Scully said.

"Which would require telling the world about this." Heidi motioned at the body. "No, John Kent will suffer a life in a prison of a very different sort. Trapped by madness and guilt. That is justice."

"And if we disagree?" Scully said.

"I hope you won't," Heidi said. "I hope you'll think about it, and you'll decide there's nothing more for you to do in Comstock."

With that, she rose and walked into the night.

By the time they'd left Heidi, it was late. Mulder had tried to talk about what happened. Scully wasn't ready. The next morning, she was.

"We can't walk away," she said when Mulder opened his motel room door. "Two people have been murdered."

He waved her inside. She followed, but only to get out of the parking lot.

"One could argue that Heidi Bannister is right," Mulder said carefully. "And they've been avenged."

"That woman is not Heidi," Scully snapped.

"She's been Heidi twice as long as the girl who came before her. Whatever she is, she's not malevolent."

"Tell that to Maurice Clark."

"The man who kidnapped, stabbed, strangled, and probably raped her?"

Scully flushed. "All right but—"

"I'm leaning toward changeling." Mulder waved at the motel room desk, papers scattered over it.

"You think Heidi is a *fairy*?"

"The lore says—"

"I don't care about the lore. I don't care what she is. Two children are dead. Maurice Clark may be committed to a mental hospital, but John Kent is still walking free. Still living with the wife he abused and the son he murdered and therefore *knows* is an impostor and will eventually turn on him. I cannot walk away and leave it at that." She turned to the door. "I'm going to speak to Sheriff Lyons."

"To tell him what?" Mulder said, following her out. "That you can take him to the bodies of two people who are walking around town? Two people I suspect will match the DNA profiles of the deceased?"

"I don't know what I'll tell him. But I'm going to make damned sure John Kent is out of that house before he can do anything else to his family."

On the way to the station, Mulder explained his theory. According to folklore, fae would replace human children with their own, creatures that would look human and then begin to change as they grew older, turn twisted and ugly and dangerous, stealing everything from their adopted parents until nothing was left and then they would repay their parents' kindness by slaughtering them in their sleep, before retreating to the fae world. That was the most common version. The most terrifying version. The story of parents who unwittingly raised monsters. Yet there were also less horrific versions, stories where they swapped out sickly human children for their own or replaced them with very old fairies, given to human families to live out their final years in a loving home.

"I think that's what Heidi and Jason are," he said as Scully drove. "Old fae. Heidi joked she felt old. Her eyes aren't the eyes of a woman not yet forty. And her profession? A historian. Which helps if you were there to witness the history firsthand. The fae lore fits as well. Fae can drive people mad, as she did with Maurice Clark. And her hobbies are music and gardening, both skills and interests attributed to fae. Jason mentioned that he asked the girl who found him whether she wanted to dance. According to the report, she said he claimed to hear music. Then he said it was gone. Fae music. From the fae world. Before he crossed over for good."

"Then why tell us about the dancing? Mocking us?"

"No, I think he was genuinely trying to figure out why he said it. It seems as if there's a transition period. He doesn't quite remember who or what he was any more than he remembers Jason's life. He's learning both. Heidi is teaching him that, having gone through it herself. The point, Scully, is that, whatever these creatures are, they didn't kill Heidi and Jason. Maurice's and John's guilt proves that. They took advantage of a tragedy to find new forms and assimilate into human lives."

"That doesn't make it right. And—"

She was about to turn the corner when she saw flashing lights down a side street. Peachtree Lane. Where the Kents lived.

"Kent's barricaded himself in there," Lyons said as they stood behind his cruiser between two deputies with rifles pointed at the house. "He let Janice out. Well, forced her out, I should say." He pointed to the distraught woman being simultaneously comforted and restrained by several people nearby. "He has Jason. I've called the state police, but they're taking their sweet time getting here, so I was just about to phone you two. If you have any experience with hostage negotiations, I'd sure as hell appreciate it."

While it was nice to have the local law enforcement actually seeking their help, this was not their area of expertise at all. Scully strained to see through the windows of the darkened house as Mulder gave the sheriff basic negotiation tips.

"The key is to get the boy out of there," Mulder said. "What happens to Kent is irrelevant at this point." He slanted a look at Scully, as if waiting for her to argue. She wouldn't. At this moment, it didn't matter if Jason Kent wasn't really Jason Kent. Heidi was right in this: Mrs. Kent didn't deserve to suffer anymore.

"We heard there was a history of domestic violence," she said.

Lyons winced. "Yeah, John could hit the bottle pretty hard. Which is no excuse. Couple times, I tried to get Janice to press charges. She wouldn't. There was no sign he ever hit the boy but..." A deep breath. "Doc says those long-healed bones are consistent with beatings. Especially the ribs. It's easy to hide stuff like that, claim the kid bruised his chest playing ball and…" Lyons inhaled again. "Doc just told me yesterday, and I planned to follow up, talk to Janice later today and now…"

"You *were* going to follow up," Scully said. "That's the important thing. Has Kent said why he's doing this?"

"He's been saying the boy isn't his. I wasn't going to get into that with you two, because he's obviously just shaken up. Jason isn't himself — which is natural, given what happened and the memory loss — and John is overreacting. I said there's that DNA testing stuff they can do nowadays, but he's heard that doesn't really work. I've said we'll do blood testing, whatever it takes to convince him it's Jason. He's not listening."

"Is he making any demands?"

Lyons said nothing.

"Sheriff?" Scully prompted.

"No," Lyons said. "He isn't asking for anything. I've offered the tests. I've offered to have the boy taken away. I've offered anything I can think of to get Jason out of there. He wants nothing. Which means I think he's just working up to… doing it."

"Killing Jason," Mulder said.

Lyons nodded.

"Let me talk to him," Mulder said. "We established a good rapport yesterday. I think I can—"

A light flicked on in the house, and Kent's voice boomed through the open windows. "Who's there? If anyone interferes, I'll break this brat's neck. I swear I'll—"

"It's just me, John. It's Heidi."

"Goddamn it!" Lyons said. "She must have snuck through the back." He brushed past the deputies and strode to the front door, shouting, "Heidi? It's Bill Lyons. Get out of there. Now!"

Heidi appeared silhouetted in a window. "It's okay, Bill. I'm just going to talk to John." She turned, as if toward an unseen figure. "That's what you want, isn't it, John? Someone to talk to. We'll have a chat over a glass of wine." She lifted what looked like a bottle as she disappeared into the darkened house. "Talk and wine. That's what you want."

"What the hell?" Lyons said, still walking fast toward the house, Mulder and Scully following. "Has she lost her marbles? Wine?" He raised his voice.

"Heidi! Get the hell out of there! That's an order."

"It's okay, sheriff," her voice floated out. "John is going to have some wine and talk. We're sitting down now. Jason is fine. Shaken up, but fine. Tell Janice that, please."

"What the *hell*," Lyons said again.

"Charm," Mulder whispered to Scully as they drew up in front of the open window. "Fae use charms to compel people to do what they want."

"What's that?" Lyons said.

"Just musing, sheriff. It is odd, isn't it? Wine and…" Mulder's eyes rounded. "Wine."

"Hmm?" Scully said, only paying half attention as she peered through the window, trying to get a better look.

"Wine. It's used…" He glanced toward the sheriff and stopped.

"Used for what?" Lyons said.

"Uh, a social lubricant. She's using it to make him talk."

Which was not what Mulder meant at all, and Scully knew it.

"We need to get inside," she said and called, "Mr. Kent? It's Dana Scully. We spoke yesterday and—"

"You can talk to John in a moment, Agent," Heidi called back. "He's just having a glass of wine. Then he'll be feeling much better. Much better."

Scully let out a curse and ran to the side of the house. Lyons shouted after her, but she kept going around the back and then, as quietly as she could, through the rear door. It started closing. Mulder caught it and slipped in behind her.

"It's poison, isn't it?" she whispered. "Damn it, Mulder—"

"I realize we haven't been working together very long," he cut in, his voice cool, "but I wouldn't allow a suspect to be murdered in cold blood, whatever he's done."

Mulder pushed past her and jogged down the hall. When he reached the end, he said, "Heidi? I know what you're doing, and you know I can't allow it. There are other ways."

Heidi appeared in the doorway so suddenly and silently that she gave them both a start.

"Perhaps, Agent Mulder," she said. "But this is our way. Now, please lower your weapons. I'd like to take Jason to his mother."

She stepped into the hall, her arm around Jason's shoulders. She prodded the boy in front of her, and he moved as if sleepwalking, his face blank with shock, his shoulders trembling. Then, he saw the agents and stopped short, blinking hard.

"He—he said he was going to kill me," he whispered. "He said I was supposed to be dead. My father said…" he swallowed. "…I don't understand."

"You will." Heidi squeezed his shoulder, propelling him forward. "Someday you will. But, for now, let's go see your mom."

As she passed, she motioned Jason on ahead. Then she dropped her voice and said, "I don't care what you decide to do about me, but leave Jason and Janice alone. Please. Just leave them alone."

Scully watched while Heidi and Jason left out the back door. Then, gun raised, with Mulder at her side, she continued on until they reached the main room. When she heard whispering, she stopped. It was Kent, whispering something she couldn't make out, under his breath. She peered around the corner to see him sitting at the table, half-filled wine glass in front of him. He was bent forward, hands over his ears, eyes squeezed shut, his voice rising now, until she could hear what he was saying.

"The music. Make it stop. Please, please, make it stop."

He kept repeating it, his voice getting louder and louder until he started to scream.

Mulder and Scully stood on the curb, watching as John Kent was loaded—screaming and raving—into an ambulance.

"Fairy wine," Scully said. "It drives people mad, doesn't it."

"That's the story."

Scully turned toward Heidi, who stood alone on the sidewalk, her arms crossed, watching them and waiting. Waiting to see what they'd do. Janice and Jason had been shuttled off before Scully came outside, the family taken away quickly so they didn't need to witness the aftermath.

"Wine can't drive anyone mad," Scully said. "Guilt can, though."

"True."

"Maybe the bodies were…" She struggled for some explanation, however tenuous and finally deflated, shaking her head. "I don't know. I don't have an explanation."

"Do you need one?"

She wanted to say yes, because she did. She needed to make sense of this. But she couldn't, and, in the end, she could only cling to the certainty that wine couldn't drive anyone mad. Therefore, while Heidi Bannister had been foolish, going into that house, she hadn't broken any laws. Even if the wine could do *something*, what would they arrest her for? One couldn't even argue persecution, when Kent had never made any previous complaint against her.

"What do you want to do?" Mulder murmured.

She paused and then said, "We have a symposium in New York Thursday morning."

He nodded, and, with one last look toward Heidi, they headed for the car.

THE END

the
truth
is out
there

DRIVE TIME

By Jon McGoran

CAMERON INSTITUTE OF TECHNOLOGY
CAMERON, MASSACHUSETTS
27th NOVEMBER, 2016, 6:32 p.m.

The air crackled, just like all the other times, and a blinding blue-white light burned with an unimaginable cold that seemed to last forever. It hurt. A lot. Even more than before. Then the light faded to darkness, and Leo Turner's eyes slowly adjusted. Hard to believe this would be his last jump. He doubted he could survive another one anyway.

Slowly, he got to his feet, head swimming, joints creaking, skin flaking off his nose and cheeks. His jeans and his shirt were singed and yet crisscrossed with lines of frost. He could smell the unique mixture of ozone and cold and the smoke coming off his clothes, his skin. He rubbed his hands together, then rubbed his arms and legs, trying to get the circulation going. He was in a small clearing in the woods, a little too exposed, but right where he was supposed to be. As soon as he was steady enough, he hobbled into a nearby thicket of trees.

He took a few minutes to get his bearings and clear his head. It seemed like so long since he had been in that part of the campus. Hard to tell how long it really was, or even what that meant anymore.

The jumps were taking it out of him, that much was for sure. But he couldn't tell what was premature aging, and what was just aging. Gruber had always insisted that the jumps themselves were instantaneous. But when the white hot cold was coursing through your veins, screaming across your nerves, charring and freezing your skin, it didn't seem instantaneous at all. When you came out on the other end, it always felt like more than a moment of your life had disappeared.

He was still catching his breath when the roaring in his ears faded enough that he heard a twig snap nearby. Holding perfectly still, he could hear the soft whoosh of a foot brushing the blades of grass.

Already, he was behind schedule. Crouching in the darkness, he felt around on the ground and closed his hands on the large, wedge-shaped rock he knew was there. He picked it up, wondering as he always did what unintended consequences his action would provoke. But this time, it didn't matter. He'd heard enough times about the possible effect of a butterfly's wings, but he didn't think it would amount to much in the wake of the crap storm of paradox he was about to unleash.

He ducked farther into the shadows and waited until a figure approached in the darkness.

He looked so young. His face uncreased, his eyes both cocky and vulnerable, unburdened by knowledge or concern for the ramifications of his actions. He strode smoothly, almost silently to the far edge of the clearing, where he hid behind a tree.

Leo swallowed but his mouth was dry. Go ahead, he urged himself. What are you waiting for? No time like the present, right?

He took a deep breath, raised the rock over his head, and charged.

He had almost closed the distance between them, when a voice to his left thundered, "FREEZE!" A shaft of light cut through the darkness, illuminating him in its glare. Before he could look at the source of it, the figure before him turned and regarded him through the darkness. For an instant, it was as if he was looking into a younger mirror. The eyes staring back at him went wide with surprise, then a voice behind the flashlight beam said, "This is Agent Fox Mulder, FBI! Put your weapon on the ground and place your hands on top of your head."

The young man in front of him vanished into the darkness. As Leo looked over toward the flashlight to his left, he heard a sound to his right. There was an explosion of stars as something cracked against the back of his head.

The next thing he knew, he was lying on his back, looking up at the night sky, the stars framed by the black trees. The man with the flashlight—Agent Mulder—was standing over him. Next to him was a man in a uniform holding a nightstick. Then the darkness closed in on him and everything went black.

CAMERON MEDICAL CENTER
CAMERON, MASSACHUSETTS
27th NOVEMBER, 2016, 7:15 p.m.

"I don't think that's him." Professor Alan Silberstein glanced nervously at the unconscious figure handcuffed to the hospital bed. Two guards flanked the doorway, one with a rifle, the other a shotgun. Both stared straight ahead, expressionless.

"You don't think so?" Mulder said, taking a deep breath and exchanging an exasperated look with his partner, Dana Scully, who was standing across from him. They both glanced over at Sergeant Francis McKean, Cameron Institute of Technology's head of security. McKean didn't react. Mulder knew McKean wasn't happy about him and Scully being there, and he was pretty sure McKean knew Mulder wasn't happy McKean had knocked the suspect out.

"There's a twelve-foot electrified security fence around your facility," Mulder said evenly. "You think two people got inside?"

Silberstein shrugged in a way that exaggerated the softness of his body, the slope of his narrow shoulders. "I don't know."

"Why don't you think it's him?" Scully asked. "Earlier you said it was."

Silberstein had reported seeing an unauthorized visitor skulking around the restricted area surrounding his facility on the university campus for the past few days. In addition to his ample guard contingent, he had specifically requested Mulder and Scully. He wouldn't elaborate on why, other than that the guy seemed "weird." Silberstein was about to conduct an important test of a super-secret defense department project called a Muon Fusion Drive. The experiment might have been making him anxious, but it was also making Mulder's superiors take Silberstein's concerns seriously.

Silberstein slowly shook his head, looking unsure. "Maybe I'm wrong. I mean, it does look just like him, but… no, he's way too old." He checked his watch. "Anyway, the experiment is set for midnight. The pre-test regimen is critical, so I should really be back at the lab."

Mulder sighed. "Okay. I wanted to ask you about that, too. Why are you doing this experiment at midnight?"

"I presume you'll be pulling a lot of electricity?" Scully asked.

Silberstein smiled. "Precisely. With the amount of energy we'll be drawing, we have to do it when demand is low."

Mulder nodded. "Thank you, Professor Silberstein. I'm sure we'll have more questions later. We'll let you know if we learn anything more."

Silberstein turned to go.

McKean paused and cleared his throat. "I need to be with the professor," he said. "If you need me, I'll be back at the lab."

Mulder and Scully watched McKean and Silberstein walk down the hallway, then Scully turned to Mulder and raised an eyebrow at the unconscious trespasser.

Mulder frowned. "What is it?"

She glanced at the two guards stationed outside the room, then led Mulder past them, into the room with their prisoner. "We need to get an X-ray to make sure there isn't a skull fracture or anything of that nature, and I'll give him a more thorough examination, but even just from a quick look there are some… anomalies."

Lying in the hospital bed, the man's breathing was steady but ragged, just this side of snoring. He had gray hair and his face was ruddy, his skin red and flaky, except for the tip of his nose, which was white.

"He has some sort of dermatitis, but examining it more closely, it looks more like exposure."

Mulder smiled. "Scully, it's been one of the mildest Novembers on record."

"Look at his nose."

Mulder squinted at the white patch on the tip of his nose, then looked up at her. "Frostbite?"

"Looks like it. And look at his ears."

Under his disheveled gray hair, the tips of both ears were missing, the edges scarred.

As they were examining his ears, he snorted and half opened his eyes. Scully took a step back, but Mulder leaned forward with a slight, reassuring smile. "What's your name?" he asked softly.

"Turner. Leo Turner," he said, his voice a dry rasp.

"What are you doing here?"

He reached up with his free hand and grabbed Mulder's lapel. "Gruber," he said, his eyes crossing slightly at the effort.

"Gruber?" Mulder repeated. "Is that a person?"

He nodded. "Bill Gruber..." he said. Then his hand dropped from Mulder's lapel and his face went slack.

Mulder gave his shoulder a gentle shake. "Mr. Turner?"

Scully pushed past him and peered into Turner's eyes. "He's out." She felt for his pulse. "His vital signs are weak. I don't see any signs of drugs, and I don't smell alcohol, but I'll run some tests for that as well."

Mulder nodded. "Good idea. I'll ask Silberstein if he knows Bill Gruber. I'll also look at the security footage with McKean, see if I can figure out how he got in."

⌀

CAMERON INSTITUTE OF TECHNOLOGY
CAMERON, MASSACHUSETTS
27th NOVEMBER, 2016, 7:42 p.m.

Mulder found McKean standing with two other guards outside a pair of thick glass doors with the words MUON FUSION DRIVE CONTROL ROOM painted on them in large block letters. Inside, he could see a large round room with two concentric circles of workstations leading down to an open space in the sunken middle, like an amphitheater. The walls were lined with electronics and the room bustled with a quiet and precise energy as a handful of grad students and lab techs in white coats made measurements and adjustments. A pair of guards armed with shotguns stood at another set of doors on the far side of the room.

McKean stood with his back to it all. When he saw Mulder, he looked like he would sprain his eyeballs trying not to roll them. Apart from that he ignored him until Mulder came right up to him and said, "Excuse me, Sergeant McKean?"

McKean swiveled his head an inch or so and raised one eyebrow. "Yes?"

"I need to speak to Professor Silberstein."

McKean shook his head. "No can do. He is calibrating the test equipment and left strict instructions that he cannot be disturbed for any reason in the next..." He looked at his watch. "...Forty-three minutes."

"I just need to ask him a quick question."

McKean smiled. "Strict instructions."

Mulder smiled. "Mr. McKean, are you interfering with a federal investigation?"

McKean bristled. "Agent Mulder, I don't understand what the hell they're doing in there, but I know it's costing millions of dollars and there's some very high-placed people in Washington who are very interested in the results. Now, if you want to flash your badge and go in there and mess all that up, you can go right ahead. From what I've heard, making enemies in powerful places isn't particularly new to you. But my friendly advice would be that you just cool your jets and wait the… forty-two minutes… until Professor Silberstein is done whatever it is he's doing in there. You can ask your question then."

They stared at each other for a moment.

"I see," Mulder said, looking at his watch. "Okay then. Well, in that case I'd like to look at the perimeter security video, see if we can determine how this guy got in here."

McKean ground his jaw, but he didn't refuse. Too much of a professional for that. He turned to each of the two guards flanking him and gave them a stern look. They somehow seemed to stand even straighter.

"Certainly," he said, turning on his heel. "This way."

Mulder fell into step behind him, matching his stride. The security room down the hall had a large bank of monitors and two uniformed guards. McKean led Mulder to a cramped alcove adjacent to it, with a miniature version of the same setup. Even the chairs were smaller.

"Seriously, I don't understand what the big deal is," McKean grumbled as he powered on the second video array. "They're going to turn on the machine, it's going to hum for half an hour, and then all the eggheads will go look at numbers for the next year and a half and say, 'Forget what we said last year about how the universe began, this year we know for sure it was something totally different.'" He laughed. "And I don't understand why these crazy scientists have to make such a big deal over a simple case of a trespasser. I brought in plenty of extra guards. Do they really have to call in the FBI?"

When he said FBI, the two guards glanced up from their monitors and over at Mulder.

"Maybe he thought you wouldn't take his concerns seriously," Mulder said.

McKean stopped and looked at him.

Mulder smiled. "Maybe he was afraid you'd think he was crazy."

McKean gave him a hard squint. The two guards looked back at their screens and they all worked in silence for a while after that.

Mulder had McKean cue up all the video from one hour prior to Turner's apprehension. He planned to start with the most recent fifteen minutes and work back in fifteen-minute chunks until they saw something or realized it was fruitless.

He started with the video from the fence camera that recorded Turner's capture. It showed Turner stumbling out of the bushes, holding a rock over his head, then Mulder stepping forward with his flashlight and his gun, and McKean coming up from the other side with his nightstick. Next he started fifteen minutes earlier. Five minutes into it, the video showed a flickering blue light, casting jagged shafts through the trees, just for a few moments, then it was gone. A few seconds later, Turner stepped briefly into the picture before wandering unevenly into a stand of trees.

Mulder and McKean were both transfixed by the sight of it.

"What the hell is that?" Mulder wondered aloud.

They watched it twice, then McKean said breathlessly, "I've seen that before."

Mulder looked at him. "What?"

"That light. Or something like it. Couple of nights ago." He shrugged. "Figured it was lightning, you know? Now I'm thinking maybe it was something else."

"I'd like to see that if you can find it. And are there any other cameras that might show different angles of what we just saw?"

"There might be," he said, shocked into cooperating without attitude.

When McKean left, Mulder watched the tapes a few more times, zooming in as Turner slipped into the trees and came out holding the rock.

There's plenty of fog or mist lit up by the blue light, but as Mulder watched again and again, he could see that some wisps of steam or smoke were visibly rising from Turner's body. When he reemerged from the trees, holding that rock, he'd been moving deliberately. There was a gleam in his eyes. It wasn't rage, not excitement. Part of it could have been fear, but mostly it's an intense, wide-eyed determination. He raised the rock over his head, as if he were going to bring it down on someone's skull. The would-be victim, if there was one, was hidden in the trees. But before Turner could do whatever he's planning, Mulder appeared with his flashlight and his gun.

Moments later, McKean ran up behind him and brought the nightstick down on his head.

McKean returned just as the video showed him clubbing Turner over the head. He cleared his throat and Mulder looked up at him.

"I got some other videos, from some of the other cameras on campus."

Mulder nodded and McKean set them up to play. One of them, from the top of the Life Sciences building, provided both decent resolution and a clear angle. The source of the bluish light was still off camera, but a few minutes later it clearly showed a figure emerging from the trees and walking across the small clearing, then stopping and looking around. Even in the dim light, the video was clear enough that they could see it was Turner.

"That's him, right?" McKean asked, looking over Mulder's shoulder.

"Looks like him," Mulder said softly. But zooming in some more, he looked different.

"He looks younger," McKean whispered.

"Yes, he does." Mulder widened the angle again and slowly advanced the video. Another figure entered the frame. The one holding the rock.

"Hey, that's him, too," said McKean.

Mulder turned and gave him a frown, vaguely annoyed at the play-by-play.

McKean glanced at him, then back at the screen, too freaked out to take offense at Mulder's expression. "It is, though, isn't it? That's the older one, about to kill the younger one. Christ, there's two of them. Maybe they're father and son."

"Maybe so," Mulder said, but somehow he knew it wasn't. Even with the age difference, the similarities were too striking, too exact.

He called Scully at the hospital to see how things were going. "Any news?"

"Nothing much," she said. "He's still unconscious and his vitals are still weak. It doesn't seem like there's any serious trauma to his head, but we're waiting to look at the X-rays to be sure. Any word on this Bill Gruber?"

"Not yet." He told her about Silberstein being unavailable, then he told her what he'd seen on the video.

"Really? So I guess there are two of them. Probably father and son."

"Could be. When he comes to we'll ask him. Meanwhile, Silberstein should be done in about five minutes. I'll go ask him about Bill Gruber."

"Bill Gruber?" Silberstein said, surprised. "What about him?"

"Who is he?" Mulder asked.

"A former colleague. A student, really. Why do you ask?"

"Tell me about him."

"I'm extremely busy here, Agent Mulder."

"Give me two minutes."

Silberstein let out a sigh. "He was one of my most promising grad students, academically. As a human being he's an egotistical ass. He's a couple years older than me, which I think rankled him, me being in charge, my name on everything. He got his PhD and landed a professorship over at Rogerstown." He lowered his voice. "It's a fine place really, but, you know... second tier. I think they're hoping his pedigree from here will help bolster their reputation. They're probably right. You know it's weird, Rogerstown is less than five miles from here, but apart from a couple of official functions each year, I never see him. Not that I'm complaining, mind you. Anyway, why do you want to know about Bill?"

"Your trespasser said Gruber's name several times before he lost consciousness."

"What's that about?"

"You tell me."

"Maybe he was spying? I've heard Gruber's working on a Muon Fusion Drive as well."

"And what is that?"

He opened his mouth, then closed it and smiled condescendingly. He gestured to the young people in lab coats staring intently at computer screens. "Most of these people don't quite understand Muon fusion, and I'm a little busy right now. I have a very important experiment in just a few hours. Maybe afterward, I can attempt to explain it to you." He smiled again. "Although if you really want to understand it, you should consider enrolling in our PhD program."

Mulder checked in with Scully and told her he was on his way to Rogerstown University. "Turns out Silberstein had a grad student named Bill Gruber who teaches there now. They're working on similar projects and I don't think their parting was particularly amicable. Silberstein describes

Gruber as having an overgrown ego. I'm starting to think Silberstein suffers from the same syndrome."

She laughed. "Yeah, I kind of got that. Anyway, X-rays have come back negative, and there doesn't seem to be any internal swelling," she told him. "But I took a tissue sample and found something interesting—a remarkable amount of cell damage."

"Like the frostbite?"

"Well, that too. But deeper, and even in the blood. Lots of ruptured and damaged cells. Almost like radiation exposure, but different."

"Interesting. I wonder what kind of radiation Silberstein's Muon Fusion Drive puts out."

Bill Gruber lived in a medium-sized white house with extra-large pillars and an excess of up-lighting. The yard was scraggly, and the place was in need of new paint.

The door opened about a foot, and for a moment it seemed as though it had been answered by a disembodied nose. Then the rest of him emerged from behind the door, a sharp, raptor-like face dominated by that predatory beak.

"Yes?"

"Bill Gruber?"

"Yes?" He glanced over Mulder's shoulder, as if searching for a clue as to what the interruption was about.

"I'm Agent Fox Mulder of the FBI," Mulder said, holding up his badge. "I'd like to ask you a few questions."

Gruber responded by not responding—no words, no movement, just bored, impatient, and interrupted.

Mulder waited him out.

"Well, I'd like to get back to my work, so perhaps you could make it quick, Agent Mulder."

Mulder smiled. "Do you know anyone named Leo Turner?"

"No. Should I?"

"He knows you."

Gruber smiled. "Agent Mulder, I am extremely well known in my field. There are many, many people who know of me, who even think they know me, whom I wouldn't recognize if they were standing in front of me with a name tag."

"Do you know Alan Silberstein?"

He smirked and folded his arms, leaning against the doorframe, like this was suddenly making some sort of sense. "I'm afraid I do. Why do you ask?"

"A man named Leo Turner broke into his lab. He mentioned your name before he passed out."

"Well, perhaps he was looking for me in order to learn something about temporal physics, and when he found out he had ended up in Silberstein's lab by accident, the disappointment was too much for the poor man."

Mulder smiled again. "Really? Professor Silberstein said you're both working in the same field."

He sneered. "Nonsense. Silberstein's a fool, chasing his tail on some misguided quest to reverse the decay of Muons, as if that would even prove anything meaningful anyway."

"I see. And what are you working on?"

He leaned forward and raised an eyebrow, "I am working on true Muon Fusion. Within weeks, I'll be announcing results that will change the way we understand the universe."

Mulder nodded, taking it in. "Silberstein has a big experiment set to take place tonight."

Gruber looked away and waved a hand as if there were a bad smell. "Nonsense. Doomed to failure. I feel bad for him in a way. He's staked a lot on this notion of his. Frankly, I don't know if his career will recover from it." He smiled when he said it.

CAMERON INSTITUTE OF TECHNOLOGY
CAMERON, MASSACHUSETTS
27th NOVEMBER, 2016, 10:17 p.m.

When Mulder got back to the lab, McKean was waiting for him in the hallway. "I found something you have to see."

He turned and strode down the hallway, not looking back to see if Mulder was following. By the time Mulder caught up with him at the security office, McKean was already sitting in front of the main array of screens. The guards who had been there were now squeezed into the alcove, monitoring the real-time feeds on the smaller screens.

"We had been monitoring all the perimeter feeds, looking for someone coming or going," McKean explained as he cued up the video. "I knew no one had crossed the fence, but I did find this."

The video screens showed a variety of views of the security fences in the darkness. If not for the rolling time imprint on the top right corner, it would have been hard to tell if they were video or still images.

"Okay, watch right here," McKean said, pointing at the screen in the upper left-hand corner.

The screen flickered, as an unseen light source on the inside of the fence lit up the night, casting a sharp shadow of the fence itself across the grass. Half the screens flickered along with it, although none shone as brightly as the one McKean had indicated. None showed the light source, either. Then it was over and all the screens went back to the dark images of the dimly lit fences, as if nothing had happened.

"What the hell was that?" Mulder muttered.

"I was hoping you could tell me," McKean said. "And there's more."

He recued the video, playing it from right before the light appeared. As soon as the flickering started, he hit the pause button, then advanced slowly, clicking through frame by frame. "This is right before the first time Silberstein reported seeing his stalker. Watch this screen," he said, pointing at one of the screens where the light was not so bright. He clicked through images of a fence and its shadow cast across the grass. Then he stopped and said, "There!"

It was the outline of a crouching man. He clicked forward and the shadow stood. Then the flickering stopped and it was gone. Before Mulder could ask him to, he recued the video, keeping the image on close-up, and clicked slowly through it. It started with an empty patch of grass and the bottom of the fence, then lit up with blue light, slowly flickering bright, then dark, then bright again, then suddenly, the shadow was there. One frame it wasn't, the next frame it was.

Mulder still hadn't managed to speak when his phone buzzed.

It was Scully.

"Turner's awake," she said when he answered it. "And he says he'll only talk to you."

CAMERON MEDICAL CENTER
CAMERON, MASSACHUSETTS
27th NOVEMBER, 2016, 10:45 p.m.

Lying in the hospital bed with an IV in his arm and an oxygen tube under his nose, Turner looked small and frail, but his eyes were clear and wide awake. Scully was waiting in the hallway outside his door.

"He asked for you by name," she said as Mulder approached. "What's that about?"

Mulder smiled. "Maybe he likes the cut of my jib."

She raised a dubious eyebrow and followed him into the room.

"Mister Turner," Mulder said brightly. "Nice to see you feeling better."

"Thank you, Agent Mulder." Turner winced as he said it, reaching back with his free hand to gingerly touch the back of his head. "No thanks to whoever clocked me on the head."

Mulder nodded, indulgently. "Yes, sorry about that. So, are you ready to tell us what's going on here?"

Turner took a deep breath and let it out. "I was originally sent here to kill Alan Silberstein. Now I'm here to save his life."

"I see." Mulder nodded slowly, processing what he'd just been told. "Sent here by whom?"

"Bill Gruber."

"Bill Gruber says he's never heard of you."

"He hasn't, yet."

"What are you talking about?"

"Do you know what Alan Silberstein is working on?"

"I'm not a physicist, but I know it's something called a Muon Fusion Drive."

"I'm not a physicist either, but I've been reading up on it." He looked at Mulder, then at Scully. "Do you know what it does?"

"Something to do with… temporal physics," Mulder said, parroting what Gruber had said, his voice going quiet as his brain caught up.

"That's right," Turner said. "It opens the door to time travel. Bill Gruber is working on something similar, a parallel track. They both end up working, although Gruber is a few months late to the party."

Scully looked skeptical, but she took a step back, almost recoiling. "They both invent time travel?"

Turner nodded slowly. "Essentially, yes. But only Silberstein gets credit for it. He wins a Nobel and makes billions. It takes decades to create the technology, and it's highly regulated and highly controversial. Anyway, I didn't know about any of this when it all began. I mean, I knew who Silberstein was. Everybody does. But I was just a guy trying to make things right with my family, trying to feed my wife and kids, keep a roof over their heads, maybe give them some of the advantages I never had, you know? But when I got out of prison the second time, they didn't want anything to do with me. And neither did anybody who was hiring. Only Gruber. And that's who sent me back here."

Scully looked at Mulder, skeptical and just a little impatient, but Mulder ignored her, waiting for Turner to continue.

Scully let out an exasperated sigh. "So you expect us to believe you're here from the future?"

Turner smiled and shook his head. "No, I don't expect you to believe that." He turned his head toward Mulder. "That's why I wanted to talk to Agent Mulder, here. I knew he was the only one who'd believe me."

Mulder smiled, skeptically. "You know about me in the future?"

Turner smiled back. "Lots of people know about Fox Mulder in the future. They sing songs about you." Mulder looked down and started to smile bashfully, but then Turner added, "Some of them are pretty funny."

Scully rolled her eyes. "Mr. Turner, could you please get to the point?"

He smiled at her, not taking offense. "Of course. It's almost eleven o'clock, but we've got time."

"Time for what?" Mulder asked.

"A guy I knew from inside, another ex-Marine, he was doing odd jobs for Bill Gruber when Gruber found out about his background and approached him about the job. My buddy said no, then he put Gruber in touch with me. He asked me about my background, my criminal record and my military experience." He propped himself up on his elbow. "He told me Silberstein's work had created a fatal paradox, a cataclysmic tear in the fabric of space and time, something like that, that Silberstein knew it and was forging ahead anyway, jeopardizing the entire universe. He said Silberstein was a very bad man and he had to be stopped." Turner's voice went quiet. "He said he needed someone to... stop him. Someone who would be paid handsomely, but probably wouldn't survive the mission." He sat back and smiled peacefully. "Here was my chance. I hadn't had a purpose since I got out of the service. I couldn't be the father I was supposed to be, couldn't provide for my family." He laughed. "The 'not coming back' part wasn't a problem, because I'd been thinking of taking myself out anyway."

Scully's hand moved closer to her gun. "You were sent here to kill Silberstein?"

He nodded. "But since then, I've spent a lot of time studying Silberstein and his work. Now I know most of what Gruber told me was lies... He didn't send me here to save the universe. He sent me here to take out the competition."

"Turner, it's not too late," Mulder said. "You haven't done anything yet. Now that you know, you can just... not kill him."

Turner smiled sadly. "It's not that simple."

"Why not?"

"Gruber knew Silberstein would be well guarded. It would take thirty men to overwhelm the security force. But in my time, the Muon fusion technology is still new. Time portals are massively expensive, and they have to be built to the exact physical specifications of the person or object going through them. Gruber had the resources to build just one."

Mulder scratched his head. "So you're the only one coming? No offense, but you seem a little frail to try to take on a dozen armed guards."

He laughed. "Well, wait 'til you see me in my prime. I assure you, we're more than enough."

"Mr. Turner, you're speaking in riddles," Scully snapped, losing her patience. "Who is 'We'?"

"Sorry. Jumps take a lot out of you, and that last one was particularly rough. Gruber sent me back here the first time on a reconnaissance mission, to get the lay of the land, see who was who, what was where. And I did that, even though it damn near killed me. At the end of three days of sneaking around and hiding in the woods, I snapped back to the future. Felt like I'd been dipped in liquid nitrogen and boiled in oil, then run through a meat grinder. But I'd already agreed to Gruber's plan, so after a day or two of recuperation, I came back again. Just for five minutes this time. It wasn't much easier on me, but I was getting used to it. Two days later, I went back again, to the exact same time, then again a couple days after that. Each time I came back, I felt like I'd left more and more of myself behind, but I knew where it was ending, I knew what was going to happen to me at the end of it. I've been back here thirty times now, and look at me…" He held out his hands and looked at the wrinkled skin on the backs of them. "I'm only thirty-six years old."

Scully put her hand over her mouth, stifling a gasp. "So what are you saying, that you've tried to kill Silberstein thirty times?"

"Oh, I killed him all right. I guess the first twenty-nine times I didn't kill him, but then we killed him, and now my own past is already changed, as if I killed him thirty times, even though he only died once. You see, Gruber figured out that if he sent me back to the same 'temporal space' thirty times, it would be the same as if there were thirty of me, just for those five minutes. And he was right. At eleven-fifty-five, we all materialize, and together, we easily overwhelmed Silberstein's guards. Of course, each time I came back I was a little bit changed, meaning the next trip, the portal was that much more out of calibration, and the trip was that much harder. I knew I wasn't going to survive this mission, but I didn't think it'd make me so… old."

"But, what you're saying… doesn't it violate all sorts of laws of physics?" Mulder asked. "What about conservation of matter, the space-time continuum?"

Turner laughed. "You'd have to ask Gruber about that. Or Silberstein. But apparently it doesn't."

"So is Silberstein dead?" Scully asked.

Turner shrugged. "Not yet in this universe. And I'm here to save him. I started to suspect Gruber wasn't telling me everything a while ago, but after my last jump, after I killed Silberstein—after we killed Silberstein—I snapped back to a world I didn't recognize, that I didn't want to recognize." He laughed bitterly. "The world I came from—where Alan Silberstein is a household name and a multi-gazillionnaire—it's cold and harsh. But the world where Bill Gruber is the big guy instead, it's horrifyingly worse. He used his power and wealth to gain more and more of both, controlling half the world with an iron fist. Governments cower under him. Most major corporations belong to him. His competitors, his enemies… they simply disappear, replaced by horrible rumors of what might have happened to them." His voice went quiet and his eyes looked faraway. "I was already dying, I could feel it. And I couldn't even find my family. I don't know if they even existed in that world. Luckily, there were still libraries, so I found one and tried to figure out what was going on. I had nowhere else to go, really. The deeper I dug, the more I realized this whole thing had been about Gruber getting the credit, getting the glory and the money. Silberstein hadn't done anything wrong, outside of being about half the asshole Gruber was—which was still pretty bad, mind you. Anyway, I knew I had to come back here one last time and undo what I'd done, stop myself—*ourselves*—before we did it. In that new future, Gruber had other portals, and I used one for a final one-way trip. It wasn't even remotely calibrated for me, damn near killed me. But I could see the end of my life rushing toward me anyway." He misted over for a second, then shook his head and cleared his throat. "I expect there's a special kind of hell waiting for me. I don't know if killing the same man thirty times counts as one murder or thirty, but I figure it's the first one the big guy gets you for." He laughed and wiped his eye with the back of his wrist. "Of course, some folks say suicide is even worse. I guess I'll find out about that, too."

He was quiet, staring into space, then he looked up at Mulder and Scully. "I tried to nip it in the bud, to stop myself when there was just the one of me here, on reconnaissance, but your friend with the police club stopped me before I could."

"Look, we can put together a search team," Mulder said. "We'll scour the grounds, and if he's there we'll find him."

Turner shook his head. "It's too late. That version of me has already gone back to his own time. And now, I imagine he has some idea of what I'm planning. The point of my original mission was to stop Silberstein, kill him before he could complete his experiment tonight. The attack will take place before the experiment. So we're running out of time. I need to be there to make sure the attack doesn't succeed." He looked at Mulder. "I need you to help me."

Scully pulled Mulder out of the room and closed the door behind them.

"Tell me you're not believing this nonsense, Mulder," she said once they were out in the hallway.

"About them singing songs about me in the future? I mean it's probably an exaggeration, but there might be a song or two, maybe a limerick…"

"This is serious. He admits he's been hired to kill Silberstein, admits attempting to do it once already."

"Actually, he admitted to trying it thirty times, and he succeeded. Now he's trying to undo what he did."

"And you believe him?"

"I don't know if I believe him, but I could see it happening. Gruber and Silberstein are both working on temporal physics, competing, both pursuing science that could potentially lead to time travel. One of them using time travel to steal glory from the other, even to kill him? I could see that happening, too. And Gruber already seems the type, frankly. Stack thirty or forty years of bitterness and jealously on there? Sure, why not?"

"Why not? Because it's ridiculous. There is no such thing as time travel."

"Not invented in our time, no. But this isn't the first time we've seen evidence that it exists in the future. And couldn't that explain Turner's cellular damage and the scarring?"

She sighed. "That could be explained by any number of phenomena. I'd like to ask him more about that, but I don't think there's anything he could say that would change my mind. We need to arrest him for the trespassing, and move him to a facility far away from Silberstein and his work. And if it turns out he tried to kill him, he should be charged with attempted murder."

She spun on her heel and returned to the room. Mulder sighed and followed her. But when they entered, they found the bed empty and the handcuffs dangling from it, unlocked. The window was open and the screen was slashed. Turner was gone.

Looking out the second floor window, through a dark mass of trees, Mulder could see the lights from the Advanced Physics Lab.

He knew that's where Turner was headed.

<hr />

CAMERON INSTITUTE OF TECHNOLOGY
CAMERON, MASSACHUSETTS
27th NOVEMBER, 2016, 11:25 p.m.

Scully stayed behind and helped hospital security sweep the building and the grounds, but Mulder sped back to the Advanced Physics Lab. He called McKean on the way.

"Don't worry," McKean said. "The fence is lit up. The guards are on patrol."

The lab was less than a mile away as the crow flies, but with the winding roads, fences, speed bumps, and angled driveways, the drive seemed to take forever. By the time Mulder got through the security gate, McKean had just discovered one of his guards knocked out cold and missing his weapon. The rest of the guards were fanning out across the grounds, looking for the intruder. Mulder joined them, working his way through the wooded area at the rear of the facility. He had just spotted a second guard lying on the ground, unconscious and unarmed, when he felt the touch of cold steel against the back of his neck.

"Still have a few tricks up my sleeve," said Turner's voice, behind him. "Hands in the air."

Mulder put up his hands.

"You know I'm trying to do the right thing, here, don't you, Mulder?"

"I believe you think you're doing the right thing."

Turner patted Mulder down and took his gun. "Okay, you can turn around now, if you want."

Mulder did. "You know, the other guards will be coming through here any second. There's no way out for you."

Turner motioned with the barrel of the shotgun for Mulder to walk toward the building. "That's okay," he said. "We're not going out, we're going in." He held up the guard's security tag. "You got to love campus security. The most powerful technology in the history of mankind and they give it the same protection as the student bookstore."

Through the darkness, Mulder could see a blank metal door with a dim yellow light bulb overhead and a green LED glowing beside it.

"Gruber lives just a few miles from here," Turner said as they marched toward the door. "I thought about just killing him. That would end this whole thing, too, and he deserves it, you know? Or he will. But technically, he's still an innocent. Plus, I can't help but think that the more you mess with time, the more messed up it gets. And if I can undo some damage instead of creating more of it, that's probably what I should be doing."

As they approached the door, Turner reached around Mulder and swiped the ID card through the slot. The door clicked open and they entered a brightly lit corridor with white concrete walls and a white tile floor.

"You don't have to do this," Mulder said. "If what you're saying is true, we can flood the control room with guards and be prepared for however many of you show up. We can even postpone the experiment."

Turner laughed and said, "This way," urging Mulder down the corridor and to the left. "Here's the thing. I hope you know I'm telling the truth, that you believe me. But I don't think either one of us is going to convince anyone else. Silberstein? No way in hell is he going to postpone his big moment. And what's-his-name, the security guy? McKean? He think's he's got everything under control." They came to a stairway and Turner gently guided Mulder toward it. "Even apart from that, you're going to have thirty special ops agents materializing at once, each one of them intent on killing Silberstein. No matter how many guys you got, they aren't going to be able to keep all of them from getting to him. Remember, I've seen it happen. It's bloody and it's fast and it's successful."

They got to the top of the steps and Turner looked at his watch—the guard's watch—and he said, "Hold up a minute."

Mulder wasn't sure if he was catching his breath or stalling for time. He thought about making a move for Turner's gun, but he didn't think he'd succeed, and the fact was, he did believe Turner. For the moment, he was willing to let things play out the way Turner was proposing.

"Here's the thing," Turner explained. "There's going to be thirty of me showing up in there, each of the thirty different times I've time-jumped through this temporal space. I'm the only one of me trying to stop this thing from going down, the only one of me who knows the truth about what this is all about. And regardless of whoever else is helping, I'm the only one who will know which one of me is the youngest. You're paying attention, right? Because this get's tricky."

Mulder nodded.

"I'm not the smartest guy in the world, but I've been thinking about this for a while now. The way I understand it, any one of me gets killed during this attack, it takes out all the older ones, too. They will have never existed, so they'll cease to exist now. I'm the oldest one, so that means if any of the others go down, I'm sure to go down. And then all you've got left is however many younger versions of me, all trying to take out Silberstein. I might be old and messed up now, but before I did thirty time-jumps I was a bit of a badass."

Mulder felt like his brain was cramping. "So what's your plan?"

Turner looked at his watch again, then looked Mulder in the eye. "I need you to keep the guards from killing me—any of me—until I have a chance to kill the first me. That'll take out all of us. And it's the only way this will work."

"Okay," Mulder said. "We go in there, and if it goes down the way you say, I back you up. If we get in there, and eleven-fifty-five comes and goes and nothing happens, you come quietly back to the hospital, and we try to figure out what's really going on."

Turner thought about it, then nodded.

At eleven-fifty-three, Turner and Mulder entered the control room through the side entrance from the utility corridor. There were half a dozen guards in the room and the same number of white-coated lab techs. They all turned and looked.

Silberstein let out a squeal, blanching as he stepped behind one of the guards. "What in God's name is he doing here?!?"

The guards raised their weapons. The lab techs stepped away from them.

Mulder raised his hands. "It's okay, everybody. Everything's under control."

One of the guards raised his rifle even farther, squinting and aiming over Mulder's shoulder.

Turner got a little farther down behind Mulder, resting the barrel of Mulder's gun on Mulder's own shoulder.

"I have a shot," said the guard.

"I have a better one," said Turner. "I don't want to take it, so don't do anything to make me."

"Okay, okay," Mulder said. "Everybody calm down."

"Are you insane?" Silberstein shrieked, emboldened by not being dead yet. "I don't know what you think you're doing, but you need to get out of here. We're about to commence one of the most important experiments in the history of mankind. You need to get that maniac out of here."

"I'm here to save your life, asshole," Turner said.

Silberstein smirked. "From what?"

"From Bill Gruber."

Silberstein's eye twitched, as if on some level that made sense. "That's ridiculous. Bill Gruber is a hack and a double-crossing jerk, but he's not a murderer. He's not smart enough or creative enough... frankly, he's not man enough."

At that moment both doors flew open and Silberstein jumped back behind the guard.

A half a dozen more guards streamed through the two doors, followed by Scully.

"Mulder!" she said. "What's going on?"

"He brought this deranged hobo in with him," Silberstein called out, before Mulder could answer.

"It's okay," Mulder said. He looked at the clock—eleven fifty-five—then turned to look at Turner, one eyebrow raised.

For an instant, Turner's face flashed with a combination of disappointment and relief, then it flashed again, and Mulder realized it wasn't Turner's expression that was flickering, it was everything. In dozens of spots throughout the control room, the air began to shimmer, barely visible. Then the shimmering turned to a crackling glow—tiny balls of lightning, blindingly bright, and each of them expanding to the size of a full-grown man. Silberstein shrieked. The guards clutched their weapons as if they were teddy bears and this was a bad dream.

Turner tucked his shotgun into Mulder's arms, holding it there until Mulder grabbed it.

"What's going on?" Scully yelled, barely audible as the air became saturated with a noise between a hum and a shriek. The guard next to her shrank in fear at the sound.

Each of the light spots, already impossibly bright, flared even brighter for an instant, so bright Mulder feared for his eyes.

Then a solid wall of wind passed through the room. Mulder's ears popped, and for a moment he thought he'd been deafened, too. Then he realized the sound had stopped. The lights were gone. In their places, there now stood dozens of Turners, all slightly different. Some were almost as old as the man standing behind him, others were barely post-adolescent. They had a variety of hair lengths, and colors, from blond to almost gray.

For a moment, the room was still except for a few pieces of paper settling out of the maelstrom. The guards and the lab techs were dazed by what they were witnessing. The Leo Turners seemed dazed by what they'd just endured. But they weren't dazed for long. The first to shake it off looked like he might have been the youngest. He had a buzz cut, fresh stitches on his forehead and a crazed grin on his face, like he thought this was fun.

The Turners attacked, some of them going after the guards' weapons, some of them going straight for Silberstein. A handful of guards formed a loose semicircle around him and grappled with the first wave of Turners. Lab workers were darting in every direction, trying to find a safe place to hide from the chaos.

"Mulder!" Scully called out.

"Don't let anyone shoot the Turners!" Mulder called back to her. As he said it, Old Turner dashed across the room toward Silberstein. Mulder felt a moment of doubt, wondering if he'd been duped, if Old Turner was trying to kill the scientist after all.

One of the guards near Mulder had Old Turner in his sites, and Mulder almost let him take the shot. Then he saw another Turner, even younger than the one with the stiches, rushing toward Silberstein, and he realized Old Turner was angled to head him off. Mulder resisted the impulse to shoot the young one. Instead, he put his elbow under the arms of the guard aiming at Old Turner and pushed them up.

As Old Turner collided with his younger version, knocking him backwards, Silberstein dropped to his hands and knees and crawled under a work station, his hands clamped over his ears and his eyes clenched shut.

Old Turner stood over the scientist, and Mulder could feel seconds crawling by. His finger felt sweaty on the trigger of the shotgun as he waited for Old Turner to either kill Silberstein or protect him.

Instead he just stood there in the middle of the brawl, motionless except for his eyes, which scanned the room.

The massive guard next to Scully was grappling with three Turners and he threw them all off with a roar, then leveled his rifle at Old Turner.

"Freeze!" the guard yelled, but his voice was swallowed up in the cacophony. Just as he pulled the trigger, Scully pushed his hands up, causing the shot to perforate the ceiling.

Mulder caught her eye for the briefest moment, when something else drew his attention. Old Turner leaped over the desks and darted across the room, a determined look in his eyes.

Then Mulder saw him—his head freshly shaved, his pink-flushed cheeks covered with a sheen of fuzz—the youngest-looking Turner so far, standing there frozen in place.

Old Turner grabbed him by the shoulder and put his lips next to the kid's ear. It was impossible to hear, but it looked like Old Turner said, "Nothing personal, kid."

Then somehow there was a scalpel in his hand and he plunged it into the kid's heart.

The room froze, all eyes on the two of them.

The fresh-faced Turner's cheeks turned white as he looked down at the scalpel protruding from his chest, then up at Old Turner. His eyes rolled up and he collapsed to the floor.

Old Turner looked sad but triumphant; relieved, resigned, but vaguely terrified. He looked down at the young man on the floor, then he clenched his eyes and put out his arms, waiting.

There was a moment of absolute stillness, then another young Turner, barely older than the dead one, wrested a gun out of a stunned guard's hands and pointed it at Old Turner. Before he could pull the trigger, he flickered with a blue white light and disappeared with a faint pop, as the air around him collapsed into the vacuum.

The gun hung in midair for an instant before it fell to the floor with a muffled thud.

The other Turners looked at each other, then down at themselves. All except Old Turner, who stood there with his eyes closed, waiting.

Another young Turner flickered and disappeared. Then a third, then a fourth. They seemed to be disappearing in age order, as the paradox of their existence chased them down, back and forth, through the temporal spaces they had crisscrossed. The universe seemed to catch on, and the pace of their annihilation accelerated: flicker - pop, flicker - pop, flicker - pop.

Silberstein emerged from under the workstation to watch the bizarre spectacle.

By the time Old Turner opened his eyes, half of his predecessors were already gone and the rest were disappearing, about one every second. Some of the older ones looked at Old Turner, questions in their eyes. Without the younger ones around, Mulder could see they looked more and more the same, more and more like the Turner he had come to know, however slightly.

Old Turner opened his mouth, but then he closed it. There wasn't time to explain. His other selves looked at him accusingly, and he looked back ashamed.

The popping sound continued to accelerate, and Old Turner watched the disappearances with a look of growing intensity, equal parts terror and exhilaration as death worked the room—his death—inexorable on its way toward him.

There were only a handful left when another sound erupted, a faint, high-pitched squeal. Everyone looked around, wondering what it was. Even the remaining Turners—embroiled in the midst of a mass murder-suicide the likes of which the universe had probably never known—looked around, confounded.

There were four Turners left, then three, when a figure darted out from behind one of the mainframes. Practically a child, it was the youngest Turner by far, his tear-streaked face flushed red, his hands clutching a pistol as he charged through the stunned room, straight toward Silberstein.

The physicist clenched his eyes and the lab reverberated with an explosive gun shot.

Then the youngest Turner stumbled and fell, his gun tumbling away from him. Bleeding from a hole in the center of his chest, he looked up at Old Turner, standing there holding Mulder's gun.

"Sorry, kid," Old Turner said. "Sometimes…"

Then Old Turner flickered with a blue-white light and vanished.

Mulder caught the gun—his gun—before it hit the floor. A wisp of smoke was still rising from the barrel as the youngest Turner released his last breath.

A few seconds later, the Turner with the scalpel in his chest flickered and vanished as well.

A few seconds after that, Silberstein started barking at his helpers, trying to get his experiment back on track. He went ballistic when Mulder and Scully told him he would have to postpone it. McKean and his men had to physically restrain him from attempting to initiate the procedure anyway, even amid the carnage and chaos. He was still arguing his point, standing over the youngest Turner's body, at midnight, when the corpse flickered and disappeared—not the victim of a temporal paradox, but simply snapped back to its own time, right according to schedule.

Mulder wondered what future the body had returned to.

Silberstein actually went quiet after that. Mulder hoped he'd finally found some sense of humility in the face of the vast forces with which he was tinkering. But probably not.

Bill Gruber was questioned exhaustively, but since he had done nothing wrong—yet—he was released without charges, or any idea of what had happened. Mulder made a mental note not to say anything incriminating if he ever spoke to the man on the phone—Gruber would probably be under FBI scrutiny for the rest of his life.

It took several days to write up the reports so they reflected a narrative that was acceptable to everyone. By the time Mulder and Scully were ready to leave, Silberstein had received the green light to complete his experiment.

"Are you sure you don't want to stay and watch?" Scully asked as they got in the car.

Mulder shook his head. "The machines will hum for a while, then they'll all go off and study the numbers. I don't think there will be much to see." He smiled. "Besides, I already know what happens."

THE END

the truth
is out
There

BLACK HOLE SON

By Kami Garcia

CHILMARK, MASSACHUSETTS
20th OCTOBER, 1977, 3:30 p.m

According to NASA, a black hole is an area in space with a gravitational pull so strong that even light can't escape. Sounds like my house. It feels like there's no way out when your parents barely speak, or if they do, it ends in an argument. It's the reason I've been standing outside my front door for ten minutes, instead of going inside. It sucks being inside there with them.

Actually, that's a lie.

It sucks because it's my fault.

Before my sister disappeared, they never fought. Before Samantha vanished, my mom didn't sit in the kitchen in the dark, staring at the wall, and my dad watched baseball games and the occasional *Star Trek* rerun with me. But everything changed one night four years ago.

One minute I was playing Stratego with Samantha, and the next, I was waking up on the floor. My sister was gone, and I couldn't remember a single thing about what happened—not a face or a voice or the sound of an intruder breaking into our house. All I remember is what happened right *before* she disappeared. I was yelling at her. She wanted to change the television channel and watch a stupid western, but *The Magician*—my favorite show—was about to start. After four years, I still hate magicians.

When I finally open the front door and go inside, everything seems normal—normal for the Mulder family anyway. Mom is in the kitchen assembling a meatloaf, which will eventually end up in the garbage, uneaten. Dad isn't there—he rarely is—he's always working late at the State Department, pretending to make a difference in the world.

"Mom, I'm home."

Mom doesn't respond until she turns toward the fridge and sees me. She stares at me for a moment like she's trying to remember my name, then holds up the pan. "I'm making meatloaf."

"Sounds good." I play along, even though I know the dish will never make it to the table.

"Dr. Bennett called. He wanted me to remind you to finish the journal assignment he gave you before your session on Monday."

"I'll get right on that," I say, welcoming any excuse to escape.

Dr. Bennett is the latest in a long line of shrinks my dad hired after I made the mistake of telling him my theory about Samantha's disappearance—which involved a mentally unstable kidnapper drugging me and abducting my sister to raise as their child. The good news is that none of the shrinks put up with me for long, thanks to a borrowed copy of *Severe Psychiatric Conditions* and my superior acting skills. Though I should give Dr. Bennett a little credit; he *did* figure out I wasn't suffering from multiple personality disorder after only two sessions.

Upstairs, I hole up in my room, where my green shag carpeting and a poster of Farah Fawcett wearing a skimpy, red one-piece offer a soothing sense of familiarity. The exercise in my therapy journal is titled "Inner Excavation," and according to the directions, I'm supposed to list the most significant events in my life over the past four months.

How much is this loser charging my parents? I need to get rid of him sooner than later.

I take a minute to choose my personal Top Five. Then I crack a rare smile and start writing.

- *The WOW Signal (proof that we might not be the only intelligent life form in the universe, which, if we were so intelligent, we would already know).*
- *Elvis Presley died (still up for debate).*
- *The Martian Chronicles was banned at school (because the teachers don't want to admit they don't understand it).*
- *I memorized all 39 ingredients on the wrapper of my favorite candy bar (while I was supposed to be reading* Hamlet *in English).*
- *Every night for two weeks straight, I dreamed that my best friend admitted she wants to make out with me, which could actually happen (also still up for debate).*

I'm only halfway through my list when I smell something burning.

I forgot to watch the clock.

In the kitchen, smoke seeps through the oven door. I yank it open, coughing as more smoke pours off of the incinerated meatloaf. I shove my hand into an oven mitt and pull out the pan. "Mom, the meatloaf was burning up. Didn't you smell it?"

She's sitting at the kitchen table staring out the window like I'm not here, like she didn't almost set the house on fire.

Again.

It's a relief when Dad finally shows up with TV dinners, which taste like smoke after forty-five minutes in the oven. We sit at the kitchen table and eat our Salisbury steaks in silence—Mom pushing greenish-gray peas around inside their aluminum compartment and Dad swallowing forkfuls of food without chewing.

Mom stares at the empty ladder-back chair across from mine, her eyes equally as empty. It's like something sucked the light out of them. It reminds me of a line from one of my astronomy books.

A black hole forms when a star dies.

Samantha was our star.

I push my chair away from the table. "I'm going to my room. I've got a paper to write about a controversial topic in recent history."

Dad's eye twitches, as he chokes down a mouthful of mashed potatoes. "So what controversy did you pick?" he asks without looking at me. "Wait. Let me guess… Roswell? Area 51?" He drops his fork and it clatters against the plate. "Aim high, Fox. If you try hard enough, maybe you can convince *all* your teachers that you're crazy."

For a second, I consider walking away without making a smart comment. But Dad hasn't looked at me once, and Mom is wringing her napkin in her lap.

"Don't worry, Dad. I wouldn't want to damage your perfectly tarnished reputation as Father of the Year." I retreat to my room without waiting for a response. I'm not interested in anything he has to say.

I drop down on my bed and grab *Children of Dune* instead of tackling the paper. If no one bothers me, maybe I can finally finish the book. I only get through a few chapters when I hear my parents shouting. I'm off the bed in seconds and press my ear against my bedroom door.

This isn't normal—not the fact that my parents are fighting; that's a daily occurrence since Samantha disappeared. But they always try to hide their arguments—whisper-shouting behind closed doors, or shifting into silent mode whenever I walk in the room.

Until now.

Mom's voice is so loud that I can hear her end of the conversation through my door.

"Why now? After all this time?" Mom asks from somewhere in the living room. Dad responds, but his voice sounds muffled.

"You don't know?" Mom shouts. "*That's* your answer?"

I crack the door.

"Lower your voice, Teena," Dad snaps.

"This is *your* fault. Every miserable second of it. And it *won't* be worth it in the end—I know that now."

What's she talking about?

I inch my way down the hall toward the living room.

"You're hysterical," Dad says, his tone full of disdain. "And you have *no* idea how bad things will get."

A chill runs down the back of my neck.

What things?

"Maybe not. But I do know how bad they are right now," Mom shoots back.

A moment later, footsteps smack against the parquet wood floor, growing louder with every step. I bolt down the hall and slip back into my room, flopping down on the bed again.

My doorknob rattles and Mom opens the door without knocking—another thing she never does.

I glance up from my book. "Hey, Mom."

"You're grounded, young man," she says, the knob rattling beneath her shaky hand.

Now I'm paying attention. "What for?"

"I saw your history test, and there's no excuse for a C."

"The one from last week?" I'm confused. "You're grounding me now?"

"No phone calls, no television, and no car until Monday." Mom ignores my question. She slams my door before I have a chance to say a word.

I have no idea what's going on, but it has nothing to do with a grade on a history test.

This is something bigger.

By Monday morning, I don't know any more than I did on Friday. My parents didn't have another fight, at least not one I heard. The house was silent as a tomb while Dad worked all weekend and Mom stared out the window. I slide into the driver's seat of our rusty hatchback, which only starts half the time. But I'm not complaining because that reduces the number of silent rides to school with Mom by half.

Today, the ignition catches on the first try, like the car wants to get away from the house as much as I do. I don't even care when I get stuck listening to "Blinded by the Light" for the ten-thousandth time this week.

Within minutes, I pull into the parking lot at Chilmark High, the sunken shipwreck inside my fishbowl of a town. It's also a petri dish that provides the ideal conditions for idiots and assholes to thrive.

Two prime examples from the football team are hanging out near the double doors as I walk up the sidewalk.

"Hey, Fox. Where's your little hen?" Adam Wilson asks, referring to my best friend Phoebe. "You snuck into the henhouse yet?" He cracks himself up, and I wonder how long it took him to come up with that one.

Phoebe is undeniably hot, so everyone assumes we're more than just friends. Unfortunately for me, they're wrong. But Adam doesn't know that, and ever since he asked Phoebe out last year (she said no), we enjoy tormenting him.

"Why don't you ask her, Adam?" I shoot back. "It wouldn't be cool for me to talk about it. You know how it is."

His smile vanishes, and he looks like he wants to throw me through a window.

Mission accomplished.

"Hey, Fox? What did you get on the Astronomy test?" Mike McGarey, a defensive lineman who looks roughly twenty-five years old, calls out.

Adam elbows Mike. "I bet he got a hundred percent."

I tutored Adam once last year, and it was the longest two hours of my life. I'd rather put duct tape on my arm hair and rip it off than do it again. "Actually, I scored a hundred and five percent because I answered the bonus question about Voyager II." Having an eidetic memory has a few benefits.

My answer throws them and gives me enough time to slip inside the building.

When I get to my locker, Phoebe is waiting, wearing jeans and a *Star Trek* T-shirt with a cracked iron-on version of the Enterprise on the front. She twists one of her blond pigtails, a style most girls can't pull off without looking like they're in middle school. But Phoebe is tall and curvy in all the right places, with naturally red lollipop-stained lips. When you factor in those attributes, the pigtails make her look like a *Playboy* centerfold from one of the magazines stashed under my bed.

She also happens to be the smartest person I know and speaks fluent Klingon, which basically makes her my dream girl.

I pull out a crumpled sheet of paper from the pocket of my jeans and wave it at her. "Scientists at Ames don't think the WOW Signal was the result of an explosion in space."

In August, a telescope at Ohio State picked up a seventy-two-second signal in space, on an internationally banned frequency. Government suits like my dad tried to attribute it to a meteor shower—or whatever space term they picked up from reading the most recent issue of *National Geographic*. But I don't trust suits; they're the kind of men who covered up Roswell.

Phoebe and I read all the data released by NASA and Ames Research Center at Stanford, my memory cataloging every page. She's the only person who knows I want to work for NASA after I graduate from college. If everything goes according to plan, I'll be at Stanford in two years—my best shot at making it happen.

"Did you see the news this morning?" she asks, without glancing at the page in my hand.

"You know my mom doesn't let anyone watch the news in our house."

She frowns and twirls her hair faster. "I thought she might've made an exception."

"Why?" I spin the dial on the lock and pull up on the handle, but Phoebe reaches out and stops me from opening it. "Something happened, Fox."

"Another signal?" My mind races. The odds of two SETI signals occurring in less than four months was something right out of *Star Wars*.

Phoebe snaps her fingers in front of me. "Fox? Get out of your head. It has nothing to do with the WOW Signal. It's about Wendy Kelly." Phoebe studies her frayed bellbottoms. "The girl from Connecticut."

My gut twists. "I know who she is."

Wendy Kelly disappeared the day before Samantha, and the circumstances were almost as weird. One minute, the twelve-year-old girl was sitting on a swing next to her best friend, and the next, she was gone.

Just like my sister.

"Did they find a…" I can't say the word.

"Body?" Phoebe shakes her head. "Wendy Kelly isn't dead. She showed up at a gas station near her house on Friday around dinnertime. She's alive."

Everything stops—the sound of lockers slamming, sneakers squeaking across the linoleum, even the high-pitched laughter of Chilmark High's chosen ones.

Friday around dinnertime. Right before I overheard my parents fighting. *Right before Mom grounded me for no reason.*

"Fox?" Phoebe touches my shoulder. "Are you okay?"

I grab her elbow and steer her toward the stairwell and down to the basement. The hallway is deserted. No one comes down here unless they have band practice or detention.

My legs turn to rubber. I lean against the wall and let my back slide down until I'm sitting on the dusty floor. "Tell me everything."

Phoebe drops her books and sits next to me, crossing her long legs. "An attendant at a gas station near New Haven found a girl wandering around near the pumps. He said she was barefoot, wearing some kind of white hospital gown. The police called every hospital and mental health facility in a five-state radius, and no one was missing."

"Was she hurt?"

Phoebe shakes her head, and her pigtails swing from side to side. "Not according to the news. But who knows? Reporters and journalists lie all the time. They're still selling that story about Elvis dying of an overdose."

Phoebe is trying to lighten the mood, but she's also convinced that Elvis Presley's death was an elaborate cover-up, and the King is sitting on a beach somewhere, drinking cocktails out of coconuts. Or, based on the sightings after his reported death, he's living in a big city like Chicago or LA, wearing a baseball cap and going to the movies like a regular person.

Sometimes I imagine my sister walking down the street, eating an ice cream cone and smiling like she has amnesia and her life just started over somewhere else. But if I really believed it, I could sleep at night.

"Did Wendy Kelly tell the guy at the gas station what happened to her, or where she's been all this time?" I ask.

Phoebe unwraps a stick of gum and folds it into her mouth. "If she did, no one's talking. The gas station attendant only did one interview before the police chased off the reporters. He said Wendy was disoriented when he found her, and she kept repeating the same thing: 'He'll find me.'"

"Who?"

"I don't know. There are tons of holes in the story."

Hope flickers inside me. "What if Wendy and Samantha were abducted by the same person?" The kidnapping is the theory Phoebe and I came up with a few years ago—and the one that landed me in therapy.

But I know someone *took* my sister.

The only question is *who*.

Phoebe stops chewing. "Are you talking about a serial killer?"

"Technically, a serial kidnapper if he's keeping the girls alive." My mind is spinning.

Samantha is alive. I just have to find her.

Phoebe twirls her hair tight enough to straighten the waves out of it. "What if it isn't the same person?"

"Do you know what the odds are on that?"

She holds up a finger, urging me to give her a second. "Roughly… two-hundred-twenty thousand to one." Phoebe doesn't need an eidetic memory to have an edge on me. It's one of the coolest things about her.

"What if random chance is operating in our favor?" I ask, altering a *Star Trek* quote just enough to make it work. "We need to talk to Wendy Kelly."

Phoebe stares at me for a moment, and her eyes widen. "You're serious? She's in the psychiatric ward, at a fancy hospital in Connecticut. They aren't going to let us visit her like she's in there with a broken arm."

"I know that."

Phoebe takes her gum out of her mouth and sticks it under the bulletin board, then unwraps a fresh stick. "Maybe we should tell your parents," she says tentatively.

"They already know. They just forgot to tell me." I grit my teeth, thinking about the dozens of times they walked by me when I was in the living room or sat across from me at the kitchen table over the weekend.

Were they going to let me find out at school from some jerk like Adam Wilson? Did they hide it so they wouldn't have to answer my questions or listen to my theory?

Probably both.

The bell rings.

Phoebe picks up her books. "Come on. We have to get to class."

We both know I'm not going.

I dig my car keys out of my pocket and dangle them in front of her. "Are you coming with me or not?"

She gives me a long look and sighs. "If we get arrested, and I don't get into MIT because I have a criminal record, I'll strangle you with my bare hands."

"Then I guess we'd better not get caught."

I reach across the seat and unlock the passenger door of the car. I don't know why I bother locking it. There's nothing worth stealing, including the car.

Phoebe opens the door and hesitates. "Fox, this is a bad idea."

She's right. Every muscle in my body is tense, like it knows I'm riding down a hill too fast, and I'm going to crash. "I agree, but it's the only one I've got."

Phoebe huffs and drops into the seat. "We probably won't even get in to see her."

"One problem at a time." Right now, I'm just praying my scrap metal excuse for a car will start. The engine whines once. Twice. Three times.

Not now.

"Come on." I slam my hand against the dashboard. I turn the key again, and the car sputters to life.

Phoebe throws herself back against the seat and shakes her head.

I'm sane enough to know that my *plan*—meaning my lack of one—is crazy. But I have to try.

I burn through town, heading for the highway. "New Haven is northeast, right?"

"You're the one with the photographic memory," Phoebe says. "Unless it was damaged along with the rest of your brain." She leans forward and turns on the radio.

"Blinded by the Light" blares again from the semi-blown speakers, and Phoebe sings along at the top of her lungs.

But I don't care.

For the first time in four years, I might be able to find out what happened to my sister—and then find *her*.

The hospital parking lot in New Haven was full of news vans, the roofs outfitted with huge satellite dishes. We agreed it would be easier to sneak inside after dark. But after a dozen games of war with an incomplete deck of cards and a few rounds of *The Hitchhiker's Guide to the Galaxy* trivia, I was going stir crazy. So Phoebe used her weapon of choice to distract me—a debate.

"There's no way." I almost laugh.

"It's possible." She leans back against the passenger door and gives me a coy smile. "A studio was going to make the movie."

"But they pulled the plug. Even if they hadn't, no one will ever remake *Star Trek* on TV. It would be like someone trying to rewrite the Constitution."

"You're wrong, but we might have to table this argument for now." She gestures at the news vans, glowing under the streetlamps. The reporters are eating Chinese carryout and chain smoking instead of staking out the front door.

"What's the plan?" Phoebe asks, tightening her pigtails like she's getting ready to wrestle down a security guard.

A guy can hope.

"I don't mean an *actual* plan," she continues. "Just fill me in on your pathetic version of one."

I consider pretending that she's wrong, and that I've thought this whole thing through. But Phoebe would never buy it. "We don't need a real plan. We sneak into the movie theater all the time. This won't be any different."

Phoebe holds out her hand as if she wants me to shake it. "Nine bucks says you're wrong, and if I'm right, I get those Enterprise blueprints you drew."

I take her hand and squeeze. "Done. But I don't want nine bucks."

"What do you want then?"

To kiss you.

Even with her hand warm in mine, I can't say it.

"Fox?"

I pull my hand away and turn off the car. "I'll let you know."

"Well, I'm not giving you my cassette player. It's a pre-order." She gets out, and we weave between the cars avoiding the reporters.

According to the map in the hospital lobby, the psych wing is on the fifth floor. Images of people wandering the halls, half-dressed and muttering to themselves, flash through my mind. We take the stairs because Phoebe says people are too lazy to walk up five flights. It turns out she's right about the stairs and the holes in my plan.

A guard is sitting in the hallway behind the double doors marked *Psychiatric Wing*.

"That must be her room," I whisper. "How are we going to get past him?"

Phoebe studies me for a moment, tightens her pigtails, and takes out a clear bottle of lip gloss that smells like watermelon. A rush of heat burns through me. Best friend or not, it's hard to hold it together when I'm imagining what it would be like to kiss her.

"I've got this," she says, rolling the little ball on the end of the bottle over her lips. It's the same thing she said the night she walked into the liquor store and bought a box of wine without a fake ID.

"You're sure you want to talk to her?" Phoebe asks softly. "You can't keep torturing yourself."

I swallow hard. "I have to know."

She nods, but to her credit, Phoebe doesn't say she understands. After Samantha disappeared, I heard it from everyone—old guys at the hardware store, the nosey friends my mom used to have (back when she still had friends), even my teachers—*I know how you feel, Fox.*

Really? Your sister disappeared while you were in the same room with her, and you didn't save her? And you can't remember what happened?

Time heals all wounds was my personal favorite—and total crap, by the way. The only thing time does is give you more time to think about them.

"Okay. Let's do this." Phoebe tugs at the bottom of her T-shirt, and it clings to her chest. I want to say thank you, but her lips are so shiny, and suddenly all I can think about is kissing her. Maybe it's the smell of fake watermelon, but suddenly I feel lightheaded.

"Fox?" Phoebe reaches for me, like she's afraid I'm going to pass out. But I reach out at the same time and catch her around the neck. I pull her toward me and press my lips against hers. I don't know what I'm doing, but it feels like this might be my only chance.

Phoebe's mouth opens just enough for my tongue to find hers. She tastes like watermelon and daydreams, and all the chances I've never taken.

She pulls back slowly, and when I open my eyes, she's staring at me—cheeks flushed and lips redder than before. "What was that?" she asks, still breathless.

If you're going to jump, you may as well do it in the deep end.

"Just something I've wanted to do for a while," I say.

Phoebe gives me a small nod. "Give me five minutes."

She pushes her way through the doors, and the smell of antiseptic and ammonia replaces the intoxicating scent of watermelon.

It only takes a second for the guard to notice her. Phoebe stops a few doors down from Wendy Kelly's room and leans against the wall, burying her face in her hands. My chest tightens, and I remind myself that she isn't really crying. The guard watches her, shifting uncomfortably in his chair.

A moment later, he stands and walks toward her. He says something and she looks up, wiping her face. I can't hear them, but his eyes are glued on Phoebe. He keeps nodding, hanging on her every word.

The guard walks her toward the water cooler—and me.

I duck underneath the window.

"I could really use a cup of coffee." The doors between us muffle Phoebe's voice.

"I'm not really supposed to leave," he says.

The guard is probably checking out Phoebe and thinking about her shiny lips. I peek through the bottom corner of the window in time to see the guard glance at Wendy Kelly's door, then back at Phoebe. Crazy girl or gorgeous girl in need of consoling? It takes him about six seconds to choose before he follows Phoebe to the elevator.

I clench my fists.

She's doing it for you, idiot.

The elevator doors close with Phoebe and the guard inside. I can still feel her lips against mine, which gives me the courage to walk down the dimly lit hallway.

A nurse's station is tucked into an alcove between the spot where I'm standing and Wendy Kelly's room. A boney woman with a sour expression sits behind the desk playing solitaire. I drop down on my hands and knees and crawl past the desk.

The curtain is drawn in front of the window into Wendy Kelly's room, and I pause, my hand closed around the knob.

What if the answers she gives me aren't the ones I'm hoping for?

What if my sister is dead?

I shake off the thought and turn the knob.

It's now or never.

I open the door just enough to slip inside. The room is bathed in the blue glow from the TV, where dots of static cover the screen.

A frail girl lies in the hospital bed wide awake—staring at the plastic blinds hiding the window to the outside world. Her long black hair looks freshly brushed.

"Wendy?" I keep my voice low.

The girl doesn't look over or react in any way. As I move to the front of the bed, I realize her lips are moving. She's whispering something, but I can't make out what she's saying.

I step in front of the blinds, hoping she sees me. The last thing I want to do is scare her. "Wendy? My name is Fox Mulder, and my sister disappeared right after you did. I was hoping you could tell me what happened."

Wendy is still whispering to herself, like she has no idea I'm in the room. I study her lips as they move, repeating the same thing over and over.

Not words…

Numbers.

"My sister was eight years old when she disappeared. I wondered—" I clear my throat, which has turned to sandpaper. "I wondered if you knew anything about her kidnapping. Her name is Samantha."

Wendy stops counting—or whatever she's doing—and her head jerks in my direction. Her skin is pale, her eyes ringed in blue-black shadows. The intensity of her gaze makes the hair on my arms stand on end.

"Number six-four-four-nine. Blood type O positive. Three cups of flour, three eggs, and one and a half cups of milk—mix and pour batter onto a hot griddle. But don't turn on the light." Her voice drops and her eyes dart to the door. "Never turn on the light."

Whoever took Wendy Kelly did something horrible to her.

I shouldn't be asking her questions, but if she gives me even one piece of information about my sister, maybe there's a chance I can save Samantha. "What happens if you turn on the light, Wendy?"

Her eyes widen and she leans forward like she's telling me a secret. "They'll come."

A shiver runs through me. "Who will come?"

She starts counting again. "Number six-four-four-nine. Blood type O positive. I pledge allegiance to the flag of the United States of America…"

The way she keeps repeating those numbers and her blood type reminds me of an article I read about a special ops unit that was captured during the Vietnam War. When the enemy forces interrogated the American soldiers, they repeated their name, rank, service number, and birthdate over and over. But Wendy isn't a soldier, and I can't think of anything those numbers could represent. Not to mention the national anthem and the pancake recipe.

My stomach twists, and I know the truth. This girl can't help me. She's broken or crazy… maybe both. I try not to think about the fact that whatever happened to Wendy might be happening to Samantha right now.

As I turn away, Wendy grabs my wrist. Her other hand is still clenched in a fist, hovering over my open palm. She loosens her fist and lets something pour from her hand to mine.

Sunflower seeds.

Wendy looks up at me, eyes wide, and her expression strangely lucid. "Not all monsters come from the dark. Some come from the light." She closes my hand around the seeds. "They're coming."

I sneak past the nurse's station and take the stairs back down to the lobby. After Wendy gave me the sunflower seeds and the warning, her features went slack and turned back to the plastic blinds, muttering to herself again.

The seeds feel warm in my hand, and I shove them in my pocket, careful not to drop any.

Wendy was trying to tell me something.

The automatic doors open and I step outside. I walked into the hospital looking for answers, and I'm leaving with even more questions.

I kick an empty soda can across the sidewalk. "Crap"

"Most things are." The man's voice comes from ahead of me. The cherry of a cigarette glows in the darkness. A man wearing a black suit and tie, with a white dress shirt, steps into the light under the lamppost.

The man takes a long drag, watching me. He's dressed like a businessman, but he gives me creeps.

"Hello, Fox."

I've never seen this guy before. Still... there's something familiar about him.

"Do I know you?" I ask. "Are you a friend of my dad's?" It's a stupid question. My dad doesn't have any friends, but he knows lots of men in suits.

The man walks toward me. He clamps a strong hand on my shoulder, and I flinch.

"We're going to take a little ride, Fox. Now I *could* tell you this whole day will feel like nothing but a bad dream when I bring you back." His fingers dig into my collarbone, and a needle jabs into my skin. "But that would be a lie."

I try to pull away, but I can't move. The world is getting darker and darker around me—like I'm the black hole sucking up the light.

Don't pass out.

But I know in about ten seconds that's exactly what is going to happen. The last thing I hear is the Cigarette Smoking Man's voice. "Don't worry, kid. The truth is you won't remember a thing."

THE END

the truth is Out there

WE SHOULD LISTEN TO SOME SHOSTAKOVICH

By Hank Phillippi Ryan

WASHINGTON, D.C.
17th APRIL, 2017, 8:40 a.m.

"Uncle who?" I knew my mother had a sister, Viveca Driscoll Koskoff, who Mom would never discuss, and a brother, Niall Russo Driscoll, the stockbroker. Who mother discussed even less. Still, I knew of their existence, through sporadic holiday cards to me, and more recently, from wedding presents. So who was this uncle she was telling me about? Father had no brother, so there was no "Uncle Scully." That I knew of, at least. And I would know.

"Not your uncle-uncle, Dana dear." Mother had mastered disdain, even over the phone. Or, perhaps, especially over the phone. I had learned to work around it. Hostage negotiation classes at the academy, all those years ago, turned out to be useful for more than talking bad guys into surrendering. Mother's other personality attribute, which I predicted would be apparent very soon, was criticism. Of me. Still she knew her stuff about the art world. Plus, she was my mother, so that trumped everything. "He was simply a close friend of your father's."

The pause, as there always was when mother mentioned father. Nothing at the academy had trained me to decipher what she was thinking in those pauses, so I had learned, over the past thirty-something years, to ignore them. I looked at the still-alien-looking diamond and gold band on my third finger left hand. Mulder would certainly laugh if I called it alien. Still, it felt alien—as in "unusual" and "something from another world." The world being Tiffany. For better or for worse, we'd said those words just a few weeks ago. So far, it was for better. Though the Bureau frowned on the relationship, we had argued we were grandfathered. If not, which of us do you want to keep, we'd asked. They were still deciding, so we were taking the downtime to move into this new apartment. The top floor of a three-story brownstone, vacant apartment below us, Downstairs Joe on the first floor, basement. Most of my possessions were still "home." Most of Mulder's were still in that room where he allegedly lived. As a couple, we were—getting there. Finding our normal.

"Be that as it may." Mother was talking again, and I may have missed some of it. I was taking notes, though, as always. "He's left you the Shostakovich."

"The dead Russian composer?" I said. I tucked the phone against my shoulder, clicked onto the computer. I could do some preliminary research as she talked. S-h-o-s-t-a—

"Well, not so much the Shostakovich, dear, as the Sitnikov."

She'd lost me completely. Delete delete delete, typing in new letters, hoping I'd spelled the name correctly. S-i-t-n-i… *Russian painter*, the web revealed, b. *19*—

The bing-bong of the apartment intercom. Which meant, if someone wasn't leaning on the buzzer again, a constant problem on our DC street corner, the intersection of 30th and P, that Downstairs Joe needed me.

"Mom? I'm so sorry." I interrupted what I'd hoped would be her explanation. "The buzzer. The Super."

"That'll be the Shostakovich," she said. "Call me back."

It took both of us, me and Downstairs Joe, to undo the screws in the wooden crate. Taller than I was, so maybe six feet high, and well, yes, wider than I am, since I am a size six (or will be again in a month or so, possibly sooner), the crate was maybe four feet across.

"What is this thing?" Joe asked. "It's wicked heavy. And who delivered it, anyway? I signed, but it wasn't the usual UPS guy, that's for sure. And where d'you want it?"

"I expect it's a painting," I said. "It's from Uncle… somebody, my mother says. Let's see if we can swivel it on the corner and move it into the—"

"Watch it!" Joe said. The corner of the wooden crate had grazed Mulder's briefcase, toppling it from the hallway breakfront. The aluminum clanged to the floor, making a ding in the hardwood. What did he carry in that thing?

Someone had worked hard to assemble the elaborate wooden crate. On each side, a thick rectangle of plywood sandwiched whatever was inside, and around the edges, stout two-by-fours held it all together with silver screws. It smelled of new wood, especially as each of the screws unwound.

One after the other, I placed each screw carefully in a silver dish (wedding present from the Director), each one clinking as it rolled into place. The crate also smelled faintly of—something else, cigarettes? It didn't matter. I had no use—*we* had no use, I smiled, remembering we were an official team now—for a clearly custom-made wooden contraption like this, mitered corners, sandpapered wood, no rough edges. Must have cost a fortune, the packaging alone. Once Mulder saw it, I predicted it would go into the basement, with all the other things I'd learned Mulder would never discard. Cardboard boxes, metal cabinets of file folders, old jackets, and twine-bound stacks of old magazines and record albums. Not one bit of it would we ever use. But we had reached junk détente. I'd mellowed, he'd mellowed. Somewhat. He was "organizing" his stuff in the basement. My possessions, already organized and accessible, would all go in my office. The third bedroom was—almost ready.

"Last one," I said. I shifted the screwdriver into my other hand, trying to get a purchase. With a tiny squeak and a bloom of wood-smell, the screw fell into my hand. I plinked it into the silver tray. "Ready?"

We lifted the two by four from across the top of the crate. It was too high to see inside—even Joe isn't that tall. We propped the long piece of wood against the wallpaper. "Careful," I warned. I sounded like my mother. "Sides next?"

We separated the left side, then the right, and were left with a six-foot-tall plywood sandwich. We could not see what was inside.

"Lay it on the entryway floor?" I suggested.

Hand over hand, we lowered the package until it was flat on the paisley swirl of the entryway rug, scooting our fingers out from underneath at the last minute.

"Okay, now let's lift off the plywood," I said. "You steady that side, I'll take this side."

We pulled the top plywood away from the package, propped it against the wall.

Bubble wrap. Layers of bubbled plastic, so thick it was opaque. Strapped horizontally and vertically with intimidating strips of clear plastic tape.

"Kidding me?" Joe said. "Your mother really want you to open this? Couldn't she have made it more of a pain? Like encased it in concrete?"

I ignored him, since Mother hadn't sent it. The package was courtesy of not-uncle—what had she said his name was, Nersky? Nemersky? I'd written it on the pad by the phone but my handwriting is so execrable, I should have been a general practitioner. I scraped a fingernail to find the end of the tape, trying to pick up a corner and peel it away.

Joe took out his faithful multi-tool, flipped out the little knife, and pointed it at the top line of tape.

"Careful," I said. "I think it's a painting."

"Of who? Of what?" Joe used his knife across the top, carefully, I was pleased to note, down the left side, then across the bottom.

The bubble wrap popped up, separated from the package, and all at once I could see color. Deep red, darkest blue, emerald green. The plastic obscured the actual picture. Whatever it was.

I reached down. "We shall soon find out," I said, and pulled at the bubble wrap, opening it right to left like a book. "Here we go."

Mulder can be predictable. His usual range of emotions is a spectrum from infra-earnest to ultra-dismissive, with bands of skepticism in between. But sometimes he'll surprise me. Not that I like surprises, but I have to admit, though I wouldn't say so to him, he's teaching me about curiosity. I gave him his space, as he looked at the Sitnikov for the first time, wondering how he'd react. Of course he'd say there was more to the painting than met the eye, something like that, but what else was new.

We stood, arm in arm, staring at the almost life-sized portrait. Downstairs Joe and I had leaned it against the wall of the entryway, the gilt-framed oil so massive we'd have to clear an entire wall to hang it properly. I considered leaving it here, in the foyer, but it needed distance, perspective, to appreciate it. Up close, it was a riot of blackened primary colors, dominated by swatches of dark red, and across the bottom what was obviously (if anything was obvious in the only partly representational portrait), a piano keyboard. After a moment, you could see the entire piano. From even farther away, you got the whole picture.

"Shostakovich," Mulder said. "Through the eyes of Alexander Sitnikov."

"So mother says."

"At the green piano, playing. See the crazy colors on the black and white keys? How his arms are positioned? How the music, like fireworks, seems to be exploding from the piano?"

"Brilliant, Watson. But the piano is red. And the oil is predominantly red and green, so I'm aware that what you're seeing is not what I'm seeing. Except for the numbers. So what do you think all the—"

He sniffed. "Smell that?" he said.

"Yes," I said. "It'll dissipate. Can't have cigarette smoke around little..."

"Heitz," Mulder said.

"Albert." I dug an affectionate elbow into his ribs. *William,* I thought. But I didn't say it. "What do you think all the numbers are?" I asked.

Mulder stepped closer, drawing me closer with him, and pointed with a forefinger, one by one, at the numbers painted into the scene.

"There's a seven," he said. "Right over Shostakovich's heart. And another seven on his ankle. Huh." He took his arm from my shoulders, and stepped closer, examining the thick oil paint and the cascade of numbers, numbers which became more and more evident the longer you looked at the thing, like one of those word search puzzles where your brain becomes acclimated to the exercise, and the answers begin to take shape where at first there were just letters. Order from chaos. Our brains were good at it.

But why would an artist paint numbers on the portrait of someone playing the piano? Some were tucked into corners, some worked into the texture of the fabric of the pianist's suit coat, some were encircled like lacquered bas-relief billiard balls, with thin brush stokes of white numbers on crimson and burgundy and cerulean. I scanned the numbers, then once again.

"Eighty-four," I said. I couldn't help it.

"Eighty-four what?" Mulder turned to me.

"The numbers add up to eighty-four. From my first count at least."

He kissed the top of my head. "Nobody likes a math geek, Scully," he said.

"You do," I said.

There was no place to put it. That was the main reason I phoned. I imagined we could save the money, whatever price the painting sold for, and use it for college tuition, or to take care of us in our old age. And if "Uncle"

Nemersky left us the painting, it was ours. He couldn't have meant to require us to keep it. Plus, according to mother, he was dead, so he'd never know.

"*How* much?" What the art dealer in New York was telling me was surprising, even though I'd looked up some of the listings of Sitnikov's other works. The artist had done some fairly obvious ones of Europa and the bull, and some Russian landscapes, a few card players, heavy-handed and pretentiously thematic, especially in the political turmoil of the seventies and post Cold War, the tightening screws of the Soviet state. But then, starting in the nineteen-eighties, Alexander Sitnikov began painting Dmitri Shostakovich. I had clicked through an internet catalog, counted four portraits of the composer, each similar to ours, with numbers and explosions and billiard ball objects. There was no photograph or representation of the painting we had leaning against the wall of our entryway. Each of the ones in the catalog would have easily paid for college, and grad school, for little whoever. Thank you, not-Uncle.

"You have *The Concert*, from what you're describing," the dealer said. "Piano, fireworks, circles?"

"Yes," I said.

"Odd," he said. "According to our provenance records, that one is owned by… a collector in Leningrad."

I paused, hearing papers rustling on the other end. "Sir?" I said.

"Forgive me," he said. "Let me clarify. Is there more than one figure in the work?"

"No," I said. "Just the one. The pianist, tortoiseshell eyeglasses, flying arms."

"Just the one," the dealer said. "I see. *The Concert* portrays four people, so that's not the work you have."

"I see," I said. Little—Dmitri?—gave me a huge kick. Ready or not, he seemed to be saying. Were we ready? Was anyone ever ready? The due date was in a week or two, mid to end of April. At least I was aware—well aware—of the provenance of this child. *William,* I thought again. *I'm sorry.*

"Just the one," the dealer said again. There was another pause. "Could you send me a photograph of it? Perhaps that would facilitate—"

More paper rustling on his end of the line. "Where did you say you were? And who?"

"I didn't," I said. I stood staring at the painting. Eighty-four. The numbers added up to eighty-four. Which was interesting, say, if he'd painted it in 1984. Clever. Or coincidental. Or, possibly, I'd added wrong, unlikely but possible. Or, more possible, I hadn't included all the numbers in my calculation. Hadn't found them all. I'll look again, I thought.

"I'll have to call you back," I said. Maybe we shouldn't sell so fast.

"But—" I heard something in his voice. "Just tell me—"

I hung up instead.

Thing was, Mulder was becoming fond of it. Fond? More than fond. He'd rummaged in the basement, and of course, had discovered, in a ridiculously short time, an issue of TIME magazine that had a drawing of Shostakovich on the cover.

"The first composer ever to appear on the cover of *TIME*," Mulder had crowed, offering me the musty periodical. It smelled of basement and damp. The Shostakovich on the cover—July 1942—was portrayed as a preppie in tortoiseshell spectacles wearing, bafflingly, a Roman army helmet. In the background, what looked like fireworks. Oh. Not fireworks. Bombs. Russia.

"From 1942?" I said. Mulder was impossible. How would he even know this magazine cover existed? Although he'd only need to have seen it once. "This issue is from 1942!"

Mulder ignored me, pointing to the cover. "Look at the headline. Fireman Shostakovich, it calls him. 'Amid bombs bursting in Leningrad, he heard the chords of victory.' "

"Nice," I said. "You know, speaking of firemen, we could give your magazines to the Smithsonian. Wouldn't they be less a hazard there than they are now?"

"And inside is some pretty interesting stuff. Read here."

Mulder was still ignoring me, and I knew the only thing to do was hear him out. And then, ignore *him*. I could get Downstairs Joe to help me clear out the basement.

"For instance," he said. "What Shostakovich said about his Eighth Symphony. He gave it a theme. Look." He pointed at the magazine cover, then read out loud the printed words I could see perfectly well for myself. "Through cosmic space the Earth flies toward its doom."

"Fun guy," I said.

"We should listen to some Shostakovich," Mulder said.

"I knew it," Mulder said. He stood at the top of the basement stairs, triumphant. He held a file folder in his hand, and no question what was coming next.

We were at breakfast, I was at least, sitting at the little table in the corner of the kitchen. Thirty seconds until my tea water boiled. That was about all I could hold down these days.

And Shostakovich had entered our lives as well. Not just Sitnikov's painting, but the music. The music of Shostakovich, his Eighth String Quartet, floated through our sun-lit room, the sorrowful notes poignant and heartbreaking. We'd listened to a lot of Shostakovich over the past few days, and now, Mulder was saying he'd found articles about—well, two things. One, that Shostakovich used codes in his music. For instance, that he'd transcribed DSCH, for Dmitri Shostakovich, into the first notes of the Quartet.

"With the note D as the letter D," he'd explained. "And musicians know E-flat is S, and then C, and B is H."

At least he'd come upstairs with research, not an X-File, which is what I had expected. But those were still at headquarters, and while the powers that be weighed our fates, they were off limits. Or out of reach, at least. Maybe things change. I considered my uneaten wheat toast. "Why does B equal H?"

These are the conversations we have.

"Who knows," he said. "I don't make the rules. I just find them."

And then, Mulder had looked up the dates of the Eighth.

"Check it out," he'd said. "Shostakovich, according to this, wrote the eighth string quartet starting July 12, 1960. Know what else happened that day? A U.S. Navy C-47 cargo transport plane crashed into the side of a mountain near Quito, Ecuador, killing all 18 souls on board."

"We're not going to Ecuador," I said.

He ignored me… what else is new. "On July 13, 1960, he was still writing. And you know what happened *that* day?"

All kinds of appropriate answers came to mind, but it was better just to let him talk.

"John F. Kennedy got the Democratic nomination for president."

"We're not going to Dallas," I said. Not again.

"All I'm saying," Mulder poked the microwave button, handed me the cup of hot water. "All I'm saying is that our painting has got to be a code, too. Music lasts, paintings last. Better than microchips or microfilm or secret letters. Anyone can see them, or hear them. But the codes only communicate meaning to those who know what they're looking for. Or listening for. The music means something. And the painting is telling us how to listen. Or, possibly, the music is telling us to look at the painting. Either way, they're connected. At least to each other, and probably to something more."

"The music means something?" I said. I dunked my tea bag, chamomile, dunked it again. "It's—sad, of course. Even tragic. This one at least. And his Fifth Symphony is—triumphant. Or military. But music is too vague to have a meaning."

"No, no," Mulder said. "It's explicit. Completely explicit. The composer must choose each note, every measure. It's deliberate, and careful, and specific, and let me put it this way. We talk about reading music. *Reading* it. And what if it's not just notes we're reading?"

He paused. Then raised his arms like a conductor. "Bum bum pa BUM," he sang.

"Beethoven? Beethoven's Fifth?" I recognized it, who wouldn't. Even though Mulder was a half-pitch off. What did Beethoven have to do with this? "So?"

"Beethoven wrote that in 1804. Or so." He pulled his chair up to the table, touching his knees to mine. "But think of those notes in Morse code. Dot dot dot dash."

"V," I said. "What do I win?"

"Beethoven's *Fifth*, right? Or, in roman numerals?"

"V," I said.

"Ha." He raised one finger. "But Morse code wasn't invented until 1890. Or so. Beethoven could not have known it was V.

"Cool," I said. "But coincidence."

"There are no coincidences," Mulder insisted. I could see that look on his face, the one he gets, a terrier with a new idea. An anaconda. A vise. He's not letting go.

"Art is about choice. Planning. Intent," he said. "It's deliberate. Choices are made. Correct? If you were putting numbers in a painting, would you use random numbers? *Random?* There'd be no reason to do that. Because art has a meaning. It *all* means something. That's why it exists. It's—communication."

I pictured our new painting, now still in the entryway, leaning against the wallpaper. I sipped, stalling. Certainly art was meant to communicate; that's why we have emotions when we read certain stories, or see certain pictures, or hear certain pieces of music. Why would the artist have chosen those specific numbers? "What if Sitnikov's meaning is the randomness of the universe?"

"You're saying the universe is random?" Mulder pointed at me, as if I were in the witness chair instead of our kitchen, and he was wrapping up a cross-examination for a mesmerized jury.

"*Someone* might think so," I said. I was losing this battle. Since the universe isn't random. The Fibonaccis. Radial symmetry. Pythagoras.

"So you agree. To know an artist, you must look at his art. There's meaning, we just don't always understand it. The Nazca Lines. The cave paintings of Chhattisgarh. The Sulawesi paintings. Think those are—random? And now we know another place to to look. In our front hall. At the numbers."

I opened my mouth to argue, but I had to admit, he had—a point. Music and math were certainly connected. I'd always loved the equilibrium, the predictability, and reassurance that every correct calculation would come out the same way every time, in every language. Math had numbers, music had numbers. And notes had letters.

"D-S-C-H, Scully," he said. "He put his name in the music. What other words could he have made? What words could you make?"

I didn't answer.

"Or what *equations*?" he persisted. "Or directions?"

"No way," I said. We didn't even discuss it, but both stood, and turned, and at exactly the same time, we headed for the Shostakovich.

"If the numbers stand for letters, we're doomed," I said. "Because you have to believe Sitnikov would be communicating—" I gestured at Mulder, giving him the benefit "—in Russian. And forgive me, but you don't know Russian, correct? I certainly don't."

"Yeah, well," Mulder said. "I agree. What if it's not words then, but math? A formula, or a molecule, or a longitude, or a—"

"Shh," I said. "I'm thinking."

The more we looked at the painting, the more the colors seemed to emerge and retreat, catch the sunlight or tumble into gloom, or an elusive glint of red would suddenly highlight, through a trick of the light or a shift in the shadows. We'd counted the numbers, together and separately, enough times to feel certain that my initial calculation of eighty-four was correct. And our research showed the painting was done around 1984.

"Nineteen-eighty-four," Mulder had intoned, as if that was undeniably portentous. "You have to admit."

"George Orwell *wrote* 1984 in 1947."

"Exactly. A clear allusion to the Stalin regime. And both Shostakovich and Sitnikov might have read it."

I rolled my eyes. "And all their names both begin with S, and they were Russian. That is the absolute definition of coincidence."

"There are no coincidences."

Another one of the conversations we have.

The phone rang.

I was closer to the mothership phone on the entryway table, so I grabbed it. Mulder drew a finger across his neck, mouthed the words "I'm not here." He was still dodging the Bureau, Mr. Hard to Get.

"Hello?" I said. The connection clicked and buzzed, as it often does, and every time I imagine the satellite transmissions and fiber optics and the music of the spheres, carrying our voices across time and space. And to whoever else is certainly listening. We're used to it.

"This is Emeson Bagdasarian," the voice said.

I looked at Mulder, shrugged. Name meant nothing.

"Who are you calling, Mr. Bagdasarian?" I asked. Maybe it was a wrong number.

"I'm calling about the Shostakovich," he said.

I punched the phone to speaker. "I'm sorry," I said. "Who is this again?"

"Emeson Bagdasarian. I understand you have a Sitnikov Shostakovich, and I'd be grateful if we could—"

Mulder's eyes widened, then narrowed, and he stared at the floor. The man on the phone was inquiring about the "price of the piece" and the "inadvisability" of sending it to auction and the "relationship of the…" But then Mulder waved his arms at me. The buzzer was ringing.

"Downstairs Joe?" I mouthed the words while Bagdasarian was still talking.

Mulder lifted his arms in victory, then touched the fingertips of his hands together, and slowly pulled them apart. The universal sign for stretch. Then held up two fingers. Two minutes. If the Bureau thing didn't work out, Mulder had a future as a mime. Two seconds later he had yanked open the door of the apartment and I heard his footsteps padding down the carpeted hallway.

"Forgive me, Mr. Bagdasarian. Someone at the door." I said. "Can you tell me again?" I looked at Shostakovich as I listened to whoever this was discuss the Russian contemporary art movement, the limitations of international commerce, and how even the existence of this school of art had been obscured until the glasnost of the late 1980s opened the doors to Soviet artists' once-clandestine garrets and studios.

Shostakovich, as always, was frozen mid-performance, his eyes wild behind those glasses, his arms, one high in the air as if just having finished a crashing chord, the other, poised, near the high end keys, ready for the next measure. The numbers, flying about like… like…

And then I realized what I should have considered. How did this guy know we had the painting? My mother knew, of course, and dead non-uncle Nemersky. Okay, fine, Downstairs Joe knew. And whoever delivered it knew. Although as far as that person was concerned, it was simply a big wooden crate. I had called that art dealer in New York, too, but had never said who I was, or where.

"Sir?" I interrupted. I was trying to place his accent, if there was one, Russian? Eastern European, perhaps. Or maybe just an affectation. Or my imagination. Mulder had used up his two minutes, and I wasn't sure how long I could keep this person on the phone. Or why I wanted to. But how did he know to call me? Us?

"And so," he went on. "As I'm sure you are aware, there is what we call a suite of paintings, all done by Alexander Sitnikov, all in the same era, and as in all realms of the art world, the sum is more valuable than the individual parts."

Mulder's footsteps again, this time coming toward our front door.

"In other words, your painting may—*may*—have some value on its own, and it's commendable if, for some reason, you'd prefer to keep it. No pressure, to be sure. And frankly, the Russian contemporaries are falling out of fashion, it happens, so the value of your little piece diminishes with every passing day."

Little? I smiled at my Shostakovich.

"But in concert," he paused, apparently so I could appreciate his bon mot, "in concert with its sister paintings, the other four, completing the set as it were, the Shostakovich suite becomes more important. We'd always wondered if there was another. There were rumors about it, and now we're delighted to hear the rumors are true. And eager to see it."

"Who's we?" I was curious, I had to admit. "How did you hear? Do you have the other ones?"

A silence. I could almost hear the sad final measures of the Eighth coming from the canvas.

"I know who does," he said.

Mulder arrived. On his face, a look of triumph. In one hand he held—of course. Why was I even surprised. He used the other hand, the one not holding the stripe-edged X-File, to signal me to get a number and then hang up.

"Sir," I said. "Forgive me. Someone at the door. If you'll give me your number, I'll call you back."

"I'll call *you*," he said. And hung up. All right then. We were keeping it, anyway.

The paintings in Mulder's X-File were color plates, as if someone had razored them from a glossy art book. I could now easily recognize them as Sitnikovs, the same chaotic colors, the same rainbow bursts of fireworks or explosions or pyrotechnics of some sort. The same subject, in part at least, the bespectacled composer Dmitri Shostakovich. And the same scattering of numbers, some in those cue ball circles, spreading out like labeled stars in a dark sky.

"Here's the story from the file. In 1984..." Mulder paused to let the date sink in.

"Yeah yeah," I said. We sat side by side on the living room couch, my added weight making me sink deep into the upholstery. He'd put the color plates on our coffee table, after shoving over a few piles of magazines and his sunflower seed repository. "I'm hearing you."

"In 1984, the body of an artist was discovered in a home in Euclid, Ohio."

"I'll ignore that," I said. "And we're not going to Euclid. But Shostakovich was already dead, so he didn't do it."

"I'll ignore that," Mulder said. "But there was no visible cause of death, and after a reasonable investigation, the cause was listed as unknown. Now, this guy had moonlighted at an art museum, which, coincidentally, was getting ready to show an exhibit of Russian art. *Nights in the City* it was called. And the same night the artist was found dead, one of the highlighted pictures at the exhibition—"

"Stravinsky begins with S, too," I interrupted.

"Show off," Mulder said. "But one of the key paintings was stolen. This one."

He touched a finger to one of the color plates, glasses guy and another person standing behind the piano. Both were, as usual, not quite grotesquely out of proportion, and impossibly vibrantly colorful. "Shostakovich number one, this one is called."

"Where is it now?"

"Hang on. But our dead Euclidean artist was not the thief; at least the painting wasn't in his home. Neither the murder nor the theft were ever solved, and his home later burned to the ground. But neither are that unusual—murder is a daily occurrence, and, pretty much, so is art theft. Where are the Picassos from the Musee Moderne in Paris? Or Van Gogh's *Poppys*, stolen from the Cairo Museum? Where are the Gardner Rembrandts?"

"Are you trying to tell me they're connected? To each other?" I asked. Mulder could see a conspiracy in a dozen eggs all looking alike. "This and the Gardner Museum heist?"

"Of course not," he said. As if *I* were the crazy one. "I'm just saying, art theft is not an outlier. Anyway, the next year, in Midlothian, Texas, another artist was found dead, no apparent cause, and soon after, another painting was stolen. This one."

He flipped a page, pointed. Explosions, piano, Shostakovich, two other people this time. Numbers. "Shostakovich two, it's called."

"Never found," I guessed.

"Las Vegas, the next year," Mulder said, nodding. "Dead artist, museum exhibition, Shostakovich three, with three people. And Atlantic City, the next year. Yes, yes, and yes. Shostakovich four. With four people. They're all in the file because the deaths were never solved. Ours is the only one where Shostakovich is by himself."

"But why did you think of it?" I was trying to follow his logic, which was often impossible. "When you heard Bagdasarian's name on the phone?

"Oh, please. I've never heard that name. I know my files, and thought of this case soon after the painting arrived. But I wanted to wait until I had it in my hot little hand, show it to you, since you'd think I was making it up."

"Who brought—?"

"Don't ask, don't tell. I still have my connections at the Bureau," Mulder said. "And Scully? You want to take a closer look at this file?"

I took the paper folder from him, not sure what I was looking for. It took me—not even a second to see it. The file was X-084084084.

"Eighty-four," I said.

"And not only that," Mulder said. "There are no photographs, not one, not anywhere, of *our* Shostakovich. The stolen ones, Shostakovich one, two, three, and four, are all owned by a blind trust. Of course, nothing's blind at the Bureau, so I'm sure we'll be able to find who's behind it. But *our* painting? There are no photographs, anywhere I could find. Or any descriptions of ours."

I could see the dark rectangular outline of our painting from my place on the couch, the colors spotted and highlighted by the glow from the tiny bulbs of the chandelier in the entryway.

"It could be a—copy? A fake? A phony? Some sort of forgery." I tried to come up with logical explanations. "But Bagdasarian called us, seemed to know all about this one. I mean—we didn't know there was this *series* of paintings. Shostakovich one, two, three, four. Only Bagdasarian told us about—"

Mulder raised an eyebrow, waiting. Waiting for me to say it.

Which I had to.

"Shostakovich Five," I said.

"V," he said.

"Coincidence," I said.

"Visitors," he said.

I wanted to believe, like Mulder, wanted to believe there was something more, but nothing worked. We'd held the color plates up to the light, turned them backwards. We'd made equations, hoping for we didn't know what, but there was no formula, no molecular design, no mathematical theory, no latitude (terrestrial or galactic), or proof of the universal string theory, or propulsion or antimatter or the twin paradox. I'd wanted to believe, but there was nothing. We'd added the numbers in each, and though each painting added to eighty-four, we concluded it might have been simply the motif that brought all the paintings together. A forger might not realize that, or might, and so we were nowhere. Shostakovich's Fifth played over the speakers. Were we looking at the Fifth Shostakovich? V?

"Mom," I said, finally having given in to the one road we hadn't taken. "Sorry to call so late, but we're looking at the Shostakovich, and—"

"The Sitnikov," she said.

"The Sitnikov. And—"

"It's odd about that painting," Mother said. "Your uncle—well, Nemersky— had it only for a few years, then he died."

"Who had it before that?" I asked. "Are you sure it's an original? And Mom, did you tell anyone you were sending it to me?"

"I didn't send it," she said.

"But did you tell anyone?"

"Who would I tell?"

"That's what I'm asking." I rolled my eyes. Mulder had unscrewed the shade from the lacquered ceramic lamp on the end table and was holding up the color plates against the bare light, one at a time. Shaking his head. Nothing.

"I didn't tell anyone," Mother said. "Why?"

Why. That was precisely the question. Mulder's file had shown a disturbing pattern, one we'd discussed, and tried, unsuccessfully, to explain. A Sitnikov painting would be shown at exhibition, then stolen, then someone connected with it would mysteriously die. Each one, unsolved. And now we had one.

"Let me just ask you. How did Uncle—you know—Nemersky—die?"

"He was old." I heard the disdain in her voice.

"Do you know if he told anyone he was leaving it to me? Us?"

"How would I know that?"

Mom was always fun to chat with.

"Hang up," Mulder said. He was holding the plates to the light, one on top of the other, overlapping.

"What?"

"Hang. Up," he said.

"Thanks, Mother," I said.

"My pleasure," she said. But she didn't hang up. "Are you all right, honey?" she finally said. "Getting enough sleep, no wine, no exertion?"

"I'm fine," I said, feeling little Alexander shift position. "We'll call you the very minute."

And then she hung up. Mulder had taken the color plates into the foyer, our big flashlight, off, tucked under his arm.

"Hold this," he said, handing me the light. He held up a photograph. "Here's Shostakovich one." He placed another one on top of that, then another, and another, until he had the four lined up together. "Okay, see? All four, stacked up. Now hit it with the light. From behind."

I blasted the mag light on high, pointed the beam at the back of the pages, then craned my arm so I could look at them from the front. "Okay," I said. "Lots of dots. Lots of people playing music, colors, a mish-mash."

"Connect the dots."

"*Really?*" I did, mentally. I was hearing the final triumphant measures of the Shostakovich Eighth playing as our background soundtrack, but perhaps I was imagining it. My brain zigzagged the dots, connecting them one way, then another. Letters, numbers, a drawing? It might be clearer if I could eliminate the other oil-painted chaos in the background. I gave up. "Nothing. Nothing I can make out, at least," I said. "Not in any way. Can you?"

"Nope," Mulder said. "But then I noticed there's only one that's the same, the red—it looks green to me, but it's red, right?—the circled number in the top right. They match, each painting, it's the only one in the exact same spot. But each painting gives it a different number."

I looked at our Shostakovich. "We have that circle, too. Ours is five," I said.

"Exactamundo," Mulder said. "So now this part is more difficult, because we can't get the light behind our canvas. And the color plates are much smaller than our original oil. But take a mental picture of the multiple images, hold that vision in your head."

"Okay." Best to humor him.

"Now imagine that Shostakovich is not lifting his arm after playing a chord. Imagine he's—directing your attention to the red five."

"Doing it," I said. It might be easier with a camera, wherever ours was. But my brain would work just as well.

"Now mentally transpose that image over this." He pointed to our painting.

I stared at the bedroom ceiling, Mulder snoring beside me. My enormous stomach made a baby mountain in the downy white comforter. Our ceiling was pale blue, the color of ice, but all I could see, in the dim glow of the nightlight and my memory, was the result of the superimposed paintings.

With the guide star of the red "five" lining up the other four paintings, the addition of our Shostakovich Five made it easy to connect the dots. Mulder had recognized the image it created from his Indian Guide days. I recognized it because I am an educated individual, as I told him. And once you envisioned the painting that way, Shostakovich himself was pointing to it. Pointing to the guide star.

That guide star number in the circle was clearly Aldebaran, the brightest star in the constellation Taurus. The other circled numbers—now, ridiculously obviously, but only if you had the fifth Shostakovich—mapped out the other stars in the Taurus constellation, their stellar magnitude recorded by the numbers. The lower the number, the brighter the star, I remembered one professor of astronomy explaining, in a system devised in second century BC. I knew Aldebaran, a red giant (Mulder kept repeating, "*red,*" as if there were some Soviet connection), is 425 times as bright as our sun, the fourth brightest in our visible sky. Whoever painted this had rounded the other stars' magnitudes to whole numbers—the Pleiades, and the other Taurii, including the supernova remnant Messier 1. Indian Guide Mulder had called it the Crab Nebula, the cluster just below the bull's bottom horn. The naked eye can only see six magnitudes, but these paintings had numbers—correctly—up to 13. Tomorrow, we'd dig out our camera, take photos of the photos and painting. And find out who'd called us about the Fifth Shostakovich.

"Are you awake?" Mulder whispered.

"No," I said.

"Do you hear that?" he said.

"Does it sound like you talking?"

"Seriously."

We were silent, listening. Nothing.

"Aldebaran," he said.

I blinked, staring at the "ceiling."

"When all else failed," he whispered, "when they trash the crop circles, cut off funding to the SETI budget, dismiss and cover up and discourage and devalue, what were—the visitors—supposed to do? Give up? No."

Mulder turned to me, head propped on one hand, yanking the comforter around us. "They—whoever they are—inspired artists, painters, and composers. They sent their messages through art, and music, and hoped someone would hear them. See them. A piece of art—a symphony, or an oil, is not fully realized until the viewer receives it, right? Until we take in, assimilate, believe, what the artist is saying to us. Maybe we can't always fully understand it. But maybe—not always, but sometimes—another entity is helping them decide what to say. Helping them communicate."

I stayed silent a moment, hearing my own heart, and Mulder's, and then the one inside me. Why did crowds gather to evaluate the enigmatic Mona Lisa? What did Guernica "mean"? The Bayeux Tapestry? Beethoven's Ninth? How often has an artist said "I don't know where it came from, I simply— thought of it." What did we mean by inspiration? Maybe it was a message from "someone." On Aldebaran?

Eighty-four. Eighty-four what? Five paintings, each adding up to eighty-four. And if our painting had been done in 1984, how many people's lives had it already touched? Why?

"Smell that?" Mulder leaped up, grabbed my hand, pulled me from our bed. "Fire."

And after most of the firefighters left—DC's finest who did their best but unsuccessfully—we stood on the corner of 30th and P with everyone else, staring at the smoking rubble of our first apartment. Mulder's magazines, gone, and his record albums. My wedding dress, such as it was, and the few wedding presents we'd received. The Shostakovich. Gone.

"So? Did you find anything? Where's Downstairs Joe?" I asked. Mulder had left me, wrapped in our comforter, under the streetlight while he shouldered through the onlookers, and checked with the deputy fire chief in the white hat.

"Not here," Mulder said.

"Is he—?" I couldn't bear to ask. The painting, and the deaths, and if something was supposed to make sense, this didn't.

"Not dead, but not here," Mulder shook his head. "We'll find him."

"You live here?" A soot-faced firefighter, turnout jacket beaded with water and mustache dripping, approached us, stepping over the swollen fire hose snaked across the sidewalk.

"Yeah," Mulder said. "Used to, at least."

"Looks suspicious," the firefighter said.

"Because?" I asked.

"See the fire pattern, starting at the basement window?" He pointed with one gloved finger. "A fire is predictable, especially one that's deliberately set. We can always tell the point of origin. It leaves a V."

"A 'V,'" I said. I didn't want to look at Mulder, whose expression I'm sure was one of satisfaction, even in a situation like this. Even though he hated fire.

"Yo!" Another firefighter was emerging from the skeletal remains of our front door, carrying a huge—

"You in the framing business?" he asked. He set the thing on the sidewalk. "We saved this, thought you might want it. It's hardly touched. Weird."

"Huh?" Mulder replied.

"Looks like a big picture frame, gold, still shiny. But there's no painting in it. Just—an empty frame."

"Mulder," I said.

"I know," he said.

"No you don't," I said. "It's time."

⌀

We decided to call her Allie. And, just between us, we knew why.

I looked up at Mulder, his green eyes shining over the hospital mask that still covered his nose and mouth. Allie was sleeping, a tiny lump of long-lashed newness on my chest. Born April 20. After we got out out of the hospital, we'd find a new place to live. Get our bearings. Worse things had happened in our lives than losing a wood and concrete structure and some possessions. I thought of William, and sent him a prayer. But now Mulder and I had each other, and we had Allie. Mom was unhappy, shall we say, about the missing Shostakovich, but happy about Allie. We didn't tell her Allie's real name.

"What time was she born, exactly?" Mother asked over the speakerphone. "She's a Taurus. The bull. I'll do her chart."

I looked at Mulder. *Taurus.* Coincidence, certainly. But what time? I had no idea, having been otherwise occupied. He shrugged and picked up the aluminum file attached to the metal tubing at the bottom of my hospital bed.

"Huh," he said. "Eight-forty. On the dot."

I told Mother the unremarkable—to her at least—news. *Eighty-four,* I thought. Coincidence.

And then I did the math. Five paintings each with eighty-four. Multiplied, five times eighty-four. I do math, I can't help it. Four hundred twenty. Four twenty. April 20. Happy Birthday, little Allie. Allie for Aldebaran.

"We should listen to some Shostakovich," I said.

THE END

the truth is out there

MUMMIYA
By Greg Cox

"Can you tell us what happened," Fox Mulder asked, "in your own words?"

"Well, it's like I was telling the officers," the homeless man replied. "I was minding my own business, sleeping it off in that alley, when *it* came lurching out of the night, just like in the movies. All wrapped up in bandages and staggering like somebody who's had a few too many, if you know what I mean. Well, I was pretty damn scared, I'll tell you that. Who wouldn't be, with something like that coming at you, reaching for you? So I pulled out my hunting knife—just for my own protection, mind you— and jabbed it right in the chest. Must have hit its heart on the first try, 'cause it dropped like a dead thing. Which I guess it already was... sorta."

"The mummy," Dana Scully said skeptically.

"You bet," the man insisted. "That's God's honest truth, I swear."

Scully had her doubts. The confessed mummy slayer, a fortyish vagrant named Eddie Noggle, who was currently occupying a holding cell at the local police station, hardly struck her as a credible witness. His record, which she had already reviewed, indicated a long history of alcoholism and mental illness. Not for the first time, she wondered why she had let Mulder drag her across three time zones to investigate... what? The murder of a mummy?

"We were skeptical, too," Police Chief Mark Johns observed. He had wasted no time escorting the two FBI agents to Noggle's cell and seemed genuinely grateful for their assistance. Bellingham was a thriving college town a few hours north of Seattle. Scully guessed that reports of wandering mummies were far outside the beefy, blond cop's comfort zone. "Eddie here has always had a few screws loose, you know? So when he showed up the other night, claiming to have stabbed a mummy of all things, we didn't take it too seriously. But then we found the… remains… right where he said, and now I don't know what to think." He regarded the agents gravely. "I'm hoping you two can shed some light on this situation, because I don't mind telling you that I'm not even sure where to begin with something like this."

"That's why we're here," Mulder said, a bit too eagerly for Scully's peace of mind. She recognized a familiar gleam in her partner's eyes and hoped that he hadn't already left common sense and rational explanations behind. "So, about those remains?" he asked. "You've left them alone as I requested? So my partner can conduct the autopsy?"

Johns nodded. "Apart from an external examination, just to confirm it wasn't a dummy or stage prop or whatever, we've put it on ice awaiting your arrival. Would you like to see it now?"

Mulder grinned in anticipation. "No time like the present."

"I was hoping you'd say that." Johns led them away, leaving Noggle behind in his cell.

"Hey, what's going to happen to me?" the prisoner called out as they left. "Am I in trouble for killing that bandaged son of a bitch?"

That depends on what we find when we examine the "victim," Scully reflected. Despite a bad case of jet lag, she was also inclined to get right down to work, if only to ascertain what exactly had transpired and whether a homicide had, in fact, been committed. She hoped that this wasn't a case of a college prank gone tragically wrong. *It's far too early for Halloween…*

"Cheer up, Scully," Mulder said, noting her somber expression. "How often you get a chance to unwrap a mummy?"

"This is a first," she admitted.

MEDICAL EXAMINER'S OFFICE

"Tut, tut," Mulder quipped. "That sure looks like a mummy to me."

Scully had to agree. Tightly wrapped in overlapping strips of linen, the body was stretched out atop a stainless-steel dissection table in a brightly lit, well-equipped autopsy room. The contrast between the apparent relic and the modern facilities was not lost on her; the bandaged form looked like it belonged in a museum or a musty Egyptian tomb, not a morgue. She wondered how old it actually was.

"So you already checked with the university, right?" Mulder asked Chief Johns as Scully prepared to examine the remains. A tray of gleaming, freshly sterilized instruments waited within reach.

"That's correct," the cop confirmed. "They're not reporting any missing mummies." Keeping his distance, he eyed the mummy dubiously. "You think this thing's for real?"

"That remains to be determined," Scully said cautiously, hesitant as ever to leap to any conclusions. Fresh blue scrubs protected her traveling clothes from the inevitable messiness of a post-mortem body. She pulled on a pair of latex gloves. "But even if this does turn out to be a genuine Egyptian mummy, we would do well to remember that ambulatory mummies are strictly a Hollywood creation. They have no basis in actual myth, history, or science… no matter what Mr. Noggle claims to have experienced."

Mulder shrugged. "So far the evidence backs up his story."

The alleged murder weapon—a serrated eight-inch knife discovered buried in the mummy's chest—had already been processed and found to bear Eddie Noggle's fingerprints. A visible gash in the mummy's wrappings also appeared to substantiate his "confession," but Scully was not ready to accept that the obviously troubled vagrant had truly killed a walking mummy in self-defense.

"*So far,*" she stressed as she began the procedure by dictating into a hand-held recorder. "Subject appears to be a human cadaver wrapped to resemble a traditional Egyptian mummy. Approximately five feet, nine inches in height. Weight: twelve pounds, fourteen ounces. Contours suggest that the body belonged to a female, but further investigation is required to verify the subject's gender…"

She began by carefully and methodically cutting the linen strips wrapped around the body, using a scalpel and scissors. This proved to be a laborious and time-consuming task as the body had been bound from head to toe in multiple layers, laid out in complex and obviously deliberate patterns. Each of the individual limbs and extremities, right down to the toes and fingers, had been wrapped separately—to allow for fuller mobility? She could only imagine the painstaking effort that had gone into preparing this "mummy."

But to what end?

As the bandages came away, a sweet odor, quite unlike the usual stench of death and decomposition, arose from the remains. She lowered her surgical mask to sniff the air.

"You smell that?" she asked aloud. "It's almost like perfume... or incense."

Mulder nodded, drawing nearer to the table to get a better whiff. "Ancient Egyptian embalmers applied spices and scented ointments to the bodies after they had been properly mummified, sometimes even washing the Dearly Departed in palm wine or milk, inside and out. The entire embalming process was quite an elaborate one, often taking as much as seventy days to complete. Rituals and incantations were also involved at various stages of the procedure, including the final wrapping of the mummy."

Scully was not surprised to find Mulder well acquainted with ancient embalming practices. She had reviewed the topic herself on the way here.

"Well, whoever made this mummy gets points for authenticity at least." She removed a small ceramic scarab that had been sewn inside the wrappings. It joined a growing collection of other small charms and amulets that she had found tucked between the layers of linen. This, too, was in keeping with traditional ancient Egyptian burial rites. In theory, the charms were intended to protect the mummy and ease its passage into the afterlife. Most of the amulets were ceramic, although a few were carved from jade, obsidian, or other polished stones. Scully admired the craftsmanship. "Although neither these bandages nor the charms have the look of being thousands of years old. I suspect we may be looking at a mummy of much more recent vintage."

"Just thoroughly old school in style," Mulder said.

"Precisely." She paused to document the location of the scarab amulet before proceeding. "A full forensic analysis of the materials may give us a better idea of when exactly this mummy was created, which might aid in identifying the body."

"So I should hold off on issuing an APB for Cleopatra?"

"Not unless you want to make an asp of yourself."

"Ouch," Mulder said, chuckling at the pun. "That's quite a biting remark."

The gallows humor helped Scully get through the tedious business of unwrapping the mummy. She kept at it until, at last, the final bandages were removed, exposing a mummified female cadaver in a remarkable state of preservation. The dry, tanned skin, stretched tightly over the bones beneath, was smooth and intact with no visible signs of decay. Blonde hair provided a clue to the victim's age and ethnicity, although Scully made a mental note to have it checked for dye. Cotton stuffing had been employed to flesh out the facial features to present a more lifelike, less sunken appearance, while the shriveled eyelids were closed as though in repose. A deep stab wound, directly above the heart, indicated the former placement of Noggle's hunting knife, but Scully also noted a longer incision on the left side of the abdomen. A parchment scroll, inscribed with Egyptian hieroglyphics, had been positioned above the incision—just as she had expected.

Old school indeed, she thought.

"You see that tattoo, Scully?" Mulder's voice held a note of excitement, like a kid who had just found an extra present under the tree. "Right where he stabbed her?"

"I do, Mulder."

The inked design was still visible despite the mummified state of the epidermis. Although damaged by the gaping knife wound, it resembled a kohl-lined human eye, stylized in the fashion of ancient Egyptian artwork and hieroglyphics.

"It's the Eye of Horus," Mulder said eagerly, "also known as the wedjat eye. Back in the days of pharaohs, it was believed to have magical healing properties, both in this life and the next."

"Doesn't look like it did this lady much good," Johns commented. The cop indicated the knife wound over the heart. "Guess even a mummy can't survive getting jabbed in the ticker."

Scully shook her head. "I seriously doubt that Mr. Noggle's knife was the cause of death, for the simple reason that this body could not possibly have been alive when it was stabbed."

Careful dissection only confirmed what she had already come to suspect, based on her earlier study of ancient mummification techniques. Most of the major organs—including the stomach, liver, intestines, and lungs—were missing and the body stuffed with gauze, sawdust, and fragrant flower bulbs to preserve its shape. The brain had also been removed, presumably via the nasal passages as per tradition, and the cranium packed with wadding as well. Only the heart, which the ancients had held to be the seat of consciousness, remained within the mummy's chest, where it had been punctured by the hunting knife—long after the lifeless body had become a mummy.

"I think Eddie Noggle is off the hook," she concluded, "at least as far as death-by-stabbing is concerned. What we appear to have here is a body that has been meticulously embalmed and mummified in the manner of ancient Egypt, but, in my estimation, somewhat more recently than three thousand years ago."

Mulder frowned. No doubt he had been hoping for something more along the lines of the curse of the pharaohs. He looked reluctant to abandon Eddie Noggle's more colorful narrative. "But how do you explain the fact that Eddie saw this mummy up and about just a few nights ago?"

"Without her organs, her brain? Be serious, Mulder," she said. "Eddie's surely seen the same old monster movies we've all seen. He probably stumbled onto the mummy by accident and his disturbed, intoxicated imagination did the rest." She called his attention back to the well-preserved corpse on the table. "Judging from the degree of mummification, and assuming that our unknown embalmer was indeed hewing to the prescribed procedure, this woman died at least two months ago, possibly longer. She was most definitely not walking like an Egyptian through that alley the other night."

"You're probably right," Mulder said, although she could tell that he still wasn't entirely convinced. He squinted at the remains. "So where do you think the mummy came from, on its own feet or otherwise?"

"It seems to me that's the real question before us," Scully said. "Did someone simply desecrate a corpse along archaeological lines, or has a deranged killer mummified his victim for some twisted reason?"

Sadly, she found the latter prospect far more plausible than, say, a living mummy. Human monsters were all too real, as she knew better than most. The grisly care and effort put into preparing the mummy exactly as was done in ages past spoke of morbid obsession, and past experience had taught her how easily such obsessions could cross over into mania. She prayed they didn't have another psychopathic serial killer on their hands.

"So you're saying we may be looking for Norman Bates," Mulder said, "not Boris Karloff?"

Scully recalled that Bates had mummified his mother in the movie, albeit without all the exotic Egyptian trappings. "If Norman was a history major," she replied. "Or an amateur Egyptologist."

"Hmm," Mulder said thoughtfully. She could practically see the wheels turning in his brain. "That suggests a possible line of investigation…"

Before she could ask him what he meant, Chief Johns came forward to inspect the unwrapped mummy. He peered at her desiccated features.

"I wonder who she was." He looked up at Scully. "Think you can identify her, Agent Scully?"

Scully saw a long day getting longer. "I can try," she promised.

"You do that," Mulder said, heading briskly for the door. "Let me know if you pin a name on the Queen of the Nile here."

"And where exactly are you going?" Scully asked.

"To consult with a non-amateur Egyptologist."

WESTERN WASHINGTON UNIVERSITY

"Thank you again, Professor, for agreeing to meet with me on such short notice."

"My pleasure, Agent Mulder. It's not often that the FBI requires my expertise."

Doctor Laila Shalabi was the History Department's resident authority on Middle Eastern history, including ancient Egypt. A handsome and stylish woman who appeared to be in her late thirties, she spoke with a hint of a foreign accent. Egyptian art and curios decorated her office on campus. Glancing around, Mulder spotted a small jade idol of the cat-goddess Bast on top of a file cabinet, as well as a miniature sphinx being used as a paperweight. Bookshelves were packed to overflowing with reference works.

But no empty sarcophagi, he noted. *Darn.*

"I must admit, however, that I'm not sure how much assistance I can be," she added. "I'm quite baffled by what you've told me of this incident, although I can assure you with some confidence that mummies do *not* go for nocturnal strolls, not even millennia ago when such funeral practices were common. My distant ancestors would have found the very notion ludicrous. Living mummies are the stuff of Halloween and horror movies, nothing more."

"So I've been informed," Mulder said dryly. "But at the moment I'm simply looking for more insight into the original practice of mummification." He inspected the professor's bookshelves. "I understand that you teach an honors course in the *Egyptian Book of the Dead*?"

"You've clearly done your homework, Agent Mulder. I wish I could say the same for some of my students." She leaned back in her chair. "How familiar are you with the Book?"

"I know that it's basically a compendium of magic spells, which originally existed in the form of papyrus scrolls." He pulled an annotated copy from the shelf and began to leaf through it. "And that those spells were intended to aid the departed in their passage to the next world."

"It's a bit more complicated than that," she said, "but that's essentially correct. There were actually a number of different versions of the Book, each with slightly different assortments of spells, depending on when and where they were compiled. The spells were often recited during the embalming process, as well inscribed on amulets, tomb walls, and even the interiors of the coffins, in order to guide and protect the dead in the afterlife."

"But none of those spells were meant to reanimate the mummy?"

"Only in the movies," she insisted again. Leaning forward across her desk, she took the Book from his hand and flipped it open to a color reproduction of a piece of ancient Egyptian art depicting a bird with a human head flapping its wings above an ornate sarcophagus. "My ancestors mummified their dead so that the deceased's spirit, their *ba*, commonly represented as a bird, could always find its way home to its body, therefore ensuring its continued existence. But we're talking about immortality in the next world," she emphasized, "not physical immortality in this one."

"Perhaps," he conceded, "but we're also talking about a civilization that endured for more than three thousand years, a long, long time ago. Who knows what arcane secrets might have been lost over the ages? You said yourself that there were alternate versions of the *Book of the Dead*, which varied in their contents. What if certain spells and rituals, perhaps more esoteric than the rest, have fallen into obscurity, unknown even to scholars such as yourself?"

She arched an eyebrow. "Do you believe in magic, Agent Mulder?"

"I believe that recorded history, or at least the 'official' version that makes it into the textbooks, seldom tells the whole story," he said. "And that the truth often has very little to do with what we believe is possible… or impossible."

"You found her? You found our Jill?"

"I'm afraid so, Ms. Broom," Scully said into the phone. "I'm very sorry for your loss."

Identifying the mummy had proved easier than expected. Working from the knowledge that the anonymous woman had died at least two months ago, Scully had zeroed in on a missing-persons report that had been filed with the local police department in approximately the right time frame. Dental records and fingerprints, provided some time ago by the family, confirmed that the body belonged to Jill Marie Broom, a college freshman who had gone missing at the end of the last school year, much to the concern of her anxious parents in Tacoma.

Scully heard muffled sobs at the other end of the line. Seated at a desk in the police station, Scully gave Jill's grieving mother a chance to compose herself, while contemplating a color photo of an attractive young woman whose short blonde hair matched the mummy's. Chief Johns could be forgiven, Scully decided, for not immediately making the connection between the vanished co-ed and the desiccated mummy in the morgue, especially since there had been no clear evidence of foul play where Jill's disappearance was concerned. Nor any known connection to mummies and ancient Egypt for that matter.

"Ms. Broom?" Scully asked gently. "Are you still there?"

"Y-yes," the other woman said hoarsely, obviously choked up. "I suppose I shouldn't be surprised. We've been dreading this call for months now, but, even still, I couldn't help hoping..."

Her voice trailed off.

"When did you last speak to your daughter, Ms. Broom?"

Scully had reviewed the rather skimpy file on Jill's disappearance, of course, but wanted to get a fuller picture in hopes of figuring out how exactly the fresh-faced young art major had ended up gutted and mummified in the manner of a corpse from three thousand years ago.

"Back in June, just before her finals. We'd expected her to head home straight after her exams, but when she didn't show up after a day or two, and we couldn't get hold of her on the phone, I knew something terrible had happened to her. The police told us not to worry, that she'd probably just run off for the summer with some friends or that boy, but Jill wasn't like that. She'd never let us worry so, no matter how... strained... things might have become."

Scully scribbled a note on a pad. "There were issues between you and your daughter?"

"Nothing serious," Evelyn Broom insisted. "It was just that... well, her father and I didn't approve her of going off on her own to a college so far away from us. We thought she should stay closer to home, especially considering her medical condition."

Scully nodded. "Jill had an inoperable brain aneurysm?"

The mummy's brain was still missing, but, judging from Jill's medical records, the unfortunate young woman had not been looking at a long life expectancy. The bulging aneurysm was a ticking time bomb within her brain. It was even money on whether she would have ever made it to her senior year and graduation.

"That's right," her mother verified. "So you can understand why we were concerned about her being hundreds of miles from home with no one to look after her. But Jill... she wanted so much to be independent, 'have a life of her own' she said, that she wouldn't listen to us..."

Scully found herself admiring the young woman, and her apparent determination to make a life for herself despite her condition, even as she empathized with Evelyn Broom's over protective instincts and present grief. How had Jill's entirely laudable quest for independence brought her to an end more grotesque than anything her worried parents could have ever imagined?

"You said something about 'that boy' before," Scully said. "Would that be the 'Bryan' mentioned in your previous statements?"

"Yes," Evelyn said. "I wish I could tell you more about him, but, like I said, Jill had become somewhat touchy where her independence and privacy were concerned." Her voice threatened to crack under the weight of her memories and regrets. "I gathered that she had met some boy, this Bryan, but that's about all I was able to pry out of her." She broke down, sobbing over the phone. "If only I had tried harder to get through to her... or not tried *too* hard..."

"I'm sure you did the best you could, under the circumstances," Scully offered by way of consolation. "And you never learned anything more about this boy?"

"I'm afraid not." Evelyn struggled to regain her composure. "Jill was a very private person, maybe too much so." She sighed ruefully. "All this time, part of me has been hoping that she really had run off on some impetuous romantic adventure, but, in my heart, I knew she was gone forever..."

"I'm so sorry," Scully repeated, wishing that she could do more to ease the other woman's pain. Perhaps closure would bring a measure of comfort in time, but Scully knew better than to guarantee that. Losing a child was a wound few people ever fully recovered from. "I can only imagine how hard this must be for you."

"Just tell me, Agent Scully. Do you know what happened to her? Did she… suffer?"

Scully had spared Ms. Broom a full description of her daughter's remains. The ghastly details would surely emerge in time, but Scully was inclined to let Jill's parents absorb the awful reality of her death before also confronting them with the fact that their lost daughter had been turned into a mock Egyptian mummy post-mortem. Possibly by this mysterious Bryan?

"Her case is still under investigation," she hedged, "but we have every intention of providing you with answers."

"Thank you, Agent Scully. Not that any answer can bring our girl back."

No, Scully thought. *Nothing could. Not even the fabled Eye of Horus.*

"One more question, Ms. Broom. Did Jill have any tattoos that you knew of?"

"No," the other woman said, sounding puzzled. "Why do you ask?"

"So the name 'Jill Broom' means nothing to you?"

Doctor Shalabi shook her head. "I'm sorry, Agent Mulder, but I don't recognize it at all. I can review my records if you like, but I'm fairly certain that this unfortunate young woman never took one of my classes in Egyptology."

"Not even your seminar on *The Book of the Dead*?"

"Especially not that one," she said confidently. "Those were not large classes."

"I see," Mulder said. Still on campus, he'd returned to Shalabi's office after receiving an update from Scully. He resolved to check Jill's college transcript and class list against Shalabi's memories, but he suspected that the professor would remember any student keen enough on ancient Egypt that she would end up mummified like King Tut.

"What about outside of class?" he asked. "Might you have run into her on campus?"

"Not that I recall," she said, "although I'm naturally saddened to hear that your 'mummy' was indeed a member of our student body. It's always tragic when a promising future comes to a premature end."

Mulder had to agree, although the particulars of Jill's sad end remained murky at best.

"We have reason to believe," he said, exploring another avenue, "that Jill was seeing a boy named Bryan before she went missing. Does that ring any bells?"

Shalabi's eyes widened. A frown troubled her features. She opened her mouth to speak, but paused, as though thinking better of it.

"Doctor Shalabi?" he prompted.

"It's probably nothing," she said tentatively. "Indeed, I'm hesitant to mention it at all, but…" She took a deep breath before committing herself. "There *was* a student in my seminar this spring, Bryan Freund, who was somewhat… intense."

Mulder jotted down the name. "Intense how?"

"Very focused. Smart and serious and very engaged with the material, which is what you want in a student, of course, but he also had some… overly imaginative… ideas regarding *The Book of the Dead* and its supposed occult properties." Her voice took on a more professorial tone. "I'm afraid his papers, as well as his contributions to the class discussions, sometimes crossed the line between serious scholarship and, well, sensationalism."

Mulder's interest in Bryan Freund was growing bigger than the pyramids. "And you didn't think to mention this before?"

"It honestly didn't occur to me until you mentioned the name," she said, perhaps a tad defensively. "And, to be honest, I'm still not entirely convinced it's relevant. The minds of eager young college students are often more excitable than disciplined; if I alerted the FBI every time one of my students got carried away with some wild pet theory, I'd need to have you on speed-dial." She sighed and rolled her eyes. "Don't get me started on all the bright young things in my classes who genuinely think that aliens helped build the Sphinx or whatever. You'd be surprised how many otherwise intelligent minds believe such nonsense."

Or maybe not, Mulder thought wryly. He resisted the temptation to debate that particular topic, and instead stayed focused on the task at hand. "But about Bryan Freund…."

She shrugged. "It's quite a leap, Agent Mulder, from a vigorous classroom debate to actually mutilating the body of a fellow student, let alone having something to do with her untimely demise. Bryan could get quite caught up in his theories, but you'll forgive me if I still can't see him as a potential butcher of women."

"Just the same, I'd like to talk to him," Mulder said. "Do you know if he had a girlfriend?"

She mustered a weary smile. "I long ago lost interest in monitoring my students' love lives. Trust me, if you've seen one stormy college romance, you've seen them all."

Mulder could believe it. "How about his address then?"

"That I can probably manage." She fished a thick printed document, about the size of a small phone book, from a desk drawer and handed it to Mulder. "The latest student directory."

It was just starting to get dark by the time Mulder got to Bryan Freund's apartment, which was located in the "student slums" surrounding the campus, smack in the twilight zone between the university and downtown. Vacancy signs occupied the windows of the low-rent housing, reminding Mulder that the fall term had yet to fully begin. He could only hope that Bryan had stayed put over the summer, perhaps to mummify his girlfriend. As Mulder approached the address, he noted that the alley in which the mummy had been found was only a few blocks away.

Only a short stroll for a mummy, he wondered, *or just a convenient place to dump the body?*

Mulder knew which theory Scully would find most plausible, but he preferred to keep an open mind. Why go to all the time and trouble of mummifying Jill Broom's body according to the ancient rites, only to discard the finished product in a dirty alley? Unless perhaps the experiment had not worked out the way Bryan had hoped?

Heavy curtains concealed the interior of Bryan's humble ground-floor apartment and whatever might have transpired there, but Mulder was encouraged to see that the student's name was still on the mailbox outside. He climbed the concrete steps and rapped on the door.

"Hello?"

He waited a few minutes, but nobody answered. He knocked again, more forcefully this time.

"Federal agent!" he identified himself, eliciting curious looks from passersby on the sidewalk. "Open up!"

The door didn't budge. Mulder strained his ears, but was unable to hear any movement inside the apartment. Frustrated, he circled around to the back of the building, where an overstuffed dumpster attracted his attention. Checking out its contents would not require a warrant…

He banged open the lid and peered inside the dumpster, feeling rather like an archaeologist opening up an undiscovered tomb.

"Eureka," he murmured.

Buried in the trash, which looked as though it hadn't been picked up for a while, were several empty cardboard boxes labeled "Natron (Egyptian)" which had apparently been mail-ordered from some New Age supplier, along with empty bottles of palm wine, exotic spices, and other do-it-yourself embalming supplies. Mulder caught a whiff of a familiar odor, not unlike incense, rising from the trash.

Smells like probable cause to me, he thought.

He considered calling Scully for backup before investigating further, but couldn't wait to get to the bottom of the mystery. Intent on learning the truth, before it could be lost or covered up as it had been so many times before, he drew his sidearm, just to be safe, and forced open the back door to the apartment. Flimsy woodwork yielded to the impact of his shoulder.

"Federal agent!" he shouted. "Show yourself!"

No one appeared to be at home, but Mulder advanced carefully through the darkened apartment, taking care to clear every corner. He entered through the small kitchen, which clearly hadn't been cleaned in weeks. Dirty dishes were piled high in the sink and on the kitchen counters. A tower of empty pizza-delivery boxes occupied one corner, threatening to topple over at any moment. Silverfish scuttled away from the intruder's approach. Just the usual student squalor, Mulder mused, or had Bryan been too obsessed with matters Egyptian to bother with housekeeping?

Shadows cloaked the living room as he made his way there. Keeping his gun raised and ready, Mulder groped for a light-switch with his free hand. He flicked on the lights—and any lingering doubts about Bryan's recent activities evaporated.

A makeshift operating table occupied the center of the room, beneath hanging fluorescent lights. The table was tilted at a forty-five degree angle—to allow any remaining body fluids to drain into the empty bucket at the foot of the table. The table was currently empty, although Mulder could make out a Jill-sized impression on the stained sheets atop the flat surface; he assumed that the former occupant of the table was presently on ice at the morgue. A tray of tools, resting on a rolling cart near the operating table, included a polished obsidian knife, a wooden scraper, and a long metal rod with a hook at the end, presumably for extracting a mummy's brain out through its nasal passages. Mulder winced at the thought.

Lifting his gaze from the operating table, where Jill Broom's lifeless remains had doubtlessly been mummified, Mulder spotted a large wooden sarcophagus propped up against a wall at the far end of the room. A stylized portrait of Jill had been painted on the closed lid of the coffin, possibly by Jill herself? He recalled that Jill had been an art major...

Was she in on this? he wondered. Facing an untimely death, had she and Bryan sought to grant her immortality through some bizarre murder-mummification pact? And had it actually worked long enough for her to make it to Eddie Noggle's alley on her own power?

Anxious for answers, he scanned the room in search of more clues. Scattered Egyptian idols and artwork reminded him of Laila Shalabi's office, while books on ancient gods and mythology occupied a significant percentage of the bookshelves. It was an impressive collection; Bryan had almost as many books on mummies as Mulder had on UFOs. The agent spotted Shalabi's name on the spine of one particularly dog-eared volume. Numerous Post-its sprouted from the text, marking page after page. The professor's views on *The Book of the Dead* seemed to have made quite an impression on Bryan—or had the absent student always been obsessed with mummies?

Mulder suspected the latter.

Time to bring Scully up to speed, he decided. Fishing his phone from his pocket, he dialed his partner. She picked up immediately.

"Mulder?"

"I'm at Bryan Freund's apartment," he told her, "which seems to be where our mummy was created." He quickly filled her in on his discoveries. "Bryan is clearly our amateur embalmer. But we still don't know how exactly Jill died."

And whether she stayed that way, he added silently.

"I'll notify Chief Johns," Scully volunteered, "but you should get out of there, Mulder. It's not safe."

"I appreciate your concern, but I think I can probably handle one off-kilter college kid if he makes an appearance." He eyed the sealed sarcophagus on the other side of the room. "Let me check out one more thing. Wanna bet Bryan's homemade sarcophagus is missing a mummy?"

"Just be careful, Mulder."

"Aren't I always?"

She sighed at the other end of the line. "Do you really want me to answer that?"

"Let me get back to you on that." He started toward the sarcophagus, working his way around the tilted operating table, but paused as his gaze fell upon four large ceramic jars lined up atop a squat wooden altar. The jars, which he'd overlooked before, were inscribed with hieroglyphics, while each of their lids was sculpted in the image of a different Egyptian deity, bearing, respectively, the head of a man, a falcon, a baboon, and a jackal. Mulder recognized the gods from his research.

The Sons of Horus.

"I'm serious, Mulder," Scully said into his ear. "You should wait for backup before—"

"Hang on, Scully," he interrupted her. "I think I may have just found those missing internal organs."

Back in the day, he knew, the embalmers of ancient Egypt had stored the deceased's entrails in canopic jars just like these ones. Mulder detoured over to the jars, turning his back on the sarcophagus. Bracing himself for what he expected to find, he holstered his gun and removed the falcon-headed stopper from one of the jars. A familiar spicy scent invaded his nostrils. He forced himself to look inside.

Sure enough, coils of dried, withered intestines filled the jar.

Jill Broom's intestines.

Mulder grimaced in disgust. In theory, Jill's liver, stomach, and lungs occupied the other jars. Everything except her brain, which the ancients had believed inconsequential as far as the *ba* was concerned. Did he need to open all of them, or could he leave that to Scully and Chief Johns?

"They're here, Scully. The rest of Jill's remains. Preserved and packed away for all eternity—"

A shadow fell across the jars. Distracted by his grisly discovery, Mulder reacted too slowly. He started to spin around, while reaching for his gun, but a hard, heavy object smacked him in the back of the head. He fell forward, crashing into the jars, as his phone flew from his grip. He collapsed amid a heap of broken pottery and embalmed innards. Consciousness fading, he dimly heard Scully crying out in the background.

"Mulder? Mulder! What is it? What's happening?!"

Then darkness claimed him…

"Where is she?" an angry voice demanded. "What have you done with her?"

Cold water splashed against Mulder's face, rousing him abruptly from dreams of dusty desert tombs. Sputtering, he tried to sit up, only to find himself bound to the operating table by thick strips of linen. The back of his skull throbbed like hell and water dripped down his face. Groggy and in pain, it took him a moment to remember how he'd ended up in this situation. He'd been checking out the canopic jars holding Jill's organs when…

"Where is she?" the voice demanded again. "Tell me!"

Mulder looked up to see the Anubis, the jackal-headed guardian of the dead, glaring at him from the foot of the table. No, he corrected himself, as his blurry vision came into focus, there was a figure *wearing an Anubis mask* yelling at him. A leopard skin was draped over the man's chest, in the manner of an ancient Egyptian priest. Mulder couldn't tell if the skin was fake or not, but he had a pretty good idea who was behind the mask.

"Bryan?"

Twisting his head to look around, Mulder saw that the empty sarcophagus was open. *Bryan must have hidden inside the coffin when I broke in,* he realized, a little too late. *Then whacked me from behind when I wasn't looking.*

Serves me right for not listening to Scully…

"Listen to me, Bryan. I'm with the FBI. My name is—"

"I know who you are, Agent Mulder," the masked student barked. "I found your wallet… and your gun." He brandished the long metal brain hook menacingly. "But what are you doing here? Did *she* tell you where to find me?"

Mulder guessed that the hooked metal rod was responsible for the lump at the back of his head. His foggy brain tried to make sense of what Bryan was asking. "Who? Doctor Shalabi?"

"No, no!" Bryan exclaimed. "Not her. I mean, Jill. *My* Jill!"

The crazed student was sounding more and more agitated. The hinged jaw of his Anubis mask opened and closed rapidly. He waved the brain hook around in a way that made Mulder more than slightly nervous.

Keep him talking, Mulder thought. *Scully knows where I am. She'll be here soon.*

Plus, Mulder still had plenty of questions that needed answers.

"Jill is in the morgue," he said. "The police found her mummy in an alley not far from here. But how did she—?"

"You found her?" Bryan sounded both relieved and horrified. "I've been looking everywhere for her, ever since she slipped away when I wasn't looking." The words gushed from his lips like the raging headwaters of the Nile. "I knew I should have kept watch over her, until her *ba* returned to her body, but I was so tired and worn out, after working so hard for so long. I had to get a little sleep and it didn't seem like the spells were working. I thought I must have done something wrong…"

Mulder struggled to keep up. "Slow down, Bryan. Talk to me. Make me understand." He strained against the unyielding bandages, but Bryan had done too good a job of wrapping him. No real surprise there, Mulder figured; the self-taught embalmer had plenty of practice binding bodies. "This was all to save Jill, right? To keep her from dying—or to bring her back from the dead?"

The jackal head nodded. "Death was waiting for her. We knew we had no future unless we took her fate into our own hands. And I knew it could be done!" He snatched *The Book of the Dead* from the shelf and held it up for Mulder to see. "The clues—the secrets—are all there, if you know where to look. Not just immortality in the next world, but here on Earth as well and for all eternity. Ask Shalabi. She knows even though she won't admit it. But I figured it out on my own and I knew it would work." Emotion raised his voice an octave. "It was our only hope!"

"So what happened?" Mulder was desperate to find out, despite his own dire circumstances. "Did it work?"

"I wasn't sure, not at first," Bryan admitted. "I thought I'd done everything right, with the charms and the spells and the ointments, but when she didn't wake up right away, I began to lose faith. I was afraid that that I'd gotten it wrong somehow, that I'd missed some crucial step, or maybe even that I'd just been fooling myself all along." He took off the mask to reveal an anguished expression. His pale face was sweaty and distraught. "How was I to know that she would rise without me there, while I was sleeping?"

Was that what had happened? Mulder imagined the mummy waking in the dark, returning to life in defiance of science and mortality. How would anyone react to that, even assuming their mind and memories were still intact? Confused and disoriented by her unnatural resurrection, with no one on hand to ease her transition, had the mummy of Jill Broom staggered out into the night, only to die a second time at the business end of a panicked wino's knife?

"But it's not too late!" Bryan ranted. His eyes gleamed with madness or obsession. He ran his hand through a disheveled mop of hair. "I know what to do now. I just need to get her back... before her spirit departs this plane forever!"

Was it possible? Mulder wondered. Could Bryan bring the mummy back to life again?

His phone rang loudly, interrupting the tense encounter. Bryan retrieved it from the floor where it had fallen before. He held it to his ear. "Hello? Who's this?"

"That's probably my partner," Mulder said. "Let's me talk to her—"

"No!" Bryan snarled into the phone. "Listen to me, whoever you are. I want Jill's body and I want it now. Bring her back to me or..." He faltered, groping for a suitably fearsome threat, and his gaze fell upon the brain hook in his grip. "Or I'll pull Agent Mulder's brain out through his nose!"

Scully gasped out loud. Her heart skipped a beat.

"Bryan? This is Bryan, isn't it?" She fought to keep her voice steady and under control. "You don't need to do anything drastic. We can work this out..."

"There's nothing to discuss," said the agitated voice that had answered Mulder's phone. "Bring me Jill, without any tricks, or your partner's skull will be as empty as my heart!"

He hung up abruptly.

"Crap," Chief Johns muttered as he drove the squad car across town toward Bryan Freund's current address. Scully rode shotgun beside him.

"That sounds like some serious crazy." He gave Scully a sympathetic look. "Sorry your partner's up to his neck in it. You can count on my department to do what we can to get him out of there safely."

"Thank you." Scully tried redialing, but nobody picked up. *Damn it, Mulder. Why couldn't you wait for me?*

Johns hit the gas and turned on his siren. "Attention all officers," he barked into the car's dashboard mike. "We have a possible hostage situation at 39 Pine Nut Lane. Dispatch SWAT team to scene immediately. Over." He glanced again at Scully. "So what do you think, Agent Scully? Do we give this wack job what he wants? I mean, the poor girl is dead anyway, and your partner is still alive… at least as far as we know."

"I'm not certain," Scully confessed. It was tempting to go get the mummy and attempt to exchange it for Mulder, but how would Bryan react when he saw that she had unwrapped the mummy, undoing all his careful preparations? "It's difficult to predict his behavior. That might just make things worse and place Mulder in even greater jeopardy."

The sky darkened as thick black clouds rolled in, seemingly out of nowhere. Thunder rumbled overhead.

"What the hell?" Johns grumbled. "Where did this storm come from?"

"Do you know how exactly the ancients removed the brains of the dead, Agent Mulder?" Bryan paced impatiently around the living room, still gripping the vicious-looking brain hook. "It's trickier than you might think. First you drive the hook up through a nostril into the brain cavity, then you have to break up the gray matter, so you can scoop it out in chunks…"

Mulder swallowed hard. Bryan seemed to be growing more unraveled by the minute, which didn't bode well for the bound agent's chances. He assumed that Scully and the cops were en route, but Bryan had the upper hand right now.

And that hand was holding a hook.

"Is that what you did with Jill?" Mulder asked, mostly to keep Bryan talking but also because he still needed to know the truth. "Remove the brain—and the aneurysm—that was going to kill her? But how could she remember you, and the love you shared, without her brain?" A possibility occurred to Mulder. "Perhaps that's why she wandered away after she woke. Because she could no longer comprehend what had happened to her."

Maybe Eddie Noggle had merely killed a mindless mummy, nothing more.

"No! You understand nothing! The brain is nothing as far as the gods are concerned. It's just meat." Bryan thumped his chest with his free hand. "The heart is where the spirit abides, and where true immortality is to be found. The ancients knew that, thousands of years before our so-called 'science.' It's all there in The Book, if only you have eyes to see!"

"All right." Mulder attempted to calm his captor. "Help me understand. Talk me through it."

Thunder boomed overhead. The lights flickered briefly.

"What is this?" Bryan glared suspiciously up at the lights. "Some sort of trick?" He leaned across the operating table and positioned the curved tip of the brain hook beneath Mulder's nose, right up against the left nostril. "What sneaky FBI tactics are you hiding in that brain of yours?"

Mulder flinched at the touch of the cold metal hook. He tried not to think about it being rammed upwards into his brain. Would that be quick and painless—or excruciating?

"It's just a storm!" he said urgently. "Thunder and lightning, that's all. Can't you hear it?"

Funny, he thought. *It hadn't seemed all that overcast before…*

A resounding crack of thunder, directly above them, knocked out the lights for good, throwing the curtained living room into darkness. For a horrifying moment, Mulder feared that the sudden black-out would drive Bryan to carry out his threat, but then a hot, dry wind seemed to invade the apartment despite the absence of any open windows. An exotic perfume pervaded the air.

"No!" Bryan gasped. "What are you doing here? Why have you come?" He stumbled backwards, away from the table. His voice was shrill. "You can't stop me, not after I've come so far. I can still save her. I can bring her back—!" Mulder heard Bryan thrashing in the dark, as though trying to fend off some unseen apparition. He knocked over the tray of embalming tools, which clattered loudly onto the floor. "Stay back! Keep away from me! Anubis, great god of the underworld, protect me from—!"

His desperate pleas gave way to a blood-curdling scream, which ended abruptly in a strangled death rattle. He crashed heavily to the floor.

"Bryan?" Mulder strained helplessly against his bonds. "Bryan! Can you hear me?"

No answer came from the fallen student. Trapped in darkness, unable to investigate, Mulder heard only his own racing heartbeat, the fading thunder, and—or was it just his imagination—the faint fluttering of wings?

A SWAT team burst through the door. Flashlights and ruby-red lasers cut through the shadows as cops in body armor stormed the apartment, securing the scene. Scully rushed in after them.

"Mulder!" she cried out. "Are you all right? We heard a scream."

"It's all right," he assured her. "It wasn't me."

The lights came back on, revealing the lifeless body of Bryan Freund sprawled upon the floor. Blood trickled from one nostril, where the brain hook had been driven deep into his skull. Glassy eyes stared blankly into eternity.

"Looks like he offed himself," Chief Johns concluded. "Crazy bastard."

Mulder wasn't so sure. "Maybe."

"Suicide is the only explanation that makes sense," Scully insisted, after the body had been carted away and Mulder cut loose from the operating table. The two agents stood in the living room, surveying the evidence of the bizarre project that had consumed Bryan and possibly Jill as well. "The storm knocked out the power, pushing Bryan over the edge. With his deranged plans unravelling, and the police closing in, he gave up and took his own life, perhaps hoping to join Jill in some mythic Egyptian afterlife. It's a sad, tragic story, but not inexplicable."

"I don't know," Mulder replied. "I couldn't see anything in the dark, but it sounded like he was afraid for his life. As though some vengeful entity had come for him."

Scully shrugged. "A psychotic break? You said yourself that he was growing increasingly unstable." She shuddered at how far Bryan's madness had nearly driven him. "My God, Mulder, he was only moments away from yanking your brain out in pieces."

"But that still doesn't explain how the mummy ended up in that alley," Mulder said stubbornly. "Unless maybe she did leave her under her own power... just like Bryan believed."

Scully sighed. Why did her partner always have to resist the obvious?

"What's more plausible, Mulder? That an eviscerated corpse woke up and walked away… or that Bryan simply panicked and dumped Jill's body when he failed to bring it back to life?"

"But why then was he so determined to get the mummy back?" Mulder asked.

"He was erratic, Mulder. Perhaps he thought he'd figured out where he'd gone wrong before and wanted to try again." She tried to get Mulder to apply Occam's razor for once and accept a more mundane truth. "There was never anything supernatural here; just a troubled young man overcome by a morbid obsession. And a doomed couple caught up in a strange *folie a deux*."

Mulder started to argue the point, but his heart didn't seem to be in it. "Maybe you're right, Scully. I hate to admit it, but I suppose this time around there really *is* a rational explanation for everything." He grinned wryly. "I guess it was bound to happen eventually."

Scully decided to let that pass.

"Let's go home, Mulder."

The flutter of wings briefly disturbed the silence of Laila Shalabi's bedchamber before her eyes opened and she woke to a new day, body and spirit joined once more. Her hand went to her chest, where the Eye of Horus was tattooed upon her flesh, above her beating heart.

It was a pity, she reflected, that Bryan had to die, but she was grateful that Agent Mulder had survived. If the gods were kind, Bryan's death would bring an end to this unwelcome investigation. There were some secrets, long buried beneath the sands of time, which were best hidden from the light of day. She would have to be more careful in the future, more circumspect in her teachings, so that she did not reveal more than she intended. Bryan had caught a glimpse of a greater truth and it had driven him mad.

She could not let that happen again.

Her brain, full of ancient wisdom, rested securely in her skull. Sacred amulets, inscribed with forgotten spells and symbols, adorned her ageless body as she rose from her bed to greet the dawn.

As she had many, many times before.

THE END

the
Truth
is out
There

PHASE SHIFT

By Bev Vincent

The Robertsons were enjoying a quiet Friday evening at home. Mel cooked steaks to go with the baked potatoes his wife, Cathy, had put in the oven when she got home from work. The adults shared a bottle of Cabernet Sauvignon. Teenager Emily had a glass of milk. Milo, their dog, gnawed on the leftover bones once the dishes were scraped clean and placed in the dishwasher.

After dinner, Mel put a tape in the VCR. Emily had already seen the movie, so she retired to her room to talk to her friends on the telephone, a recent addition that Mel was starting to regret.

Halfway through the film, a blinding white light illuminated the yard outside their living room window, an intense flare that lasted several seconds. At first, Mel thought something had exploded, but there was no sound other than an alarming hum that reminded him of overworked electronics.

The instant the flash of light in the back yard cut off, the power in the house went out, too. Mel headed for the circuit breaker box, which was mounted on the outside wall of their dining room, but he couldn't get the patio door open. He felt around the perimeter to make sure he'd removed all the locks and pins, but the sliding window refused to budge.

Milo started barking, but, in the darkness, no one could tell at what. Emily emerged from her room, complaining that her call had been interrupted. Cathy rummaged through a drawer in the kitchen and came up with a few candles, which she placed around the living room. This was hurricane territory, so they were reasonably well prepared, although the batteries in Mel's big flashlight were dead. He fumbled around in the laundry room cabinets for replacements and finally got it to work.

He went to the front door, intending to circle around the house to the breaker box. Try as he might, though, he couldn't get a firm grip on the doorknob. He could tell where it was—he could see the reflection of flickering candlelight in the brass fixture—but he couldn't feel it.

He was confused, but not defeated. There was still the garage door. With the power out, the automatic opener was of no use, but he couldn't even get the door to budge an inch after releasing the locking mechanism.

He was perplexed by his inability to get out of the house, but didn't want to alarm his family. He strolled back to the patio window to see if their neighbors were affected by the outage, but everything beyond the glass pane was blurry and indistinct.

"Never mind," Cathy said. "The power will come back on eventually. This is nice, sitting around by candlelight." She suggested opening a second bottle of wine. It was a Friday night, so Mel thought, why not? Their problem—assuming it persisted—could wait until the light of day.

Emily returned to her room, grumbling and complaining. Milo barked some more and twisted his head at the front door for a while, but eventually returned to the T-bone under the kitchen table. Cathy was right, Mel decided. It was sort of nice.

The first night was, anyway.

<hr/>

WASHINGTON, D.C.
7th MAY, 1996, 7 a.m.

After partnering with Fox Mulder for a few years, Special Agent Dana Scully was used to his mysterious summonses. She showed up at Dulles without any idea where they were headed or for what purpose. He'd only said that they were going someplace warm.

She found him at the airport, sitting near a bank of payphones, cracking open sunflower seeds with his teeth and depositing the shells into his jacket pocket. He handed her an airline ticket and a boarding pass. She glanced at the documents.

"What's in Houston?" she asked.

"Besides killer Tex-Mex and the Oilers?" Mulder shrugged.

"You don't know why we're going?"

"I have no idea," Mulder said. "That's part of the fun, right?" He told her they were looking into the disappearance of a family, without supplying any details. "We'll know more when we get there," he said.

"Is this an officially sanctioned case?" she asked as they walked to the gate.

"Skinner and I have an understanding," Mulder said. "After all, he keeps the X-Files going to stir up the people he reports to. He thinks we make them nervous. Maybe even scared."

"You're not talking about the Director, are you?"

Mulder smiled and shook his head. He pantomimed smoking a cigarette and raised an eyebrow. "Besides. Skinner owes us after we helped save his job."

Scully nodded. "So what makes this situation an X-File?"

"After you read this, you'll know as much as I do," he said, handing her a manila folder.

Though they sat in adjacent seats on the three-hour flight, there were too many people nearby for them to discuss the contents of the file. She scanned the documents and turned to her partner with a quizzical look after she read the final page, but waited until after they landed and picked up a rental car before asking any questions.

"You found the file folder in your office?"

"On my chair."

"And you have no idea who put it there."

"Nope."

"Your special friend?"

His irregular informant, the man he thought of as X, had been maintaining radio silence for the past several weeks. Considering their history, Mulder didn't trust the man's allegiances or his motivations. "Maybe."

"You're sure this isn't some kind of wild goose chase? We've been down that road before."

Mulder shrugged again. There were so many unknowns in their work.

HOUSTON, TEXAS
7th MAY, 1996, 11:15 a.m.

As Scully negotiated the spaghetti maze of roads around Houston Inter-
continental Airport with the car's air conditioning blasting, Mulder flipped
through the contents of the manila folder again. It didn't bear the normal
markings of an X-File—it was unadorned except for a single, neatly
printed word on the tab: the name of the city they were now approaching.

The first sheet was the top half of a page ripped from a copy of the
Houston Post dated two weeks ago. An item near the middle was outlined in
thick black marker, a three-column-inch report about a family missing for
a week from a Houston neighborhood. Their relatives were asking anyone
with information regarding their whereabouts to please contact the Houston
Police Department's Missing Persons Bureau.

Next was an article about a mysterious incident two years ago in
suburban Pittsburgh. The residents of a high-rise apartment had been
trapped inside the building for over a week, unable to communicate with
the outside world. Mulder had recognized the font and style of the article
immediately—it came from *The Lone Gunman*, a monthly periodical to
which he had a lifetime subscription. The report featured a photograph of
a concrete building and the magazine's hallmark overblown prose and
rampant speculation as to the cause of this enigmatic occurrence, along
with lurid details and first-person accounts about how the residents had
survived their unexplained incarceration.

The final document was a two-page spread from a very early issue of *The
Lone Gunman*. In enormous letters, the centerfold article proclaimed a
GOVERNMENT COVER-UP of ALIEN EXPERIMENTS on INNOCENT
AMERICANS. There were grainy photographs of alleged military vehicles
on the outskirts of a small town in Alaska. A rudimentary map of the state
indicated the town's location with an enormous arrow.

Mulder read the article aloud. It suggested that aliens had cut the town
off from the rest of the world for several weeks while performing unspecified
experiments on its population. Martial law had been invoked once the
outside world became aware of the town's plight, and the National Guard
was dispatched—except it wasn't really the National Guard but rather

specially trained Black Ops soldiers whose main objective was to take control of the story and prevent it from making headlines. They had set up camp on the edge of town until the mysterious force confining the town's residents vanished. They had then (according to the authors of the article) descended upon the town like an invading force.

Tempers had flared among the entrapped populace during their confinement and several people had been killed. Others died in the aftermath, though the circumstances were vague. None of the town's surviving residents were willing to discuss the incident with journalists. Most denied that anything unusual had happened. The article contained the standard paranoid disclaimers about how much risk the reporters were taking by disseminating this information, but it was the magazine's mandate to expose these things whenever they came to light.

Nothing in the file drew any connections between the two earlier incidents and the recent disappearances, but the implication seemed obvious.

Mulder's cellular phone chirped. He pulled it from the pocket of his suit coat and yanked out the antenna. "Mulder," he said. He listened for several seconds. "Yes, I know the shadow government might be listening." Another long pause. "I wanted to ask about a couple of articles you published." He looked at Scully and shook his head. "If you want to get the word out, then you need people to listen, don't you?" He closed his eyes. "No, I understand that. Just give me a second. What can you tell me about the incident in Alaska in 1989? Yes, that one."

While Mulder listened, Scully navigated the freeway leading into the city, occasionally glancing at a map on the dashboard for directions.

"Okay," Mulder said. "And the apartment building in Pittsburgh a couple of years ago. Did you ever connect the two incidents?"

Mulder held the phone away from his ear so Scully could hear the loud, excited voice on the other end of the line. When it started to die down, Mulder attempted to speak again. "Okay, thanks. If you come up with anything, get back to me, all right?" He disconnected the call.

"Which one was that?" Scully asked.

"Not your boyfriend," Mulder said with a grin, "if that's what you were wondering. I think I just made Langly's head explode." He grabbed the map from the dashboard and looked around to orient himself. "Take this exit," he said. Then he made another phone call.

A police cruiser was waiting for them in the parking lot of a strip mall three blocks from the interstate. Hot, sticky air engulfed Mulder and Scully as they got out of their rental vehicle and flashed their FBI credentials at the officer seated behind the wheel. The cop, who looked to be in his late twenties, got out with apparent reluctance. "My lieutenant said to cooperate with you," he said.

"We appreciate that," Scully replied. She was already starting to sweat in the unaccustomed humidity and it was barely noon.

"Don't know what all the fuss is about. Family goes on vacation and suddenly it's a big deal."

"You know that for a fact?" Mulder asked.

The cop shrugged. "It's not like there are bodies or reports of violence or anything else suspicious."

"You checked their place out?"

"Sure. The dispatcher sent me over there after someone reported them missing."

"When was this?" Scully asked.

"Dunno. Two, maybe three weeks ago? I could check my notes."

Mulder said, "That would be helpful."

The cop pulled a small, spiral-bound notebook from his back pocket and leafed through the pages. He went all the way back to the beginning and then paged through it again. Finally, he stopped. "Here it is," he said, scratching his head. "Nothing suspicious."

"That's it?"

"That's it." He confirmed the date for them.

"Any follow-up?"

He shrugged again. "None was requested."

They let him return to duty.

"Houston's finest," Mulder said. "Mostly harmless."

"What now?"

"Now we check out the place for ourselves. See how unsuspicious it really is."

The Robertsons lived in a quiet urban neighborhood on the south side of U.S. 59, one of the three main thoroughfares that transected the city. The street was tree-lined and, perhaps, gentrified. A few cars were parked next to the curb, but most were in driveways or garages. The yards were well maintained. However, thanks to the city's virtually non-existent zoning regulations, there was a service station at one end of the block and an antiques store near the other end.

Scully pulled up in front of the house, using street numbers painted on the curbs for navigation. Before getting out of the car, she surveyed the neighborhood. A resident across the street pushed back the living room curtains and looked out, but attentive—or nosy—neighbors weren't unusual for this kind of community.

The single-story house was about as nondescript as they came. Nothing about the place registered in Scully's mind. Even its color was hard to pin down. It was unsettling, in fact. There were plenty of trees around it, casting shadows, but there was more to it than that. If she blinked, she could almost convince herself that the house didn't exist.

"Excuse me," a voice called out. "Excuse me."

Scully turned, expecting to see an older lady with gray hair, perhaps with a yappy dog on a leash. Instead, she was greeted by a woman about her own age. She was wearing a business suit, and her makeup was restrained but expertly applied.

Scully glanced at her partner, but he was already halfway up the walkway to the front door. "Yes?" she asked.

"You look official. Are you looking for the Robertsons?"

Scully flashed her credentials. "Do you know them?"

"Oh, sure," the woman said. "Everyone knows everyone around here."

"We have a report that they're missing. When did you last see them?"

The woman tilted her head to one side. "Huh. You know, I'm not exactly sure. It's been a while."

"Three weeks?"

"Maybe. That long? It's funny. Now that I think about it, you might be right."

"They didn't say they were going anywhere? Vacation? A cruise?"

The woman shook her head. "Not that I recall. Isn't that strange?"

"Have you seen anything suspicious?" Scully noticed that the woman didn't look at the house.

"Um. No. Not that I recall. Listen, I'm going to be late for my appointment. Nice talking with you." She turned on her modest heels and headed toward her car, which was parked in the driveway.

Scully shook her head. It had been a strange encounter. Not many people thought it was nice talking with them, and the woman seemed to be having problems recalling things.

She circled around the rental car and started up the stone walkway toward the front door. Only then did she realize that the grass on the front lawn was long and straggly, and a sickly color of pale green. Fast food containers and faded newspapers were strewn across the yard. She couldn't believe she hadn't noticed before.

Scully scrutinized the house. At first it looked like the clapboard exterior could use a coat of paint, but when she blinked it appeared to change color. The whole thing seemed strangely out of focus. The windows, instead of reflecting the noon-day sun, were dark and blurry, as if they were absorbing all the light in their proximity. She detected a strange odor that reminded her of the aftermath of a lightning strike, and the air felt fully charged with static electricity. The rotating roof ventilator was motionless and, though Scully had noticed several in the trees and on the ground near their car when they parked, there were no birds around the house. A preternatural silence enveloped them, as if they were cut off from the rest of the world.

Scully frowned at Mulder as she approached him.

"Interesting, eh?" he said when she reached the front door. "Wait until you try this."

"Try what?"

"Open the door."

"Mulder, we don't have a warrant."

"Don't worry about that. Just try the doorknob."

Scully reached for the knob. It felt warm and fuzzy, but she couldn't get a grip on it. It had substance—her hand didn't pass through it—but she couldn't close her hand on it to turn it.

"What's going on, Mulder?"

Mulder gave her one of his childlike grins and put his shoulder against the door. She could see where the solid oak pressed against the material of his suit coat, but he didn't seem to be making real contact with it. He pounded on the door, but there was no sound.

They crossed the lawn to the living room window. Scully thought at first that she detected motion within, but everything was out of focus, as if she were looking through a thick quartz crystal instead of glass.

"Do you think there's anyone inside?" Scully asked.

"I tried calling," he said, "but the phone doesn't ring. No busy signal or disconnect message. Nothing." His smile had been replaced by a more serious look, one Scully recognized.

"I suppose you're about to tell me that this part of Texas is a hotbed of alien activity."

"Farther west, maybe," he said. "Not here."

"I'm going to canvas the neighbors," Scully said.

While she was gone, Mulder circled the house twice. He couldn't see through any of the windows—it was like the glass had been somehow corrupted. In the backyard, he threw a rock at a sliding glass patio door, but it simply struck the pane without making any sound and fell. There was an audible thud when it hit the ground.

A while later, Scully rejoined him on the front steps. "A lot of people aren't home. Those who were don't remember anything unusual," she said. "Which is in itself strange, because everyone I spoke with knew all the details of everyone else's lives on the street. No one found it odd that they hadn't seen the Robertsons lately until I brought it up. A couple of people said there might have been a bright light one night a few weeks ago, but they weren't sure. Might have been a dream, one woman said. Have you ever encountered anything like this before?"

Mulder shook his head. "I think the phenomenon is similar to what happened in Alaska and Pittsburgh. Something is blocking people from getting in or out, and it's also preventing people from noticing that anything out of the ordinary is happening."

"But how? And who? No, wait, don't tell me. I know what you're going to say."

"I think this house is out of phase with reality."

Scully opened and closed her mouth. "Okay, I take that back. Sometimes you say things without seeming to take into account the fact that I have a degree in physics. 'Out of phase with reality.' What does that even mean?"

"How would you explain this?" Mulder asked. He lobbed another rock at the living room window. "Or how would your friend Mr. Einstein, for that matter?"

Scully was silent for a few seconds. "It must be some sort of force field."

Mulder smirked. "Have you ever encountered a force field anywhere besides in comic books? Especially one that fits the shape of a house exactly, right down to the doorknob?"

Scully didn't respond.

"And if it is a force field, what's generating it? And why here?"

"I don't know, Mulder. Maybe it's a geomagnetic anomaly?"

Mulder's phone rang again. He barely got a chance to say his name before the person on the other end launched into a monologue. Finally, Mulder was able to interject. "Slow down. Yes, that's right. Maybe so." He listened some more. "I was thinking the same thing. Do you think he can help?" He nodded. "We'll be here."

"What was that all about?" Scully asked after Mulder hung up.

"A friend of our *tres amigos* back in Virginia has some gear they think might help. He's on his way."

They sat in the car with the A/C running while awaiting the arrival of a man named Sampson who ran a Radio Shack at the Galleria mall.

"Do you think the Robertsons have been trapped inside the house all this time, like those people in the apartment building?" Scully asked. "If we believe that story, which I have to say sounds mighty far-fetched to me. And as for the town…"

"Stranger things have happened."

Scully raised her eyebrows, but didn't reply.

"It's possible that time is moving at a different rate for them. Three weeks for us might be three days for them, or three hours. Maybe it's suspended altogether. We can only hope. Can you imagine what it would be like to be stuck at your place for three weeks?"

"Or yours," Scully said. "You'd die of starvation after a couple of days."

"I could survive on my fish for a while."

"Mulder," Scully said, making a face. She took a breath. "Where do these wild theories of yours come from, anyway? You always seem to have an explanation. Phase shifts. Really?"

Mulder grinned. "I can't take responsibility for that one. When I talked to Langly the first time, he mentioned that as a possible theory behind what happened in Pittsburgh. He hadn't made the connection to the Alaska incident, though, so they're going back through their files to see if they can find any evidence of a similar phenomenon."

"I wonder about those guys," Scully said. "I wonder a lot. Like, what do they do for money?"

"I think Frohike hires himself out at dances," Mulder said.

Scully's jaw dropped. "You're not serious."

"Don't ask questions unless you want answers," Mulder said.

A few minutes later, a dented, yellow AMC Pacer adorned with fringes of rust pulled up behind them. A man wearing a tight black t-shirt, a cowboy hat, boots and the shortest shorts Scully had seen on a grown man in her life emerged. Mulder and Scully got out to greet him.

"You Sampson?" Mulder asked. He reached for his credentials.

"You don't need to show me those," Sampson said with a drawl. He looked around as if to see if anyone else was watching. "This the place?"

Mulder nodded. They went to the front door, where Sampson spent several minutes taking readings on a small gadget that looked to Scully like an off-the-shelf voltage meter. He tested the doorknob and tried rapping on the door. He peered into the living room window, with his hands over his brow to block out the afternoon sun.

"This is pretty awesome," he said after a while. "Never seen nothing quite like it."

"Can you help us?" Mulder asked.

"Sure. I think so. Maybe we should wait 'til the sun goes down, though? Wouldn't want to draw too much attention to ourselves."

"I think we could strip naked and do jumping jacks on the front lawn and the neighbors wouldn't notice," Mulder said. He pointed to the litter strewn across the overgrown yard. "Something about this place makes people not pay any attention to it."

"You sure?" Sampson asked, and for a second Scully was afraid he was going to put Mulder's hypothetical idea to the test.

"We'll be okay," Mulder said.

"Okay. You're the boss. I'll jes' get my gear out of the car."

The Pacer's voluminous storage area held several large metal cases. Mulder helped him carry them to the front lawn, breaking out in a sweat from the elevated humidity.

"Told you we should'a waited 'til later," Sampson said. "It'll be cooler then." He paused. "A little."

"Just show us what to do." He took off his jacket and slung it over his shoulder.

"This is delicate paraphernalia," Sampson said. "You guys go buy yourselves a cup of coffee and a donut and give me some time to get everything in place."

"I am kind of hungry," Mulder said. "Any recommendations?"

Sampson told them about a taco truck that was usually parked in a lot a few blocks away, but Scully vetoed that idea. "We'll find something. With air conditioning."

They had a quick bite in a family restaurant near the highway. When they got back, Sampson was putting the finishing touches on a series of small instruments that encircled the house. Each one had a set of flashing LEDs and a pair of what appeared to be tiny radar dishes.

"Each one communicates with the next one in the circuit," Sampson said.

"What exactly do they do?" Scully asked.

"You wouldn't understand."

"Try me."

"We're working under the assumption that a phase modulation is affecting the fundamental structure of the constituent molecules of the house, right?"

Scully nodded, but said nothing.

"Well, this here is gonna fix that."

"I'm glad you explained it," Scully said. "It's all so clear to me now."

"What next?" Mulder asked.

"I flip this here switch."

"And then?"

"One of you gets to go inside."

"Why just one of us?"

"Everyone has his own elemental field, you see, and if too many people go inside, the whole thing might collapse onto itself."

"I take it that's not good."

Sampson grinned. "You got that right, Mr. FBI Man. It's not going to last long, neither. You're gonna have to be quick about it."

"How long?"

"Five minutes." He squinted, as if doing complicated mathematical calculations in his head. "Maybe ten."

"I'll do it," Scully said. "Assuming this works."

"Good thing it don't run on faith," Sampson said.

Scully stood at the front door waiting for an indication from Sampson that he was ready. She had a drill ready to pull the cylinder on the lock.

"You might wanna leave that hunk of iron behind," Sampson said, indicating Scully's sidearm.

"Why?"

"Can't say exactly what'll happen when I flip this switch. The less metal you have on you, the better, that's all."

Scully exchanged a glance with Mulder. After giving it a moment's consideration, she put her gun down on the doorstep. They weren't expecting any trouble inside, as far as she knew. Assuming she got inside. Assuming this cowboy knew what he was doing.

Sampson nodded. "Ready?"

"Ready."

"Here we go," Sampson said. "Hold onto your hats."

He flipped the switch and a gentle humming filled the air. Scully couldn't see anything happening with the instrument array, but when she touched the doorknob, it was solid and real. She could grip it. To reassure herself, she rapped on the door and felt the hardwood beneath her knuckles. "Hello? Is anyone in there?"

Receiving no answer, she quickly drilled the lock and pushed the door open. Once inside, the first thing she noticed was a foul odor that reminded her of decomp. She glanced around the entrance and headed left into the kitchen, the apparent source of the smell. The kitchen table was heaped with empty cans and frozen food containers. Dirty dishes were stacked in both sinks, and bulging garbage bags were piled up in one corner next to a dog's dish. The refrigerator door hung open and the pantry was bare. It looked like everything edible in the house had been consumed. Time had not been standing still after all.

She rounded the corner into the living room. Here, she found three people huddled together on a sofa. She assumed they were the Robertsons and their daughter. Scully wondered why they hadn't responded to her voice or the sounds she'd made moving around in the kitchen. Wielding her FBI credentials, she announced, "I'm Special Agent Dana Scully. Are you all right?"

The people on the couch didn't give any indication they'd heard her. She advanced a little farther into the room, checking around the corner to make sure no one was lying in wait. She was acutely aware of the absence of her sidearm.

Once she was sure the room was clear, she stepped toward the sofa, standing right in front of the Robertsons. They seemed to be conscious, though weak and bedraggled. The daughter, Emily, stared right through her.

Scully leaned over to touch the man's shoulder, but she experienced the same sensation as when they'd first arrived at the house. She wasn't really making contact. He was "out of phase" with her, assuming Langly knew what he was talking about. Sampson's gadget may have fixed the problem with the house, but it didn't fix the family. Or, she thought, maybe the family had been trapped inside in the same way that she and Mulder had been kept out, and Sampson's array had inverted everything, house and people.

She'd already spent two or three minutes inside, so she probably didn't have much time left. She couldn't drag the Robertson's outside, since she couldn't touch them, and she definitely didn't want to be caught inside the house when Sampson's field collapsed.

With time running out, Scully made an impulsive decision. She dashed out the front door, stopping only long enough to pick up her gun. "Mulder," she called. "Help me get these inside."

The empty metal cases that had contained Sampson's equipment were light enough for her to drag two toward the house by herself. Mulder paused for a second, but then leapt into action, gathering up two more.

"I wouldn't recommend that," Sampson called after them.

Scully went through the front door first, with Mulder on her heels. As soon as they were inside with all four metal boxes, the house began to shake and bright lights flashed all around them. They smelled something reminiscent of burning electronics. Mulder felt tingles run up and down his spine, and watched as Scully flickered into a negative image of herself and then back to normal again. He was beginning to think Sampson was right when the shaking stopped and a pungent odor filled the air.

Scully heard a moan from the living room. When she stepped into the room, Mel Robertson looked at her. "You're." He stopped to catch his breath and to swallow. "Here."

"We're here," Scully said, "and we're going to get you out of this place. Mulder, give me a hand."

They carried the Robertson's daughter through the front door first. "Call an ambulance," Mulder yelled at Sampson.

Sampson was tending to his electronic gadgets, which were now emitting plumes of smoke. "Have to find me a payphone," he said.

Mulder pulled out his cellular phone and tossed it to the man. "Use this."

"Don't these give you brain cancer?"

Mulder shook his head. "Make the call."

They went back inside and brought out Cathy Robertson and then her husband. Scully stayed with them while Mulder checked out the rest of the house. He found nothing to explain how the family had become trapped inside. Nothing to account for the mysterious force field, which Scully's actions had apparently short-circuited.

"How did you know what to do?" Mulder asked when he came back out.

"I didn't," Scully said. "I couldn't think of any other option."

"Risky," Mulder said.

Scully nodded and returned her attention to the Robertsons. Before long, two ambulances and a police car rolled up in front of the house. The EMTs took over from Scully. "They're dehydrated and famished," she told the medical technicians. "I don't know when they last had anything to eat."

Mulder noticed that Sampson had taken advantage of the confusion to round up his equipment, throw everything in the back of his car and vamoose.

Once the patients were ready to transport, Scully got into the back of one of the ambulances, leaving Mulder behind to explain the situation to the Houston Police Department. She wondered how that conversation would go.

WASHINGTON, D.C.
8th MAY, 1996, 9:15 a.m.

The next day, back in DC, Scully sat in front of her computer and filed her report.

> The Robertsons are expected to recover once their electrolytes
> have been balanced and they start ingesting solid food again. The
> daughter in particular seems averse to eating, perhaps because of
> the nature of some of the things they were forced to consume

during their as-yet unexplained confinement. After three weeks without power, some of their food had undoubtedly spoiled. It is difficult to imagine what sort of lasting psychological effects this incident will have on these individuals.

Agent Mulder believes the "phase shift" that trapped the Robertsons in their home was caused by alien forces conducting sociological experiments on this family. He also believes that at least two other incidents in the past [see attached documents] are additional instances of the same type of alien testing after isolation. He speculates that these experiments are becoming more tightly focused: first a town, then an apartment building and, most recently, a single-occupancy dwelling.

We discovered nothing during our investigation that can confirm this theory. There is still a very real possibility that this phenomenon has a scientific explanation. However, with the permanent disruption of the alleged force field that prevented access to—or egress from—the Robertson's house, no evidence remains that can be subjected to rigorous testing. Who brought the situation in Houston to our attention in the first place is also unknown.

The incident, therefore, remains unexplained. Further investigation is unlikely to produce any fruitful results.

Scully sent the document to the printer.

Mulder was at his desk, reviewing reports from the Houston Police Department. They were eager to sweep the entire incident under the rug, and thus far no newspapers had picked up the story. He was looking forward to the next issue of *The Lone Gunman* for their take on events.

"Another one for the files, eh, Scully?"

"I honestly don't know what to think about what happened, Mulder." She got up from her desk and stretched. "There must be a rational explanation... but what?"

Mulder waved the police report. "I don't want to put you off your feed or anything, but…"

"What?"

"Did you know that the Robertsons had a pet dog?"

"Yes. I saw its bowl in the kitchen."

"Did you see a dog in the house?"

"No." Her eyes widened. "You don't think…?"

"They're considered a delicacy in some cultures."

"Oh, yuck. Those poor people. No wonder the thought of food is making Emily queasy."

"Yeah, that could be it," Mulder said, tossing the file onto a pile on his desk.

"What?" Scully said. "What else did you find out?"

"Sure you want to know?"

"Tell me."

"Really sure?"

"Come on. Spit it out."

Mulder smirked. "Interesting choice of words. Apparently Cathy Robertson's mother lived with them, too…"

Scully felt the blood drain from her face. Her legs went weak and she had to sit down, resting her head in her hands. All of a sudden, her breakfast wasn't resting so easily in her stomach anymore.

THE END

the
Truth
is Out
There

HEART
By Kendare Blake

HOLMDEL, NEW JERSEY
23rd JUNE, 1995, 11 a.m.

Arthur Linninger was not the sort of man who enjoyed making waves. He was not the sort of man who enjoyed being seen at all. Every morning, Arthur would rise, and walk down the hall and into the kitchen, to cook and eat one fried egg, with prune jam spread over buttered toast. In the afternoons, depending on the season, he would tend to his garden, or organize and re-organize the old photographs, cans of paint, seedling trays, tools and other items that cluttered the corners of his basement and attic. It was an ongoing task. No matter how carefully he tried to organize, items accumulated in these spaces as if they had wills of their own. He had heard it was the same for other people. In the evenings, he would sit in a cozy chair and read, or watch some television. When he grew tired, he made sure to put the book back on its shelf. Arthur hated to leave things out of place. And he never left the TV or the lights on when he wasn't using them.

It was an unimportant life. He had no illusions about that. But it was also an unobtrusive life that harmed and inconvenienced no one, except for the very basic, fundamental harms that all lives caused. That gave Arthur a sense of comfort, a sense of accomplishment on those days when he stared in the mirror too long, at cheeks that sagged from rarely smiling, or at his fading, wispy, widow's peak of hair. He was soft and insignificant, but he was not a bother.

So when a ventricle exploded in his heart one sunny, spring morning in May, the only sound that escaped him was a soft, "oh!" Barely more than a gasp.

He would have simply lay there and died, wondering what mess his body would make, and who would have to do the cleaning up after it, had that little boy and his mother not seen his shoes, sticking out some distance from behind his hedge.

"Look, Mommy, look!" the boy shouted, and Arthur closed his eyes.

"What, Chris?" he heard the woman ask, and then heard her suck in a great gulp of air. The little boy yelped, as if he'd been choked.

"Don't go too close," she said. "We don't know what happened."

There was nothing else for what seemed like a long time. Only pain and pressure in Arthur's chest, and the blackness behind his eyes—not terribly comforting. He was going to die, he thought, and not alone like he always supposed he would, but right in front of someone, and at least he wouldn't lie there and rot. But then the woman spoke.

"Sir? Are you breathing? Just hang on, I'm calling 911."

"No, no," said Arthur, softly. "Please don't. It's quite all right."

It was then that the woman came to him, and knelt by his side. Poor, unobtrusive Arthur, who, when jostled in line at the supermarket, always gave way. His habits brought out contempt in some. Particularly the bold. And the young. But in other people it stirred a compassion that was almost akin to fondness. Alas, the mother of the boy was one of such type.

"Don't be brave now, or stubborn," she said, without pausing to give Arthur room to explain. "Something has obviously happened here, and you need help." She took his hand.

Arthur lay on his back, feeling her hand and the burning pressure in his chest. It would have been a fine day. Sunshine and no breeze to blow things around. A nice red strip steak on his refrigerator shelf for supper. Now the hedges would stand half done, and if the wind kicked up, the trimmings would find their way onto the Kempsons' lawn. He moaned.

"We're on Pinehurst Drive," the woman said. "I don't know what happened. I don't know who he is. My son and I were out walking and we just found him lying here."

He felt a tugging on his arm.

"Sir? What's your name? They want to know your name."

"Arthur," he said quietly. "Linninger."

"What?" she asked loudly, as if he'd suffered a ruptured eardrum instead of a ruptured ventricle. "No, hey, Christopher, it's all right. Just… don't go anywhere. Stay where Mommy can see you."

"Linninger," Arthur said again. "My name is Arthur Linninger."

"What's your house number, Mr. Linninger? They need it for the ambulance. It's on its way."

"753," he said. "753 Pinehurst Drive."

He wanted to say, "I wish you wouldn't," but of course it was too late. The hospital was only four miles away. The sirens would come, and draw people out of their homes, into their yards and driveways. Arthur could swear that he heard them approaching even though the woman was still on the phone.

He didn't open his eyes when the paramedics came. The woman had stopped talking. She'd called her son and Arthur could hear the boy's shirt rumpling as she squeezed him. She had let go of Arthur's hand. It was too still. Too cold. She didn't want to be touching him if he was dead.

The paramedics shouted. They told him to open his eyes and he did. They asked him questions, and he answered. He tried to be stiff and light when they lifted him to the gurney, but it still jolted and rattled.

Once they secured him inside the ambulance, his condition worsened. The paramedics shouted louder. It was hard for Arthur to separate one word from the next. It was dark, but he didn't know anymore whether or not his eyes were closed.

At the hospital they cracked open his chest. He was not asleep when they did this and he was afraid. The pain was terrible, but distant. Almost like cold. As if rather than spreading his ribs and putting their hands inside, they had thrown in a bucket of ice. One of the doctors climbed on top of him. The doctor rode the gurney, and Arthur, into the trauma room with his fingers knuckle-deep in tissue. No one seemed to care that Arthur was awake. They didn't seem to care much about Arthur at all. It was bad, and they had nothing to lose. Arthur looked at the doctor crouched above his open chest, and then looked down into his open cavity. He could see the white of his own ribs. He could see how shiny and slick he was on the inside. The doctor's eyes seemed to say that Arthur wouldn't remember any of this later, but it seemed to Arthur to be an awful lot to forget.

They gave him a new heart without asking. He hadn't thought they could do that. Arthur pursed his pale lips on questions as the doctor went on about damage too extensive to repair, and fast decisions, and Arthur's good overall health. The doctor said he had every chance. That he was lucky. The only question Arthur posed was to ask who the donor was.

"Someone whose family wishes to remain anonymous," the doctor said. It was not the same doctor who had ridden him into the emergency room. That fellow had a generous black beard and eyeglasses that hid steely, regretful eyes. This one was younger and clean-shaven, with tan hair clipped so close it seemed to melt into the edges of his tan skin. He seemed very pleased with himself. Arthur did not think he could get any further answers out of him.

Two weeks later, almost to the hour, a Checker Cab dropped Arthur off at the end of his driveway. He stared up at his house for a few moments as the cab drove away. His house was a small, white rectangle with dark gray trim, and window boxes filled with purple pansies and yellow snapdragons. Someone had come into his yard while he was away and finished trimming his hedges. The clippings had been disposed of, and the edges clean and even. Arthur blushed furiously, but he stood a moment with his hand on the leaves as a show of appreciation in case whichever neighbor had done it was watching.

There wasn't much in his refrigerator that he could stand to eat. Hospital food was so bland, and he felt certain his stomach would reject anything made with proper butter or cheese. He had to be very careful, the nurses said, of vomiting, or straining while on the toilet. Arthur looked from shelf to shelf. His lovely red strip steak had turned a faded shade of brown. Almost green. He threw it out. What a waste, he thought. They had kept him in the hospital for too long. He'd felt just fine after nine days, but they kept him anyway. They said he had good insurance. That he shouldn't worry.

That night, after he had eaten his can of vegetable beef soup and watched a little bit of Jay Leno, Arthur stood in front of his bathroom mirror. He'd buttoned his blue-striped pajama shirt to just below his sternum. Just below his incision. It was still covered… a long, white rectangle of tape and gauze. Two weeks ago, he thought, I saw my own heart. He touched the edge of the gauze with a forefinger. His own heart had looked red, and wet, and quivering. As vulnerable as anything. It was gone now. Someone else's was nestled in its place, pumping along, doing the job that his old one should have done.

Arthur pressed his hand over the bandage. It felt to him like the worst kind of imposition.

19th SEPTEMBER, 1995, 1 p.m.

Arthur did not reject his new heart. Of course he was a very good patient, always careful with his meds, and with his activity levels. But even so, the young tan doctor was impressed by his recovery. He said the utter lack of inflammation was nothing short of extraordinary.

"You're staying away from too much red meat?" the doctor asked on one of Arthur's recent follow-ups.

"Yes," Arthur replied. "Except when the heart wants it."

"What do you mean?"

"Last week I found myself at Louie's, over a plate of medium rare ribeye and two lobster tails."

"Arthur." The doctor frowned. He put his chart down and clicked his pen to put back in his pocket. "You cannot have rare meat. Or shellfish." He took his pen back out and clicked it again. "Next you'll be telling me you went out for sashimi."

"No," Arthur said, quietly. "I've never liked lobster anyway, and I've never had sushi."

"Look," the doctor said. "Your recovery is going extremely well. And I know that patients with such good prognoses can feel a little bit like… they have a new lease on life. There's no reason you can't celebrate. Just take it slow. Take it easy for the next six months, all right?"

Arthur nodded. He did not tell the doctor what he secretly suspected: that the reason his new heart was adjusting so well was simply because Arthur himself was so accommodating.

Arthur took a taxi from the hospital and asked to be dropped at the park a mile away from his house. He'd taken to walking more often, partially for the health benefit, but also because his house felt smaller and smaller, and his neighborhood more provincial. It was a place where nothing happened. Nothing more exciting than a new sedan replacing an older one. Nothing more scandalous than Mr. Wilkes blowing leaves onto Mason Thom's lawn. It was a stable place in which to live an ordered life. It didn't suit his new heart. Over the past weeks, Arthur had come to the conclusion that the heart had belonged to a young person. It pounded too hard sometimes. It made him restless.

When he reached his own street, Arthur waved to Mrs. Kempson from the sidewalk. She was returning from the market with a few plastic bags of fruits and leafy greens. The neighbors had been warmer to Arthur since his scare, as he'd heard them refer to it. They kept a more watchful eye. He thought it would bother him more than it did.

Mrs. Kempson was an attractive woman, barely into her thirties, with an ass that looked barely into its teens.

Arthur lowered his hand quickly to his chest, afraid that Mrs. Kempson would somehow hear his thoughts. But she only smiled, and went about her own business.

In the morning, Arthur walked down the hall to the kitchen and prepared his breakfast eggs and buttered toast. A fresh jar of prune jam sat on the countertop. He still bought it, out of habit, he supposed, but he hadn't touched it for weeks. He'd simply lost the taste for it.

"The fiber in prune jam is better for you than the fat in an egg," he said as he ate. "You would think that a heart would have better sense."

Someone knocked on his door. Arthur paused, and set down his toast. It was too early for the postman, and he rarely had hand-delivered mail. He nudged the edges of his pajama collar together and went to the door, stopping first to peer through the curtains.

Two people in suits were standing on his front steps. Rather shabby suits, though Arthur didn't know how he knew that. One was a woman with red hair. She was very pretty, if a bit serious. The other was a young man with bored-looking, squinted eyes. Both smiled at him through the window with closed lips.

"Arthur Linninger?" the woman asked, and Arthur quickly opened the door. "Yes?"

"I'm Agent Scully with the FBI." She showed him her badge. "This is my partner, Agent Mulder. We'd like to ask you a few questions."

The new heart burned in Arthur's chest. It did not like the badges. It did not like these people. But Arthur opened the door and stepped back to allow them in at once.

"Thank you," said the young male agent, and Arthur closed the door behind them.

"Can I offer you some coffee?" Arthur asked. "Or tea?"

"No, thank you," said the female agent.

"I apologize for my appearance. I never expect anyone so early."

"It's almost ten o'clock," said the male agent. Agent Mulder.

Arthur glanced at the clock on the wall.

"I'm sorry," he said again. "I don't usually sleep this late. I had a heart transplant some time ago, and it's made some… changes."

"Changes in your behavior you mean," Agent Mulder said. "Sleeping at odd hours, craving foods you've never craved before. Surf 'n' turf, perhaps?"

Agent Mulder didn't seem bored to Arthur anymore, even though his expression had hardly changed.

"How did you know that?" Arthur asked, but the agents didn't reply. They exchanged a look.

"Lucky guess," said Agent Mulder. "I just meant that recipients of organ donation will often find themselves taking on some aspects of the donor. Aversions or fondness for scents or colors, changing sleeping habits, tastes in food. Like surf 'n' turf, for example."

"That's very interesting," said Arthur. "If you'll permit me a moment, I'll just get dressed…"

"That won't be necessary, Mr. Linninger," said the female agent. "We only need a few minutes of your time."

"All right," said Arthur, tugging at his collar.

"Can you account for your whereabouts on the evening of June 23rd?"

"I was here," he said. "I'm always here."

"Can anyone verify that?"

"No, I… live alone."

"What about the afternoon of September 13th?" she asked.

That was less than a week ago. He'd been at his appointment with his doctor.

"I was at Presbyterian Memorial Hospital," he said. "My doctor can tell you. Dr. Rankovic."

"Have you had any other strange symptoms, following your transplant, Mr. Linnanger?" Agent Mulder asked. "I mean aside from the cravings for steak and lobster."

Arthur shrugged. He gestured to the wall clock.

"I sleep later," he said. He thought of his urges toward Mrs. Kempson, but decided not to mention it. "I don't care for avocados anymore."

"Nothing else?"

"Nothing. Agents, can you tell me, please, what this is about?"

"Mr. Linninger," said Agent Mulder, "over the course of the past month, two people under suspicion in the death of your heart donor have been murdered. We have reason to believe that one or several of the organ recipients may have been involved."

"The recipients?" Arthur asked.

"Your particular donor gave tissue to six recipients. Both kidneys, one lung, and two pieces of liver. And of course a heart, to you. At this time we're only following up with the remaining recipients."

Arthur looked bemusedly from one agent to the other. Surely it was some kind of joke.

"Are you aware of the phenomenon?" Agent Mulder asked. "Of organ recipients taking on the aspects of the donor, left-handed people become right-handed, develop similar allergies, seek out friends of the donor despite having no knowledge of their acquaintance?"

"I believe I have read something about that." Arthur said nothing more. It would have been rude to ask the agents to leave. But he did not want to encourage their continued presence either.

After a moment of silence, the agents moved back toward the door, and Agent Mulder handed him a card.

"If you're approached by anyone strange, Mr. Linninger, or if you experience any other symptoms or changes in behavior, I can be reached at this number anytime."

"Of course, of course," Arthur said. "Thank you, agents."

Arthur escorted them through the door, and saw them down the front steps.

"Agent Mulder," he said, feeling safer seeing the backs of their jackets, and possessed of a sudden curiosity. "The other recipients. Are they well?"

"Not a rejection among them," Mulder said, without turning around. "Their doctors say it's extraordinary."

Arthur tried to forget about what the strange FBI agent had said. He showered, and dressed, and thought he might turn his afternoon walk into a trip to town and the farmer's market. He would buy himself a roasted chicken breast and a couple of zucchini squash, and chop them up with tomatoes from his own backyard plants.

When he arrived in town and saw the agents get out of a blue-gray car and walk into The Local Yolkel, he knew he ought to keep on going, cross at the crosswalk and turn left at the pharmacy. Whatever wild goose chase those agents were leading themselves on, it was none of Arthur's business. A light sheen of sweat prickled the back of his neck and under his arms. The sky was clear above his head, and the sun was hot. He could easily slip into the Yolkel through the side entrance and splash himself with some water in their restroom. He could buy a cola at the counter and take it to go.

As soon as the light turned, Arthur walked quickly across the street and entered the diner. There was more sweat gathering on the back of his neck, even inside, with the air conditioning.

"Hello, Arthur."

Arthur, startled, smiled quickly. It was only Gretchen, head waitress at the Yolkel for nearly ten years. She brushed past him, and wiped damp fingers on her apron. Since his transplant, Gretchen made a point to greet him whenever she saw him. She kept his coffee cup perpetually full, and took it upon herself to substitute egg whites for eggs in whatever Arthur ordered. She was kind, and she was presumptuous. And with the heft around her middle and the cigarettes she smoked, she was sort of a hypocrite.

"Your usual stool's open," Gretchen said. "Do you want a menu?"

"Yes, thank you."

It worked out quite nicely. Arthur always sat at the end of the counter, between the partition to the kitchen and the booths. The agents were seated not far away. He could hear them on the other side of the partition. They wouldn't see him unless they got up to use the restroom, and perhaps not even then. Cardiac infamy or no, Arthur was still an easy man to miss.

"Turkey soup today."

"I would like a cup of that, please," said Arthur. "And a diet cola, to go."

He settled onto his stool, and listened.

"You sure you're feeling okay, Scully?"

"I'm fine, Mulder. It's barely a bump."

"The third bump this month. One more and coach is going to have to bench you."

Arthur folded his hands on the counter. The male agent spoke with fond familiarity. Perhaps Arthur would be unlucky. Perhaps they had some rule, to never discuss their work over lunch.

The female agent, Agent Scully—Arthur had had such a difficult time recalling her name that morning—sighed.

"Something on your mind?" Agent Mulder asked.

"I'm just wondering whether we should be concerned," she replied.

"About what?"

"About any of this. Joel Brown, Nicholas Murray, they were violent men who did violent things."

"And they had violent things done to them."

"By good people," Agent Scully said. "Amy Miller, suburban wife and mother to a three-month-old? And Ben Lewis didn't have so much as a speeding ticket before he drove Murray and himself into the Hudson. While Brown and Murray have been under suspicion two dozen times between them. Arson, assault. Known associates of the Antonelli crime family for a decade. Try as I might, Mulder, I can't conjure up any sympathy for the victims here."

"All the more reason to get to the bottom of this. Before more good people are sitting in cells. You don't want to see poor old Arthur Linninger in front of some judge in his pajamas, do you?"

Old Arthur Linninger? Arthur trembled, and took a sip of his diet cola. He didn't feel so very old.

"Mulder, you dragged me all the way up here on this ridiculous hunch, and we still have no evidence to suggest that Mr. Linninger, or Mr. Bolvic, or Ms. Wilson are—or will be—in any way involved."

"Two dead thugs, killed by two people with no previous offenses, whose only link to them or each other is a shared organ donor that was offed by the two thugs? Scully. That's more than a hunch."

Arthur touched the purple scar on his chest. He felt the ridges and rises of it. It was ugly, and sinister. Sometimes when he stared at it in the mirror he imagined it was not a heart inside, but some lab-created creature, and the purple eruption down his sternum was not a scar but the first visible pieces, pushing its way out.

"Hush," Arthur whispered, and stroked it through his shirt.

"It might not be the only link," Agent Scully said. "But the only known link. Maybe we're missing something here."

"Missing what?"

"Whatever explains the connection between these people. The motive. Something other than an urge for revenge from beyond the grave brought on by rogue donor tissue."

Her voice had dipped low to border on sarcastic. Though Arthur had seen her only briefly, he could imagine very well the weary, bemused expression on her face. She'd had to say similar things, in a similar tone, many times before.

"Scully, transference of traits from donor to recipient is a documented phenomenon. You heard Mr. Linninger. His sleeping patterns have changed, and his tastes in food. The look on his face when I said surf 'n' turf… anyone can tell you Mickey Leeds was down at Moretti's for steak and lobster tails every Saturday night. How much do you want to bet that old Arthur had his craving on a Saturday night? Around 8 p.m?"

Arthur thought back to his meal at Louie's. It had been on a Saturday night. The restaurant had been crowded. Almost full. It had been loud, and active as an ant hill. He'd never cared for places like that. He also didn't care for the way Agent Mulder kept referring to him as "Old Arthur."

"Even so," said Agent Scully, "developing a taste for seafood is a far cry from kidnapping the murderer, or stabbing him in the throat."

"Kidnapping, violence; for a day in the life of Mickey Leeds, it was par for the course. Donating organs to save lives doesn't seem to have changed his."

"Mickey Leeds is dead, Mulder. Beaten and executed in an alley nearly three months ago."

"And now, two of his four murderers are dead," said Agent Mulder. "With two of his transplant recipients somehow involved. Explain that to me, Scully."

Agent Scully sighed.

"I can't," she said.

"If I'm right, Leeds will be going after the Royce brothers next. We should put a tail on Arthur Linninger."

"A tail? Mulder, that man barely leaves his house."

"Here you go, sweetie."

Arthur had been so lost in thought and in the agents' conversation that he nearly startled off his stool when Gretchen set down his soup. It sat wobbling in a small, white cup beside two packets of saltine crackers. To Arthur's eyes it was thin. It was yellowed water with celery pieces and ragged bits of turkey settling to the bottom.

Gretchen set down a second plate. A salad. He hadn't ordered one, and he didn't want it, but he smiled at Gretchen and she winked, like it was the most helpful thing in the world. As if it was healthy, buried as it was underneath three ladles of French dressing. There were names for women like her. Busybody broads. Gretchen was most certainly a busybody broad.

To be polite, Arthur took a bite of the salad. The lettuce crunched so loudly in his ears that he almost didn't hear the agent's phone ringing.

The conversation was brief, and rather curt. Agent Mulder answered the call with his name, and then said only, "When?" and "We're on our way."

"What is it?" asked Agent Scully.

"Richard Bolvic was just murdered," he replied, and Arthur recalled the last name. Bolvic. Hadn't the agents mentioned Bolvic among the list of other organ recipients?

"How?"

"He was beaten unconscious and shot in the back of the head with a small-caliber pistol."

"Just like Mickey Leeds," said Agent Scully.

"Not quite. Bolvic put up a fight. There's blood on the scene, and neighbors said they saw two men matching the Royce brothers' description nearby at the time of the murder. Local PD is out to make the arrest, but I'd like to be there to question them."

Arthur listened as the agents gathered their belongings and dropped cash on the table. He kept his head low and sipped his soup, but like he knew they would, they walked right past without seeing him.

"Mickey Leeds," Arthur said. He didn't know how many times he'd said the name since he left the diner. He couldn't seem to stop saying it. Mickey. Mick.

"Mick," he said. He imagined that his heart beat more attentively when he said it, but of course that was only his imagination.

Other names, too, flickered through his head as he went about his evening's business, chopping chard to wilt down with parmesan cheese and putting away clean dishes from the dish rack.

Bolvic. Ben Lewis. Murray and Brown. The Royce brothers.

"Whoever you were," Arthur said to his heart, "you led a far more interesting life than the one you'll lead now."

But then, that wasn't exactly true. Or at least it didn't have to be. Couldn't Arthur, even old, stodgy Arthur, pick up and go wherever he pleased? Wasn't his house bought and paid for, left to him by his mother and worth at least a quarter million dollars? With property values what they were, even that dull, gray-shuttered rectangular box had to be worth at least that.

"Yes," Arthur whispered.

There were so many things in the world outside. Streets lined with glass buildings so you could admire yourself from all sides. Cathedrals full of stained glass and spires that pointed straight to God. Boats on the harbor. Proper shoes made of proper leather, not the machine-stitched loafer monstrosities that Arthur wore. Decent food that arrived at the table on plates, rather than having to be painstakingly assembled every single night on his own.

"Ah."

Arthur looked down. He'd cut himself along with the chard. It had happened so quickly he'd hardly felt it, but blood had already come to the surface and spattered onto the edge of his countertop. He wiped the drops up with a damp dishcloth and carried the mess to the sink, then held his finger under running water until the cut looked clear.

"What is so horrible about the life I've led?" he asked, aloud. "It's been quiet, yes, but filled with small pleasures. I've been a man unto myself. No one has had to bother themselves over me, and none who know me have had complaint. I've been," he said, "accommodating."

Arthur shut off the water and pressed the dishcloth against the cut. It came away only slightly pink. He was about to walk down the hall for a small bandage and to throw the cloth into the hamper when something outside his window caught his eye.

It was full dark. It was late. In the weeks preceding, he had fallen into the habit of eating his dinner so late that occasionally he would miss the start of the ten o'clock news. No matter how he tried to hold to his old routine, the time slipped by. The attempt had begun to feel as useless as purchasing the avocados, and holding a slice of one in his mouth, only to spit it down the garbage disposal.

He thought he'd seen something moving near his back hedge, just to the right of where the old gate joined his property with the Ramseys'. But there didn't seem to be anything there. It had probably been one of the city raccoons. He'd seen one in the early evenings, climbing up and over the hedges and fences, making its way through his yard to wherever it made its den.

Arthur sighed.

"I'd better bind this up, or I'll ruin the rest of the chard."

Arthur walked out of the kitchen, and around the corner. He reached into the bathroom and turned on the light, then flipped the faucet on to run and closed the door slightly. He did not go inside, but instead, walked calmly into the darkness of his den. It seemed like a curious thing to do, and when he looked down, he noticed that he had somehow picked up his knife off of the cutting board.

He wouldn't have heard the door open if he'd still been in the kitchen, or standing near the bathroom sink, but Arthur was a quiet sort, and knew the sounds of his home very well. Someone was inside. They were making their way through the dining room after coming in through the back door. That one had always had a soft squeak in the summers, when the wood tended to be damp and would swell. No doubt Arthur's intruder would have liked to be privy to that little tidbit.

Arthur should be afraid. He should be trembling, or finding a phone to call for help. Instead he gripped the knife, and his heart beat faster and stronger. It was not surprised.

A shadow fell down the hallway as a man crept closer to the slightly ajar door of the bathroom. When he stepped into view, Arthur could see that he was the sort of strong that would best be described as due to heft, from sheer size rather than any time spent exercising. The sides of his fine cranberry-colored shirt bulged over the top of his belt. In his left hand he held a gun. But he paused outside the bathroom door and put it away, quietly replacing it with wood handles, and a thick piece of wire. Arthur had seen enough movies to know what that was.

He thought they would wait until the thug opened the door. Instead they cut as the intruder's arm reached forward. The knife went through shirt and wrist down to the bone just as easily as it had sliced into Arthur's finger. Then it was out again, and the pointed end went into the man's right bicep. The wire and the wood thumped onto the rug, and after a few well-placed footprints to the crotch, so did the intruder.

"Jacob! Jake!"

It was more than a little sad to watch the man's hands bat feebly against them as they searched his pocket for the gun. And then it seemed such a surprise, when the second intruder came around the corner and was shot in the face. He went down so quickly. And it was such a small gun.

Arthur toed the tangle of wire away across the carpet though the man made no move to grab it. He merely sat, and shook, and bled, and stared at his fallen comrade.

"You killed him," he said. "Jake." And he wept.

"What were you going to do with that?" Arthur asked, and toed the wire again. "Cut my throat? Use this," he held up the gun, "to put a hole in every organ to keep me down?"

"Should have done that the first time. Instead we gave you mercy."

"Putting your fists in my face until my nose caved in, that's mercy. I could taste my own nose, in the back of my throat, but that's mercy."

"That was Anthony. You know how he gets." The man dug into his pockets. Arthur saw this, and wondered what he had inside. "It was business. You should have honored that and stayed dead. We should have gutted you like a fish, like the boss wanted."

He was up in an instant, flash of steel in his hand, trying to make good on his promise. Arthur thought he moved very fast, for a man of his size and bulk. The knife missed, but Arthur was still slammed up against the wall of the hallway. Every picture rattled. He worried one might fall and break. He didn't realize he'd put his kitchen knife into the man's gut until he felt the warm skin and blood against his knuckles.

The man staggered back, and slumped down onto the carpet again. The small knife was still in his hand, but looked very useless.

"You shouldn't have killed Jake."

"Jake shouldn't have killed me." The gun raised in Arthur's hand. "Good night, Royce."

"Fuck you, Mick."

Arthur flinched when the gun went off. He couldn't look at the paintjob that Royce's head did on his hallway wallpaper. He couldn't look when the gun went off again, and again into the other intruder for good measure. Arthur couldn't look, until the FBI agents kicked against the front door.

"FBI! Open up!"

"Of course," Arthur said at once, and then said it again, louder, in case Agent Mulder hadn't heard. He hurried to the door and turned the deadbolt, then stepped back to allow the agent inside.

"Mr. Linninger are you all right? We heard gunshots."

"Yes, yes," Arthur said.

"Don't move!" Agent Scully was suddenly there, pointing a gun at him. She'd apparently come through the still open back door. "Put down the gun, Arthur."

Arthur looked down. He was still holding the gun, and the blood-covered knife. He dropped them at once.

"What happened here?" Agent Scully asked.

"I don't know," Arthur replied. "They broke into my home. They were going to kill me. That gun is theirs, and they had that wire. They were going to kill me," he said again.

Agent Scully bent over the two dead men, checking for pulses or signs of life. After a few moments, she straightened, and sighed.

"I'm going to call this in," she said.

Arthur thought she looked rather tired. She'd undoubtedly had a very long day, and had seen so many dead men. He ought to offer her a cup of tea, with honey and lemon, if only he could find his voice.

Everything happened so quickly after that. The police arrived, and photos were taken. Someone wrapped him in a blanket before he had time to decline it. There were lights everywhere, and he could see his neighbors, most staring moon-faced out of their windows, and some in their pajamas on their driveways and lawns. He wondered what they must be thinking. They must have asked themselves when it was that Arthur Linninger had become so much of a bother.

Arthur sat through it all, very quietly, except when his statements were needed. His ears perked up when he thought he heard the agents talking about the soul, and how much of one could be attached to bodily tissue, but the conversation didn't last long. Agent Scully seemed to be in no mood for it.

They took the bodies out in bags. Arthur was glad to see them go, but he would need new carpet, and new wallpaper in the hall. Or perhaps, he thought, perhaps he would really sell the place. He had a good enough excuse to do so.

Agent Mulder came and sat beside him.

"You'll have to go down to the station tomorrow," Agent Mulder said. "And answer more questions. If you'd like, you can stay the night at a motel. Either way there will be an agent out front for the next few days, just to make sure you're all right."

"Oh no," Arthur said. "That won't be necessary. Let the agent go on, and do more useful things. Get home to their family."

"You're not afraid?"

"But I don't need to be, do I?" Arthur asked. "It's over. All four are dead."

Agent Mulder regarded him curiously.

"How do you know that?"

"I don't know," Arthur lied. "I just do."

"All right." Agent Mulder stood to go. "We'll pull the car." Before he left, he held out his hand, which Arthur shook, gladly. Agent Mulder held it tight, and leaned in close, as if they were sharing some great secret. "You take care of that heart now, Arthur."

"Oh yes, Agent Mulder," Arthur said, and touched the raised ridges of his scar.

"I am its home now."

THE END

the truth is out there

MALE PRIVILEGE
By Hank Schwaeble

HORN, ARKANSAS
2nd DECEMBER, 2006, 9:37 a.m.

Constable Roy Pratt sat in an oversized chair behind a sprawling, glass-topped desk in the spacious office, rambling in a folksy, somewhat perturbed manner about all he could recall of the night before his small township's world seemed to turn upside-down, but Mulder was having a hard time keeping his eyes off the man's rather impressive breasts. A double-D, if he had to guess. Complete with smooth and fleshy cleavage that looked, to Mulder at least, like a genuine suffocation threat were the man to nod off in the wrong position.

A stab in his calf, painful enough to make him flinch. It was Scully—the point of her shoe. She glared at him, same crossed leg at the ready, reloaded and twitching.

Mulder coughed. "Go on," he said. He pretended to adjust his pant leg, rubbing the spot and forcing himself not to wince. He glanced at Scully and mouthed the word *ow.*

"Well, like I was sayin', I don't remember much else." The constable lowered his eyes to his chest, tugged at the plackets of his shirt. "Hey, I'm sorry, but the damn thing won't button any higher. And the T-shirt was making my nipples sore as hell."

Scully interjected, cutting Mulder off. "So the last thing you do remember that night was the bell?"

"Yes. I remember the bell ringing. From the tower in the square. Twelve times, for midnight. That's supposed to signify the beginning of the official Horn Township Annual Fall Fair. Well, the fair doesn't actually start then, but that's like the kick-off of the season. Tradition is that couples kiss while

the bells are going. I remember pulling my wife closer, kissing her, then…
it was morning—" the man fanned his open hands, indicating his body "—
and I was like this."

"You, and virtually every other man in town, as I understand it," Mulder
said.

"Pretty much. Everyone except my son, Brandon—as you know. Didn't
seem to happen to anyone younger than him, though. Thank God. But
someone already talked to him. Without me present, I might add."

Scully nodded. "A CDC representative has made contact with everyone
on the list. I'm sure you understand that your son, being eighteen, is legally
an adult. Agent Mulder and I will need to do a number of follow-up
interviews so we'll want to speak with him ourselves, if you don't mind."

"We might need him to talk about things he might not want to discuss in
front of his father," Mulder added. "Or mother. You understand."

"I can get him down here whenever you want," the man said, drumming
his fingertips on his desk. His gaze seemed to recede into his thoughts.
"Just let me know."

"Are you certain there weren't any symptomatic persons who weren't at
the event?" Scully asked.

"I'm sure. Pretty much the whole town comes to the Sadie Hawkins
Dance. Like I said, it's a kick-off. The start of our big fall festival."

"Does that bring in a lot of money?" Mulder asked. "The festival?"

The man's eyes narrowed and he cocked his head. "Money? No. It's all
free. Put on by the township. For the townsfolk."

"What do the townsfolk get?"

"Different things. Dinners, live music. Parade. Sometimes we even throw
a luau. Apple in the mouth and everything."

"And it's all paid for by City Hall. Sounds generous. Though if the other
city buildings are half as nice as this one, Constable, I don't doubt your till
can take the hit. For such a small town, you must have some tax base.
What's your major source of revenue?"

"Revenue?"

"Money. Your little town seems to be doing quite well. What do people
here do for a living?"

"Oh, well, we're sort of the region's best kept secret. Lots of entrepreneurs
and such, people running businesses through the internet. We boast more

lottery winners per capita than any other town in the state. People here like to keep a low profile. Money can attract unwanted attention."

"I see. And the festival is your way of spreading the wealth around?"

"What can I say?" The man lifted his hands and fanned them apart, eyebrows raised, mouth a tight arc. "If you've ever been stuck living in a small town, you'd know they can get really boring. So we try to let everyone blow off some steam and have a good time. Sure, we've been very fortunate. That's why we measure the tenure of our residents not by years, but by generations. Nothing wrong with letting everyone know how much they're appreciated."

"I guess that explains the town's slogan. Is it true that your *residents never leave for long and always come back*? Imagine the irony if there were a zombie apocalypse. Speaking of which, I couldn't help but notice you also have quite an impressive arsenal."

"You know us southerners. We appreciate the value of superior fire-power."

Mulder nodded, looking to Scully with an arched brow and amused frown before letting his eyes drift to the wall behind the Constable, taking in first the enormous longsword hanging there—an ornate and well-maintained antique with a scrolled guard and leather handle, a large medallion at the end containing a green jewel of some kind—then settling on the image next to it, a gigantic blood-red boar with angry black eyes emerging from a patch of tall grass, a bright moon above it. A huge pair of double tusks protruded from its lower jaw, lips peeled back in a snarl. It had caught his attention when he first walked in, the piece taking up a good chunk of the space, a framed print behind glass, the work of some talented computer graphic artist, oversized and menacing. The caption at the bottom read, "Never Yield" in bold, stark letters, more like a threat than a command.

Scully flipped up a sheet of paper in a folder, scanned the page below it. "And you have no idea who sent the anonymous email notifying the CDC of your town's... health issues?"

"None," the man said, his jaw clenching. A little too tightly, Mulder noted.

"Were you ever planning on notifying any higher authorities?" Scully said. "It's my understanding you hadn't even notified anyone from the state. I don't see why you would be so reluctant to get help for such a serious medical situation."

"Agent, do you have any idea how embarrassing this is? And do you really think anyone feels better because a bunch of nerds with clipboards are crawling all over town?"

"They're just trying to figure out what's going on," Scully said. "We all are. I think you'd agree all parties have done a good job keeping this out of the news."

The constable shrugged, offered a grudging dip of his head. "I'll give you that. But no one's exactly been cured so far and I had to fight to keep them from restricting everyone to their homes. Only reason I'm helping you is because they backed off. The people here don't need that."

Scully was about to say something, but Mulder spoke first. "I'm curious, Constable. How did the town get its name?"

"Horn? From what I'm told, it was originally called Horn of Plenty. I guess at some point, everyone decided that was a mouthful. Look, can we take a break? I need to go pee."

"Of course," Scully said, standing.

The man circled around them and left the room. As he passed from view, Mulder called out, "Hey, if someone left the lid up, don't look at me."

"What's gotten into you, Mulder? Why are you being so rude, not to mention crude?"

"Oh, come on. You have to admit it was funny."

"I would have thought you'd be taking this seriously."

"I am. Okay, maybe I crossed the proverbial line a few times, but if that constable were to lie any more than he already has, his skirt would catch fire. I'm hoping that if I keep tossing jabs at him like that, he'll slip up and let me see through that poker face. He's hiding something. Don't tell me you don't think so."

"Maybe you're right. But we have to be sensitive here. These people have had their lives upended. Not just the men, their entire families."

"Didn't you tell me the effects were temporary, and could be reversed even if they weren't? I think that makes it safe to joke about. It's just some shrinkage and man-boobs we're talking about."

"I said early indications were they were *likely* temporary, and could *probably* be reversed with treatment if they didn't spontaneously self-correct. That's not the same thing."

"Look, even if I'm wrong about Pratt, the experience is probably a net good for the men of this town. What better way to stamp out sexism and advance the cause of equality for all than have them walk a mile in your pumps?"

"Gender politics and social justice issues notwithstanding, you antagonizing them isn't going to help anyone figure out what caused these men to undergo a massive, sudden sexual metamorphosis. They weren't too keen on the CDC coming in to begin with."

Mulder shrugged. "One thing about southern men, they don't get easily offended by ribbing if it's something they consider fair game. If anything, it's expected. Wrong word about football, on the other hand…" Seeing her expression, he held up his hands. "I know, I know, I'm supposed to be just along for the ride. Wouldn't want to upset the CDC."

"It is their show, Mulder. I'm merely a bio-terrorism liaison. You wanted to come, remember?"

"Can you blame me? How many times do you get to see something like this? On the government's dime, I mean. Except maybe by mail order in a plain brown wrapper. Plus, I was holding out hope that the barbeque down here lived up to its reputation."

"Well, we won't likely be here for long. The massive amounts of hormones in all the male bloodstreams seem to indicate it's as much a cause as an effect, and the fact everyone affected was at the same event is a strong indication that someone delivered an agent there, likely through the beverages. Why are you giving me that look?"

"I'm having a hard time believing this comes down to somebody having slipped some estrogen into the punch bowl. If that's all it took, do you really think this would be the first time an entire male population took an unexpected walk on the wild side?"

"No, but the fact is these men have received a massive boost in female hormone levels, both estrogen and progesterone, caused by *something*. The blood work looks practically the same across the board. An agent of some kind triggered that, and it was likely something administered to them at or around the same time. But I will admit I'm at a loss to explain how it could happen. Normally changes like this would take months, not days."

Mulder tipped his head from side to side, unconvinced regarding her take. "What about the constable's kid who hasn't shown any effects? What did his tests show?"

"Brandon. Normal, according to the labs. The working hypothesis is that his body is producing maximum testosterone, a combination of his age and exercise habits. You have to remember, Mulder, spontaneous sex change is not unprecedented. There was one widely reported case in Myanmar in 2005. Of course, in this case you have dozens of men showing advanced stages of hermaphroditism at the same time. The primary concern in this instance is that it was an act of intentional contamination."

"Look around, Scully. Do you really think some international terrorist outfit would be able to sneak into a town like this? Somebody from the next county stops here for gas, the people at the corner diner are gossiping about it before his tank is full."

"That's exactly why we're here. If a delivery system sophisticated enough to avoid detection under these circumstances is at someone's disposal, there are plenty of those up the chain who want to know about it. That's also why this is being kept very low key. We don't need another Ebola-type panic."

"I guess." He placed his hands on his chest, pressing in various spots. "I just hope you guys didn't drop the ball on whether it was contagious."

"That's why you and I are just now getting here, after ten days of on-site observation. And speaking of getting here, why *are* you here, Mulder?"

"Me? *You* invited me, remember? Said you could use a hand."

"I informed you I had to go on an assignment to Arkansas, you invited yourself. I only agreed after you promised you wouldn't be asking the locals about extraterrestrials. If Skinner wasn't on vacation, I doubt he would have let you come."

His mouth curved into a pout. "That hurts. And here I was, just trying to be a team player."

"Look, I have been asked to work up a medical profile on the constable and both deputies. A forensic nurse from the Center is supposed to meet me to assist. It will likely be quite boring, and certainly won't be quick. There's no need for you to sit through it."

"Do you want me to see if I can find out if anyone has any ideas as to who may have had a reason to do this?"

Scully tilted her head to glance out the doorway. "Only if you can manage not to antagonize people in the process."

"In that case, I was thinking I'd check out the library, anyway. Never know what you're going to find stashed in the archives. And the one in this town happens to look like it might house a few Faberge eggs."

"That's actually a good idea, Mulder. There might be information that isn't reflected in the medical records, maybe a viral outbreak from decades ago that could help explain what's going on."

"Or…," Mulder said, turning up his palms. "…why the state university's mascot is a monster pig with gigantic tusks."

Before Scully could respond, the constable walked in. "There's a lady out there asking for you." He jerked a thumb over his shoulder, causing his shirt to slide over too far, exposing a nipple. "Sorry."

"No apologies necessary," Mulder said, standing. "Though just out of curiosity, when you say 'lady,' do you mean a cisgendered—?"

Scully sat forward, her voice a bit amped. "Agent Mulder was just leaving."

"She's right, I am. While I'm gone, Doctor Scully here will be asking you a few questions. But don't worry, nothing with stirrups, I'm told. And she's promised to keep me abreast."

Ignoring Scully's look, Mulder headed for the door. He stopped at the threshold and turned back. "I do have one more thing to ask, though, Constable."

"Yeah?" Pratt sat down behind his desk, fiddling once again with the opening of his shirt. "What's that?

"That razorback on your wall, you ever see one like that in these parts? Gigantic, with those elongated tusks?"

Constable Pratt looked over his shoulder, then back at Mulder. He blinked a few times, like he didn't understand the question. "It's a mascot. It's not supposed to look real."

"Mulder—"

"Just showing my interest in the great state of Arkansas," Mulder said, waving Scully off. He raised a fist, palm out. "Go Hogs."

"That was here when I took over for my predecessor. I went to Ouachita Baptist."

"In that case, go Tigers," he said, before nodding to Scully and backing out of the room.

"I apologize for my colleague. His sense of humor can sometimes be inappropriate."

"*Pfft.*" He waved a hand. "You don't have to apologize. A little teasing never hurt anyone. Sort of lightens the mood."

The man leaned back in his chair, swiveled it a bit. "And hell, any man who knows that OBU are the tigers is a-okay in my book."

"You haven't been answering your phone."

Mulder looked up from the book he had laid open on the table, one of several. "Scully! Glad you're here! This basement is like a fortress, probably lead in the walls." He pulled a chair over and gestured for her to take it.

She was standing at the foot of the stairwell, overlooking the rows of tables and walls of shelves. "We're needed back at the Constable station."

"In a minute. There's something you need to see."

"You look like you've been busy," Scully said, stopping at the end of the table. "Did you find something on the town's medical history?"

"Medical history? No, not exactly. But look at this." He slid a book in her direction. On the left page was a large drawing of a serpentine creature with an enormous head and large tusks. It was raised up, its posture suggesting it might strike or lunge.

"Mulder, what the heck is this? I thought you were looking for a history of disease or epidemics."

"Yeah, there really wasn't anything to suggest that. But tell me, what does that look like to you?"

"I don't know… nothing real."

"Just, tell me what it looks like."

She gave an exasperated shrug. "A dragon?"

Mulder snapped his finger. "Exactly. But you know what it really is?"

"Mulder—"

"It's a *Gowrow.*"

She stared at him. "This is what you've been down here researching this whole time?"

"I'll take that look you're giving me to mean you're intrigued."

"Intrigued about what?"

"Since you asked, the Gowrow is an Arkansas legend, a creature native to these parts. Specifically, native to this *county*. It was last reported by witnesses a century ago right in this area, not ten miles from where we're standing."

"What does any of that have to do with what's going on here? With assisting the CDC? Which is why we're here in the first place."

"I'm, uh, still working on that."

She looked down at the assorted books, the heavy, jumbo volumes of old newspapers. "This is why you volunteered to help, isn't it? You knew about this. You came here to investigate this Gowrow legend."

"Okay, maybe that was in the back of my mind. But think about it for a moment, Scully. This town is just a few miles from where the creature was last reported. Multiple witnesses, newspaper accounts with remarkable detail, even this artist's sketch based on the descriptions."

"You said that was a hundred years ago."

"I said it was a century ago. I found one more reference fifty years prior, possibly another fifty years before that. And do you know when the anniversary of that hundred years is? Tomorrow."

"Mulder, I'm sure this legend is all very fascinating, and maybe later we can discuss it in depth. But we came here to do a job, and right now—"

"There's something else. Remember what Pratt said about there being more lottery winners here than any other town in the state? He was wrong. From what I can tell, there are more lottery winners here than any other town in the *country*. Not just per capita. More *total*. I found over a dozen before I quit. It would be easier to count the number of people who haven't won."

"Well, he did say it attracted people with money."

"But that's the thing—I see no evidence the town has attracted anyone. All the winners were living here when they won. And I can't find any record of anyone moving in or moving out. When he said they measured people's residency by the number of generations, he wasn't kidding."

"I'll admit that's really strange, but—"

"It's more than strange. We're out here in the middle of the hills of Arkansas, deep in the wooded countryside, over an hour drive to anything approximating a even a small city, yet what do you see? Huge homes, perfectly manicured lawns, new SUVs and mini-vans. That can't all be from lottery money. Did you notice the floor upstairs? How many small-town libraries have Italian marble floors like that? Looking through the town's history, I can't find any industry that would support a growing economy of lotto winners with money to spend. I can't find any 'internet entrepreneurs' operating here. And what fills the local government coffers? Property taxes are less than my water bill. There are no factories, no tourism. Mining operations ceased almost two hundred years ago. And do you know how well outfitted this town's law enforcement is? They have a tank. There was a story in the local newsletter. Three officers and a crime rate lower than Mayberry's, but they have a tank. Where does the money for stuff like that come from?"

"We don't know anything about this town's history. And more importantly, I just—"

"Ah," he said, snapping his fingers, then holding his index finger up. "That's a good point. Remember when I asked about the town's name? And the constable said it used to be called Horn of Plenty? Look at this…" He spun a large binder of old newspapers around until the open pages faced her. "What he didn't say was that the town was originally a French settlement, which was apparently also wealthy yet vanished overnight. Almost three hundred years ago on the dot. Poof. Then it was resettled fifty years later, with the new residents calling it Horn of Plenty. Again, it seemed to become a haven of wealth almost immediately."

"What are you getting at, Mulder?"

"Do you know the one thing dragon legends have in common across the globe? *Treasure.* They were believed to be guardians of it, protectors. That's why they were so hunted. Maybe that's what drove the first settlers here off. Maybe that's what made the next ones stay."

"And you think that's what's behind this town's fancy homes and nice cars? Dragon gold?"

"I'm saying maybe the way to figure out what's going on here is to look at the town as a whole. Not just medically."

"That's what I've been trying to tell you, Mulder. It's why I came to find you. We may already know who did this."

"Who?"

"Brandon Pratt. He walked into the constable station less than half an hour ago and said he wanted to confess, but only to the FBI and no one else. That means you and me." She let her gaze slide over the table again, shaking her head. "So if you can tear yourself away from this, maybe you can ask him if a Gowrow was involved."

The teenager behind the table in the interview room was tall and awkward, long arms and obtrusive elbows fidgeting on top of the table, skinny stovepipe legs bent and bouncing on the balls of his feet underneath. He was wearing a varsity jacket and jeans and a nose that would look at home on a vulture. The first thoughts Mulder had when he entered the room had to do with just how ugly the kid was.

He was holding a piece of paper in front of him, over the table. The teenager started to get out of his chair, but Mulder motioned for him not to bother.

Scully introduced herself first, badge and credentials out, then Mulder. She took a seat. Mulder looked over at the small two-way mirror and remained standing.

"Constable Pratt—your father—said you had something you wanted to talk to us about," Scully said.

The boy nodded and swallowed, the small point of his Adam's apple bobbing up and down.

"No need to be so nervous," Mulder said. "It's been months since Agent Scully here has bitten anyone."

"Why don't you just tell us what's on your mind, Brandon?" Scully said.

The teen cleared his throat. His voice was a raspy whisper, like he had a sore throat. "I have a statement I prepared." He tilted the paper up and began to read.

"My name is Brandon Amos Pratt. I am eighteen years old and fully competent to make this statement. I placed an unknown combination of ingredients into the three bowls of cider at the Sadie Hawkins Dance last month. For that I am very sorry. I did not know what the contents were. I believed I was spiking the drinks with strong alcohol. I was given the concoction by Dani Crumb. She told me it would be fun to see everyone drunk since this is a dry county. She lives with her mother off of Laurel Creek Road, east of town. She made me promise not to tell, but I was not aware of her intentions. I do not wish to answer any questions. I wish to remain silent and say nothing further. If questioned I will ask for legal counsel. Thank you."

The boy set the paper down on the table and looked first at Scully then at Mulder before lowering his gaze to his lap.

The door to the interview room opened. Constable Pratt leaned in, holding onto the knob. He put a hand to his shirt to keep it closed. "Guess that's it, Agents."

Mulder and Scully looked at each other and stood. Mulder reached for the piece of paper on the table.

"Do you mind if I take that?"

The boy hitched a shoulder, avoiding eye contact. Mulder took the sheet and followed Scully out of the room.

"The Crumb woman and her daughter live about seven miles from here. It's technically just outside the Horn Township, which means it's out of my jurisdiction. Plus, with me and my deputies like this and under voluntary quarantine, you probably want to treat this as federal anyway. I can call the county sheriff and have them meet you out there if you want to go pick them up."

Scully nodded without committing. She looked over to Mulder, who was studying the statement.

"What do you think, Mulder?"

"Where did he get the pen and paper?"

After a beat, the Constable said, "Are you asking me?"

"Yes. Who gave him something to write with?"

The man stared at Mulder for a moment, like he was uncertain what he was being asked. "You mean, for the statement? He brought that in as it was, already written."

"Oh." Mulder turned to Scully. "In that case, we should head over there and take the daughter in for questioning. Anything we should know about the daughter? Or the mother, for that matter?"

"Typical troublemaker. You know the type. Dresses weird. Antisocial. No respect. I'd be careful, though. The mother, she's, well… she's a witch."

"Not very nice?"

"No, I mean, she's a *witch*. Like, casts spells and all that crap. And she doesn't like cops. I wouldn't take any chances. Treat it like a felony apprehension. I'll have the sheriff's department meet you there. Use extreme caution. Knowing her, I'm sure the place is booby trapped."

"I think we have enough around here that we don't need to be trapping more," Mulder said, trying to avoid Scully's glare. Before the Constable could respond, he added. "Just give us the directions, or something to plug into our GPS."

Pratt proceeded to do just that, adjusting his breasts and punctuating his sentences with occasional grunts of discomfort each time he did.

"All right, Mulder," Scully said, shifting the rental car into park "I think we both can agree Brandon wasn't telling the whole truth back there."

Mulder stared out the passenger window through the break in the trees. "He wasn't the only one."

They were parked at the entry to a winding dirt drive. The trek from the center of town had taken about ten minutes, twisting winding roads that cut through thickly wooded terrain. But much of the focus was on not missing turns. Most of the roads weren't marked and some were hardly visible.

"Pratt?"

"He told you the kid wanted to talk only to us, right? That's why he had to say Brandon brought the statement already prepared. Except the paper wasn't folded, or crinkled. And it's awfully convenient you didn't see him when he came in."

She shook her head. "Pratt told me he was in the interview room, that he would only speak with the FBI. That's when I came to get you."

"Pratt or one of his deputies wrote that statement. No teenage kid would use those terms. Certainly not that one."

"But why? To get us to arrest them? Bring them into Horn?"

"Maybe. But didn't he seem determined that we wait for the county sheriff's department? Do you see anyone?"

"No." Scully picked up her phone. "I suppose we could contact them ourselves, but either way we'd have to wait."

"Your call," Mulder said. "I'm just along for the ride, remember?"

Scully got out of the car, looked at Mulder, then checked her weapon. He followed her down the path until they spotted a cracker style farmhouse with a deep porch and large windows.

"If we knock, she may try to run," Scully said. "Do you want to take the back?"

Mulder pulled his weapon, checking the chamber, and started to veer to the right. "Always my favorite side." Scully rolled her eyes at the comment…

The dusting of fall leaves crunched beneath his shoes as he made his way around the edge of the property. A light breeze rustled through the trees, swirling the leaves and washing over his face as it passed. The earthy aroma of the surrounding woods gave way to something else. Something sharp. Something herbal.

Just past the edge of the house, he saw them. But what they were doing remained unclear. Two women, one young, a girl, really, and another Mulder assumed was her mother. They were beneath the canopy of a massive oak tree, inside a large circle of stones, punctuated along the perimeter by hammered metal bowls flickering with blue flames.

The woman was on the ground in a lotus position, palms up, hands resting on her knees. She wore a long flowing dress of off-white fabric, possibly hemp, and a wreath of flowers on her head. Her dark hair spilled down her back, halfway to the ground.

Directly over her head, a large sword dangled from a rope, tip down, swaying only slightly in the breeze.

Behind the woman stood the girl. She was dressed in a loose blouse of similar material to the woman's dress, but wore jeans. The sleeves of her top draped from her arms. Her feet were bare and tensed, her toes curled and digging into the ground beneath her.

For good reason. In each of her outstretched hands was a length of rope. The ropes extended in a tight line to each side, needled in both directions through a looped piece of metal staked in the ground at the edge of the circle. From there the ropes angled up to where they fed through a pair of iron rings suspended from a hefty branch. They seemed to be tied together by a smaller rope that was wrapped around the handle and hilt of the sword. The sword hung from the section of rope between the two rings.

The girl holding the rope ends, arms stretched wide, was straining, adjusting her grip every few seconds. She was facing the side of the yard Mulder was using, but her eyes were closed. Before Mulder could back away, she opened them and whipped her head in his direction.

"Don't come any closer! If I let go of these, she'll die!"

"Whoa, whoa!" Mulder said, holstering his weapon. He raised his voice enough that he thought Scully might hear, but not so much he thought it would be obvious. "Nobody needs to die."

He maneuvered directly in front of her, trying to move closer without being obvious.

"Stay back!"

"Let's talk about this." He looked at the woman seated at her feet, trancelike, beneath the blade. "Is that your mother?"

The girl's eyes flashed and she bared her teeth in a grimace. Her grip slipped and she let go of the rope and then grabbed it again. The sword dropped a few inches. It started to sway more.

"You're Dani, right?"

Beyond the girl and the tree, Mulder saw Scully corner the house from the opposite direction. She seemed confused for a moment about what she was witnessing, then gestured to him in a way he assumed meant she wanted him to keep the girl talking.

"Like Dani California?" he continued, trying to keep the girl's attention. "Was your 'Papa a copper,' by any chance?"

The girl grunted and clenched her teeth. "It's short for Danielle, asshat."

"Hey, no need to get testy," Mulder said, showing his palms. "That's not even my favorite Chili Peppers song."

"I can't talk and hold this much longer," she said, puffing clipped words.

Scully had made her way to behind the tree. She nodded to Mulder, pointed to the rope on one side. Then she pointed to him, mouthed the word *you*, and pointed to the other side.

"Why don't you just let me move your mother? Then you can let it down gently and talking won't be a problem."

He took a tentative step forward. The girl shouted, almost screaming.

"*Don't* break the circle! The sun hasn't completed the journey!"

Mulder dropped his gaze to the circle, followed the perimeter of it. The shadow of the sword formed a line like the hand of a clock. That line was about six inches away from a particularly large stone with white markings on it.

He glanced up at the sun, peaking through a sizable gap in the branches of the oak. Then he looked back down at the shadow. Then over to Scully.

Scully signaled to him then sprinted toward the girl. It was too late to change plans, so he did the same. Dani's eyes widened, her mouth gaped and she started to yell something. But before she could, it was over. Scully grabbed one end of the rope just as Mulder grabbed the other.

"*No!*" Dani cried out and slammed the edge of her fist against Scully's chest. "You ruined it!"

"Mulder!"

Mulder reached over, extending himself as far as he could, and took the rope from Scully, who was fending off Dani with one hand and clearly straining not to lose her hold in the process.

The sword pendulumed from side to side, dropping a few more inches. The tip of its blade was now only two feet or so above the woman's head.

"Jeez," Mulder said. "Is this a sword, or an anchor?"

Scully wrapped the girl up, lifting her off the ground. A few moments of kicking and twisting and jerking, and the teenager seemed to give up. A loud hiss escaped her mouth and she sagged.

"Dana," Mulder said, shifting his attention to the sword as it dangled. "Meet Dani."

The girl shook her head. Her body slumped as if boneless. Scully let her slide to the ground. "You ruined it."

Mulder felt the rope slip and reset his grip. The sword dropped a few more inches. "Would it help if I told you we're from your government and we're here to help you?"

Scully slowly let go of the girl. She moved to the woman who was still in the lotus position and tried to drag her from beneath the sword. She wouldn't budge.

"Mulder," Scully said, placing two fingers against the woman's throat. She looked up at him. "This woman has no pulse."

"She may not have a head if we can't get her to a different spot, and fast. This thing feels like it was forged out of spent uranium."

"What did you do to her?" Scully said, turning back to the girl. "Is she drugged?"

The girl snorted, shook her head.

Scully was about to ask her again when the woman opened her eyes and sucked in a loud breath. She inhaled and exhaled a few times, looking around. Her gaze circled from Scully to Mulder to Dani then back Scully.

"Are you okay?" Scully asked. She pulled out her cred case and showed the woman her ID. "I'm Special Agent Dana Scully, this is Special Agent Mulder. I'm also a medical doctor. We need to move you. Are you hurt?"

"For crying out loud," the woman said, untangling her legs and crawling out from beneath the sword. "Can't someone perform a simple protection spell these days without the FBI getting involved?"

The tip of the sword was sharp enough that Mulder pricked his finger touching it. A tiny dome of blood bubbled and he stuck it in his mouth.

"What is it with this town and swords?" he said, gently setting the longsword flat on the ground.

"It's a powerful shape," the woman said. She stretched out, twisting her neck back and forth. "The symbol of intersection, dividing the world into its four elements. It's why Christian imagery is so compelling. Combine that with the qualities of metal, and it is both a talisman and a weapon."

"And having it aimed at your head?"

She closed her eyes, rubbed her temples. "True peril enhances the power of faith. The great goddess of day and night responds to the ultimate show of trust between women, granting the strongest protection possible."

"You were trying to protect Brandon?"

The woman paused. She fixed her eyes on Dani. "Yes. For my daughter."

"And you ruined it!" Dani said. She raked her hands down her face, then threw her arms up. "We have to do something!"

"Brandon is fine," Scully said. "He's being watched by a CDC official as we speak."

"Are you sure?"

"Yes. I just talked to her on the drive over. He's sitting in a room and she could see him through the glass."

"I don't believe you!"

The woman held up a hand toward her daughter, gentle but firm. "Dani is right. They sent you here because I made it impossible for anyone from town to set foot on my property—even that detestable father of his. And it worked. That was a potent spell you disrupted. You only get one chance."

"What were you protecting him from?" Mulder asked.

"Telling you would be a waste of words." She swept her hand in a gentle fan across the grass. "Only someone who wants to believe can see the truth."

"If you keep talking like that," Mulder said. "I'm going to assume I'm being punk'd."

"But you admit you were the ones who contaminated the beverages at the dance?" Scully said.

"Contaminated? Ha. That entire *town* is contaminated. I was doing them a favor."

"I doubt they see it that way," Scully said. "Look, Ms. Crumb—"

"Althea. And of course they wouldn't see it that way. Who do you think it was that contacted the CDC in the first place? It sure as Hades wasn't them."

Scully paused. She passed a look to Mulder.

"You sent that email?" he said.

"Of course! The last thing any of them wanted was outside attention. A medical emergency was the only way I could get anyone to care without SWAT teams kicking down my door. Plus, it was supposed to be a way to thwart their centennial. Put an end to this town's legacy."

"Only it didn't work on the one who mattered!" Dani said.

"Slow down," Mulder said. "What were you trying to protect him from?"

Althea let out a huff of air. "This town. This town and its vile ritual."

"Does this by any chance involve a creature called a Gowrow?"

The woman's eyes arced from one side to the other. "Ugh. What an ugly, hick pronunciation. It's called the *Gu-r'har*. From the secret language of the Druid High Priests. Roughly translated, it means the Young Man's Curse."

Scully spoke up. "Althea. This is a serious matter. I think it would be best if you and your daughter came with us back to the constable station so we can sort this all out."

"Are you arresting us, Agent Scully? That's rich. Hand me over to Pratt and the rest of that criminal gang called Horn."

"This is a federal matter now. Nobody will be handing you over."

"Sure. If you say so."

"Would I get to see Brandon?" Dani said. "I mean, actually see him? I have to know he's okay. I haven't been able to see him since the quarantine. I've been worried sick. I think his dad must have taken his phone."

"Yes. I promise we'll let you see him."

Dani looked like she was about to cry. She turned to her mother. "Maybe they're right, Mom. Maybe bringing in the FBI and all those other people stopped them."

Althea shook her head. "You know they would never just give up."

"Why?" Mulder said. "Why would they never give up?"

"Because the town owes all its prosperity to this. Good health, long life, abundance."

"By sacrificing a boy to a dragon every hundred years, they get all that?"

"It's not a dragon," Althea said. "And it's every fifty years. And who said anything about sacrificing a boy to it? That's not what I said. The boy *is* it."

"What do you mean? You're saying Brandon is the dragon?"

"Not a dragon! And no, not yet he isn't. But unless you do something, in a little less than half an hour he will be."

Mulder crouched low, looked her in the eye. "What happens in half an hour?"

"The same thing that happens every fifty years. A young man from the clan—in this case, the town—is taken to the lair of the *Gu-r'har* where, as the sun touches the horizon, he is to do battle with it until one is no longer living. If he loses, he dies and the chain is broken. The clan is no longer enchanted. If he wins, he becomes the *Gu-r'har*, and spends the next five decades in his lair."

"You don't know that, Mom," Dani said. "None of us has ever seen it."

"That doesn't seem like great odds," Mulder said. "Sending a teenager in to beat a dragon, with, what, a sword like this one?"

"It's not a dragon! And after so many years, the creature has no real fight left. It is not that hard to defeat. But only a young male can take its place."

"And if he refuses?"

"Not an option. They brainwash the chosen one. He spends a year— quite a long time in the life of someone so young—as the town hero, a champion. He has everything handed to him he wants. Girls are thrown at him. He gets his pick."

"Mom! Brandon's not like that! I told you! He wouldn't do that!"

"Dani," Scully said. "Brandon signed a statement that said he spiked the punch at your request. Is that true?"

"What? No! And it wasn't the punch! It was the water tower. And I don't believe you. He would never say something like that about me."

"My daughter suffers from the same sort of naïve outlook so many do about how the world works. In her case, it's the notion that the heart conquers all. She thinks she's his one true love."

"I am! You just can't stand him! You never approved of us! You're as bad as the town people you hate so much! You think he's just some player, trying to take advantage of me! It's not like that!"

The woman looked at Scully and then Mulder, shrugging. "Kids. Always rebellious. Even after I put myself beneath the sword for her."

Mulder said, "I think Agent Scully is right. Maybe we should all head in to town and sort this out. Brandon is there, and we can get to the bottom of this. Even if you're right, the constable and his two deputies aren't going to try anything with us around, not with the CDC in town too."

"I'm telling you," the woman said. "With the circle broken, Brandon will not be there."

Scully stared at her, pursing her lips. Then she pulled out her phone and tapped the screen. She spoke for half a minute, turning away.

"I just called the CDC investigator at the station. She said she was watching Brandon through the glass and that he hadn't left the room since she showed up. He was bored and fidgeting but clearly still there. Apparently the constables all left to get dinner."

"See, Mother! Maybe it did work!"

Scully's phone buzzed and she swiped the screen. She turned the phone out toward Dani. "I told her to take a quick picture so you could see."

Dani stared at it. Her mouth contorted and her nose crinkled. She looked at Scully with alarm in her eyes.

"Is this supposed to be some kind of joke? That's not Brandon. That's his cousin, Tanya Herman. Constable Pratt's niece." A gust of wind snarled through the yard, swaying trees and swirling leaves. "The mean kids all call her Tony He-Man."

Scully sped the rental sedan down the winding hillside, tires screeching at the curves.

"It's almost dusk," Mulder said. "Let's hope we don't arrive just as Brandon gets all toothy and scaly."

"You really believe her, Mulder?"

"It does explain everything. Why the town was so unhappy for the CDC to show up, why the media blackout was so easy to maintain, why Pratt was so quick to send us out here. There's obviously something they didn't want us to see."

"I don't know. Does Pratt strike you as the kind of man who would sacrifice his son? We're taking her word for it. Who do you trust?"

"Me? The only one I trust is you, and only a little. But there's one way to find out."

Scully frowned. "Maybe you're starting to make me paranoid. But something seems off."

"It's not paranoia if they're out to get you. It's just a heightened state of awareness. Is that why you had what's-her-name text you that picture? Smart move, by the way."

"The whole thing just wasn't adding up," she said nodding. She slowed the car as it approached a bridge. "This must be it."

She parked and they climbed down a slope beside the bridge, finding a trail along the water, just as Althea had described it. The sun was low on the tree line, starting to dip below. The angled light cast a reddish glow over the surrounding woodlands. They hiked for several minutes until they saw the rotted wood hull of a boat protruding from the water.

"South at the sunken boat," Mulder said, repeating Althea's directions. "Then over the ridge."

The climb was steep, but not too far. The ground was slick with fallen leaves and loose rock. Mulder was able to reach the crest first, then grab the trunk of a thin birch tree and pull Scully the rest of the way.

They waded through forest for a few yards. Where the trees broke, the ground dipped into a clearing. At the far side of the clearing there was a large opening in the hillside—less the mouth of a cave than a jagged, rocky hole in the slanted ground.

A young man knelt about ten yards in front of the hole. He was leaning on a large sword, head bowed, as if in prayer.

"Blond teenage boy with a sword," Mulder said. "Unless that's Excalibur and not the one from his father's office, I'm guessing we found Brandon."

"Do you honestly think a dragon is going to emerge from that cave?"

Mulder squinted at the opposing hillside. "Well, a Gowrow, maybe."

"Whatever is going to happen, we should put a stop to it before it goes any further."

"Oh, come on. Aren't you dying to see?"

"The question isn't whether I'm dying to see, it's whether we risk that boy out there dying so we can see."

"Gee, when you put it that way. So, what do you suggest? Take him into custody as a material witness? No one's ever accused me of being a slave to procedure, but we're already treading on thin ice by not arresting the Sorceress Crumb or her daughter, even though they confessed."

"Well, we have to do something."

"Aha! Admit it. You do think a dragon may come out of there!"

"It hardly matters—"

A sound bellowed from the hill, something deep and shrill, like metal twisting and scraping. The boy in the clearing pushed himself up and moved back, lifting the sword with both hands, clearly straining to keep it raised.

Scully started to say something else, but stopped, gagging.

"What in God's name is that stench?"

Mulder coughed, lifted the lapel of his coat over his face. "Does that smell like sulfur to you?"

Another loud roar, closer this time. Mulder could feel the vibration through his shoes.

"Mulder, whatever that is, we have to get that boy out of there."

Nodding, Mulder drew his weapon. Scully did the same. They each checked their chambers and headed down into the clearing.

The sound again. Louder, closer. It resonated deeply enough Mulder could feel it in his chest. He and Scully picked up the pace. He was opening his mouth to shout Brandon's name when something large exploded out of the hole. An arm, or front leg. Gray and black and taloned. It slammed down onto the rocky surface and its claws dug into the stone. In the darkness of the opening, Mulder saw a flash of white. Teeth.

"*Brandon!*"

The boy didn't react, transfixed on the opening in the ground. Mulder shouted his name again, this time joined by Scully. The boy jerked his head around. He stared for a second before looking back to the hill, then looked over to his right.

Another roar, this time higher pitched. The claws let go of the rock and yanked back into the darkness.

A percussion thumped the air and buffeted Mulder's ears. Scully stumbled, hands to the side of her head. Just above the hole, an explosion threw rock and dirt, pieces rising and falling like a fountain, leaving a burst of smoke to be pushed off by the breeze.

Whatever was emerging from the hole had pulled back from view and was now out of sight.

Through the ringing in his ears, Mulder heard another sound, a grinding hum over a crunching roll. He turned to see a dark blue tank smash through some small trees, crushing them beneath its tracks.

The tank fired again, this shot slamming into the hole and sending another spray of rock and dirt into the air, another cloud swirling into the wind.

Everything was a faint peal now, Mulder's eardrums numb. Scully was shaking her head, knocking her palm against the side of her skull and stretching her jaw. Behind the tank, Mulder saw the constable's deputies, rather zaftig and buxom in their ill-fitting uniforms, wielding AR-15s.

The tank creaked to a stop. The top opened and Constable Pratt appeared. His cheeks were flushed and his eyes glowered.

"Goddammit! What the hell were you thinking? You screwed it up! We had it! For the first time ever, we had a chance!"

Mulder could barely hear the man, but he was shouting just loudly enough to get through the buzz. He looked over to Scully, who was poking her ear with a finger. She shook her head and shrugged.

"You were trying to kill it?"

"Hell yes I was trying to kill it! Did it look like I was wanting to take a picture of it? And now it's gone! *Gone*! Deep down into the bowels of the Earth, way too far to ever reach! For another fifty years! Fifty years! God*dam*mit!"

"Constable," Mulder said in a voice he was certain was too loud but seemed quite far away. "We're completely lost here." He glanced over to the boy, who looked bewildered, the end of his broadsword on the ground and the handle pulling down on his arms like the weight was stretching them. "What's going on? Why did you lie to us about Brandon?"

The man climbed out of the vehicle and used a pair of metal rungs on the side to get to the ground. He cupped his breasts and winced as soon as he hit the ground.

"Because you would have messed it all up! You still managed to! You were supposed to go out to the Crumb place and wait for the Sheriff's Department, remember? But *no*, you had to stick your big federal noses where they don't belong."

Scully spoke up. "Constable, we were told Brandon was in danger, and that you were the one putting him in harm's way. You passing your niece off as him made that seem highly credible."

"Althea!" Pratt said, looking away and mopping his face. "I told you she was a witch and not to trust her, didn't I? Why would you listen to *her*?"

Scully made eye contact with Mulder, rattled her head in confusion. "What are you saying?"

"It was her family that started this damn curse to begin with! Something about a French woman hanged for sorcery, nobody remembers exactly what. But every fifty years the thing comes out, and if there's no first-born male past puberty waiting for it, it goes on a rampage. And every fifty years, someone tries to break the curse by killing it! Or starting a hundred years ago, we have. Who knows what they did before that. We only have the stories."

Mulder tried to process what he was hearing. "I thought the thing brought your town its wealth."

"Yeah, sure. But the curse makes that money expensive."

"What curse?" Mulder said.

The man sighed, studied the ground near his shoes. Then he told them.

They didn't quite arrest her, since they weren't sure of what federal charge they could make, but Mulder and Scully took Althea into custody and brought her back to the constable station. She didn't resist. Neither the constable nor his deputies could set foot on her land, due to a permanent spell of some sort. At least, that's what Pratt told them. Scully humored him.

The woman sat in the interview room with an expression that was part bored, part agitated, and one hundred percent unapologetic.

"Your daughter could be facing a lot of trouble," Scully said, seated across from her.

"Doubtful. You have no traces of anything in the water, no evidence from a lab, no possible mixture of chemicals that could induce the reaction you would be testifying to, and no witnesses. She's a minor who you can't speak to without a guardian or a lawyer present. If you think you can convict her on one comment, good luck. Try explaining the rest, while you're at it."

Scully looked to Mulder, who was standing up, leaning against the wall, hands in the pockets of his black coat.

"You're probably right," he said. "But what will your daughter think when she finds out you were the reason it didn't affect Brandon, whom she obviously is quite fond of?"

Althea's eyes narrowed. "I don't know what you're talking about."

"Sure you do. You're the reason he didn't have the sudden identity crisis all the other men did. You were hoping he would be killed. That's why you passed a spell that made him immune. And that's why you tricked your daughter into a more powerful spell, one you couldn't do alone. Admit it—that dangling-sword stuff wasn't protecting him. It was protecting the dragon."

The woman lowered her eyes but said nothing.

"That thing was an ancestor of yours, wasn't it?"

"Mulder…" Scully said.

"It was two birds, one stone. You didn't want your daughter falling in love with Brandon, some old feud, I would venture, since you hate just about everyone in the town. But you also had to make her think you were trying to help, so she wouldn't hate *you*. That's why you told her Brandon would become the creature if the spell failed, paving the way for her, or maybe her daughter, to keep protecting it the next time, after you're gone, thinking it's the boy she loved. What you didn't tell her was that if no young man showed up, the Gowrow would destroy the whole town, just like it did with that first settlement. And, of course, you always intended for the spell to work, just not in the way she believed. You'd get points for trying, and in the end you'd succeed in protecting the dragon, and getting rid of her suitor, all at the same time."

She slapped her hand against the table. "*Gu-r'har,* you imbecile! The women of my line have been protecting them since before dragons were ever imagined!"

The room stayed quiet for a long moment. Althea pulled back into her seat and took a few calming breaths. "I want a lawyer. And if you repeat any of those… those *filthy lies* to my daughter, I'll sue your asses off for slander."

Mulder started to keep going, but Scully stood and pulled him out of the room. She shut the door behind them and stood in the hallway.

"It's done, Mulder. You know that. Even giving her a speech could taint what we have. Which, I'll concede, isn't much. But rules are rules."

"I suppose," he said, scratching his cheek.

A squeal erupted from down the hall. Mulder and Scully rounded the corner to see Dani near the front entrance, arms around Brandon's neck with her feet in the air. The boy spun, swinging her as she peppered his face with kisses.

"I guess she was wrong about that, too," Mulder said.

Scully's mouth tightened but her cheeks dimpled. "What now, Mulder? Do we get the U.S. Attorney's office involved?"

"Nah. Let her stew in there for a bit while we see if the local barbecue is still open."

"So, we treat it as an X-File?"

"Think about it, Scully. Do you really want to testify about what went down? Let's face it, your theory about an unidentified cave-dwelling species of crocodilian sounds even more far-fetched than a dragon. Besides, do you really want to drag those kids through it all? I think it's safe to say these people have been punished enough."

They walked past the teenagers, who only paused briefly to acknowledge them before returning to their displays of affection.

Outside, the full moon was floating above a dark, distant hill.

"Sort of brings new meaning to the old saw about being a nice place to visit," Mulder said, pointing to the statue in the town square. "'*Our residents never leave for long and always come back.*'"

He placed a hand on Scully's shoulder as they started down the sidewalk. "How many towns do you suppose have a slogan that doubles as a curse?"

THE END

the
Truth
is out
There

PILOT
By David Liss

I t was the sort of case that Dana Scully usually let her partner investigate on his own time. No crime had been committed, so there was no forensic or detective work to be done. It had all the telltale signs of a waste of time, the sort of inquiry that on the surface looked like nonsense, and closer examination would prove it to be exactly that. On the other hand, the witnesses lived just west of Baltimore, so without traffic it was less than an hour's drive from the J. Edgar Hoover building. It had been only a few months since Scully's sister had been murdered, and sometimes the grief still hit her hard, especially when she was alone in an apartment that now felt too large and too vulnerable. Keeping busy seemed like a better idea than restless solitude, so Scully had volunteered to ride along on a Saturday afternoon.

For Fox Mulder, this was a typical weekend. Following up on insubstantial leads or chasing internet rumors was all part of the game. Most of it went nowhere, but you had to look closely at a lot of losers to find the occasional winner, and he had a gut feeling the trip was worth his time. The story was just idiosyncratic enough to contain something substantial.

"There are multiple witnesses," Mulder explained as they drove along the highway. Weekend or no, he wore a dark suit that served as his FBI uniform, and he looked all business. The sun was out, and the spring weather was just inching past cool. It had all the makings of an enjoyable day. "It was before nine at night, and most of our witnesses were already outside."

"Drinking beer," Scully noted. She wore dark slacks, a white blouse, and a dark jacket. Not a pantsuit, but close. "Your witnesses are drunk teenagers."

"Maybe," Mulder conceded as he made his way along I-695, "but being drunk doesn't disqualify you as a witness. There are six people who have gone on record as having seen bright lights flashing in and around the house where our principal witness lives. The lights are described as being both like clouds and like blue lightning."

Scully sighed. "Mulder, there are countless natural phenomena than can cause electrical discharge."

"That's true, but the witnesses also said they heard a mechanical whine at the same time. And then there's Howard Nagel's story, which you have to admit is interesting."

Scully leafed through the folder as Mulder drove. "That's one word for it."

They spoke to four of the six neighbors first. The other two were gone for the weekend, and it soon became clear that two more voices were not going to shed much light on what had been observable from the outside—clouds of light, flashes of electrical discharge, mechanical whining. No one saw anything else out of the ordinary, and while the sights and sounds were admittedly unusual, ultimately there was nothing overtly suggestive of alien or paranormal activity.

Howard Nagel, Mulder hoped, would have something more interesting to report.

"Don't get your hopes up," Scully said as they walked up the driveway of the neat suburban home. The grass was a little long, the bushes a little in need of trimming, but it was otherwise well maintained. "He's a teenager. Their brains are developing. Embellishing, even hallucinating, is not at all unusual in adolescence. With a witness like this, part of being objective is being skeptical."

"You're already dismissing the witness and we haven't heard what he has to say," Mulder observed. "That's not very objective."

Howard Nagel was a short and thin 15-year-old with wild hair in need of washing. He had a sunken chest, bad posture, and a kudzu-creep of acne across his face. He wore a faded black t-shirt with a picture of Yoda on it. He was, in other words, a classic teenage geek, and even Mulder began to lose heart only seconds after he opened the door.

If the agents were not impressed with Nagel, he seemed delighted with them. When they flashed their badges, his sad face brightened, like he had been visited by rock stars. His eyes were darting back and forth between the two of them, but then settled on Scully and lingered there.

Mulder had seen this before. A certain kind of man always found Scully's serious appearance especially alluring. He watched as Howard looked away from her, then risked a glance back. His eyes went slightly wide, then he blushed and looked away again.

Still holding out the badges, Mulder identified himself and his partner.

"You're Mulder and Scully!" the kid said excitedly. "That is so cool!"

"You've heard of us?" Scully asked, more than a little surprised.

"No. I mean, not really. You'll see." He seemed pleased with himself.

"We wanted to ask you some questions about what you witnessed the other night," Scully said.

"Sure," Howard said. "I mean, I don't know why the FBI would be interested, but I'll tell you what I can."

Inside the house, Howard offered to take Scully's coat and bring her a lemonade, which he served in tumblers featuring a uniform insignia from a popular science fiction show. Mulder, meanwhile, took stock of the house. It was not terribly large, and it was clean and neat, but still radiated an air of neglect. The furnishings and curtains all had a faded look to them.

"Where are your parents?" Mulder asked as they sat.

"Dead," Howard said neutrally. "It's been almost eight years, so don't feel awkward. They were both professors at Johns Hopkins, and they were in a car accident coming home from a faculty event. Honestly, I hardly remember them anymore."

"You live here alone?" Mulder asked.

"With my sister," Howard explained. "My aunt came to live with us after the accident, but when Jennifer, my sister, turned 18, she took over. Now it's just the two of us." He looked at Scully. "Anyhow, I appreciate you coming out to hear my story, Agent Scully. I make up a lot of stuff, but not this."

"You make up things?" Scully asked.

"I'm a writer," Howard said. "At least, I want to be."

"Science fiction?" Scully asked, professionally neutral.

Howard nodded enthusiastically. "I especially like stories in which there's some kind of romance between people and machines. That's my signature move."

"Maybe we should hear about what happened to you," Mulder prompted. "We can hear about the machine romance later."

Turning to Scully, Howard began to tell the story about how he'd been in his room, working on one of his stories, when he'd noticed the flashing. At first he thought it was coming from outside the house, but then he realized it was all around him. Suddenly, he was face to face with himself. A replica of Howard Nagel was staring back at him.

"I panicked," Howard admitted. "I threw myself back onto the bed, and I may have covered my eyes for a few seconds. And then I realized that this must be a visitor from another world. He'd taken on the shape of the first person he'd seen—me."

"I think I saw that in a movie, once," Mulder suggested, arching an eyebrow.

"Exactly," Howard said, brightening toward Mulder for the first time. "I figured I had a responsibility to be an ambassador for my planet, so I sat up, ready to greet the visitor, but by then it was gone."

"Vanished?" Mulder prompted. "Dematerialized? Beamed up, maybe?"

Howard shook his head. "No, he must have slipped away when I wasn't looking. The thing is, for a few seconds, my room was different. It was still my room, but not exactly the same. All my poster, collectables, comics— they were gone. Then my sister came in, and she was acting all weird. She was scared, like something was wrong with me. She kept asking what had happened to me, like I had some horrible wound or something."

"Were you bleeding?" Scully asked.

"No," Howard said. "I felt fine. But then there were more flashes, and everything seemed normal again."

"When you spoke to your sister," Scully asked, "what sorts of injuries did she say she saw on you?"

"That's the thing," Howard said. "She didn't remember any of it. She said it hadn't even happened."

"Lost memory," Mulder said, taking notes. "Interesting."

"Uh huh," said Scully, looking at her watch. "Did your visitor leave any evidence of his visit? Some kind of mechanisms? Signs of energy discharge? Ray gun? Ectoplasm?"

"Ectoplasm is ghosts, Scully," Mulder said.

"I don't want to rule anything out," she told him, her face a mask of patience that her partner recognized immediately and unambiguously as impatience.

Mulder knew she was done here. By now she had dismissed Howard as a sad, lonely nut case, making this story up entirely or suffering from a delusion. Suddenly an afternoon of laundry and crossword puzzles didn't sound so depressing after all.

"There was one thing," Howard said. He got up and went to a desk drawer from which he took out a manila envelope. He handed it to the agents. The look on his face demonstrated the smug satisfaction of someone who had proved himself right in the face of doubters.

On the envelope were the words: *DO NOT OPEN, HOWARD. GIVE THIS TO MULDER AND SCULLY.*

"Well, that's something," Mulder said. He watched Scully trying to figure out when Howard could have written their names on the envelope and slipped it in the drawer. Her uncle had long ago taught her some sleight of hand, and she was pretty good at it, but Mulder didn't think anyone was *that* good. He'd had his eye on the kid and the environment the entire time they'd been in the house. He would have noticed if Howard had gone across the room and opened a drawer.

Mulder examined the envelope's exterior, and showed it to Scully. "Nothing up its sleeves," he said.

"We should take this back to the lab and examine it before opening it," Scully said.

"That would be smart," Mulder agreed. Then he tore the envelope open. Inside was a glossy 8" x 10" photograph. It was in color, but grainy, like a still from a video camera. It showed Mulder and Scully sitting with Howard in the living room.

"Holy crap!" Howard shouted. "That envelope's been sitting there for days!"

Mulder smiled at Scully.

Scully rolled her eyes.

"I've seen a magician make an elephant disappear," Scully said on the drive back to DC.

"On TV," Mulder noted. "You can make anything look real on TV."

"My point is that it was a trick. A very good trick. The kid has a lot of talent, but it was still just a trick. We know he likes to make up stories."

"Writing fiction doesn't make someone a liar," Mulder told her. "And even if it did, I don't think Howard Nagel has the confidence to pull off something like that."

"You can't know that after just meeting him."

"Sure I can," he said. "I'm very sensitive."

"So, if it's not a trick, what is it?"

"That's really the question, Scully." He rubbed his chin thoughtfully. "Some kind of time travel, maybe? A psychic projection from the future imprinted on film. That could explain the electrical discharge. And the doppelgänger. Howard, or maybe an astral projection of Howard, was visiting himself."

"That's a good theory," she said, her tone making it clear she thought it was a ridiculous theory. "Another possibility is that the photo was a decent parlor magic trick."

"How do you explain the lights witnessed by the neighbors?" Mulder asked.

"He rigged up some sort of apparatus. Mulder, he's a lonely teenage boy. He's obviously smart, but he has social difficulties. Like a lot of kids in that position, his imagination and intelligence can lead him into some weird places."

"Like fabricating a story that witnesses will circulate, so two FBI agents can some out to his house where he can secretly videotape them, transfer that videotape to photo, and slip that photo into an envelop in a drawer across the room?"

"You'll forgive me if I find that a little more convincing than time traveling astral projections. My theory is unlikely, but at least it's not impossible."

"Sometimes the impossible is a lot more probable than the unlikely," Mulder said.

"And other times," said Scully, "it's not."

Mulder continued to try to follow up with the case on the internet, but there were no new sightings, no new developments or evidence, so he simply filed his notes and moved on. He forgot about Howard Nagel entirely until, a week later, two events refreshed his memory. He called Scully down to his office in the basement of the Hoover building.

"What're you working on, Scully," he asked when she walked in. He didn't bother to look up.

Scully leaned against the door jamb. "Just catching up on my filing, but you could have called to ask me that."

"That's true," he agreed, still leafing though the folder, "but these conversations are much more meaningful when they're face to face. Hey, do you remember a couple months back when you infiltrated that former leper colony that I thought was a secret facility for breeding alien/human hybrids, but you were sure was simply where equally secret, but much more mundane, experiments were conducted on radiation exposure?"

Scully arched an eyebrow and folded her arms. "It rings a bell."

"Did it look anything like this?"

Mulder put his feet down and handed Scully a picture from the folder. It was a glossy 8" x 10" color photo depicting Scully and an older man with wispy gray hair. The man's face was marked with lesions, showing clear signs of leprosy. The image caught the two of them in the woods, pausing briefly to converse.

Her eyes went wide. "Where did you get this?"

Mulder smiled. He now had her attention. "I don't suppose you noticed any security cameras out in those woods?"

"No," she said, lost in thought as she took her glasses out of her coat pocket to examine the photo more closely. "It was a secret facility, so there might have been cameras, though I'd be surprised if they were in this particular location. The image does have a grainy quality that suggests a captured video image, but I doubt it's from a security camera."

"Because?" Mulder made a beckoning gesture, waiting for her to put it together.

"Because it's in color, and security cameras almost never capture color images. The photo isn't overexposed, so you can see it's night, but the lighting is strangely bright. You can see the red of my scarf clearly. Anyhow, the resolution is too good for a security camera, and it's fairly close up, so we would have had to have been standing directly in front of it."

"My thinking exactly. It's kind of like that photo we got in Maryland, isn't it?"

"They're photographs," Scully said, her body posture shifting defensively. "They're similar by nature."

Mulder, however, was on a roll. "So, remember what I was up to while you were at the old leper colony?"

"I seem to recall you were trapped on a train car that contained a concealed bomb on a timer."

"Correct," said Mulder.

He now handed Scully another photo, which showed Mulder pointing his gun at a man who claimed to be an NSA agent. Like the first photo, it had the grainy quality of a video still, but was much brighter, being from a well-lit space.

"I looked over that car pretty carefully," said Mulder. "I was trying to find a bomb, after all, but I don't recall seeing any security cameras."

"Even if there had been one," said Scully, "and even if the cameras had recorded in color, this quality here is simply too good. Like the other one, it's close in, and you're clearly moving here, but the image isn't blurry."

"I agree, Scully."

Scully sat down as she continued to examine the photo. The skepticism was gone. Scully was now clearly alarmed. "Mulder, where did these pictures come from? How did someone get video of us when we were places no one should have been able to see us?"

"I received them this morning in the mail," Mulder said, "along with this note."

He handed her a piece of yellow legal pad paper. It contained a single line in a neat hand. *Intrigued? There's more where that came from. And better. Howard.*

"I'd say it's time to give our friend Howard Nagel another visit," Mulder said.

"I would agree with you, but that's the other interesting development," Mulder said. "Howard Nagel's house was destroyed in some kind of explosion. He's presumed dead."

The neighbors were gathered at a respectful distance outside the quarantine zone. It looked like they would be allowed back in their neighborhood soon enough, since the guys in the hazmat suits had taken off their hoods, and there were cops and firefighters walking around without any protection.

The preliminary reports had been either inaccurate or deliberately downplayed. There hadn't been an explosion. Howard Nagel's house had been obliterated. It looked like a hand had reached down and pulled it out of the earth—that is, if the hand had been red-hot. The ground still smoked, but none of the neighboring houses appeared to have sustained any damage.

Mulder parked outside the yellow tape, and he and Scully ducked under and flashed their badges. In the distance they saw the coroner's office trying to collect badly damaged remains. There wasn't a whole lot to work with.

"What's the FBI's involvement here?" asked a middle-aged guy with broad shoulders and a weight-lifter's physique. The badge around his neck identified him as ATF agent Tim Flumph. "We're pretty sure this was an explosive device of some kind, though beyond that, I'm stumped. But I don't see any signs of terrorism."

"This is part of an ongoing investigation," Mulder said. "Can you walk me through what happened?"

Flumph didn't know very much. Howard Nagel had been seen coming out of the house that morning to collect the newspaper. A few minutes later, the neighbors heard not an explosion, but a loud popping sound, and when they came outside, they found the house was simply gone.

"Did you find any photographs that survived the explosion?"

Flumph laughed. "The entire house was more or less incinerated. We found some remains, but it's going to take weeks to identify what's left of this guy. You want to find photographs?"

"Maybe near the crime scene," Mulder prodded.

"Like porn, you mean?" Flumph asked. "Are you looking for porn?"

"Not really," Mulder said. "Why, did you find some?"

"No, but kids that age, they sometimes like porn," Flumph explained.

"I read about that," Mulder said. "But I'm looking for anything unusual at all. It can be pornographic or not."

The ATF agent shook his head. "Didn't find anything. But you two, you're good with this sort of case, aren't you?"

"How do you know that?"

Flumph shrugged. "Word gets around."

"What do you think caused a crater like this?" Scully asked.

"Could be anything, really," Flumph said with a shrug. "Something in the explosion family is most likely."

"You don't say." Mulder folded his arms.

"The real question," the ATF agent said, "is *who* caused it. My money is on Howard Nagel."

"I thought you found—"

"We found remains," Flumph said. "Might be Nagel's. Might be someone else's. Too early to tell. But if you find Nagel, I want to talk to him."

"Of course," Scully said.

"That's an unusual name," Mulder said. "Flumph."

"It's Italian," the ATF agent said with a wink. "The 127th most common surname in America."

Mulder and Scully drove to the local police station where Howard's sister Jennifer was giving a statement. They found her in an unlocked interrogation room, clutching a Styrofoam cup of milky tea that looked ice cold.

She was in her early twenties with dirty blonde hair pulled into a shoulder length ponytail. She wore a white blouse and conservative gray skirt, and Mulder supposed she'd come directly from some sort of office job.

"I can't believe everything's gone," she told Scully, who sat across from her. Mulder was a little off to the side, letting his partner do her thing. Grieving people often opened up to her more readily than to him. He had no idea why.

"Our parents were killed in a car accident eight years ago," Jennifer said. "Everything I had from them—it's all destroyed."

Mulder was about to open his mouth, to mention that her brother was also gone, but Scully gave him a quick look, and he kept quiet.

"Tell me about your parents," Scully said.

"They both worked at the Applied Physics Lab at the university. That's where they met. They were busy—really focused on their work—but they loved us. Howard doesn't remember them as well as I do."

"And now he's gone too," Scully said. Her voice was sympathetic, but she was probing.

Jennifer turned away. "Yeah."

"Do you know what might have happened? Was your brother experimenting with explosives or any kind?"

"No, he wasn't into anything like that. I tried to get him to study science, to be like mom and dad, but he just wanted to write his stupid stories."

"Did he have any enemies?" Mulder asked. "Problems at school? Conflicts with bullies?"

"At the college?" the Jennifer asked.

"I thought he was fifteen."

The sister nodded. "He graduated high school last year. He was saving up for a proper four-year college and going to the local community college in the meantime. He was really smart—smart enough to skip grades—but he got distracted in high school. He wanted to just write his stories, and sometimes forgot to do his assignments, so his grades weren't good enough for scholarships."

"Did he talk to you at all about the incident from a couple of weeks ago?" Mulder asked. "With the lights?"

"Not really," she said. "To be honest, I didn't really want to hear about it. I thought he was just getting carried away with one of his stories. That happened sometimes. He'd get so lost in his imagination, he would lose his grip on reality."

Scully nodded gravely, like she understood all too well.

"Howard told us that you seemed alarmed when you saw him, like he was hurt, but then you didn't remember," Mulder prompted.

"Yeah," she nodded. "He seemed so sure we had that conversation, but it never happened." She took a moment to wipe her eyes with a tissue. "Why would someone blow up our house? I don't get it. Promise me you'll find whoever did that."

Scully patted her hand, which seemed to Mulder a great way to avoid promising anything.

As they walked back to the car, Mulder said. "She doesn't seem all that broken up. And she spoke about Howard in the past tense."

"That happens a lot. You know that."

"But houses don't just vanish leaving a smoking crater a lot. That's more unusual."

"I admit that," Scully agreed, "but there are any number of plausible natural causes for something like this, and that's not even accounting for explosive devices. I don't see that there's anything to follow up on."

They were about to get into the car when Flumph came over and put a hand on Mulder's shoulder.

"So, have you decided you're working this case?" he asked.

"I don't think so," Mulder said, "but keep us in the loop, especially if anything strange shows up?"

"Strange like porn?"

"You'll know it if you see it," Mulder said.

"Got it. At the same time, you let me know if you find Howard Nagel." He handed Mulder his card. "Call me immediately. This guy might be dangerous."

"It was the exploding house that gave it away," Mulder said.

They opened the car door and Scully found an envelope waiting for her on the passenger side. When she opened it, she found a photograph of them about to get in the car, Flumph placing his hand on Mulder's shoulder. Attached to it was a note.

Want to know what happens next? It said. *Want to know what the Smoking Man is up to? Want to know the truth about the government and aliens? I've seen the future, but it will cost you.*

"Neat magic trick," Mulder said.

Scully raised her eyebrows. "Someone is going to a lot of trouble to wow us with what is impressive sleight of hand. The question is why. And how do we contact whoever is doing this?"

"I have a theory," Mulder said.

He turned over the envelope and showed Scully the phone number that had been scrawled on the back.

It was a DC number, so they waited until they were back in the Hoover building to call. The phone answered right away.

"Hello, Agent Mulder," said a voice he recognized at once as Howard Nagel's.

"How'd you know it wouldn't be Scully?" he asked.

"It's more your style to take the lead on this."

"And how do you know that, Howard?" Mulder asked.

"I know more than you'd believe."

"You knew how to completely destroy your house without harming your neighbors' property," Mulder said. "That's a neat trick. Whose body will the authorities ultimately identify?"

"Look, I didn't blow the house, if that's what you're thinking. They are trying to get me. I was just playing with you guys at first. I thought it was fun, but now it's become more serious. I have to use what's available to me, and that means I have to charge you."

"Charge me for what?"

"The goods. I was going to give this stuff away—just like playing with you, because I love you guys and all. But now I need money, so you'll have to pay up. Sorry, Agent Mulder, but that's how it has to be now. I'd like to meet and show you something. Something far more impressive than those photos. I'll give it to you for free, but the next installment will be very expensive."

"You're trying to blackmail government employees?" Mulder asked. "Do you know how little we make?"

"It is not blackmail," Howard said. "I'm not threatening you. I'm simply offering to sell you something in my possession. It's not like I mean to do anything bad if you don't want it."

"How do you know we won't arrest you for destruction of property?"

"Because you don't have any proof that I've committed a crime," he said. "Like I said, I didn't destroy that house."

"I could report you to the ATF," Mulder said.

"Go ahead," Howard said. "But don't report me to that man *pretending* to be an ATF agent. That's all I ask."

Mulder thought it best to defer on that one. "Where do you want to meet?"

A few minutes later, after making another call, Mulder hung up the phone. "The ATF has no Agent Flumph in its employ."

"And that surprises you?" Scully asked. "It's a made-up name."

"Maybe," Mulder said. "But I think there's something else going on."

When they got down to the garage, Agent Flumph was leaning against Mulder's car, flipping through a copy of a pornographic magazine—the kind with pictures of airbrushed women and interviews with famous athletes. He was holding the magazine at a crooked angle and staring.

"You hear from Howard?" asked Flumph.

"No, have you?" Mulder asked—deadpan.

Flumph folded up the magazine. He pressed his lips together in a thin smile. "Let's stop playing around, shall we?"

"Sounds good," Mulder said. "Who are you really?"

"Who do you think I am?"

"That question doesn't make me feel confident that we're no longer playing around."

"Go ahead," Flumph said. "Guess."

"If I had to come up with something," Mulder said, "I'd propose that you're with some sort of time traveling law enforcement agency. Maybe one who comes from an era where there is no pornography."

Flumph smiled. "Right church, wrong pew. If you hear from Howard, let me know. I'll make it worth your while."

Howard looked different. His clothes were neat, and his acne had cleared up. He looked to be the same age, but also older, more mature somehow. Mulder's first thought was an identical twin, but Jennifer had said it was just the two of them and there were no other siblings. She had no reason to lie that he knew of. Of course, that didn't necessarily mean anything.

They sat down at a table, and Howard folded his hands and smiled smugly. He was completely unlike the twitchy, uneasy kid they'd met only a couple of weeks ago. Maybe that had been an act, but Mulder doubted it.

"What happened at your house, Howard?" Scully asked.

He shrugged. "I wasn't home. I have no idea. I'm just glad no one was hurt."

"They found remains," Scully said.

He shrugged again. "I don't know who that could be. I was the only one who might have been there, and as you can see, I'm right here."

"Unless," Mulder said, "you are a future version of yourself, and you came back in time and killed your earlier self."

"Nice theory, except if I came back and killed my younger self, then my older self could never have come to kill him."

"That is assuming that time is a connected whole rather than isolated pockets of autonomous reality. Time travel paradox has never been proved to exist."

"It's never been proved not to exist," Howard countered.

"That's the *I'm rubber and you're glue* of scientific arguments," Mulder said.

"What is it you want to show us?" Scully said wearily.

Howard reached into his bag and pulled out a videotape. It had a commercial cover, which featured close images of both Mulder and Scully. Mulder was holding a gun. Scully looked fetching and alarmed, or possibly seductive. Above their faces, in vaguely spooky type, were the words THE X-FILES.

Mulder took the tape and examined it. He kept his expression carefully neutral. "Who are Donald Delaney and Jill Henderson?"

"Actors," Howard said. "They play Agents Mulder and Scully in the hit show, *The X-Files*. That's the pilot episode right there."

Scully took the videotape and examined it. "What exactly is all this? What are you hoping to prove by making this thing?"

"Nothing," Howard said. "Take that with you. Watch it. Let me know if you'd like to see more. I have the entire run available. You want to find out what the government is really hiding?"

"Where did this come from?" Mulder demanded.

"Nothing I say will matter until after you've seen it," Howard said. "So go watch it, and then you'll believe me when I say I have all the answers to all the questions that drive you."

"Including the truth about my sister?" Mulder asked cautiously.

Howard nodded. "But it's not really what you're expecting."

Mulder stood up, ready to force Howard to say more. Scully, however, was there to restrain him. She began to pull him out of the coffee shop.

"I look forward to your call," Howard said. "But don't be too long. There's someone out there who doesn't want you to see what I've got."

They watched the episode in Mulder's office. When it was over, they stared at each other, unable to find the words.

"That was weird," Mulder said.

"What is this?" Scully asked. "I mean, that was us, but not really. Most of that was just like what happened, but it was a little off too. There were things neither of us actually said. And I never owned some of those clothes."

"They were a little sexier than your usual style," Mulder observed.

"And that scene where I come into your motel room? I would never have said that. It was so trampy."

"I thought that was dramatically effective," Mulder said.

"I'm serious," Scully said. "How do you explain this? Could it be cutting edge special effects? But I can't imagine any special effects that look so realistic, and if it is fabricated, it would have cost a fortune to create. Why would anyone go to the trouble? And all of that assumes they knew exactly what happened in that case, right down to the things we said when no one else was around."

"I'm scrapping my time travel theory," Mulder told her. "The math is complicated, but there is a lot of compelling evidence to support the theory of parallel realities. Each possible alternative reality is generated simply by the possibility itself. Who is to say there is not a reality in which we are fictional characters instead of actual people?"

"And, what? Howard, or one of the Howards, is a visitor from a different reality, and he happened to bring his collection of TV videotapes with him?"

"That's where I'm going with this, yes. Look, Scully, this tape followed reality pretty closely. You can't deny that. And there were scenes that we weren't part of. We got to see what other people were up to. And that bit at the end with the Smoking Man. Pretty chilling, right? This show could give us the clues we need to figure out what we're missing."

"Why would it?" Scully demanded.

"Because if it's a TV show, it has to have narrative coherence. You can leave the characters hanging, but not the audience."

"Mulder," Scully began.

But Mulder was busy calling the contact number Howard had given him.

"Impressed, Agent Mulder?" Howard asked.

"Gibsonton, Florida," Mulder said. "What happened to the missing conjoined twin?"

"You want another freebie?" Howard didn't sound pleased.

"Answer the question, or there's no deal."

"Great episode," Howard said. "Season two. The Enigma ate him."

Mulder slammed down the phone. "You were right, Scully. The Enigma ate him."

"But how could Howard know that?" Scully demanded.

"Because it's on the show, and the show contains elements that are unseen to us. Don't you get it? If we can watch this thing, we'll know so much more about where we've been, and maybe even where we're going. For the first time, we can be ahead of our enemies."

"Mulder, you can't believe in any of this."

"The evidence is right in front of us," he said. "How can you deny it?"

"Because I can't accept that I'm just a fictional character, played by an actor, out of someone else's imagination."

"You're not, Scully. You have free will. The actors, their writers, aren't creating us. They are simply a representation that happens to coincide with our reality. If there are an infinite number of universes, in which all possible outcomes are represented, then there has to be at least one in which our actions appear as a fiction television program. There's another universe in which there's a different show that diverges dramatically from our reality, but this tape doesn't seem to come from that universe. And since the universe it comes from is so useful, we should take advantage of that."

"But they've already made this show. Doesn't that mean that I've already made all my decisions elsewhere, and if so, I don't have free will."

"This television show doesn't change how much free will is real or an illusion. We could be on a different timeline, so these tapes represent some kind of past events. If you could travel back in time to meet Lincoln, the fact that you know his biography doesn't mean he no longer has free will. The truth is going to be the truth, and ignoring a tool like this, because it makes you uncomfortable, is insane."

Mulder picked up the phone again and called Howard. "How much do you want?"

"$50,000 per season," Howard said.

"How long did this thing run?"

"Twelve years," Howard said. "The last two were pretty great. I'll throw in both the movies for free if you buy the whole run. The first film's pretty important for the mythology."

"I don't have that kind of money."

"You don't have to buy them all at once. My only stipulation is that you buy them in order. No sneaking ahead."

"I'll take the first two seasons," Mulder said.

"I'll call you back with the meet time."

Scully blanched when Mulder told her how much he was prepared to pay.

"My father's left me some money. It will clean me out, but I don't care. I need to see what's on those tapes."

When they called Howard later that day, however, he did not answer, and Mulder went home with a briefcase full of money.

Howard called him the next day. "They're after me," he said. "I need help."

"Who's after you?"

"The people who blew up the house."

"Why did they do that, Howard?"

"They were trying to destroy the machine I use for traveling, which they did. They were also trying to kill me."

"But they got the wrong Howard," Mulder speculated. "This reality's Howard?"

"That's my guess," said Howard. "I never meant for anyone to get hurt. I made contact with you guys because I'm a fan. I thought it would be fun. It was just a physics project. My dad helped me, and now maybe I'll never see him again."

"Why don't you let me put you in protective custody?" Mulder asked. "At least until we can figure this out."

"So you can try to track down my videotapes? Forget it. If I'm stuck in this universe, I'm going to need cash. Pay up, or I bet I can find someone else who will."

"Are you threatening to go to the supporting cast?" Mulder asked.

"That's exactly what I'm doing," said Howard. "Get me the money, and get it to me quick or I'll find another buyer. I bet Krycek would be willing to fork over top dollar."

Howard was hiding out in a farmhouse in rural Maryland. After getting the directions, Mulder went and picked up Scully, and they drove along rural roads for almost an hour.

They saw the column of smoke when they were more than a mile out. What had presumably been a barn was now a smoking hole in the ground.

"It looks like the inter-dimensional police got here first," Mulder said.

A little farther up they saw Flumph leaning against a car, magazine under his arm, looking at the smoke.

Mulder got out of the car and walked over to him. "You killed him?"

Flumph shook his head. "Sent him back to where he belongs. I destroyed his video collection, though."

"We still have the pilot episode," Mulder said.

"You can see if you do when you return to your office," Flumph told him.

"How do you know we won't arrest you right now?" Scully demanded. "You seem very smug."

"Arrest me for what?"

"Impersonating a federal office," Scully said. "Destruction of property."

"You can't link me to any crimes," Flumph told her. "And I'd vanish from the system long before you could slap those pathetic charges on me." He opened the door of his car. "I need to return this to the rental place and get back home." He shook his head at the wonder of it all. "Cars you can rent. Amazing."

"Let me ask you something," Mulder said. "Is *Flumph* really an Italian name where you come from?"

"Let that be part of the mystery," Flumph said. He closed the door, turned on his car, and drove away.

Mulder watched him go and then turned to look at the smoldering ruins of the barn.

"Think what we could have learned," he said.

"Even if any of that were true," Scully said, "how could you stand to watch it. Would you really want to see your life, your *future*, as a television program?"

"Once we saw it, the future would be altered. But I don't care about that. I care about the past and the present. Now they're as hidden as they've ever been."

"Then maybe we should look for the secrets the old-fashioned way," Scully said.

Mulder nodded and turned to get back into the car.

As they drove away, he turned to his partner. "Did you think fictional Mulder was a little funny looking?"

"I don't know what you mean," Scully said, but she seemed unwilling to look him in the eye.

THE END

the truth is out there

ROSETTA

By David Sakmyster

"**M**ulder, you need to wait!"

Fox Mulder stepped out of his car and scanned the path that led through the wheat field, winding up to the lone farmhouse about a hundred yards away. Scully's voice in his ear was as welcome as it was frustrating. *Wait?* He couldn't wait. Not any longer, not now when he was so close.

A single light beckoned in the faraway room behind the porch, under a sagging roof and a rusty weathervane. Dusk had just settled over the South Carolina hills as he arrived from the western approach, a dirt and gravel driveway, while his partner waited up on the hill within binocular sight.

"Scully, this is it. If we wait, we could lose the informant."

"An informant you don't know anything about, Mulder. None of this makes any sense. You could be walking into a trap." She was about a half mile away, on the ridge in her Prius, with a laptop and satellite uplink to another ally's location.

"She's right," Byers' voice sputtered in Mulder's ear, making him wince and wonder if they really should have brought the Lone Gunmen in on something this sensitive. "Everything about this stinks of a trap, Fox. We should be able to hack the nearest geosynchronous satellite overhead, easy as taking popcorn from a kid at a ballpark, but this thing's giving us all sorts of problems. Frohike's about to kick his computer across the room. This encryption is like nothing we've ever seen."

"That only strengthens my argument," Mulder said, drawing his gun and his flashlight. "If they're going to such lengths to block this discovery, then this could be it, the key to everything." He took a breath and a moment to get his bearings. "A NASA informant with real-time information from the Rosetta probe, which just made a tricky but successful landing on comet 67P-Churyumov-Gerasimenko two days ago, claims to have recovered photos and readings of… an extraterrestrial nature."

"Mulder…" He could hear the disbelief in Scully's voice, all too familiar.

He wasn't going to be deterred. "This informant's taking a great chance, risking everything to get the truth out before the European and American space agencies lock it down and hide it from the public."

"But Mulder," Scully's exasperated voice came back again. "We've been through this before. Why? Why would they do that? If they actually found something up there, way at the edge of our solar system, why hide what could be the single most important and energizing discovery in history? Something that could justify their budgets, make them the focus of so much of the world's attention? This is what they live for."

"I disagree, Scully. They have another mandate. There's another level of secrecy controlling everything the space agencies have ever done. They know what's out there, Scully. They always have, and this might be our one chance to prove it."

"Mulder, are you hearing yourself?"

He acted like he didn't even hear her. "Having that proof, getting our hands on what they've been hiding all this time? It would change everything, Scully."

Mulder crouched, moving fast, focusing on that window light while keeping his eyes open, scanning the cloudless sky. "Once he trusts me and hands over the intel, we can upload it to the Lone Gunmen to disseminate over the web, and then he's clear. We're clear—and they have nothing on us anymore. Nothing on the X-Files. It has to be now. If they get to him first, it's over."

"You're trying to make this about us, but it isn't, Mulder. Look at the facts. You know nothing about this man. We couldn't find his identity in NASA's directory, and the timing—so soon after the probe's landing, it's all too suspicious."

"Or it's perfect. Trust me, Scully. Everything he told me in a text message yesterday fits with all the anomalous rumors I've been studying about the Rosetta Program."

"Here we go," said Byers in an enthusiastically sarcastic tone.

Mulder imagined the three of them—Byers, Langly, and Frohike—sitting in a dark room surrounded by wires and servers, all hunched over multiple laptop screens.

"Think about it, Scully," Mulder said as he approached, head down, skirting through a darker section of wheat stalks toward the rear of the farmhouse. "Think about the name of the program, *Rosetta*."

"Yes, we've been through this."

"I haven't," said Langly, sounding like a kid who had walked in on his parents during a fevered debate already in progress.

There he is, Mulder groaned as Scully continued in her best academic tone.

"The Rosetta Stone, a granite stele dating back to 156 BC, was uncovered by archaeologists in the Nile Delta in 1799. On its surface was the same text inscribed in three separate languages—Demotic, Greek, and Ancient Egyptian Hieroglyphic. Finally they had something that provided the key to translating the ancient Egyptian language. It opened the way to understanding thousands of years of history and providing insight to a long-vanished culture."

"Exactly," Mulder chimed in, slowing his footsteps, going for stealth. The air was crisp and clear, but prominent was the absence of noise—any noise, bugs, crickets, scampering animals. He hesitated. Something about all this unnerving silence was familiar. He had a sudden sense of déjà vu, something taking him decades, back to his youth… to a night in his room, waking, sitting upright and having that same sense of absolute quiet. Except… knowing there was something outside the window. Something heading toward…

Don't think about her… Not now.

He shook free of the unnerving feeling and returned his focus to the present. "I think you have to ask the larger question."

Langly cleared his throat. "Uh… why choose that name for this particular space mission? Why Rosetta?"

"Bingo," Mulder said absently. "Why make this expedition to a distant comet about language, about decipherment, about something so critical as communication between an ancient race and a new one? This is supposed to be a joint space mission focused on the study of a celestial body's geology and offering insights into the early formation of the solar system. But instead NASA and the ESA made sure to include among its cargo something called the *Rosetta Disc*, a tablet with thirteen thousand pages of text written in… wait for it… more than twelve hundred languages."

"Well," Byers said. "That's certainly interesting. But not necessarily a smoking gun."

"And," Frohike said, "we know smoking guns."

Mulder was undaunted. "Then there are all the Egyptian names they have for everything on this mission. *Osirus* for the camera module, *Philae* for the lander."

That disquieting feeling again, and with it—the fleeting glimpse of something he had seen as a child, but had quickly forgotten. Outside his bedroom window: a jackal-headed human in silhouette.

What was that? He felt every muscle tighten in his chest, and his lungs strained to take a simple breath. *Why have I not remembered this before?*

The entire image shuddered suddenly like a photo held by trembling hands, but then it was gone, and he resumed his focus on the present.

"You have to ask, why? Why the references to ancient Egypt, its language and reflection of lost culture and history? And then why include a sample of every language we know of on board that craft?"

"Mulder," Scully's voice came, "they've done this sort of thing before."

"Yes, with the early Voyager probe, where they made sure to include golden phonograph records that could play sounds and images of Earth's life and culture. It was essentially a message-in-a-bottle tossed into the cosmic ocean, hoping to encounter intelligent life out there and let them know about us." He took a deep, clear breath. "But that just proves my point. Voyager was flung wily-nilly out beyond the solar system, a welcome ship, for all intents and purposes. But Rosetta should be different. A mission to a lifeless rock on an elongated orbit around our sun? Why include all that other data? Why go through all the effort to load it with such a key translation program if not for the direct purpose of communication with something unknown that might be out there?" He took a breath and paused his approach, so close now to the house and its mysterious occupant. "What do they know that we don't?"

"I don't have an answer to that, Mulder. Maybe they're just being symbolic, but that doesn't bear on this case. What we're doing—unsanctioned, without FBI backup, and no offense to your friends in their van—"

"Secure basement," Frohike corrected. "Vans are too conspicuous."

"Whatever, I don't like it, Mulder. It's too dangerous. This has happened before. They've used you and your obsession for the extraterrestrial, for conspiracies and informants—to play you. To play all of us for fools."

"She's right about that," Frohike said. "We don't like being made to look foolish."

Mulder bit his tongue, stifling a response to the contrary.

Scully continued. "What if it's all a setup to discredit you and the X-Files once and for all, in such a way we never recover from it?"

"Got to take that chance, Scully." Mulder crept the last few feet to the edge of the porch. "I'm going into this with my eyes open."

But was he? Something about this didn't sit right with Mulder either, and as he neared the entrance, he felt a strange vibration in the earth, traveling up his legs.

"Mulder?"

"What?" He flinched, shaking his head. "I'm sorry, I know this is a crazy time to say this, but I'm getting a strong déjà vu sense here." He pointed to the door with his flashlight, and saw it trembling in his grasp.

"Maybe that's your common sense kicking in, Mulder. You should think this through some more."

Mulder shook his head, and then saw it all again in a sequence of flashes:

He was a young boy, sitting up in bed as a humming sound dug into his ears and ground into his heart.

Another flash and what at first seems like an alien visage looming at the window shifts to a jackal-headed figure, rising and tapping a staff against the glass.

Young Fox Mulder screams and he's—

Back in the present.

"What the hell? I don't remember that, I don't…"

"Don't remember what, Mulder? What are you talking about?"

He frowned and then the humming ended and the vibration stopped. "I don't know. Whatever it is—was—it's gone now."

"Mulder, you're scaring me."

"Us too," said Langly. "So, back to this informant. I want to believe, like you, but…"

Mulder cleared his throat, then advanced up the stairs. "He's said all the right things, including the little known fact that Rosetta, which launched in

2004, detoured from its original mission and did a flyby of Mars in 2007. The informant told me there was something there that they found in the Cydonia region. That during the 1976 *Viking* mission they discovered an anomalous pattern on the surface that, decoded, indicated the trajectory of the CG comet. *That* was the genesis for this mission, and in 2004 the *Opportunity* mission discovered something else from that same area on Mars, something they had to investigate. There's been speculation that it recovered data from the Russian Phobos-I probe, lost in 1988, but we have no idea what they found. Now, almost thirty years later, Rosetta has landed exactly where they told us to go."

Langly's voice broke through the ensuing silence. "Cydonia was the place where all the hoopla started about the Martian Face and other anomalous structures NASA denies exist on that surface."

Scully broke in. "Structures that have since been disproven as eroded geological features, Mulder. Coincidences and tricks of light and shadow." Her voice sounded tired, pained, losing her professional edge.

"That's the official story," Mulder hesitated at the threshold. "This informant claims he has access to the undoctored images, the actual data that's behind the true mission of the Rosetta Program."

The single light flickered inside the farmhouse, and Mulder caught a shadow passing by the window in the room.

He shuddered, *was that a jackal's head?* "I can't wait any longer, Scully. Any luck with the satellite, guys?"

"Almost there," Frohike said. "Damn this encryption. Never seen anything like this, the entire thing is just... oh, we've almost got it, but still can't access all the sub-functions. Can you wait?"

"No," Mulder said. "Do your best, I'm going in."

"Mulder!" Scully insisted. "Your com is starting to break up. There might be a dampening field in there too. If we can't hear you..."

Too late. He made it to the door, turned the handle and with a last glance up at the distant, cold constellations and a certain speck hundreds of millions of miles away, Mulder entered the farmhouse.

Scully trembled in her seat. The vents were pumping out warm air, but it wasn't enough. Nothing about this was right, from the farmhouse location to the intel, to the loss of Mulder's signal and their inability to hack into the satellite. She needed those infrared sensors, needed to know what Mulder was up against. What if she was right and this was all a huge setup and enemy agents lurked in the wheat fields or upstairs or in other parts of the farmhouse? Mulder was a sitting duck, and she was no help out here. Her only hope would be to call Skinner and beg for a favor, to send backup that would only arrive too late.

Damn it, Mulder. She never should have let him talk her into this, but like on so many other cases, she had let his unbridled enthusiasm push her past the point of logic or reason. Way beyond caution, here she was, alone and vulnerable on some hilltop ridge while her partner walked into almost certain danger.

She reached for the gun on the passenger seat, feeling the reassuring comfort of its grip. She tapped and adjusted the Bluetooth in her left ear.

"Mulder? Can you hear me?"

Static and broken words, something that sounded like *"He's… all shadow. Can't see… face. Making… contact…"*

Byers' voice broke in. "Agent Scully, we've got it. Frohike's broken the code, it's… wow, amazing. We're all in awe here of its complexity…"

"…and my skill in breaking it," Frohike added. "Just look at this section here—"

"Shut up," Langly said, "she doesn't need to hear it."

"All of you shut up," Scully quipped. "Get me eyes on that farmhouse, something's wrong."

She started the car. Static crackled again, and now she could hear another voice: a somber monotone rolling over Mulder's.

"He's made contact?" Byers spoke. "I can't make out what they're saying."

Scully paused, foot on the gas, listening. "Neither can I. Mulder? Can you hear us? Are you safe?"

More static.

Damn it.

She eased the car forward, down the path, still with the lights off. She'd go in as quietly as possible.

Her smartphone lit up.

"Data transmitting now," Byers said. "Sending satellite imagery to your phone."

A blurry image appeared, grainy and tinted green.

"Infrared?" Scully asked.

"Coming online momentarily," Langly said. "Almost have it."

"I can't wait," Scully said, realizing she sounded like her partner. She accelerated, headlights off, driving by starlight, keeping to the tinted edges of the gravel road as she rounded a bend and rolled toward the lone light at the end of the drive.

She peered through the windshield as it started to fog up unexpectedly. *Come on, not now.* In that lighted room she could see two figures, both standing still, facing each other like mannequins in a department store window.

For an instant, something in that room shifted, and one of the figures changed: morphed into an Egyptian hieroglyphic-like image of a dog-headed humanoid. The one facing Mulder... Again the crackling in her ear. Just a few words. "...Guiding the souls... Opening of the way... Cydonia..."

"Byers, can you boost that signal or do anything about the interference?"

"One thing at a time. We've almost got infrared for you."

She glanced at her phone again, just as the static cleared for a brief couple of seconds.

Brief enough for her to hear clearly:

"Scully, we were all wrong! We—"

"Mulder?"

In the ensuing blast of static, as she slowed the car and braked right before the main porch, she took her eyes off the pair of figures in the window to look down at her phone's screen.

The farmhouse from above sat perched in the field, and now the infrared feature was activated, picking up...

But... that couldn't be right.

"Mulder?"

She swallowed hard, looking from the window back to the phone. "Mulder, *there's only one heat signature in that house!* You're alone."

That's when the gunshot popped in her ear, and the light inside the room went out.

She burst through the door, flashlight in the hand over her gun, beam pointing this way and that, scanning for targets, scanning for...

"Mulder?"

Nothing at first. Shadows. A standing lamp, a coat rack, a wicker couch and a TV set against the back doors. The beam swept back and forth as she held her breath, listening. She hoped the Gunmen wouldn't babble in her ear now and shatter her focus.

What was that gunshot, where was—?

A body on the floor!

She started for it, crouched and aimed the light again.

"Mulder?" She recognized the coat, the gun in his limp fingers. Setting the flashlight on the floor facing ahead, she reached for him. Still warm. Reached for his neck, searching for a pulse.

Weak, but still there.

"Damn it, Byers can you hear me?"

Static crackled back.

She had to call for backup now, emergency medical assistance. She held up the phone's screen, and now saw the two heat signatures, hers and Mulder's, but then…

A sound, creaking on the floorboards to her right.

She dropped the phone, snatched up the light and aimed along with the gun's sights.

A furtive shadow darted out of view.

"Who's there? Show yourself. I'm armed!"

A clicking noise from around the corner, toward the kitchen area. Scully rose on trembling legs. *What was this? Something that gave off no heat, something Mulder had been talking to?* She had heard it too.

Crackling again in her ear, Byers' voice. "Company's on its way…"

"What?"

"…multiple… inbound… minutes…"

Damn! She knew it was a trap… or else Mulder was right and the informant had been followed and they'd run out of time.

She turned back to Mulder, aiming the light over his body, looking for gunshot wounds, feeling for blood. She'd have to turn him over, and was about to when bright lights suddenly stabbed through the windows, making her wince.

Raising the gun, she squinted, using the lights to scan the room for the other figure, for anything. She thought she caught a glimpse of a dog-headed figure standing in the corner—but then the front door exploded inward.

Men in black, with helmets and guns out, laser sights all stabbing toward her, lighting up over her heart. She directed her gun to the ceiling, then crouched and set it down slowly beside Mulder.

"Back away, Agent Scully," came a familiar voice.

Director Skinner stepped out of the corner where she had seen the figure. Trench coat waving behind him, his spectacles flashed in the beams from the headlights.

"Sir?" Scully stared incredulously at the director. "How did you get here? Were you following us?"

Skinner raised his hand and made a motion. The other agents quickly moved in, took Scully's gun and dragged her away from Mulder. "Agent Scully, we've had your partner under surveillance ever since he received a communication from an ex-NASA employee, one who had been previously fired for trying to sell state secrets to the Chinese."

"Sir, none of this makes any sense, and even if you did have this intel, you just let Mulder walk into this situation? He's been shot, for God's sake. He needs help."

Skinner blinked at her as she struggled against the men. "Agent Mulder knew the risks. We gave him plenty of rope in this case, just enough to hang himself."

"What are you talking about?"

"We wanted to see how far this obsession of his would take him. The informant was fed fake information. The comet, the Mars flyby. Everything, including falsified photographic images, the kind of alien structures and elaborate geometric figures that Mulder would be sure to see as his proverbial smoking guns."

"You were here, sir? With the informant?"

Skinner made a pained face. "Mulder was unhinged, Agent Scully. He actually believed they *chose* him, picked him out from among all of the humans on this planet, picked out one believer and chose this NASA man to act as liaison."

"I don't understand. Why would Mulder—?"

"He pulled a gun on me, Scully. I had no choice."

"*No choice?* Sir, that's Fox Mulder lying there. He was your friend, not just your employee. You know him, you know the sacrifices he's made, the persecution he's suffered for his beliefs. His lifelong search for his sister. I can't believe you'd subject him to more of this pain. And for what?"

"For this, Agent Scully." He spread his arms wide. "To see if he'd really lost his reason, to see if he was no longer in control of his senses, and if not—if he had become so obsessed as to deal with traitors and dangerous enemies of state, then we had to know. Not only that, he could be a danger to the FBI, and especially to you, Scully, his partner."

"I don't believe it, sir. And my safety was for me to judge. I could handle it."

Skinner shook his head and knelt beside Mulder. Placed his hand on Mulder's forehead.

"I can help him," Scully said. "Let me…"

"Too late, Agent Scully." Skinner shook his head slowly. He stood, head bowed.

The other men released their grips on Scully. She stumbled forward, and in a wave of disbelief and shock, she dropped to her knees beside her partner.

"I'm sorry it happened like this," Skinner said, stepping away. The lights dimmed, pointing away, leaving her to let her eyes adjust. Absently, not sure of what to do, her left hand slid into her coat pocket, settling on the smartphone.

Something crackled in her left ear, and for a moment she had no idea who could be talking to her.

Then she heard Byers' voice, pieces of his words. "*…almost there… have to get out… approaching from…*"

Frowning, she removed her hand, and glanced at the screen…

…The visual app that still showed the satellite infrared imagery.

The scan that made her heart skip, and in the next instant she lunged over Mulder, reached around his chest, into his coat and found the gun in his holster, withdrawing it rapidly and pointing it at Skinner's face.

"Who the hell are you?"

She stood up, gun trained on him even as she expected a dozen red beams to bear down on her with a force of an equal number of gunshots, but none came, and instead she raised the smartphone to eye level, then turned it so Skinner could see—the two bright reddish-blue smudges side by side on the screen.

"It's just me and Mulder in here, *sir*."

Skinner smiled as he backed into the shadows, shadows that for a moment took on the shape of a jackal-headed, pointy-eared figure, then all at once the lights winked out and Scully was alone with Mulder, who groaned and sat up.

"Mulder?"

He blinked, shook his head and tried to smile. "Where is he?"

Scully fumbled for her flashlight, found it and turned it on, aiming the beam around the room. "Mulder, I don't understand what's happening. Skinner was just here, and before, you were talking to someone. I believed this was all an elaborate hoax to close the X-Files so whoever's doing this can then operate with impunity. Somehow they set all this up, messed with the satellite imagery, set up a distortion field on our communications… but now I don't know. Maybe they're playing with holograms, or we've ingested some kind mind-altering drug…"

Mulder shook his head, tried to stand, then got there with Scully's help. "Now you're sounding like me, Scully. As much as I appreciate that, you couldn't be further from the truth."

"What do you mean?" She aimed the light again, waving it all around, searching for Skinner, for anyone. The door was still broken in, the wind whistling inside. "Where did they go?"

"Who, Scully?" In the dim flashlight illumination, color was returning to his face. Whatever had happened had knocked him unconscious, clearly, and maybe put him in shock, but he was recovering now. "Check your satellite feed again."

She pulled out the phone. "Impossible. It's just…"

Mulder smiled. "You and me, Scully?"

She met his eyes, opened her mouth, about to ask when something shifted in the shadows. Her eyes darted in that direction.

"We're not alone," she finally managed.

Mulder's smile widened. "I've been saying that for years."

"Who are you?" Scully aimed the light, but it flickered as soon as it contacted the dark form, its energy and brilliance consumed by the blackness then expelled in a pattern of electrical sparkles and pulses high-lighting the figure's outline.

"*What* might be the better question, Scully." Mulder stood, arms outstretched, palms out. "We were interrupted before. I didn't see it, didn't realize the truth until too late." He bowed his head and reached out to Scully, gently putting pressure on her wrists to lower her flashlight and gun.

"I pushed too hard," he said, "thinking I was dealing with a regular informant. I paid the price, but I understand now."

"Understand what, Mulder? What are we looking at?"

"The Rosetta probe sent back more than just images. It made *contact*, Scully, with something out there on that comet. Something that traveled back along with the probe's radio signal, something that in turn probed our servers, got into our networks and accessed countless databases. It sought out a suitable contact, a contact it felt it could trust."

Scully turned to him with an incredulous look. "It found you?"

"Found *us*, Scully. That's as near as I can determine. Why else did it create this facsimile, this whole story, to get us out here? And you said Skinner was here? That clinches it. This is something else entirely. You and I? *We're* their focus. We received the invite, and we came."

Scully tore her eyes away from the incomprehensible figure. "But why? Why us? And what do you mean, 'something else'?"

"I'm not sure yet, but I've seen it before, I know I have." He strained his eyes on the electrically outlined shape, trying to locate a feature or anything to root his focus. "It may be that it sought out compatible minds it knew would spread its message instead of hide it. Or it may be that it learned from a previous encounter and this time wanted something subversive, outside of the program that may have turned a deaf ear to the last invitation."

"What do you mean? The Mars visit?"

"Maybe they were put off that their message had been hidden. They wanted to take no chances this time around. Maybe the importance is too great, and they didn't want their effort to be wasted again. They gave us a chance forty years ago, and we chose not to honor it but keep it in secret, too scared or cautious."

"Not sure I would do it differently, Mulder, given the uncertainties. If this is really first contact, there has to be concern. What do we really know about what's up there?"

Mulder shook his head. "I'm not sure, but I think I know the answer to the obvious now. To the question of why Rosetta."

Scully's arms trembled. It seemed as if the figure was holding its breath, listening to their next words with rapt attention, as if everything depended on it.

"Just like the Rosetta stone and the breakthrough key that led to the decipherment of the ancient language, we're making it clear to them this time around that whatever they've left on Mars for us, we're ready to listen. We're ready for the key. We've shown them, with our thousands of languages and historical precedents, that we're open to analysis of an ancient culture, open to accepting whatever they may have known, whatever they may have been."

His hand still on her wrist, it dropped and she put the gun away and took the flashlight with her other hand so she could then reach for his hand. Their fingers entwined, clenched as they faced the shadowy being that sparkled and coalesced again, turning first into a Skinner look-alike, then into a faceless man wearing an astronaut suit, then a man in a black suit and dark glasses, then into a jackal-headed Egyptian deity

Static crackled in their ears. Langly's voice came again, clearer this time, but still chopping out. "...*inbound agents. Almost there.*"

Scully reluctantly pulled her hand away from Mulder's and checked her phone. Red dots were indeed approaching now, a short distance away from the farmhouse, but moving fast.

"We're about to have company, Mulder. Real company."

Mulder pulled out his phone with his left hand, held it up and pressed the start key on the record app. "I think it knows that, and I think we're about to get an earful."

The thing before them, appearing for all purposes as Anubis himself, god of the Dead (or guide of the Dead) opened its mouth—and out came a pouring forth of verbiage. Words streaming out in an unrecognizable language.

"What language is that?" Scully asked.

"Several, I'd say. Dozens in fact…" Mulder cocked his head, listening intently as the being kept speaking, the phrases coming faster and faster, the words changing pitch and quality every few seconds. "Mimicking everything on that Rosetta disc, I'm guessing."

Mulder caught a few snippets of languages he recognized: French, Portuguese, finally something in English. He held his phone steady, recording it all.

"What is it saying?" Scully asked, daring to take a step closer, still questioning this experience, questioning the validity of any of this, looking for signs of duplicity: staged effects or projectors.

Mulder shrugged. "Not sure, but it almost feels like it's extending an invitation—or a warning. Like in airports where everything important is spelled out in several languages on signs or spoken over the intercom."

Scully was about to question something more when she caught sight of her phone—and the red surge bearing down on the farmhouse. "We're out of time."

The words abruptly ceased, and then the figure just winked out of existence, the black snout seamlessly blending in with the shadows as red beams intruded and men rushed in.

Mulder quickly tapped a button to send the data off to Frohike, and then dropped his phone in time to raise his hands and kneel beside Scully as the bright lights and guns converged upon them.

Hours later, as the sun was making its appearance out the Director's office window, and dawn began to spread over Virginia, the agents faced Skinner's wrath.

"Can you tell me why, Agents Mulder and Scully, I have two different space agencies breathing down my neck, three international committees clamoring for my head, your resignations, and a full accounting of what you were doing in South Carolina? An unsanctioned intervention infringing on all sorts of sensitive mission information, international protocols, and long-range technological parameters that could set back space exploration and funding for decades?"

Mulder sat up from his slouching position, glanced at Scully, then turned to his boss. "No, I don't think we can, sir."

Skinner's complexion turned an even angrier red. "Excuse me, Agent Mulder?"

"I'm sorry, sir, but this had nothing to do with you or the FBI. It was a side project of mine, one which I warned Agent Scully here to have no part in, yet she, in her infinite desire to help, couldn't be kept away."

"Agent Mulder, that is…"

"Reckless, irresponsible, and in all ways detrimental to my career. Yes, sir, I'm aware of that, but as I've said, this was done on our own time, outside of FBI knowledge. You have no responsibility here."

Skinner removed his glasses and glared at them. "That has no bearing on the fact that I'm still ground zero for the veritable storm of hell coming at this office from all directions. What did you two step into?"

Scully stood up. "Sir, we may have encountered something that proves beyond a doubt…" She glanced at Mulder, thought unfinished. "Aren't you going to interrupt me?"

Mulder shrugged. He looked beaten, exhausted. Eyes unfocused, as if staring a long distance into the past. "Your call, Scully. Cat's out of the bag at this point, I'd say. Or soon will be." He got up wearily and stood beside her. "If that's all, sir? I'm sure we have real work to do, new cases to investigate, theories to disprove and that sort of thing. Or is the X-Files in danger of being shut down again?"

Skinner stared at him, at both of them, weighing the situation. He leaned back in his chair, then turned to look out at the slowly rising sun. Took a deep breath and let it out slowly. "Fine," he said without turning around. "Get back to work. I'll handle this, and I'll also be doubling your workload since you seem to have all this free time to get into trouble with every other agency except your own." He returned his glasses to his face, spun slowly in his chair, and then blinked at both of them. "Go!"

Mulder took Scully's arm and led her out of the office. Out in the hallway, he turned and faced her questioning eyes.

"Mulder? What do we have? I'm still reeling from that experience last night, but I don't know what to make of it. After firing your gun you were knocked out by an electrical blast that for all we know could have just been a high-powered Taser. We have no other evidence, nothing to say it wasn't all some elaborate setup, as I originally thought. And what's more, the Rosetta probe has now malfunctioned. It's gone dark—conveniently falling into a shadowed part of the comet's cratered surface where it can't receive sunlight enough to charge its batteries. It may be lost forever." She looked exasperated. "Again, what do we have?"

"We've got *something*, Scully."

"What?" She saw the phone he fished out of his pocket. "The message you recorded? Wasn't it just gibberish spoken in a hundred different languages?"

"I was wrong before, Scully."

"You, wrong? That might be a first. Which part?"

"About it choosing us. It didn't."

"No?"

"No, not us. *Me.*" He restarted the recording, let it play a few seconds, then paused it. "That part there, I remember it exactly. I've heard it before."

He played it, and Scully listened. "Sounds Arabic."

"Ancient Egyptian is my guess," Mulder said, "although no one really knows what that sounded like."

"But you said you heard this before?"

Mulder closed his eyes, and this time saw it again: the scene from his childhood, only now he remembered the rest of it. Rising out of bed, glancing to the window, where outside, the jackal-headed visitor tapped the glass, then turned its snout to the direction of…

Samantha's room.

Inside, his sister dozes fitfully, not even stirring with the sound of the creaking door as Mulder pushes inside.

Then he's at her bedside, and an elongated jackal-shaped shadow glides across the room on a shaft of moonlight.

Samantha's muttering in her sleep.

Those same guttural words.

Mulder's lips are moving along with hers, whispering the words too.

Only this time, he's translating…

"Open the way, open the way…"

Mulder blinked again, and was back in the present, where Scully looked at him curiously. "Open the way? That's…"

"An Egyptian phrase," Mulder said, beating her to it. "Associated with Anubis, god of the dead, who led the souls to the next world. Or to heaven, or…"

"The stars." Scully frowned. "I don't understand, Mulder. You say you remember this same phrase, but assuming it's not just a dream and it really happened…"

"It did happen, Scully. Maybe it was a dream, but I remember it now. And now I'm rethinking everything. The message from the comet, the Rosetta Program, even Samantha's abduction. Maybe it had nothing to do with extraterrestrials."

He looked up at her, eyes suddenly pained and near to tears, expressing the loss of faith, trust, and worst of all, *belief*.

"Maybe it has everything to do with death. And the ultimate question, expressed by every culture and in every language."

Scully met his eyes, and finished his thought: *"What happens when we die?"*

Mulder put his phone away.

He glanced down the hall, then back to Skinner's office. He trembled and for a moment felt the floor vibrating, heard a humming in his ears… and then it was gone. He met his partner's eyes. "They're going back there, Scully."

"Where?"

He brought her around a corner and into the public lab. Found a workstation and called up the NASA website. Scrolling down, he expanded a window entitled "UPCOMING MISSIONS."

Watching her face for a reaction, he pointed to one of the bulleted lines about halfway down, a nondescript series of numbers and letters prefacing a certain mission.

"What am I looking at?" she asked, peering over his shoulder.

"This mission, it wasn't there a couple days ago, and now it's been slotted in." He clicked on the link, which brought up mission parameters—*Mars*. Numbers that seemed…

"I recognize those coordinates," she said.

"Cydonia," Mulder said with her. He met her eyes. "NASA might have gotten the message too. We're going back."

She pulled away from his look and studied the screen, the mission timetables. "Five years from now, we'll know?"

"Maybe," Mulder said. "If we trust that they will actually tell us the truth this time. Or if not, maybe we can get a real contact on the inside."

"Don't start that again."

Mulder forced a grin and clicked off the mission page. As it dissolved, a background page of the Rosetta mission took its place, with a news flash: *Rosetta probe to reactivate as comet's trajectory now predicted to pass into sunlight in six months, to provide new images and data transfer…*

He met her look and raised an eyebrow. "Maybe we won't have to wait five years, Scully. I have a feeling we have some unfinished business. What are you doing six months from now?"

THE END

the Truth is Out There

SNOWMAN
By Sarah Stegall

ALEXANDRIA, VIRGINIA
9th MAY, 2001, 5:39 a.m.

Special Agent John Doggett cupped his hands around the thick coffee mug, warming them. He squinted out at the empty parking lot through the window of the 24-hour diner; snow blurred softly, insidiously against the glass. Now and then snow turned to sleet, then back to snow, just the right combination to turn the roads to glass. He checked his watch for the third time, trying to remain calm.

When the burly man slid into the bench opposite him, Doggett's hand snatched for his gun. Then he stopped. "Sir."

"You're getting soft, Sergeant. You weren't watching your six." The man jerked his head towards the back of the restaurant. "The cook let me in the back. His boy was one of ours."

"Beirut?"

The man nodded. Nothing more needed to be said; the Marines who had come out of that disaster knew words would never cover it. "We have about ten minutes. I can't be seen here, I'm supposed to be somewhere else. I can give you the sitrep, and then you'll have to decide to fall in or not. My plane leaves in twenty minutes."

"I don't understand this, Lieutenant Salvert—"

"Captain. It's Captain Chuck Salvert now." A hard expression came and went across Salvert's weatherbeaten face.

"Congratulations, sir, and it's long overdue," Doggett said. "But I haven't heard from you in three years, and now you wake me up at four in the morning to meet here because you've got an urgent mission only I can help with. I'm with the FBI, not the military."

Salvert glanced around and leaned forward. "I can't trust anyone in the military chain of command."

Doggett was shocked. Chuck Salvert was as by-the-book a commander as he'd ever known. "What's going on?"

"Two weeks ago, a six-man Marine recon team deployed on Mount Rainier in Washington state to test a new long-range communications array, one which could function in the event of a terrorist strike in the most extreme weather conditions. Their last radio check was three days ago, on the night before they were supposed to return. There has been no word since."

"Search and rescue?"

"Covert op, Sergeant. We can't even alert the Park Service."

"With respect, sir, it's been a while since I did any mountaineering. And this isn't my area, sir. I'm assigned to… an investigative unit, not a fugitive task force. So far, nothing you've told me indicates a crime has been committed."

"Dammit, Sergeant, I—" The captain locked hands together. "Something's wrong. I know it in my gut. And I need someone I can trust."

Doggett turned his head, staring at the black glass of the window. He saw not his own rawboned face, but the face of a younger self, scarred and bloody, being pulled from a collapsed barracks, hearing the screams of dying men, smelling the burned cordite. "Your gut's good enough for me, sir."

Salvert glanced at his watch. "We leave in fifteen minutes. I chartered a flight."

Doggett let his surprise show. "Not a Marine flight?"

"I want this off the radar. Do we need to swing by your place?"

Doggett looked offended. "Please, sir. My bag is in my trunk."

Salvert reached over and clasped Doggett's hand. "Thank you, Sergeant."

"Special Agent," Doggett said firmly. "I'm not in the Corps anymore."

"There's no such thing as an ex-Marine." Salvert grinned, revealing a missing canine tooth. Doggett remembered the stories about that; some stories said he'd lost it in a man's throat during a particularly nasty fight in Lebanon.

Doggett wasn't sure about that one. "Semper fi."

LIBERTY RIDGE, MT. RAINIER, WASHINGTON
10th MAY, 2001, 2:31 p.m.

Doggett leaned into the straps of his pack and thrust his boots into the snow in front of him. He panted, the icy air burning his throat. Behind him,

Chuck Salvert trudged up the steep incline, putting his feet in Doggett's bootprints.

"Want me to take point, Sergeant?" Salvert said. He spoke easily, hardly winded by the effort.

"No, sir, I'm good. But I need some direction."

Salvert pulled a laminated map out of his parka. Doggett recognized the military-grade precision, the contour lines nearly on top of one another on this incline. "We're at about 6,000 feet here," Salvert said. "Their last report said they were about 1,500 feet higher."

Doggett glanced up. The clouds parted enough to allow the sun to strike the mountain's peak. Mantled in permanent white, the most dangerous volcano in North America was a postcard-pretty image of Cascade beauty.

They had spent the morning climbing up the Liberty Ridge approach, following the route taken by the missing team. The trail climbed up a narrow file of rock. On either side, the land fell away to the edge of the forest. Even in the middle of the afternoon, with bright sun shining down, the shadows under the trees looked dark and forbidding.

Doggett glanced ahead. He stiffened when something caught his eye.

"Forward on this heading about five hundred meters, then we should hit the climbing trail for Carbon Glacier," Salvert said.

Doggett wasn't listening. He crouched down, peering closely at the snow. "What is it?"

"Tracks." Doggett pointed. In the snow before them, blurry footprints climbed from the trees to the trail, and then turned uphill. "Someone came out of those trees and entered the trail ahead of us."

Salvert stood braced against the wind, and now his sidearm was in his hand. "One man, it looks like. Moving fast. Maybe two hours ahead of us."

"This is not a coincidence," Doggett said. He slipped off his pack, which was outfitted with a rifle carrier on one side. He unzipped it and brought out a Remington rifle.

Salvert cocked an eyebrow. "Left your M16 at home, Marine?"

Doggett checked his scope. "You didn't give me much notice, sir. Lucky thing I keep my hunting rifle in the trunk of my car."

Salvert leaned forward, shading his eyes.

Doggett did a slow recon through the rifle's scope, paying special attention to the point where the stranger's tracks had left the woods.

"If this guy reaches our men before we do… if they're hurt or vulnerable…" Salvert didn't have to finish his thought.

"No hostiles sighted, sir," Doggett said. He lowered the rifle. "Do we proceed?"

Salvert nodded at the slope ahead. "I want to catch up with this guy before he finds our men." He strode past Doggett, heading up the mountain with grim resolve.

Doggett slung his rifle on his shoulder, and surveyed the terrain: a narrow trail with drop-offs on either side, totally exposed. From a tactical point of view, it sucked. They followed the stranger's footprints, now half-erased by the wind, up the spine of the mountain.

Suddenly, a low howl sounded in the woods to their left. Doggett flung himself off the trail, rolling to a stop as he brought the rifle up to his shoulder, scanning the trees. Salvert fell to the ground beside him, drawing his sidearm. The howl broke off, followed by several loud raps, as of wood striking wood.

"What the *fuck*?" Salvert said, his voice low. "Who is that?"

"I don't know, sir," Doggett said softly. "But it would be better not to talk right now."

Long, tense minutes passed, and then they heard an eerie whistle. This was followed by several whooping sounds. More rapping. Cold seeped up from the ground, but Doggett did not move. He heard something large and heavy moving away through the woods: breaking branches, the whisper of snow dumped to the ground from a disturbed branch.

Doggett cautiously stood up. He shifted the rifle so the butt was on his thigh, the barrel pointing to the sky. "Should we check it out? Could it be one of the missing men calling for help?"

"I doubt it." Salvert looked up at the sky, frowning. "We've maybe got two hours of daylight left, and the coordinates of their last camp are ahead of us, not off in the woods." He re-holstered his weapon. "We proceed, but if we don't find our men ahead of us, we'll check this out on the way down."

He strode past Doggett, taking the lead. Doggett stood for a long moment, unwilling to lower his weapon. He recognized the feeling creeping over him, making him uneasy.

They were being stalked.

LIBERTY RIDGE, MT. RAINIER, WASHINGTON
10th MAY, 2001, 4:17 p.m.

Doggett felt the temperature dropping almost with every step. Breaking trail through snow was exhausting, so he and Salvert switched off the lead. It was mid afternoon when they came to Thumb Rock, a black rock spire pushing through the snow, with the trail detouring around it.

Doggett spotted a cluster of seeds off to one side—no, not seeds. Sunflower seed shells, the kind left behind by hikers eating trail mix as they walked. These sat on top of fresh snow; whoever had left them was on the other side of the rock.

Doggett halted, raising his fist in a silent order. Salvert stopped behind him, saying nothing. In a few terse hand signals, Doggett guided Salvert to maneuver around the spire, while he stayed on the trail. Rifle at his shoulder, Doggett strode forward and rounded the rock. At the same time, Salvert jumped forward from the other side, his gun in his hands.

Between them, a dark, shaggy figure rose from a half-crouch.

"Federal officer! Let me see your hands!" Doggett yelled.

The figure continued to rise, shapeless and distorted. Doggett let his breath out, finger tightening on the trigger.

Then the figure shrugged, the parka fell from its shoulders, and a familiar voice asked sardonically, "Is it okay if I keep my gloves on?"

Shocked, Doggett immediately lowered his weapon. "Mulder? Is that you?"

Former Special Agent Fox Mulder wore heavy ski pants, a quilted vest over a sweater, and a knitted wool cap. Snow dusted his shoulders. A heavy pack lay at his feet. He held an open bag of sunflower seeds in one hand. "The one and only," he said.

Salvert, still training his gun on the man in front of him, said, "Who is this?"

"It's okay, sir. I know this man. Mulder, what the hell are you doing out here?"

Mulder shrugged. "Same thing you're doing. Hunting for some missing men."

Salvert stepped closer and raised his gun to aim at Mulder's head. "Who told you about them? Who is your source?"

"Easy, sir," Doggett said. "He's okay, really. He's a former FBI Special Agent, Fox Mulder. I've worked with him before." He flicked a glance at Mulder. "I trust him."

"Touched, I'm sure," Mulder said.

"I don't like it, Sergeant. How did he know about this mission?"

Mulder reached into his jacket. Salvert tensed, but Mulder brought out a microcassette recorder. "This message came to me through semi-official channels," he said, and hit PLAY.

Doggett leaned closer to hear over the whistle of the wind.

"Hey, honey, it's me. Sorry I didn't catch you at home. How're you doing? What did the doctor say? I'm going nuts worrying about you. Call my mom if you need help. But don't call me, because—what the hell?"

A moaning howl echoed out of the tiny speaker. Doggett heard confused sounds, orders being shouted. Then the howl stopped and the voice was back. *"Sorry, babe. I think the moose are in season out here."* There was a short, nervous laugh. *"Anyway, don't call me back, I'll call you."* There was a click, and silence fell.

"The time stamp makes it the last known transmission from your missing men. The woman who gave it to me thought her husband was on a training mission in South Carolina." Mulder held out the bag of sunflower seeds first to Doggett, then to Salvert. "Seeds?"

"Give me the tape," Salvert said. "That is an unauthorized transmission."

"Take it." Mulder tossed the tape to Salvert. "It's a copy anyway."

Salvert zipped the tape into a pocket. "Take point, Sergeant. I want this man between us."

Mulder shrugged, picked up the pack at his feet and slipped his arms through the straps. His breath frosted in the air. "Funny, you haven't even asked why I'm here."

Doggett glared at Mulder. "Okay. Why are you here, Mulder? Because some wife is anxious about her husband? This isn't an X-File."

Salvert said, "What's an X-File?"

"Didn't you hear the sound on that tape?" Mulder said. "That's a Sasquatch call. I knew right away the caller wasn't in South Carolina. That call has been recorded several times in the Sierra Nevada and here in the Cascades. It's—"

Doggett stared. "Are you fuckin' *kidding* me?"

"What is he talking about? Sasquatch?" Salvert said. "Is he talking about *Bigfoot*?"

"Mulder, we're out here on serious business," Doggett said.

Mulder raised his hands. "You heard it yourself, both of you. I know *I* heard it."

"That tape could be a complete fake," Doggett said. "Even if—"

"Not the tape." Mulder swept a hand out, encompassing the shadowy woods closing in from either side. "You heard it just a couple of hours ago."

"Like the guy said, a moose or elk in mating season," Salvert said.

"It's not mating season—" Doggett began.

"Enough of this bullshit," the captain snapped. "I don't want to hear another word. Sergeant, I'm disappointed in you. I can't believe you're actually arguing with this idiot."

"It's not like that, Captain," Doggett began.

"Forget it," Mulder said. "This isn't the time or the place. It's getting dark, and most cryptozoologists believe that Sasquatch is nocturnal. I don't want to be out in the open when he is."

"Shut up!" Salvert said.

Mulder shrugged and started forward behind Doggett. Silently, the trio marched single file up the narrow trail.

The sun dropped lower, and finally Doggett halted, looking around.

"What's the hold-up?" Salvert called.

"We're at the camping point, sir," Doggett said.

"Carry on, then. We need to be squared away by sundown."

"Yes, sir."

Salvert charged past him, his boots punching through the pristine snow.

"Who the hell is that guy?" Mulder said. "And why does he keep calling you 'Sergeant'?"

"He was my lieutenant in Beirut." Doggett's eyes went cold and flat.

Mulder looked at him quizzically. "You were in the barracks that were bombed. Assistant Director Skinner told me."

Doggett stared past him, past the snow, into another time and place. "I was," he said shortly. "That man pulled me out of the rubble with his own two hands."

"So," Mulder said. "You trust him."

"I owe him my life." Doggett looked at him quizzically. "Why shouldn't I trust him?"

"Have you asked yourself why this rescue operation is so hush-hush?"

"Mulder, you're—"

Out of the woods to their left came a long, low wail. Doggett whirled, reaching over his shoulder for the rifle.

Mulder put a hand on his wrist. "Wait."

Ahead of them, Salvert stood with his gun in both hands, facing the woods.

"I don't believe that's Bigfoot," Doggett said.

"Then who? Or what?"

The low-pitched wail came again, followed by knocking sounds, like wood on wood. Twigs cracked. Then silence.

Salvert put his weapon away. "Let's pitch camp." Salvert eyed Mulder. "We've only got room for two."

"Oh, I can cozy up," Mulder said.

"We don't need to," Salvert said. "Sergeant, take first watch." He turned and began stamping out a place to pitch the tent.

Night fell swiftly, hastened by the heavy cloud cover. There was no moon, no starlight. Doggett took first watch while the others bedded down in the tent. He hugged himself and stamped his feet, staring out into the darkness. All he could see was a wall of scurrying white.

A sound behind him, like footsteps crunching in snow. Doggett spun, unslinging his rifle. He strained to see into the darkness. Was that a moan? A growl? Nothing. Or something—a shadow inside a shadow, flitting out of sight.

"Who's there?" he called.

Nothing answered, but he could not shake the feeling something was out there, something was watching him. Planning.

Waiting.

———*———

LIBERTY RIDGE, MT. RAINIER, WASHINGTON
11th MAY, 2001, 7:43 a.m.

Bleary-eyed, Doggett shoved through the tent opening and forced himself to stand upright. He did a few stretches, looking at the white landscape. Behind him, Fox Mulder moaned as he crawled through the opening.

"Coffee. What I'd give for coffee," Mulder muttered.

"Sure," said Doggett, bending down to touch his toes. "Tell room service to send up scrambled eggs, bacon, and toast. Whole wheat for me."

"You're an evil man," Mulder said pitifully. He groped his way upright.

Above, the wind shoved heavy clouds towards the top of the mountain, where they snagged and built into ominous masses. Salvert was nowhere in sight. Doggett glanced over at Mulder, who was stamping his feet and slapping his arms to warm up. "How is Agent Scully?"

Mulder continued looking off across the snowfield. "Getting ready for a baby shower, last I heard."

"Good."

"I sent a teddy bear. What did you get her?"

Doggett shook his head, amused. "I haven't decided yet."

Mulder hunched his shoulders, drawing inward. "She's the one who sent me that tape," he said.

Doggett squinted. "So she's your 'semi-official' source?"

"The Marine's wife is a friend of hers."

There was a short silence. Doggett cleared his throat. "Shouldn't you... be with Agent Scully right now?"

Mulder threw him a dark look over his shoulder. "What do you mean?"

"I mean, she's your partner. Was your partner," Doggett said, feeling awkward. "Do you really need to be out here, instead of with her when she's so near her time?"

Another silence, and Mulder's voice, low and harsh. "It's better for her, for the baby, if I'm not with her right now."

Doggett nodded. "Well, do me a favor. While we're working with the captain, lay off the spooky stuff, okay? No stories about Bigfoot or the Abominable Snowman or whatever."

"That's what the Russians call him, you know."

"Call who?" Doggett bent to brush snow off his pack.

"We call him Bigfoot or Sasquatch. But to Russian intelligence, he was just the Snowman."

Doggett straightened. "Russian intelligence? They believe in this bullshit?"

Mulder gave Doggett his sunniest smile. "It's not bullshit. They had a secret task force on it in the 1950s. They shut it down and destroyed the files. Or thought they did."

"Just keep it to yourself, will you?"

"Okay if I mention it when it stomps through our camp?" Mulder gestured. "Tracks, Doggett. Pretty damn big ones."

Doggett looked where Mulder was pointing. Sure enough, the snow showed large depressions leading to the tent, circling it, and leading away. "Snowshoes," he said. "Someone on snowshoes checked us out last night." He bent close, then put a hand down beside the closest two tracks. The tracks were deep, long, and wide—twice the size of his own bootprints.

Mulder knelt. "If this was a man on snowshoes, he was a hell of a big guy. Even a man with a heavy pack wouldn't make that deep an impression."

Doggett straightened. "Probably a bear, drawn by the smell of our food."

"A bear that came all the way to the tent, smelled the food inside, and made no attempt to enter?" Mulder said.

"If a bear could smell the food, he could smell the guy standing guard," Doggett said stubbornly. "Don't mention this to the captain. We've got six good men missing up here, and I'm not going to waste the day figuring out how a bear left tracks in the snow."

He ducked into the tent, leaving Mulder staring at the huge tracks circling the tent. "It wasn't a bear," he muttered.

They had been climbing for an hour, fighting their way uphill on a thin slice of bare rock, when they heard the sounds again.

A low-pitched wail warbled out of the trees to their left. All three men stopped instantly. Doggett, in the lead, gripped his rifle. In the rear, Salvert unholstered his gun. All three faced the sound.

"Who's there?!" Salvert demanded. "Identify yourself!"

The wail cut off, to be followed by the knocking sound they'd heard before. Then silence for five minutes.

"What *is* that?" Doggett felt the hairs rising on the back of his neck, a focused intensity descending on him that he had not felt in a long time.

"Still think it's a bear?" Mulder asked Doggett, eyes on the treeline.

Salvert brought his weapon up and fired. The shot echoed through the frigid air, bouncing off the wall of mountain ahead of them.

Mulder slapped Salvert's hand down. "What the hell are you doing?"

"I won't be intimidated," Salvert said.

"You don't fire a weapon without knowing what you're firing at," Mulder said. His eyes blazed with anger.

Doggett stepped up beside Mulder. "Sir, for all we know, that could have been one of our own men, calling for help."

"That wasn't a call for help," Salvert said. "That was a challenge. Ever hear a cougar roar?" He slipped the safety back on his weapon, holstering it. Without a backward glance, he started up the trail.

The eerie wail broke out again, and Doggett flinched. Mulder turned and they faced the treeline.

"About twenty meters inside the treeline, I think," Doggett said. Ahead of them, Salvert plowed on, ignoring the sounds. "It's moving parallel to our line of march."

Mulder glanced at Doggett. "We're pretty exposed out here."

"It's better than being under the trees with whatever is making that noise."

Another wail, this time from behind them. Both men spun around, but the trees were as dark and mysterious as ever. The cry was answered from the left.

"Two of them," Mulder said. "They're flanking us. What do you think, Agent Doggett? Are we being stalked by a moose?"

"I don't think it's Bigfoot," Doggett said quietly. "Maybe someone else. Maybe someone who wanted this mission to fail, and made sure it did."

Mulder squinted at him. "What are you thinking? Sabotage?"

"I'm thinking terrorists. I'm thinking Russian or Chinese intelligence. I'm *not* thinking of seven-foot-tall apes covered in hair, Mulder."

Both men kept their eyes on the forest on either side of them. Ahead of them, Salvert forged on alone, refusing to slacken his pace for the others, taking no rest stops.

Throughout the next two hours, as they trudged through the snow, the wails and knocking sounds emerged periodically from the forest.

"They want us to know they're following us," Mulder said during a rest stop. "So much for the secret mission."

Salvert shrugged. "As long as they leave us alone, I don't care."

An hour later, they found their first corpse.

Doggett saw Salvert fall to his knees; he left the trail and plowed through the snow at top speed. Mulder floundered behind. Doggett stopped next to Salvert, who was sweeping snow off a lumpy figure.

It was a man, lying face down. Male, Caucasian, dirty blond hair in a Marine buzz cut. Salvert dug under the man's neck to bring out his dog-tags.

"Staff Sergeant Carstensen," Salvert said quietly. "Poor bastard. But I don't understand why he isn't wearing his parka."

Mulder cleared snow off the man's feet. "He's not wearing his boots, either. Just one sock on his left foot." Together, the men cleared the remaining snow. Carstensen had also been wearing khaki boxer shorts and a T-shirt; there was no sign of cold weather gear.

Doggett stared. "This doesn't make any sense. Why would he come out in this weather without proper gear?"

"Maybe someone killed him and took it," Salvert said.

Doggett's gaze met Mulder's. "There's no sign of injury. This man froze to death."

"He was running from something," Mulder said. "See where his right foot is cut and bruised? And he fell facing downhill."

They all glanced up the slope, where the mountain's peak loomed regally against the sky. Salvert stood and cupped his hands. "Hello! Can anyone hear me?" Silence answered him. "Maybe they're farther on."

Mulder leaned close to Doggett. "I'm worried about what he was running from," he said.

Doggett stood. "Sir, shouldn't we call this in?"

Salvert shook his head. "We maintain radio silence. We can't do anything more for this man; we may as well go on and find out where the others are." He got to his feet, dusting snow off his pants. With one last sad look at the dead man in the snow, he tromped off uphill.

Doggett took off his pack and opened it up. He pulled out a spare T-shirt and draped it over the head of the corpse. His actions were gentle, respectful. "What do you think, Mulder? Did your Sasquatch do this?"

Mulder looked down into the woods. He said nothing.

———— *Ø* ————

LIBERTY RIDGE, MT. RAINIER, WASHINGTON
11th MAY, 2001, 11:21 a.m.

Salvert was in the lead again when he stopped. "Twenty meters, dead ahead!"

Slogging up the track, Doggett stared. Hours of hiking through snow had left him bleary-eyed with exhaustion. "What?"

Salvert pointed to a snow-covered hump. "That's a tent." Without waiting for the other two, he charged off the trail into waist-deep snow.

"What tent?" Mulder said. Doggett said nothing, following the captain.

When they caught up to Salvert, he was digging with his hands at the base of a mound of snow. "Downes! Matthews! It's Captain Salvert!"

Doggett grabbed Salvert. "Stop! Sir! You're disturbing the scene."

"What are you talking about?" Salvert said. "You think this is a *crime* scene?"

Mulder tramped past Doggett, circling the hummock.

"We won't know until we look," Doggett said. "We don't know how Carstensen died. Mulder and I, we know how to process a crime scene. Give us a minute."

Reluctantly, Salvert stepped away.

Mulder gestured to Doggett from behind the mound.

Doggett slogged over. "Find something?"

"Here, where the mound sheltered the ground from the snow a bit. Tracks."

Footprints led away into the trees. "How many?"

Mulder squatted. "Two guys in bare feet, one of them running that way, the other headed into the trees."

"Barefoot?" Doggett stared. "Like the other guy we found."

"But running *away* from one another. What does that mean?"

Doggett turned and walked in his own tracks back to the mound. Beyond it, Salvert was bent double, walking slowly, looking for more tracks. Doggett swept a hand across the snowy surface. Underneath, he saw a smooth expanse of white ripstop nylon. Suddenly his hand thrust through an opening. "Hey!"

"What is it?" Salvert trotted up.

The men worked to clear snow from what emerged as a three-foot-long slash in the side of the tent. "Is anyone there?" Mulder yelled.

Working swiftly, they uncovered a strange scene. The standard-issue white Marine tent, about six feet long and four feet wide, had been ripped open in several long, vertical gashes. Peering through them, Doggett saw backpacks, sleeping bags, and other equipment laid out neatly, covered with a thin dusting of snow.

"What do you see?" Salvert said impatiently.

"Equipment, clothes. A plate of food, frozen now." Doggett craned to see the stacks of equipment. One box sat with the lid half-off; the stenciled label on it said "Direct-Decibel Energy Broadcaster." More radio equipment was neatly arranged on a folding rack. The tent was neat, orderly, showing no evidence of violence and no sign of the men who had occupied it.

Doggett lifted a rifle from the snow. "M16," he said. He turned to Mulder. "Standard issue for Marine infantry. It hasn't been fired." He looked at the edges of the tears in the ripstop nylon. "I don't get it. If something ripped into this, why does it look so clean and neat inside?"

"There's no blood." Mulder reached into an inside pocket of his parka and brought out a pair of glasses. Settling them on his face, he slid a hand along the edge of one tear. "These are clean cuts."

"I see boots, hats, and parkas. Why would they leave their gear behind?"

"Maybe whatever tore open this tent didn't give them a chance," Mulder said. He straightened. "These slashes weren't made by claws."

Doggett bent down to look. "He's right, sir. Looks like someone sliced into this tent with a knife."

Salvert's hand came to rest on the Ka-Bar on his vest, standard Marine issue. He glanced around. "Someone attacked my men?"

"No." Mulder shook his head. "This tent was cut open from the *inside*."

Doggett stared. "From the inside? That doesn't make any sense."

"It does if they panicked," Mulder said.

"Marines don't panic," Salvert said.

Mulder stood back to let Doggett take a closer look. "Anyone can panic, given the right circumstances. I've read about this before."

"Where? When?"

"The Ural Mountains in Russia, in 1959. Nine experienced hikers cut open their own tent in the middle of the night and fled in all directions, leaving their boots, clothes, and equipment behind in sub-zero weather. Their bodies were found weeks later, with injuries that could not have been made by human beings. The authorities merely said they'd died of some 'compelling natural force.'"

"I never saw that in the X-Files," Doggett said. Salvert stared at him, but he paid no attention.

"The FBI never investigated it," Mulder said.

"But you think it was, what, the Abominable Snowman?"

Mulder half-smiled. "Funny you should say that. The Russians called their investigation 'Project Snowman.'"

"So?"

"So those hikers that died? One of the last entries in their journal was, 'From now on we know there are snowmen.'"

Silence reigned for a moment, and a few snowflakes eddied down out of the sky. From the trees far below came a knocking sound. The men looked at one another.

Salvert stared at the ripped tent. "There's another set of tracks headed southwest. Two men."

"Mulder and I will take those," Doggett said. "Maybe they found shelter."

"I'll take the others you found. We'll meet back here in thirty," Salvert said, turning away.

"Aye, captain," Mulder said mockingly.

Doggett and Mulder followed the second set of tracks. The ground rose a little and then sloped down sharply, past outcroppings of granite. Now and then one or the other of the running men had slipped in the snow, but then scrambled to his feet and continued.

Mulder halted and Doggett stopped beside him. "Why did he swerve here?" Mulder asked.

One set of footprints suddenly veered to the left, then zig-zagged back to the first heading. A few yards farther on, the footprints made a U-turn, backed on themselves, then U-turned again, fleeing down the mountainside.

Doggett looked around. "He was being chased."

"Herded." Mulder gestured. "Something was herding him into that."

Below them, the white-fissured surface of a glacier gleamed. Half a mile across, it glistened blue and white and silver under the cobalt sky, winding away down the steep canyon.

"Carbon Glacier," Doggett said. He shuddered. "Ever since we got here, I've felt like I'm being watched."

"Not watched," Mulder said. "Stalked."

Doggett hesitated a long moment. "You carrying, Mulder?"

"I'm no longer authorized to carry firearms." Mulder's voice held a bitter tone.

Doggett reached back to his waistband. He pulled out his Sig Sauer P226. "I didn't give you this. Or the full clip in it."

Mulder took it in his gloved hand. "Not much use against a six-hundred-pound Sasquatch," he said. "But thanks." He pulled the slide back to load a round into the chamber.

As soon as they started down the slope, clouds crossed the sky and cast a gray shadow over the entire landscape.

"Hold it," Mulder said. He pointed to their left.

Huge tracks came up from below, emerging from a pile of rocks and crossing the trail of footprints ahead of them. One of them had obliterated the running man's footprint.

"It was tracking him," Mulder said.

"It? I think it was a 'he,' Mulder. Some foreign agent with a sniper rifle—" Mulder stopped short and Doggett plowed into him. "Hey!"

A body lay sprawled in the snow at the foot of a granite outcropping. The man was African-American and wore only shorts and a khaki T-shirt; his dark skin showed through the light dusting of snow. "Cover me," Doggett said, kneeling.

Mulder stood above him with the Sig in both hands, watching their back trail. Doggett turned the body over gently, then winced.

Something had bashed a hole in the man's forehead; it was a bloody mess of hair and brains and gravel from the slope. The man's shoulder also had an odd configuration; Doggett decided he'd dislocated it. Blood had pooled and frozen under the man.

"ID?" Mulder asked.

Doggett fumbled around inside the frozen T-shirt and found the Marine's dog tags. "Downes. He was the radio operator."

"There's blood and hair on these boulders," Mulder said. "He probably tripped and fell on them."

Doggett stood. "It would have been pitch dark and snowing. They couldn't have seen where they were going."

"Couldn't even see what was chasing them," Mulder said.

"What about the other man?"

Mulder nodded downslope, where the white wall of the glacier loomed high. "More tracks. Looks like he was running for the ice."

A roar from behind them made both men spin around, bringing weapons to bear on the shadowed slope they had just descended. "Who's there?" Doggett yelled.

Another roar answered him, and a huge boulder came rolling and crashing down the hillside. They leaped out of its way, just as another boulder half the size of a car smashed downhill. Something very angry roared again, and then Doggett was running, scrambling heedless and headlong. Mulder fought to remain on his feet but fell, and the two of them rolled and slid, grunting as they hit rock outcroppings. More boulders rolled down; one the size of a beach ball soared past them, thrown as easily as a softball.

"Get behind those rocks!" Doggett yelled. He pointed at a jumble of naked rock at the base of the glacier wall.

Mulder scrambled behind one, then Doggett slammed into the wall, bounced back, and staggered to his feet. Something roared again, and Doggett heard something big coming down the hill.

"Mulder?"

"Back here," came a muffled reply.

"Where?" Turning, he tripped and fell forward past a huge block of stone into a split in the wall of ice, his rifle clattering on the floor. Finally he rolled to a stop.

And came face to face with a dead man.

⎯⎯ 1 ⎯⎯

CARBON GLACIER, MT. RAINIER, WASHINGTON
11th MAY, 2001, 1:52 p.m.

The dead man's eyes were open, staring. He'd been in his mid-twenties, fit and trim, with black hair. There was no sign of injury, but the blue tint of his lips and the glaze of ice on the man's eyes told Doggett he had frozen to death. The man wore only winter pants. His bare feet were black with frostbite. There was no other sign of injury.

"He froze to death, too." Mulder was kneeling beside the corpse, holding the Marine's dog tags. "This was Lance Corporal Criscione."

They stood in a narrow slit in the side of the half-mile-high glacial wall. Near the entrance, the ice was white and blue, but after a few yards darkness closed in.

"What's in his hand?" The dead man's right hand was fisted around a small box.

Doggett winced at the sound of breaking knuckles, then Mulder stood up holding the object. It was the size and shape of a TV remote control. He frowned. "This is calibrated in decibels, but those numbers don't make sense. They're below the threshold of human hearing."

"We'll worry about it later." Doggett reached for the control and stashed it in a zippered pocket.

A huge shadow crossed the opening, blocking the light for a moment.

"Can't get out that way," Mulder said quietly.

Doggett glanced at the body on the floor. "Maybe there's another way out." Doggett slipped a mini flashlight out of his pocket and aimed it. The walls closed in, narrowing, but then turned a corner.

Mulder led the way deeper into the ice cleft, then halted. "Feel that?"

Doggett felt a breeze in his face, indicating another entrance somewhere farther on. A deafening roar thundered through the corridor. Bits of ice showered down on Doggett, and he felt dizzy for a moment.

"He's coming in," Mulder said. Together they half-ran through darkness lit only by the beam from Doggett's flashlight. "Scully had much better flashlights," Mulder panted.

The passage turned and turned, meandering like the trickling stream of meltwater that ran down its center. Doggett rounded a corner, following Mulder, and stopped.

Peering out of the darkness at him was a grotesque apparition: a shaggy, muscular human-like creature with lanky hair and broadly simian features, lit only by the tiny beam of Mulder's light. Doggett instantly brought the rifle to his shoulder, his finger tightening on the trigger.

Mulder put his hand on the rifle. "Wait."

"But it's—"

"It's dead."

Doggett hesitated, and Mulder stepped forward. The creature was huge, maybe eight feet tall if it had been standing, but it lay in a niche in the wall of ice. Mulder set his hand against the creature's face. Now Doggett could see that the thing was encased in the glacier. Ice compression had crushed and squeezed the corpse into a bizarrely contorted position.

"There's another," Mulder said quietly.

Doggett saw another hairy creature frozen into the ice; this one had breasts. The eyes were open, staring, glazed in frost.

"And another." A gray-furred one this time, with open wounds in neck and shoulder looking dull red in the half-light.

"Who are they? How'd they get here?" Doggett said. He swept his light over the surface of the ice. A young, skinny female lay curled in a heap of fur; another large male lay on his back, jaws open in death, showing ivory fangs the size of his thumb. "Were they caught in an avalanche?"

"I think this is a tomb."

"A tomb?"

Mulder pointed. "See the arms crossed over the chest? See the flowers on that one? There are Neanderthal burials in Europe that show that much care for the dead." He placed his hand flat on the ice face, an inch from the snarling fang of one of the dead creatures. "These bodies were buried in the glacier."

"You think they're Neanderthals?" Doggett felt a shiver go over him; it had nothing to do with the cold.

"You know they aren't." Mulder's eyes were dark with emotion. "They're Sasquatch. Why won't you admit it?"

A muffled roar rumbled down the passageway behind them. Ice flakes showered them.

Doggett faced back along the way they'd come, his rifle leveled. "It's here."

Paying no attention, Mulder held the flashlight up to the ice. "These bodies are probably hundreds of years old," he said. "Maybe thousands. I can see more of them back behind these, deeper in the ice."

Another smashing sound, and the patter of falling ice. Doggett felt the rough floor trembling under his feet. "We need to get out of here."

Mulder paid no attention. "This explains so much," he said, gazing into the ice. "This is why no one has ever found any bodies, any evidence of Sasquatch. They hide their dead. And this glacier is the perfect place." He put both hands on the wall, staring upward towards the point where the narrowing walls met. "They'll be safe here until the glacier grinds them into dust."

A growl rumbled ominously through the tunnel behind them. Doggett felt the hairs stand up on his neck.

"Gotta go," Doggett said, stepping backwards, eyes on the dark tunnel behind them. "Go towards the light, Mulder."

Mulder half-laughed. "Heard that one before." But he stepped away from the wall. "This way."

As he stepped backwards, following Mulder, Doggett felt the floor tremble under his feet again. Was the approaching creature, whatever it was, that heavy? Air puffed against the back of his head. "Mulder?"

Something moved in the passage. For a moment, Doggett glimpsed a massive, shambling presence at the edge of the light. He clutched the rifle in both hands. Then a hand landed on his shoulder and he flinched.

"Hurry!" Mulder said. "Don't look behind you!" Doggett saw the glint of a gun in his hand. Mulder wasn't looking at him, but over his shoulder. Doggett heard pounding footsteps behind him. "Come on!"

Hand over hand, Doggett climbed the broken ice, slipping, gaining ground, fighting his way up the slope. Then suddenly Mulder was kneeling, braced, firing over Doggett's shoulder.

Doggett scrambled up and out of the ice cleft. A low, menacing rumble floated out of the darkness under the ice. He glanced around; they had emerged on the same side of the glacier, a little farther down the slope.

"Hey!"

Doggett whipped around, then stared upward. At the top of the ridge above the glacier, a figure waved. "It's Salvert." Doggett waved back. "Stay there, Captain!"

But Salvert was already headed down the slope towards them, sliding and skidding. Doggett retreated to a pile of snow-covered boulders, Mulder right behind him.

Suddenly there was a great, grinding CRACK from the glacier and the ground heaved. Mulder and Doggett staggered.

"Go back!" Doggett yelled at Salvert, but if the man heard him he paid no attention. Doggett could see he was carrying a backpack. "What the hell is he doing?"

Salvert half-ran, half-slid to a stop. "Did you find the men?"

"Downes and Criscione, sir." Eyes still on the opening in the ice, Doggett fished out the object he'd found in Criscione's hand. "Criscione was carrying this. I don't understand. He left his M16 behind, but took this."

Salvert took it, nodding. "Good work, Sergeant. This is what I was looking for."

Something in his tone, some shift in emphasis, had Doggett turning, staring. "Sir? Did you find the missing men?"

Salvert hefted the backpack. "I found what I was looking for. My mission is over."

Doggett stared. "You found the other men? We only found three so far."

Mulder half-laughed. "Oh, come on, Doggett. You're not that naive. Do you honestly think a Marine captain is going to come all this way for a few good men?"

"Yes," Doggett said, his face turning to stone. "Yes, I do."

"You weren't looking for the men. You went back to the tent, didn't you?" Mulder looked at Salvert. "What's in the backpack, Captain?"

Salvert answered with a glare. Doggett looked from one man to the other. "What's going on here?"

"What were they testing, Captain?" Mulder said, almost taunting. "A weapon? Did it work so well it killed the men who tested it? You didn't come here to rescue your men. You came to rescue an experiment, didn't you? Were they the experimenters? Or the victims?"

Doggett felt horror creep over him as he saw Salvert's mouth tighten in a grim line. "Sir?"

"He's crazy. The mission failed, that's all. Good men died, but that wasn't our intent."

"What's in the backpack, sir?"

Mulder stepped back, pulling the Sig out of his pocket.

"Classified, Sergeant." Salvert said. "Need-to-know basis, and you don't need to know."

Doggett had been pointing his rifle skyward. Now he brought it down, pointing at Salvert's feet. "I'm not a sergeant anymore, Captain. I'm a special agent of the Federal Bureau of Investigation, and I have jurisdiction in a National Park."

"Especially in a murder case," Mulder said. "And this was murder."

"Open the backpack, Captain Salvert," Doggett said. His tone brooked no refusal.

Salvert looked from one man to another, then shook his head. "It won't matter anyway," he said. He tossed the backpack at Doggett's feet.

A sound of colliding boulders came from the glacier wall.

Doggett knelt and unzipped the backpack. It was a standard issue Marine patrol pack, white to blend with the snow. There was only one object in the pack. He drew it out—a large oval box with a membrane over one flat side.

"What is this, sir?"

Salvert said nothing, but raised his hand. He was holding the silver control, and now he pushed a button. A red light on the front end winked on.

Terror slammed through Doggett. He dropped the box. "What—?"

Mulder stepped back, his face pale and sweaty. "What is that?"

A low, moaning wail broke from the ice field above them. Another crack exploded from the glacier, echoing from wall to wall. All three men staggered as the ground rocked. Doggett fought to stay upright, and was amazed to see the captain grinning.

"It works," Salvert said.

CARBON GLACIER, MT. RAINIER, WASHINGTON
11th MAY, 2001, 2:39 p.m.

John Doggett had not known fear like this since Lebanon, a cascade of horror robbing him of mind and will. He shook all over; his rifle fell to the snow. Despite the cold, he felt sweat break out.

Beside him, Mulder had fallen to his knees. Though he still held the Sig, he didn't seem to be able to raise it. He fell sideways, shaking.

Salvert's head turned to follow Mulder's movement, and Doggett saw something glinting in his ears. But it didn't seem very important. What mattered was his need to run far and fast, away from this terror...

Salvert bent and picked up the rifle. He stepped calmly past Doggett and tugged Mulder's gun out of his limp hand, tossed it away. Then he stepped back two paces, raised the silver control, and pressed a button. The red light winked off.

Instantly, the fear and panic that had held Doggett helpless disappeared, as if he was waking from a dream. He heard Mulder cough, then scramble to his feet.

"Sorry about that, Sergeant," Salvert said. His entire demeanor was different—still the bulldog Marine, but wary. He reached up and plucked earplugs out of each ear, holding his gun on the men. "I really didn't want to have to do this, but Mulder's right. And because he's right, I can't let either of you walk out of here."

"Sir? Captain, I don't understand. I know you. You pulled me out of that disaster in Beirut. You cared about these men."

"Yes, I did." Salvert sounded genuinely regretful. "But sometimes men have to be sacrificed, for a mission. You understand that, John."

A long, angry rumble like distant thunder echoed through the valley, the sound bouncing off the glacier above them. Salvert looked up. "I have to go.

My mission is over. And if it's any comfort, Sergeant, you and my men died in the service of your country."

Mulder struggled to his knees, then to his feet. "Murder," he gasped.

Salvert shrugged. "It's war. Sergeant Doggett knows that. Do you know that two thirds of Afghanistan is mountains? Not just any mountains, the Himalayas. And those mountains are full of glaciers. Do you know what happens when an entire glacier breaks up? No one does. Imagine the devastation downstream, disrupting enemy plans, enemy movements. Imagine the psychological impact: our armies can destroy glaciers! Who wants to go up against that?"

"Break up a glacier? You're insane!" Doggett said.

Salvert's expression was sad. "It's just science, John." He hefted the oval box. "Build a speaker small enough to broadcast at low enough frequencies, and it'll break up a river of ice the way a surgeon breaks up a gallstone with ultrasound."

"You fool!" Mulder said. "That's why the readout was calibrated so low. You have no idea what you're doing."

Salvert raised the control. "You mean the side effects? The fear, the terror? Yes, that was a wonderful bonus. We didn't know about that."

Doggett looked at Mulder. "What's he talking about?"

"He's talking about infrasound, sound below the threshold of human hearing. At ultra-low frequencies, humans can no longer hear sound, but they can feel it. Humans perceive infrasound as fear, panic, paranoia. Everything we just felt. One of my psychology professors researched it. He went insane." Mulder stepped forward, fists clenched. "Did they know? Your six good men? Did you tell them what would happen when they set it up, when they turned it on?" He gestured at the silver control.

A bolt of hot anger surged through Doggett. "By God, he's right, isn't he? Your machine made these guys so crazy they cut their way out of their own tent, went running off into the night to freeze to death!"

"You set them up." Mulder sneered. "You weren't trying to break up a glacier. You were developing a terror weapon!"

A low whistling moan from high up the ridge caught Doggett's attention. Was something moving up there?

"I didn't think the machine would work at all," Salvert said. He stuck the earplugs back into his ears, carefully seating each one. "No one knew it would affect our men. I mean, ultra-low frequencies? Who can hear that? Elephants? Whales?"

Mulder looked past Salvert. "How about a Sasquatch?"

"Wha—" Salvert turned, raising the control.

Something white, moving very fast, slammed into him. At the same moment, a thunderous crack from up-canyon echoed down the valley. Doggett staggered back.

Salvert's high-pitched screams mingled with a roar and a sickening, cracking sound like branches—or bones—breaking. Doggett lurched forward, but Mulder caught him and hauled him back. "No! It's too late!"

Two figures rolled on the ground, fighting. Suddenly there was a scream, cut off, and a scarlet gush of blood across the snow.

"Sir!" Doggett lunged toward the pair, but out of the flurry of white a huge head, shaggy and red-eyed, turned towards him. For an eternal moment, Doggett locked eyes with something out of a nightmare.

"Doggett! Come on!" Mulder grabbed at him. "The glacier is breaking up!"

Doggett fell backwards. Snow rolled over him, and for a suffocating moment he thought an avalanche had caught him. A strong hand grasped his, pulled. Mulder hauled him to his feet. "Run!"

Doggett looked back just in time to see a ten-story-high section of the ice wall fall away. Splitting as it fell, it slammed to the ground, exploding into a cloud of ice splinters. The shock of the impact staggered him. The wind caught the snow and threw it in their faces.

"Where's Salvert?" Doggett yelled over the roar.

"The Guardian got him," Mulder said. "Come on!"

The men scrabbled up the steep slope they had come down only an hour before. Boulders rolled and bounced down at them; one rock the size of his head rolled over Doggett's left hand and he yelped in pain. Finally they collapsed, panting, at the crest of the ridge. Lying flat, Doggett stared down at the glacier.

The wall of ice was a maze of fissures and cracks. Snow geysered up here and there as huge chunks fell from the face. As Doggett watched, one wall a hundred feet high sheared away; for a moment Doggett saw clear, pure ice exposed for the first time in thousands of years. Were there figures in there, frozen forever in death?

Mulder tugged at him. "We've got to get farther away!" Mulder was covered in snow, even his eyelashes were white, but his expression was grim. "This will trigger avalanches all over this mountain!"

Doggett staggered to his feet, then followed Mulder as he fought his way back towards the abandoned camp. He put one foot after another in Mulder's tracks, noting dully where larger tracks crossed his, not caring.

Light bloomed before him, and he turned that way like a moth chasing flame. Shouting, something shoving at him, and then falling, falling. Doggett fell face down into soft, comforting snow and all was darkness.

ABANDONED CAMP, MT. RAINIER, WASHINGTON
11th MAY, 2001, 7:49 p.m.

Doggett woke to the smell of coffee. He lay outside the ripped tent. The sun lay low on the horizon, nearly set.

"Here." Fox Mulder shoved a cup of hot coffee in his hand. "I got the stove going. They left it in good condition."

Doggett looked over his shoulder, back towards the glacier. A cloud of ice and snow hung over it like smoke, and a dull rumble sounded now and then.

Mulder sat holding the cup in one hand, the Sig in the other. "The law of unintended consequences."

"What?"

Mulder tossed his coffee; it made a dark smear on the snow. "Whoever developed that infrasound generator didn't know what it could do."

"I don't think the captain knew," Doggett said.

Mulder looked at him, and his eyes were cold and dark. "I think it was working on Salvert as well as us."

"But he was wearing earplugs."

"It wouldn't matter. You can't hear infrasound, but you can feel it."

Doggett stood. "He saved my life in Lebanon; he was a good man."

"I think whatever demons you carry with you, whether it's fear or a will to power, infrasound unleashes it. I think Salvert just became more of what he was."

"I'm not sure what to put in my report," Doggett said. He picked up his backpack, brushing snow off of it, tightening the straps. "I don't even know what to put down as cause of death. These poor bastards froze to death, that's clear enough, but I don't know what killed Salvert. All I saw was a blur of white. An avalanche?"

Mulder's gaze was steady. "You know what it was. Why can't you believe?"

"I only saw a blur of white," Doggett said stubbornly. He rolled his shoulders to get the stiffness out of them. "I guess you're going to say it was Bigfoot."

Mulder turned away. "Whatever put those bodies in that glacier was protecting them. It was guarding sacred territory."

Doggett glanced around. "What happens to this stuff? What happens to the men?"

"I don't know about you," Mulder said. "I'm walking out of here. I don't want to spend another night on this mountain."

"Copy that." Doggett said. "We can at least tell the Marines where to recover the bodies." His face clouded. "All but the one in the glacier. And Salvert."

"Salvert?" Mulder said coolly. "Salvert who?"

THE END

the truth is out there

VOICE OF EXPERIENCE

By Rachel Caine

WASHINGTON, D.C.
13th OCTOBER, 1993, 7:15 a.m.

It wasn't Fox Mulder's usual habit to sit outside with his coffee, but today was an especially fine day for October in Washington D.C.... clear skies, soft breezes, temperatures so gentle they might have been imported from Hawaii. It would have been a shame not to enjoy it before plunging into the depths of the Hoover building, where he shared his basement office with Dana Scully. So he'd joined the ranks of those enjoying their caffeine on the café patio, and the combination of roasted coffee and the morning paper made him feel almost normal.

Almost. But then, being someone who waded neck-deep in the weird and grotesque meant he never was *quite* normal. And he was pretty sure he preferred it that way.

"Fox?"

It had been a long time since he had heard the voice, but he didn't mistake it for an instant. A woman's voice, mellow and sweet as dark cherries. Besides, she'd been one of the few outside his own family who'd ever called him *Fox*.

He looked up from his coffee to see Gina Sherman standing in front of him, with the morning sun a halo around her head. The breeze teased her dark hair out into a banner. For a flash of a second, she was *exactly* the same as she'd been five years ago; the illusion passed, and he saw changes in her: a little more weight, a few more lines.

She also sported a glittering diamond wedding ring, and a very obvious pregnancy.

"Gina," he said after a frozen moment, and stood up to slide the other chair out at his table. He wasn't quite sure how to feel about seeing her.

Pleased? Cautious? Something between the two? "You look great."

She sank into the wrought-iron chair and put her own drink down. She gave a little sigh of relief, rested one hand on the curve of her stomach, and smiled at him with what looked like rueful understanding. Still the same dark red lipstick he remembered.

"Well, this is awkward," she said. "I know we didn't exactly part as friends, Fox, but… I was wrong about so much, and when I spotted you I just *had* to try to make amends. I was a different person then. Please forgive me for making it so hard on you. It wasn't your fault how things ended." She laughed a little nervously. "Sorry. I've been practicing that speech for a while."

It was a lot to take in at once, and Mulder wasn't sure he wanted to do this. Not on what had started out such a perfect day. *Didn't exactly part as friends…* that was one way to put it, but it hardly described the train wreck of the end of their relationship. He regarded her in silence for a moment, nursing a perfectly reasonable caution. Then he said, "It was a good speech. How's Roy?"

"Roy's good." Gina had always had a beautiful smile, but now it was luminous with joy. She was a classically pretty woman, one to turn heads and inspire passion, and he still wasn't immune, even after so much exposure. "Roy's *great*. We're both so excited about the baby!"

"I'm happy for you both," Mulder said. He meant that, honestly. There was a guilty flutter of relief in the pit of his stomach that she wasn't still the angry, bitter woman he'd faced at the end of their time together, but mostly, he was glad to see her this way: healthy and joyful. Gina wasn't right for him, but she deserved this. "When are you due?"

"Two more months," she said, and laughed a little breathlessly. "I think this kid's going to be a professional wrestler. Big, heavy, and man, can he *kick*." She sipped tea, and her large china-blue eyes watched him over the lid of the cup. They were still a little tentative. "How about you?" she asked. "Still chasing ghosts?"

She meant that in a lot of different ways, of course, but he chose to take it in a professional way. "Still working on the X-Files," he said. "I have a partner now."

"Really? They drafted someone into the basement with you? How crazy is he?"

"Scully's not crazy," he said. He didn't correct her mistake, because frankly, he couldn't guess what her reaction would be to a female partner. He knew what it *would* have been, five years ago, and he wanted to avoid pushing his luck. "Are you still living in town?"

"Roy and I have a place over in Adams Morgan. You're still at the old apartment? What am I saying, of course you are. Fox, it's so good to see you. I can't believe how badly I treated you; it was like I was a crazy person. I've picked up the phone a dozen times to try to apologize, but I wasn't sure you'd give me a chance."

There was nothing in her face but sincerity, and as they talked on, there was no trace of the possessive, distraught woman that he'd broken up with years back. This Gina was content. A wife. A soon-to-be mom. She chattered on about the baby, plans about the birth, decorating his room. She and Roy were still debating names, and he suggested a few completely ridiculous ones. When it was time to go, he gave Gina Sherman—no, Gina *Wettig* now—a gentle embrace. *Scully would be so surprised,* he thought. *Me, acting like a responsible adult.*

He was a little shocked himself.

He and Gina exchanged business cards. She was, he was mildly surprised to see, employed in the Department of Transportation as a structural engineer. She had the degree, but when he'd been with her, she hadn't had any interest in using it.

Things had changed for both of them. For the better.

He entered the office whistling, and found Scully already behind her desk. She looked up at him with a slightly wary expression, to which he returned a smile.

"Christmas is officially on the way, according to the in-store music," he said. "Time to dust off the case file on Claus and see if we can catch him this time. That whole naughty and nice thing is classic sociopath territory."

"You're in a good mood," she said. He could tell it both soothed and alarmed her, because she wanted to feel comfortable with him. So far, they'd settled into a guarded, fragile trust, with flashes of friendship. It wasn't reluctance on his part; he liked smart people, and she was always the smartest one in the room. Including this room.

But that didn't mean he could absolutely trust her. She'd been assigned to help shut down the X-Files. He respected the fact that she'd come into it her own person, making her own judgments, and he didn't feel the need to prove himself. The X-Files would convince her, if she gave them a chance.

While they had a certain admiration and respect going, being easy with each other, being seamless, would take time. And work.

"Anything new come in today?" he asked, as he sank down in his office chair—an upstairs reject, like everything in the room.

"Another haunted hotel," she said, and made finger-quotes around *haunted*. "How many haunted houses does this make?"

"That depends, are we counting saloons, prisons, bed and breakfasts…"

"Never mind. I'm doing a point-by-point on why it's not worth pursuing."

"You take all the fun out of life." He picked up a baseball from the corner of his desk and tossed it to her. She ignored it, and it hit the wall behind her and rolled into the shadows. "Okay, Scully, the rules of catch are simple. You actually catch—"

She held up a single, stern finger without looking up. She was writing, and he shut up and watched. Part of what made her so intimidating was her focus, and right now, it was off of him and on the papers in front of her. Standard, dry FBI language, he was sure, about something that would be anything but standard, or it would have never ended up abandoned on their doorstep.

While she did the work, he shot rubber bands up at the pencils he'd previously darted into the ceiling. One fell with a clatter and narrowly missed Scully's desk.

She didn't bother to look up. "If you hit me with one of those, I'll stick it somewhere uncomfortable," she told him. "And as someone who regularly dissects the human body, I can find some pretty uncomfortable places."

"But, I'm high on life, Scully." He thought about telling her about his morning meeting with Gina, but since he'd never told her about Gina, that seemed like a long, and probably too intimate, conversation. "And caffeine."

Scully tapped a fingernail thoughtfully on the contents of the folder she was reading, and scribbled more notes. He watched. It was always interesting to see so much going on in so small a space.

The pen-scratching stopped, and he aimed another rubber band for a dangling pencil. It hit right on target. The pencil clattered down on his desk, with the FBI seal facing up. Double points.

Scully dropped her notebook on his desk, along with the file.

"Aw, come on," he told her, and gave her his best smile. "We could at least take a look."

"This isn't a horror movie," she told him. "It's an old, badly maintained hotel with a generous-pour bar and a guest cruising for a coronary. There's no mystery here. Just overheated imaginations."

"Disappointed?"

She shot him a look that strongly implied she wasn't. "We've been chasing amateur videos and badly faked photos for weeks now. Bored is more accurate."

"Enjoy the time off." He wasn't worried. Things would pick up. They always did. One thing he could always count on: The weird never stopped coming.

To fill the time, Mulder organized case files, and Scully knocked off early to do some shopping for her sister. He was just finishing up for the day when his desk phone rang. He picked it up and held it between his cocked head and shoulder while he juggled files back into place. He thought about answering *Aliens 'R' Us, we never close,* but settled for "Mulder."

"Agent Mulder, this is Assistant Director Walter Skinner. I need to see you in my office. Now." Skinner? Skinner was just a face to him. Not their direct supervisor; just someone he saw in the halls. Why was he calling?

Plus, Skinner spent too much time with that old cigarette-puffing son of a bitch, the one with the cold, lizard-flat stare.

Mulder slammed the file drawer and took a firmer hold on the receiver. "Scully's gone already, but if you give her thirty or so, I'm sure I can get her back—"

"I don't need Scully. Just you," Skinner said, and hung up before Mulder could ask anything more.

Mulder drank the last dregs of a soft drink, grabbed his coat, and locked the office on his way upstairs to what he always thought of as the Penthouse. Not that spacious, but Skinner had windows. Windows equaled power.

Skinner's assistant spotted him as he entered, and halted Mulder with one dramatically upheld finger. He waited as she placed an intercom call. "He's ready for you now," she said then.

Why was he seeing Skinner, and not Section Chief Blevins? Not that he preferred Blevins, who hated the whole concept of the X-Files, but the FBI was a bureaucracy. There was no such thing as random change.

"Close it," Skinner said when he entered. The assistant director was seated behind his desk. Mulder did a quick assessment of the rest of the office, and sure enough, there was a barely seen figure in the darkest corner. Too dark to see who it was, but the bitter smell of smoke lingered in the air. "Sit down, Agent Mulder."

That didn't sound good. Sitting usually went hand in hand with more serious conversations. Reprimands, mostly, and Mulder couldn't think what he'd done to earn one.

"I've had a call from Metro police," Skinner continued. "They're waiting in the lobby to take you in for questioning."

"Questioning?" Mulder took a second to ponder that, but he came up blank. "About what?"

"A woman died today with your card in her coat pocket. Gina Wettig." Mulder felt his whole body tighten, like he'd been punched.

Skinner's eyes narrowed. "You knew her?"

Skinner had a law background; most of the higher-ups did. He wouldn't ask a question unless he knew, or strongly suspected, the answer. No point in lying. "I—we lived together. Briefly. About five years ago. How did she—"

"How did your relationship end?"

Mulder pulled in a deep breath before he said, without evasion, "Badly. She took it hard. We had problems."

"Including a restraining order, filed by her," Skinner said. "That doesn't look good."

"Sir, that order was vacated two days later, and I never spoke to her again until we ran into each other this morning. We had a cup of coffee. Exchanged cards, that's all." Mulder swallowed a suddenly ashen taste. "What happened to her?"

"Metro hasn't shared details," Skinner said. "But you're in the clear. You never left the building after you arrived this morning, according to the security logs. I expect their questions will just be pro forma." He frowned. "I've contacted an FBI lawyer to meet you there. Do not offer any unasked-for information. Do you understand?"

He felt hot all over now. "Sir, Gina Wettig is—*was* a federal employee. Transportation Department. That puts it in our court."

"No," Skinner said. The light glinting off his glasses made it impossible to see his eyes. "Even if there is an investigation, you will not participate. Do you understand?"

Mulder's mind was elsewhere, on the sound of a dark-cherry voice saying his name, the glint of gentle sunlight on dark, windblown hair.

"Mulder? Do you understand?"

The curve of her growing, unborn child under her protective hand. *Oh God. The baby.* He swallowed hard, and heard his suddenly dry throat click. "What about her baby?"

Skinner looked down at his desk blotter.

The Cigarette Smoking Man, if that was the shadow lurking in the corner, didn't move or speak, and the reek of stale smoke made Mulder sick.

Skinner might have said something, but Mulder was already on his way out, past the assistant, to the elevators. Down to the lobby, where two plainclothes DC Metro detectives waited.

He didn't even break stride as he passed them. "Let's get this over with."

WASHINGTON, D.C.
14th OCTOBER, 1993, 12:45 a.m.

Skinner was right; they didn't suspect Mulder, but that didn't stop them from pounding away at him through the evening, and the late night hours.

The restraining order from five years ago, added to the recent contact, was enough to keep them at him. But they couldn't connect the dots and finally his lawyer—a thirty-something preppy boy with Georgetown written all over him—shut them down.

The cops had told him nothing he didn't already know. When they left the room, he finally asked the prepster.

Sometime after he'd left her, Gina Wettig had gone back to her house, where she'd been found dead by her husband, when he returned from work. That was all the lawyer knew. And when they got to the lobby, the lawyer peeled off to his next case, and Mulder found Scully waiting.

She'd changed out of her FBI suit and into a sweater and jeans, and came to her feet when he was escorted past the security barrier.

"You all right?" she asked. He nodded, but it was a lie. "I'll get you home."

"Thanks, but my car—"

"A.D. Skinner asked me to come get you," she said, which was a little bit of a surprise.

He shook his head. "What? Why?"

She stopped him when he headed for the front door. "Not that way. Out through the back. The press is here, and it's a mess."

"Press?"

Scully sighed, and he heard the regret and anger in it. "Mrs. Wettig was pretty and pregnant, which makes the case a media magnet. They're waiting to pounce on anyone who's remotely connected."

"Do they know—"

"Who you are? No. The police leaked that there was an FBI agent being interviewed. But so far, not your name. We're just exercising extreme caution."

She walked him out and down the dark steps in back of the building. The FBI badge on the dashboard had scored her a spot close to the door, and he sank into the passenger seat with relief. "Sorry," he said. "I didn't mean to screw up your day like this."

Scully started the car and pulled out from the curb with only a single, worried glance at him. He adjusted his seat back to accommodate his legs, which put him a good foot back from Scully's position. That was good. He didn't want her reading him right now.

She'd been right about the press; there was a traveling caravan of them camped in front of the police station, with anchors doing on-site standups under portable lights. Salivating over every detail of Gina's death, spreading uninformed opinions like viruses. He had a bad moment imagining the same circus at his door, but the FBI had a steel wall around all agent information. Even if he *was* the embarrassing inbred cousin of the Bureau family, they wouldn't want him paraded on national TV. Family loyalty.

"Tell me about the case."

"Mulder, I'm not sure it's a good idea—" She must have known it was useless, because she checked the warning. "Mrs. Wettig was at work that morning, and then she went to lunch with a friend, who dropped her back at her house around two thirty. Her husband found her at seven."

"The lawyer called it a suicide." It just didn't make sense.

She gave in with only the briefest hesitation. "He found her in her car, in the closed garage, with the engine still idling. The forensics show that she'd run a garden hose from the tailpipe into the car interior and locked the doors from the inside, garage and car. The ME is ruling it suicide pending toxicological tests."

"No," he said. Gina's smile: luminous, full of joy. Sunshine and the smell of light jasmine perfume. The idea of her dead in that car was obscene. "The baby." He knew the answer but hoped, still.

Her hands clenched on the wheel. "The baby didn't survive." He heard the tightness in her voice. He had a sudden vision of her, remote and professional in her scrubs and face shield, observing what had to be a wrenching, difficult autopsy.

Gina's autopsy.

"It wasn't suicide, Scully," he said, and had to clear his throat. "I don't care how it looks."

"Metro found it hard to believe, too, but it was only her prints on the duct tape, the hose, the doors." Scully paused for a long few seconds, and then said, quietly, "I'm sorry. From what Skinner said, I know you had... history."

Mulder closed his eyes against the onslaught of streetlights stringing past. "She *didn't* kill herself," he said. "Scully, I saw her. I talked to her. She was happy, and she loved that baby. I could *see* it." His stomach churned.

Scully said nothing. They were almost at his apartment now. Silence filled the car.

"She's a federal employee. FBI has jurisdiction, if they want it," Mulder finally said.

She was already shaking her head. "Skinner says hands off, Mulder. It's a conflict of interest. I'm sorry, but—"

"Did they talk to her husband? Roy?"

"I'm sure Metro did."

"I don't care. I need to see him," he said.

She shot him a look. "He's just lost his wife *and* his unborn child. And Skinner told you not to. You can't disobey a direct order."

He felt his lips go thin and hard. "Watch me."

"Mulder—"

"Please, Scully." *I need to trust you, Scully. Do this for me. Please do this.*

She drove for a few moments in silence, then turned right on 18th toward Adams Morgan, where Gina had said she and Roy had a house, and a room they were decorating for a baby boy who'd never arrive.

It was probably significant that Scully didn't even need to look up the address.

Gina's husband wasn't asleep, and he answered on the first knock. Gina's age, more or less, trim but going bald. And he looked ten years older than the last time Mulder had seen him. His skin seemed loose, and his face had a corpse-gray blankness.

"Fox Mulder," he said. "My God." No anger, at least. Just dull surprise.

Scully stepped in between them. "FBI Special Agent Dana Scully. I'm sorry for your loss. We'd like to talk to you about what happened to Gina."

Wettig left the front door open and walked into a dim living room, switched on a single lamp and sat under its glow. Scully settled on the couch near him, and Mulder took a chair in the shadows. Better to keep his distance and stay out of Roy's easy reach, in case that empty recognition turned to something else.

The house smelled feminine, a familiar scent of vanilla potpourri and a hint of jasmine perfume. Gina's ghost still lingered. She smiled down from wedding photos on the walls, silently laughed from a framed photo on an end table.

"Thank you for seeing us, sir," Scully said. Her voice was quiet and gentle. "Can you tell me a little about your wife?"

"Ask your partner."

That earned Mulder a quick glance from Scully. "I'd rather ask you, sir," she said. There was just enough warmth in her voice, and a delicate touch of compassion. "You know her best."

"Knew," Roy said. His voice sounded rough with grief. "*Knew* her the best."

It was common law enforcement procedure that the first person looked at in any death was the spouse. Roy had found the body, and it wasn't unusual for a killer to arrange discovery to cover up their crime. But it was hard for a killer to hide their fear, or their arrogance.

Mulder couldn't see any of that in Roy. The grief looked sickeningly real. It had mutated him down to the bones, made him bent and fragile.

"I'm most interested in Gina's state of mind, sir. Was she worried at all? Distressed?"

Wettig picked up the framed photograph and held it. "No. No, she was fine. I kissed her goodbye in the morning. She was *happy*." He squeezed the frame so tightly that Mulder heard it creak. Roy put the picture down and carefully wiped his fingerprints off the glass. "We had to go to a doctor to get pregnant. We'd been trying for two years. Why would she... why would she kill herself? Kill our baby?"

All his body language was right. All his stumbling inflections. Even his lack of affect was consistent with shock and extreme grief. *He didn't do it,* Mulder thought.

But someone did. Roy was right, Gina had been happy.

Scully gave it a minute before she said, "Tell me about yesterday."

Roy wiped at his eyes and looked down at his fingers, as if surprised they were wet. "She went to work. Then to lunch with her friend, David Samuels. I stopped at the store to pick up—to—pick up—tomatoes, for the sauce, she was making Italian, and when I got here I opened the garage and all the smoke came out, and I saw the car, I saw her in the *car*..."

Wettig's faltering voice stopped. He sat in silence. Scully leaned forward and put her hand lightly on his shoulder.

"I tried to give her mouth to mouth," Wettig suddenly blurted. "She tasted like burned cigarettes." His stare was focused in that middle distance again, and rocked slowly back and forth.

Scully exchanged an appalled look with Mulder. "We'll leave now, Mr. Wettig. But I'm leaving my card. And—I'm so very sorry."

Maybe it was the sympathy, but Wettig suddenly snapped back to focus on her again. It was a little unnerving, how bright and frantic his gaze seemed. When she started to turn away, he grabbed her arm. Hard. Mulder felt the impulse to move, but he stilled it. Scully could handle herself.

"I'd rather someone had killed her," he said. "Isn't that sick? I can't stop thinking it. I'd rather she was murdered than... than this. Than it being her fault."

Scully gently loosed his grip. "I'm so sorry, sir," she said again. Wettig picked up the photo, and held it in both hands against his chest.

"She was *happy.*"

Mulder followed Scully outside, where he took a deep, slow breath. Beyond the porch light's glow it was oppressively dark.

Scully turned toward him, and her expression was grave. "Tell me about Gina."

So he told her, there on Gina's porch. From the first date to the doomed end. The bad breakup and worse epilogue. He didn't spare himself in it. He'd done his part to make it bad, and he knew it.

"Did you love her?" Scully asked him, when silence fell. She was staring off into the distance, at the dark houses. Somewhere, a dog barked, but it was sleepy and tentative.

"No," he said. "I wanted to. But I didn't."

"Do you think that meeting you yesterday set her off?"

"I don't know," he replied softly.

But he could no longer be sure.

✗

WASHINGTON, D.C.
14th OCTOBER, 1993, 7:00 a.m.

The next morning, Scully came back to pick him up at his apartment, since his car was still in the garage at work. They both looked straight out of an FBI recruiting brochure. Professional armor.

"Gina's friend Samuels lives in Georgetown," she said as she put the car in gear. He took the file off the dashboard. It was a new one, still crisp and clean, and inside he found a dot-matrix-printed photo of an older man with a kindly, lined face.

"He's a writer, with eight books in print. After the first one was a failure, he hit with the second, and every one after. The last won the Pulitzer. He teaches at GW, but he doesn't have a class until eleven. We should still be able to catch him at home."

She was right; Samuels was still there when they rang the bell. He looked more distinguished than the grainy photo: silver hair, a lined face, sharp silver-gray eyes. The professorial look was completed by a tweed jacket with leather elbow patches. It was almost too perfect.

"Mr. Samuels? FBI Special Agents Scully and Mulder. May we have a word?"

Samuels raised his brows, "Whatever about?"

"Gina Wettig," Scully said.

He frowned. "Oh. Oh, yes. Please. Come in. I'll make more tea."

He bustled off down the hallway. Mulder closed the door and took in the details of Samuels' small house as they followed.

It was housekeeper-neat; frames marched in regular order down the hallway. On one side, matching framed book covers. On the other, photos of individuals he assumed to be the professor's friends or family. Almost like matched sets.

In the homey kitchen, Samuels filled an electric kettle and plugged it in. "Poor Gina," he said, as he retrieved cups and saucers. "I heard on the news it was suicide. Was I wrong? How is the FBI involved?"

Something in Mulder's profiler radar pinged, but he wasn't sure why. Something was out of tune.

"How well did you know Mrs. Wettig?" Scully asked.

Samuels busied himself with wiping the counter. "Gina is in my writer's group. It meets every Wednesday evening. She's relatively new."

The kettle whistled, and Samuels took it off boil and poured, then carried the cups to the table to set them in front Mulder and Scully. "Milk? Sugar?"

"This is fine," Scully said. She focused on Samuels. "I understand you saw Mrs. Wettig shortly before her death."

Samuels nodded and stirred his tea. "As I said, she was new to our group. I like to take new members to lunch to get acquainted. I took her to Ernesto's—do you know Ernesto's? Marvelous place. I had lasagna, and I think she had a salmon salad... but I don't suppose what we ate would be relevant." Excess detail. Embroidering. Mulder's radar pinged again. "I understand her poor husband found her. How horrible that must have been for him! Can you imagine?"

"Did you notice anything odd about her behavior at lunch?"

"Well, yes, frankly," Samuels said. "She said she'd run into an old flame that morning, and that upset her. I'm afraid she broke down for a few minutes, but she'd calmed by the time we were done, and I took her home." Samuels' gray stare seemed to have zeroed in on Scully. "You haven't touched your tea."

Scully took the teabag out and put in on the saucer, and took one small sip before putting the cup back down. "Was Mrs. Wettig afraid of anyone?"

"Not that she mentioned." There was something in the way Samuels was looking at his partner that made Mulder's nerves crawl.

The man's pupils were getting wider. Darker.

"I don't understand what happened to her. Agent Scully, you must be about Gina's age. Can you imagine being so... so lost that you would kill yourself? *And* your unborn child?"

Scully seemed thrown. Her mouth opened, but nothing came out. She covered it with a sip of tea and got back on point. "So you didn't see any signs that Gina might have been suicidal." Her fingers trembled on the handle of the cup. Not like her.

"I'd hardly have left her alone if I had. Tell me, Agent Scully, have *you* come face to face with death?"

Scully didn't speak. And she didn't look away.

Shift the ground, Mulder thought; Scully was a good interrogator, and she knew better than to let subjects drive the conversation.

But she didn't shift the ground.

She didn't say anything.

"You must see such terrible things in your line of work. And so much of it must be so terrifying." Samuels' voice was quiet, almost soothing. "You seem like a very empathetic person, Agent Scully. It must bother you."

Mulder tried to draw focus by clearing his throat. "When you dropped her off, did you see anyone else at her house?"

"No." Samuels didn't look toward him. "No one."

"So, just to confirm… that means no one can verify what time you left her house, either."

That got Samuels' direct attention. "What are you implying?"

Samuels' eyes met his, and for an instant Mulder felt disoriented, as if he'd been hit by a brilliant spotlight. It made no sense; he'd sat across from cold-blooded serial killers and kept his pulse rock steady, but now it was racing.

Scully didn't speak. She was sitting back in her chair, and seemed shaken.

Keep it together, Mulder told himself, and somehow, he recovered. "So according to you, Gina went from being just fine to breathing exhaust in just a few minutes, and no one can verify when you—the last person to see her alive—left her house? I'm not a writer, but that seems like a significant plot twist. Unless you've got an alibi."

Samuels' eyes had gone flat as silver coins. "As a matter of fact, I do have one," he said. "I went straight to teaching a class of forty students. They're not especially bright, but they will remember the test I gave." He turned back to Scully. "I did not kill poor Gina, if that is what your partner is implying. I hope that *you* believe me."

Scully didn't answer. It felt wrong. All of it.

Mulder broke the silence by jostling his teacup and spilling a hot wave of amber liquid over the tablecloth. "Oops," he said. "Sorry."

Samuels glared at him. Eyes storm gray, pupils like pools of night. Something suddenly yanked at Mulder, and he felt himself... unraveling. It was just a split second, because he managed to look away, but it shook him hard. Mulder's radar wasn't just pinging now, it was howling.

Samuel suddenly smiled. "Ah. *You're* the one she met that morning. She told me about you. No wonder she was upset."

Mulder burned to say, *She wasn't upset when I left her,* but he swallowed it. Samuels wanted engagement, and he couldn't give it to him.

"Come on, Scully, let's go." Scully didn't get up. He pulled her up anyway. "We'll be in touch," he said.

He hustled Scully down the hall to the front door. They passed the row of framed book covers. Samuels' name was larger on each, ramping up from first to last. A sign of his ever-growing acclaim.

And across from each book cover hung a matching photograph... each person pictured young and vibrant. *There's something here,* Mulder thought. He didn't have a logical reason, but the skin was cold on the back of his neck, and he wasn't like Scully. He didn't just follow the line of logic like a road map. He took shortcuts.

Samuels was horribly, fundamentally *wrong.*

"Mulder?" Scully's voice seemed as uncertain as her steps.

He got her out the front door. She took in a convulsive gasp, as if she'd been holding her breath, and grabbed for the porch railing. Her face was almost gray.

"Tea," she whispered. "Maybe the tea...."

Mulder doubted she'd been drugged, but he banged back through the door, straight to the kitchen. Too late. David Samuels was at the kitchen sink, rinsing out the teapot. The cups were already cleaned and sitting on a dishwasher rack.

Mulder grabbed the tablecloth he'd spilled his cup on, and whisked it off the table. "I'll have this dry cleaned," he said. "Sorry for the mess."

"Agent Mulder."

Mulder knew he shouldn't, but he turned and met Samuels' eyes. It was like being caught in a silvery, quivering web... and then Samuels blinked, and he was just a kindly older man again.

"Do be careful with that," Samuels said. "It was my grandmother's. Sentimental value."

Mulder had had enough of the dancing. "What did you do to Gina?"

"I didn't do anything," Samuels said, and gave him a gentle, chilling smile. "I'm just a writer, Agent Mulder. And the tea is just tea. There's no need to waste taxpayer money on tests."

"Thanks for the advice."

"Speaking of advice, do drop by any time. I'm a good listener. And you have such a *lot* on your conscience." Samuels' head tilted slightly to the side. "So many losses. Your partner's fear runs deep, but you… you might well be the most troubled man I've ever met."

The words might have held a tinge of concern, coming from anyone else. Not from Samuels. It was more… appreciation, as if he'd discovered a dusty, valuable vintage of wine in his cellar.

"Stay away from Scully," Mulder said.

Samuels smiled. "I never touched Gina. In fact, I plan to honor her memory in my next book. I will make her immortal. That's what a writer does."

For a brief, black second, Mulder thought about punching him. Then he turned away with the tea-stained tablecloth clutched in one hand.

Scully was still on the porch. She had some color back in her face. "Thank God," she said. "I was about to go in after you. What the hell happened in there, Mulder?"

"I don't know," he said. "But I think we need to go shopping."

Mulder bought all of Samuels' books that the bookstore had in stock. Once they were headed for the office, Scully said, "What are you looking for?"

"Oh, come on, Scully, who wouldn't want to read… *a darkly compelling, emotionally raw tale of love and loss?*" He started with the earliest of the books in hand, flipping pages as Scully drove. The dedication caught his eye. *To Betty-Anne Nilan. Gone before her time, but never forgotten.*

"You're a big reader, Scully. What do writers put in dedications?"

"Usually thanks to their parents, friends, agents, that kind of thing."

"Or to someone they've lost?"

"Sometimes."

The book he was looking at was Samuels' second one, and his first success. Mulder checked the dedication in the next one. *Jeannette Oroco. Gone before her time, but never forgotten.*

The next book was dedicated to George Terrell. The next, Farah Ismaili. The latest one, *Sea Birds,* was dedicated to Roy Hauser.

Gone before his time.

"Anything?"

"Maybe," he said. He wasn't ready to put it into words and expose it to the merciless glare of Scullyvision… despite what had just happened, she'd dismiss it outright.

He shut the book and said, "We need to find his other books."

An hour of research in the FBI archives turned up news articles and obituaries matching each of the dedications. The earliest, Betty-Anne Nilan, had died in a one-vehicle car-versus-tree, ruled accidental.

Jeannette Oroco's death was more obviously troubling: suicide by bridge. Her broken body had been fished out of the Potomac two days after bystanders failed to talk her down. Witnesses claimed her last words were, *It's all gone, and I can't get it back.*

George Terrell had slashed his wrists, after polishing off an entire bottle of expensive single malt. Farah Ismaili had taken an overdose of sleeping pills. And Roy Hauser, to whom *Sea Birds* had been dedicated, had put a shotgun in his mouth.

Now, Gina Wettig was dead, too.

"Scully." His voice sounded raw to his own ears, and she looked up quickly from her desk. "See if you can find the dedications of his other books."

"Why?"

"Humor me."

It took some phone calls to a friendly Washington librarian, and in a few minutes, four more pages creaked slowly out of the office fax machine. Scully retrieved them and brought them over. "What do you think you're going to find?"

"Three of those will be to someone gone before their time. One won't be."

Scully cocked her head as she read through the faxes. "How did you know that?"

"Logic, Scully. His first book failed. The other seven succeeded."

He read the dedications. The first book—the one that had bombed— was a more mundane entry, to his parents. Then it got interesting.

Mulder took the three other names and matched them against newspaper article databases available through the FBI mainframe. *Bingo*. Three more dead friends. One had been ruled accidental, but could have been suicide. The other two were clear. Mulder sent all the articles to the dot matrix, tore them off, and handed them to her without comment. Scully read with intense concentration, one after another, then put them down on the desk. Her blue eyes met his. "I'll admit it's suggestive."

"Suggestive? Come on, Scully. Seven books. Seven dead. Eight, counting Gina, and he already told me he'd be *honoring* her in the next book."

"Correlation, not causation," she said. "His inscriptions link them, yes. But how did he *cause* them to commit suicide? How do you explain the first book? There's no death linked to it."

"He found his muse, Scully."

"Dead people are his muses?"

"In a way. Tell me what you felt at the kitchen table."

She froze for a second. He didn't think she was even aware of putting space between them, or of folding her arms in body language that was clinically defensive. "I got dizzy, Mulder. Maybe it was the tea. Low blood sugar. Being up all night."

"What did you *feel*? Forget about logic. Forget about science. Give me your gut feeling."

He was afraid she'd retreat back into her safe, scientific shell, but his partner let out a slow breath and said, "It felt like he was inside my head. Looking for…"

"Looking for what?"

"Fear." For a second, something shivered in her eyes that made him go cold. "It felt like something was… pulling at me. Trying to tear a piece away."

"I felt that too. Only he was looking for something else in me."

"What?"

"Guilt."

That earned him a long, searching look. "Guilt about Gina?"

"I think that's what he does. We throw around the term *emotional vampire*, Scully, but this guy? He's the real thing. He sucks it right out of his victims like a spider."

She was shaking her head now. The crack he'd seen in her was already filled in, plastered and invisible. "How can you prove something like that?"

"To start with, the odds of Samuels knowing that many suicidal people are astronomical. And I'll bet you cash money that not one of them left a note. He wouldn't want them stealing his literary thunder."

"Most suicides don't leave notes," she said. "A lack of one is not dispositive. You need more than that."

Not *we*. *You*. Unconscious disassociation. He struggled with a black surge of anger. After the encounter with Samuels, Mulder was having trouble keeping all his emotions in check. Samuels had rattled all the boxes, and the monsters inside had listened.

All my fault. If I hadn't run into her, hadn't spoken to her, she'd still be alive. She'd wanted *his* child, five years ago, and he'd pulled away. *I did this to them. Somehow, meeting me made it happen.*

"I need Gina's file," he said to Scully.

"Mulder—"

"You want me to find proof? I need to look at everything."

She obviously didn't like it, but she got the folder on Gina Wettig's death. He reached out, but she kept hold, a silent tug of war. "Skip the autopsy," she said. "Promise me."

He didn't promise, and she finally let go.

Right up front, neatly attached on the left side, were the crime scene photos: Gina, her face and eyes flushed cherry red. Her left hand clutched the end of a garden house, and her wedding ring still glittered on her third finger.

He forced himself to take it all in, to memorize every detail of her agonizing death, and that of her defenseless child. *She was happy when she left me.* He still believed that. He *had* to believe that.

The autopsy came next, and he forced himself through the horrific photos and details of that, too. When he'd finished, he shut the folder and allowed it all to rush through his mind again. All their history. All their intimacy. All their sound and fury and sorrow.

Something David Samuels had said in the kitchen whispered back to him. *I will make her immortal.* As if words could replace Gina's joy, her vibrance.

There had to be proof out there.

He stood up and yanked his jacket from the back of his chair, hard enough to strain its stitches. The move was sudden enough that Scully, absorbed in typing up notes, jerked upright.

"Mulder? Where are you going?"

He could tell from her anxious tone that she thought the file had upset him. It had, but something else had upset him far more: the thought of letting Samuels get away with it.

"Out," he said. "I'll be back."

"You're not going to—"

"Confront Samuels? Like you said. No proof." He gave her a bleak little smile. "Relax. I just want some air. Want a coffee?"

He read her doubt, and the exact moment she decided to take him at his word. The relief almost hurt as Scully turned back to her report. "If you're picking it up, try to make it something better than break room coffee."

"I hear that new place is good. Mocha?"

"Maybe just cream and sugar."

"You disappoint me, Scully. Aim higher."

She smiled, seeming reassured by the easy banter, which was what he had intended. He didn't want her tagging along. His sedan was still in the garage, and he drove it across to Georgetown, checking maps along the way.

He never said he was going *straight* for coffee.

The waitress at Ernesto's remembered Samuels well. She also remembered Gina. "It's so sad," she said immediately. "I cried and cried when I saw it on the news. So shocking, you know? I mean, she was sitting *right over there*. Such a pretty lady! And the baby, why would she do that to her own baby? You'd have to be a monster, right? That's what they're saying on all the news shows. That she was a monster?"

Mulder let that go, with an effort. "So you did see her with Mr. Samuels at lunch yesterday?"

The waitress was still vigorously nodding. "She was really happy, you know? Glowing. I mean, you couldn't help but smile when you set your eyes on her. I just can't understand it."

"Did anything strange happen?"

"Strange?" The waitress' brown eyes looked off into the distance, and a frown crumpled her forehead. "At the end, I guess. She was laughing and happy and then she just… wasn't, like a light went out in her. I've never seen anybody do that before, change like that."

"Did Samuels touch her?"

"No. He just—he was staring at her, that's all…" She shifted a little, uncomfortable, and leaned forward. She dropped her tone to almost a whisper. "I thought maybe it was *his* baby, to be honest. That they were, you know. More than just friends."

Mulder had no doubt the baby was Roy's, but he understood what she was saying. He'd seen that avid hunger in Samuels' eyes. It hadn't been passion for Gina herself. It had been greed for what she had. What she felt.

The bastard had killed Gina as she'd sat here in Ernesto's, in full view of the waitress. It was the perfect crime. Even people who'd witnessed it hadn't *seen* it.

They would all blame the victim. *She was a monster. You'd have to be a monster, right?*

Despite what the waitress reported, the expedition hadn't borne any fruit that Scully could—or would—accept. It was still just his gut, and that wouldn't be enough.

He called and told her he was on the way with the coffee, just in case she started to doubt him. The line at the new place was ridiculous, so he picked up diner coffee.

"Scully?" he kept his tone deliberately light and calm as he carried the cups into their basement office. "Caffeine delivery. Come and get it…"

The lights were on. Scully's computer was still running, though the screensaver had kicked in… cartoon aliens in a cartoon UFO, bouncing from corner to corner of the monitor. He'd installed that himself.

She wasn't here.

He put the cup on her desk, and waited. It dawned on him a few seconds after he took his first sip that her coat was missing from the rack.

Mulder called security. Scully had logged out of the building just ten minutes ago. He tried her cell. She didn't pick up. "Scully," he said to the recording. "Call me back. Let me know where you are. Hey, your coffee's getting cold." He tried for humor, but there was a gnawing anxiety in the pit of his stomach.

He called her apartment. Answering machine. He left the same message, minus the humor.

Then he talked Tech Services into giving him the last number that had dialed Scully's office phone. The reverse directory gave him name and address of the caller.

David Samuels.

The churning turned to nausea.

It only took two rings before Samuels' pleasant baritone said, "Mulder?"

"I want to talk to Scully."

"She's indisposed."

Mulder took a slow, deliberate three-count. His hand hurt where it squeezed the life out of the telephone receiver. He hardly recognized his own voice; it came out low and grating. "I'm coming for you."

Samuels said. "You're always welcome."

GEORGETOWN, WASHINGTON, D.C.
14th OCTOBER, 1993, 4:17 p.m.

It was late afternoon, and the sun shone brightly in a cloudless sky. Birds sang in the spreading trees. A swinging wind chime clinked gently in the breeze at the corner of the porch.

It didn't look like the lair of a monster. *Maybe it isn't,* Mulder thought. *Maybe we bring all the monsters with us.*

He didn't bother to ring the bell, just walked down the hall of the dead and the books they'd fueled to success. David Samuels sat quietly, alone, at the kitchen table.

Mulder pulled his sidearm and pointed it directly at the older man's head.

"You'll find her in the bedroom," Samuels said.

Mulder's mind flashed red, and he visualized taking the shot. He visualized it so hard that he imagined the kick of the energy through his hand and up his arm, the deafening slap of the explosion on his ears. The Rorschach test of blood and brains on the wall behind Samuels' limp body.

It was so real he thought for a split second that he'd actually fired, and spent the next fraction of a second struggling not to. He took his finger off the trigger and lowered the weapon.

"Did you hurt her?"

Samuels' gray eyes were wide and wet as the sea. "Not much. I only took a little."

The weapon came up again, and Mulder's muscles jumped with tension. "A little *what*?"

"Fear," he said. "She had enough to spare."

Mulder moved down the hall. There were two rooms. One held an office: a desk, a computer, books on shelves. The other was a bedroom, and Scully was curled on her side on the mattress, fully dressed in her FBI suit and sensible heels. Her eyes were shut, and her skin pallid, but when Mulder put his fingers to her throat, he felt the steady beat of life. He sank down on the bed beside her with his hand resting against her skin.

Samuels had followed. Mulder sensed his presence in the door.

"I told you," the man said. "She's alive."

"How did you get her here?"

"I told her she'd better come get you before you did something unwise. She believed you'd come to kill me. What does that say about the two of you?"

When Mulder turned, he found that the man had already walked away. Mulder followed him back to the kitchen, where he found Samuels putting water in the electric kettle. More tea. So civilized.

"Are you going to shoot me, Agent Mulder?" Samuels nodded to the gun Mulder still carried as he put cups and saucers on the table. "Because I think we both know that would end your career."

"Maybe I don't care."

He looked up, and that was a mistake, because Samuels was looking at him, and those eyes, those gray eyes as pale as a spider's web, *had him*. He couldn't move. Couldn't look away.

The electric kettle hissed, and the hiss rose to a moan.

"Oh, I think you *do* care. Very much," Samuels murmured, and those pupils expanded. They grew black and huge and empty, and Mulder felt the unclean rummaging in his mind, *no,* his soul, all his locked and hidden boxes uncovered, all his guilt threatening to spill out in an uncontrollable, poisonous wave.

He would have pulled the trigger then, but somehow the gun was no longer in his hand.

The kettle was whistling.

"I think you care all too much. How you carry it all, all that guilt? Your sister. All those you've lost. All those you've failed. And Gina... she had an excess of joy, delightful but shallow. But you. So dark. So *rich.*"

The kettle was screaming.

Samuels reached out and touched Mulder's hand. The contact blew through him like grounded lightning, and if his guilt had been leaking out before, now it was a big-screen full immersion horror show, all his flaws and faults and griefs laid relentlessly bare, every lie, every wrong, every unforgiveable sin.

Samuels took in a wet, deep breath. If he spoke, Mulder couldn't hear it over the screaming of the teakettle, the screaming in his head. He felt everything he was draining from him like blood from an open wound.

He was going dark.

Going empty.

He remembered Jeannette Oroco's last words, before jumping to her death. *It's all gone, and I can't get it back.*

In that last, silent moment, Mulder wondered what emotion Samuels had tapped from Jeannette.

He wondered if it had been love.

There was movement in the corner of his vision. A smear of motion, a slender hand gripping a teapot, a glittering arc of steaming liquid flying through the air, and in the next second Samuels screamed, a thin and inhuman sound, and clawed at his eyes.

Mulder fell back in his chair. The tidal pull was gone.

Samuels' face was mottled red and steaming, and liquid dripped from the point of his chin, as if it the flesh was melting. His eyes were squeezed closed and covered by shaking hands.

It took a frozen second for Mulder to recognize the electric kettle still clutched in a hand in the corner of his vision, and to put it all together.

Scully had thrown hot water in Samuels' eyes.

She dropped the pot with a crash to the floor and lunged at Samuels. She flattened him on his stomach and pinned him there as she pressed her sidearm to the back of the old man's head.

He was crying. Whimpering.

"Scully," Mulder said. His voice came from a great distance. "*Scully.*"

She looked up. Her blue eyes were dazed, her pupils pinpoints, and she looked… she looked feral. He remembered Samuels saying, *I only took a little.*

He swallowed hard. "Don't. Don't kill him, Scully."

She fought it, and for a long moment he thought he'd lost… and then she holstered her gun and went for handcuffs instead.

She wasn't gentle about it. She left Samuels writhing and whimpering on the floor, and backed off to lean against the chair where Mulder still sat. She panted, and he could smell the anger on her.

He grabbed her hand, and held on, held on as an anchor against the empty space and silence inside.

"It's okay. We're okay. Right?" Scully whispered.

Police sirens howled.

He saw the flutter of Gina's hair in the wind, the luminous curve of her smile, but it was remote now. A fading memory.

We're okay.

He didn't think he was, but he knew he would be.

His grief was nothing but a blank, empty ache, and the idea that he would be okay...

That was the worst part.

THE END

the
truth
is out
there

XXX

By Glenn Greenberg

SAN FERNANDO VALLEY, CALIFORNIA
8th MARCH, 1999, 11:35 a.m.

She sat on the plush sofa, watching him as he knelt by the side of the glass-top coffee table in front of her. He had already poured two glasses of red wine, and was now lighting the two long white candles he had placed on either side of the table, secured in their ornate silver holders. He wore a black sport coat, gray slacks, a collared white shirt, and a silk burgundy tie. His thick dark brown hair was perfectly coiffed. She'd never seen him look so dashing.

Flashing that warm, inviting smile of his, he reached into the inner pocket of his jacket and pulled out a shiny black box. He lifted the lid to reveal a beautiful pearl necklace inside. She looked deeply into his eyes, hoping that she was conveying the pure, unadulterated love and longing that a moment like this would inspire. He removed the necklace from the case, walked behind her, put it around her neck, and fastened it. She closed her eyes, to let the moment wash over her. She could feel him coming closer, his warm breath on her neck. She turned around on the sofa to meet him. Their lips touched, then began a tender dance that grew steadily in intensity, their tongues finding one another and intertwining over and over again. Eyes still closed, she could feel his hand moving from her shoulder to the zipper on the front of her skimpy French maid outfit. His fingers arrived at the tab of the zipper and began to pull it down. She reached out to unfasten the buckle of the belt around his waist.

"Cut!" a commanding male voice called out from the other side of the room. "Okay, let's change angles."

The moment was over. But she knew that once she heard the word "Action," it would pick up again, and she would have to commit herself far more fully— far more intimately.

Just another day on the job for Ashley Ford, adult-film superstar.

She watched as her director Bob Berkley began to guide his crew in adjusting the cameras and lights to continue filming the big scene for his latest erotic extravaganza.

Ashley began to walk off the living room set, heading to her small dressing room to touch up her hair and makeup, when she was approached by her co-star, Tim Gordon—not his real name, just as Ashley Ford wasn't hers. His smile was gone. He looked dead serious.

"You all right?" he asked in a soft voice, to avoid being overheard by the various crew members passing back and forth.

"What do you mean?"

"The stuff we just shot—you were totally flat," he told her. "Our characters are supposed to be madly in love, but you didn't seem to be into it at all. How am I supposed to play against that? You're destroying the realism of the scene."

"I'm fine," she insisted coldly.

"Well, then put some *life* into it, will you? We're shooting the *main* stuff next." He stormed off, heading back to the living room set, leaving her scowling.

Deluded jerk, she thought. *"The realism of the scene." What does he think, we're real actors making a real movie?*

She felt tempted to storm off herself, to refuse to continue working with this ridiculous diva. But the director and producers and the crew were counting on her.

And besides, she needed the money.

Moments later, she was back on the set, standing before the cameras, stripping down to her bra and panties as Tim Gordon began to loosen his tie. She was still pissed off at him—he was the *last* person she wanted to be intimate with at that moment—but it was her job. She didn't have to enjoy it, but she would go through with it.

Suddenly, Gordon began to sway, as if he couldn't maintain his balance.

"Are you all right?" Ashley asked him, stepping closer, afraid she'd have to hold up her much taller co-star to prevent him from collapsing to the floor.

"What's the matter?" Berkley called out from his director's chair.

Gordon couldn't answer, at least not verbally. He started to make gurgling noises. Ashley couldn't help but gasp when she saw streams of blood start to flow from his nose, his ears, his mouth, and even his eyes. He looked bewildered, dismayed, and terrified, all at once. Whatever resentment Ashley may have felt toward him minutes earlier was replaced by the impulse to do something, *anything*, to help him.

But she had no idea what to do. And even if she did, there was no time to do it—his bloody eyes bulging, Gordon suddenly clutched the sides of his head, and then there was a single, loud, wet *pop*. And then his head simply wasn't there anymore. It had exploded in a burst of blood, flesh, bone, and brain matter. Ashley watched as the rest of Tim Gordon's body tumbled to the floor in a lifeless heap.

Berkley slowly came up beside her. They stood together, director and star, looking at the mess in front of them.

"Not again," they said in unison.

⎯⎯*X*⎯⎯

FBI HEADQUARTERS
WASHINGTON, D.C.
10th MARCH, 1999, 8:03 a.m.

Special Agent Fox Mulder sat behind his desk, fully immersed in the research laid out in front of him. Suddenly, from out of nowhere, a voice addressed him.

"That must be some really interesting reading," it said. Startled, Mulder looked up to see that his partner Dana Scully had arrived at the office they shared—she had already taken off her coat and settled in at her own desk without him even noticing.

"What is it?" Scully asked. "*The Making of Debbie Does Dallas?*"

"Actually, you're not that far off the mark," Mulder replied as he handed her a file. She began to leaf through it.

"Last month in Los Angeles," he began, "a male adult-film star named Jon Harper—professional name Jon Longfellow—died mysteriously on the set of the film he was working on. Witnesses reported seeing blood streaming from his eyes, ears, nose, and mouth shortly before his head… burst."

"Burst?" Scully asked skeptically.

For emphasis, Mulder put his fists together in front of him and then quickly moved them apart while spreading his fingers out wide to simulate an explosion and making the sound "*Boooosh*."

"The bleeding could have been the result of a recent head trauma," Scully replied. "Or he may have had a blood-clotting disorder—some form of severe hemophilia or aplastic anemia. He could have had a myelodysplastic syndrome, or preleukemia. Even a severe enough nosebleed can cause blood to dribble out of the eyes and mouth." Then she frowned. "The exploding head part is a bit harder to explain," she admitted.

Mulder pressed on. "The autopsy and his medical records showed no history of any head trauma. Given his line of work, he was getting blood tests regularly. No diseases or drugs or any other type of foreign substances in his system. By all accounts, he was a physical-fitness nut and very much focused on maintaining his health."

He let that hang in the air for a moment, then continued. "Following Harper's—or Longfellow's—death, the entire adult-film industry shut down temporarily, until health officials could determine that it wasn't related to some sort of contagion."

"No wonder you've seemed so down lately," Scully replied, barely keeping a straight face.

Mulder brushed it off. "The industry got the all-clear to resume production earlier this week," he told her. "Everything seemed to go back to normal… until two days ago, when another male performer, Timothy Gordon Marshall—professional name Tim Gordon—died the *exact same way*. And interestingly enough, at the time of his death, Gordon was working with the same director, the same female co-star, and many of the same crewmembers that Longfellow had been working with when *he* died. All of those people are currently fine. And here's the kicker: Tim Gordon had no involvement whatsoever with the earlier film—no exposure to Longfellow."

"So what are you thinking, Mulder?" she asked. "That these deaths, whatever caused them, were by design?"

"I'm thinking, Scully, that this is right up our alley—especially since the fine folks upstairs saw fit to put us back on the X-Files after Jeffrey Spender's run. And I'm thinking we should try to get some actual work done before they change their minds again." He turned to his computer and started typing on the keyboard. The website of National Airlines came up on his screen. "I'll get us on the next available flight to L.A."

"Guess I'll go home and pack," Scully replied. "Call me with the flight information."

She got up out of her chair, grabbed her coat, and headed for the door. Then she turned back to face her partner again. "Oh, Mulder—who's the female co-star who was working with both men?"

Mulder looked directly at her. "Ashley Ford. Why?"

A hint of a smirk crossed Scully's lips. "That's what I thought," she replied. "More up your alley than mine."

"What do you mean?" he asked flatly.

"I've been an FBI agent—and your partner—for years now, Mulder. If I didn't know by now who your favorite porn actress is, I'd be pretty lousy at both." She flashed a winning smile at him and walked out of the office.

"Sheer coincidence," Mulder murmured as he turned back to his computer.

SAN FERNANDO VALLEY, CALIFORNIA
11th MARCH, 1999, 10:25 a.m.

Mulder and Scully got out of their rented car and approached the two-story, nondescript warehouse in a fairly isolated section of Chatsworth. Walking through the main entrance, they found the place quiet and unoccupied, with the sole exception of a maintenance worker with a screwdriver. He was kneeling beside a wall in the small lobby area, screwing on the cover of an electrical outlet. The man was heavy-set, with a round, doughy face and curly brown hair. He glanced up briefly at the two FBI agents, clearly curious about their sudden arrival.

"Excuse me," Mulder said, flashing his badge. "This is where they were filming the adult movie, right?"

The worker nodded. "One of the big companies, X-Plicit, rents the place," he replied. "Main studio's down there," he added, cocking his head toward a large door at the end of the main corridor. The worker then turned his attention back to the electrical outlet.

The agents headed down the corridor to the door, which was blocked by yellow barricade tape with the words "Police Line—Do Not Cross" emblazoned on it. Mulder stepped past the tape and opened the door. He and Scully entered a vast chamber filled with lighting and sound equipment, cables, and, in the center of it all, a living room set that included a sofa, a fireplace, and a glass-top coffee table with partially melted candles and two half-empty glasses of wine. On the floor near the sofa, there was a discarded French maid outfit. It was clear what kind of scene was being shot at the time of Tim Gordon's death.

Mulder gazed around the entirety of the room. "If these walls could talk," he commented.

Scully stepped over to the set to examine it more closely and replied, "They'd probably say, 'What were they filming in here, a porno movie or a horror movie?'"

There was dried blood splattered everywhere, along with dark clumps of hair, pieces of bone, and shriveled bits of brain. "I'll get some samples," she told Mulder as she reached into her shoulder bag, pulled out a pair of rubber gloves, long tweezers, and several clear plastic storage bags. "Of course I'll want to examine the body itself."

"We'll head over to the coroner's office after this," Mulder replied. He began to slowly walk around the set, studying its details. He tried to envision where everyone was, what everyone was doing, at the moment when Tim Gordon's life suddenly ended. The shock and dismay they must have felt when they saw his head burst, the terror and revulsion when they realized there were pieces of him on their own bodies.

"Who are you?" a male voice suddenly demanded from behind him. Mulder turned to see a tall, out-of-shape, middle-aged man with dark hair that was graying at the temples. He was accompanied by a shorter woman, about five foot three, with long brown hair and large soulful eyes shielded behind a pair of black horn-rimmed glasses. The man was wearing an expensive-looking purple dress shirt with gray slacks and black loafers. The woman was wearing a bulky sweatshirt, loose-fitting jeans, and sneakers. She seemed uncomfortable, as if she wished she could be anywhere else.

Mulder flashed his badge again as Scully came up beside him. "Special Agent Mulder, FBI. This is my partner, Special Agent Scully. We're looking into the death that occurred here this week. And you are…?"

"Bob Berkley," the man replied. "I run the company that was filming here when it happened."

"X-Plicit Entertainment Group," Mulder said, nodding. "Were you on set at the time, Mr. Berkley?"

The older man's face froze up momentarily, until he looked away and replied with obvious reluctance, "I was directing the scene."

Now Scully spoke up. "You were also directing when Jon Harper died, weren't you, Mr. Berkley?" Mulder couldn't help but be amused by the fact that Scully declined to refer to Harper by his stage name.

Berkley looked back at the two agents with a spark of anger and defensiveness in his eyes, though he remained calm. "Yes, I was," he answered, his voice betraying no emotion.

"Do you remember anything—*anything*—unusual that was happening on set at the time of each death?" Scully asked. "Anything they have in common?"

Berkley sighed deeply. The expression on his face turned to anguish and frustration. "No," he answered. "Both times, there was nothing out of the ordinary. Both times, it just came out of *nowhere*." He took a long pause, then began again, his voice quavering. "When it happened to Jon, I'd never seen anything like it in my life… and in a million years, I never thought I'd have to see it again. These were guys I'd worked with many times. Good guys. They didn't deserve this." He cleared his throat and wiped his eyes.

Mulder figured this man was either genuinely distraught, or he was a far better actor than any of the performers who starred in his movies. Instinct and training led Mulder to lean toward the former. "Why are you here now?" he asked.

"Karen," Berkley began, indicating the bespectacled woman beside him, "forgot her purse in the dressing room when we evacuated the set after… what happened to Tim. She didn't want to come back here alone to get it. I told her I'd meet her here."

Mulder glanced at the woman, Karen, and finally took a good look at her. There was something familiar about her, though he was certain they had never met before. She was not wearing any makeup, her hair was unkempt, and her clothes gave no hint of her figure. But she was still attractive, as far as Mulder was concerned. She was just downplaying it at the moment, for understandable reasons.

Then it clicked. He imagined her with generous amounts of eyeliner, mascara, and lipstick, with her hair perfectly blown out and sprayed, and without the glasses, and it was now very obvious who she was.

"Ashley Ford," Mulder said to her. She winced, ever so slightly, presumably disappointed that she had been recognized.

"That's my professional name, yes," she replied with a hint of defiance in her voice, as if bracing herself to be judged for her chosen career. Mulder could tell he had struck a nerve, though he had not intended to do so. He struggled to reconcile the fact that the woman standing before him was the same one he had seen many times before, though in a very different context. Up close, in person, she was nothing like the vivacious, fun-loving, free-spirited dream girl she had always appeared to be on screen. In real life, she was… just another human being. And at the moment, a very vulnerable one.

"All right," Mulder began. "Karen, Ms.…."

She hesitated, clearly reluctant to reveal her real name to a stranger. Finally, she relented and said, "Porter."

Suddenly a cell phone rang. Berkley took his phone out of the right pocket of his pants and checked to see who was calling him. He looked concerned as he took the call, turned away from everyone, and walked across the room. Berkley then pulled a small black notebook and a pen out of his left pocket and wrote in the book extensively as he conversed with his caller.

Mulder began again. "Ms. Porter, how well did you know your two co-stars?"

"I worked with each of them a bunch of times," she replied. "Tim and I, we got into the business around the same time. Jon was already established. I didn't really socialize with them outside of work, though."

Berkley returned, shoving the phone back into his pocket. "Sorry," he said. "That was my office. There's another industry-wide shutdown because of what happened to Tim. My partners are waiting for me there now, to discuss what we're going to do to minimize the financial damage to our company. If you don't have any more questions for me, I'd really like to get back."

"I think we're good for now," Mulder said. "We'd like to keep talking to Ms. Porter."

Berkley pulled out his wallet, took out a business card, and handed it to Mulder. "I want to know what happened just as much as you do," he told the agents firmly. "Any way I can help, just contact me." He gave Ashley Ford, a.k.a. Karen Porter, a quick peck on the cheek, said to her gently, "Hang in there, babe," and left with a determined stride.

Karen glanced around the blood-spattered set and shuddered. "Look," she began, "I just came for my purse. If we have to continue this, can we at least do it outside? Being in here is… very upsetting."

Mulder glanced over at Scully, who shrugged. "Sure," he replied.

Moments later, they were in a small storage room off the main corridor that had been converted into a dressing room. Mulder and Scully stood and watched as Karen, sitting in a chair near the makeup table and a large mirror, stared down at the floor, frowning as she worked to recall the details stored in her mind.

"Like Bob said, it happened pretty much the same each time," she told them. "We started to film the… " Karen paused briefly as her eyes fixated momentarily on the gold cross that Scully was wearing around her neck. Karen then continued. "To film the uh, *main action*, if you know what I mean."

"I think we do," Scully replied. Mulder had little doubt that his partner appreciated the other woman's effort to keep her explanation as PG-rated as possible.

Karen picked up again, turning to Mulder. "And each time, we didn't get very far into the scene before…" She sniffled and wiped away a tear that rolled down her right cheek. "That's all I can tell you."

Mulder nodded sympathetically. "Thank you, Ms. Porter. If we have any more questions, we'll be in touch." Karen rose from her chair and headed for the door to leave.

"Ms. Porter," Mulder called out. She turned, warily, to face him. He walked over to a small table and picked up a black and red leather purse that was sitting on top of it. Mulder held it out to her and grinned. "I left mine in the car," he said, "so this must be yours."

Karen giggled, her face red with embarrassment, as she accepted the purse—the whole reason she had come back to the warehouse in the first place. "That's the first laugh I've had in days," she told him. She took his hand and squeezed it gently. "Thank you, Agent Mulder." Then Karen turned and left, her mood much brighter than it had been just moments before.

A trace of Mulder's grin lingered on his face as Scully headed for the door. She cast a sidelong glance at him as she passed him by and murmured dryly, "You're never going to wash that hand again, are you?"

Mulder brought the hand that Karen Porter had squeezed to his nose. He could smell the lingering scent of whatever fragrance she had been wearing. It was quite pleasant.

"Maybe not," he replied with a smirk as he followed Scully out of the room.

LOS ANGELES COUNTY DEPARTMENT OF CORONER
11th MARCH, 1999, 6:45 p.m.

Scully sighed as she lifted her head from the microscope at her temporary work station. Mulder was on the other side of the laboratory examining X-rays of what was left of Timothy Gordon Marshall's head. He seemed to sense that his partner was ready to deliver her report, and looked over at her.

"I have to concur with the coroner's initial findings," she told him. "Marshall, like Jon Harper, had no blood disorders. There are traces of marijuana in his system, but no other drugs, prescription or illegal. Not even Viagra."

At that, Mulder nodded, impressed. "In this business," he noted, "a hard man is good to find."

Scully rolled her eyes and continued. "Based on what's left of his head—which isn't much—along with the bloodstain pattern on the set, and the eyewitness accounts, it's clear the explosion occurred from the inside. But even allowing for the possibility that some sort of miniature bomb was somehow planted in his head without him knowing it, there are no traces of any metals or wiring or chemicals—or burn marks—that would indicate the presence of such an explosive."

Mulder thought for a moment. "You've heard of spontaneous human combustion," he said.

"Mostly from you," she replied. "But Mulder, spontaneous human combustion—if it even exists—is when someone suddenly burns up without an apparent source of ignition."

Mulder nodded. "Maybe this is some sort of variation—spontaneous *detonation*." A wave of enthusiasm rushed through him. "Scully, we could be dealing with a totally new phenomenon, something unprecedented."

She looked at him dubiously. "Why now?" she asked. "Why here? Why the porn industry?"

He shrugged his shoulders. "I didn't say I had all the answers, I'm just putting forth a theory." He then felt a grumbling in his stomach and looked at his watch. It was nearly 7 p.m., and they hadn't eaten since around noon. "And now I'm experiencing spontaneous starvation. How about we take a dinner break?"

"You go," Scully told him. "I want to keep at it for a while, see if there's anything I missed. No offense, but somehow I prefer the notion of a micro-bomb."

Mulder ended up at a family restaurant that was just a ten-minute drive from the coroner's office. He couldn't resist the place, given its name: Astro. It was charmingly old-fashioned, with a distinct retro style. Mulder half-expected to pick up a newspaper and read about the latest goings-on in the Kennedy administration. Seated at the counter, he scanned the menu.

"Agent Mulder?" he heard from behind him. He swiveled around in his chair and saw Ashley Ford—Karen Porter—at a nearby booth, looking at him curiously. And she wasn't alone. A little girl with darkish blonde hair was sitting next to her. Mulder smiled sheepishly, got off the chair, and walked over to the table.

"I'm not following you around, I swear," he assured her.

"I guess even FBI agents have to eat sometime," Karen replied. There was now an easiness, a look of comfort, in her eyes. If she was at all troubled by his presence, she didn't show it.

"The coroner's office is nearby, my partner and I have been there since this morning," Mulder explained. He then looked over at the little girl, who was scrutinizing him closely.

"Who are you?" she asked.

"This is Agent Mulder," Karen replied. "He's like a special policeman. He works for the government."

"You catch bad guys?" the little girl asked.

Mulder grinned at her. "As many as I can."

She nodded and smiled back. "That's good."

"This is my daughter Rachel," Karen told him. Mulder wasn't surprised—the kid looked like a miniature version of her.

"Very nice to meet you, Rachel. How old are you?"

"Seven," the girl answered enthusiastically. "Do you want to have dinner with us?"

"Rachel!" Karen blurted out with an embarrassed laugh, her cheeks turning beet red.

Mulder chuckled and pointed his thumb back toward the counter. "I, uh, actually have a spot over there. But thank you for the invitation, Rachel." His eyes shifted to Karen. "I don't want to invade your privacy. Enjoy your meal."

But as he turned away, Karen said, "You're welcome to join us." He looked back, uncertain. "Really," she added. Next to her, Rachel was nodding, looking very hopeful. Mulder grinned again and sat down at the booth.

Mulder ordered a cheeseburger and fries, Karen a chef's salad, and Rachel a dish of spaghetti with meat sauce. As they ate, Mulder turned to the little girl.

"Knock knock," he said to her.

"Who's there?" she replied.

"Boo."

"Boo who?"

"Awwww, Rachel, don't cry!"

She laughed and tried to respond in kind, but it was clear she didn't *quite* grasp the concept of the knock-knock joke. When Mulder asked, "Who's there?" she said, "Orange." When he replied "Orange who?" Rachel answered, "Orange balloony-head!"

Mulder had to admit, that was original, and he smiled at her warmly. Karen was clearly enjoying watching the exchange.

Eventually Rachel pulled out a small electronic game that monopolized her attention, which allowed Mulder and Karen to converse uninter-rupted—albeit with carefully chosen words. No telling what the child might pick up on.

"I really appreciate you not being judgmental about my job—at least not to my face," she told him. "That hasn't really been the case the other times I've had to deal with folks in law enforcement."

Mulder shrugged. "None of my business." Besides, he thought, who was *he* to judge? Especially given the stash in his apartment—much of which featured her.

"I admit, I have mixed feelings about it," she continued. "To be completely honest—and this is going to make me seem so evil—when Jon and Tim died, each time, a small part of me actually felt… *relief*. Because it meant I wouldn't have to do the scene. Isn't that terrible?"

"You can't control how you feel," Mulder replied. "If you could, you wouldn't be human."

"I'm not ashamed of what I do for a living," she said. "But I don't brag about it either. I do my best not to be recognized on the street, at the super-market, at Rachel's school. The bottom line is, it's good money, I'm a top earner, and I need to support myself and my child. It's just the two of us."

"What do you intend to do when you're no longer a top earner?" he asked. "It doesn't last forever."

"I don't know," she admitted. "Other than be the best mother I can possibly be." She kissed Rachel on the forehead. The little girl's attention never shifted from her game.

Finally, dinner was finished, the check was paid, and the three of them stepped out of the restaurant and into the night air.

"Thank you for joining us, Agent Mulder," Karen said with a smile. "This was nice."

"My pleasure," he told her—and it was true. He genuinely liked this young woman, and appreciated getting to know her a bit as a real person. Mulder then looked over at Rachel. "You be good, Orange Balloony-head." She laughed and waved goodbye.

"I hope you find out what happened," Karen added as she turned and walked away with Rachel in tow. Mulder watched as they kept on walking down the street away from the Astro. He wondered why they weren't parked in the lot behind the restaurant, which had plenty of empty spaces.

"Where are you parked?" he called after them.

"My car's in for repairs," Karen shouted back. "But it's okay, we live within walking distance. Ten, fifteen minutes at most."

"Don't be silly," he insisted. "I'll give you a lift."

"This is us," Karen said from the passenger seat. Mulder parked in front of a small one-story house on a quiet street in what appeared to be a peaceful middle-class neighborhood. As he walked mother and daughter toward the front door, he noticed a man standing farther down the night-shrouded sidewalk, just beyond a blanket of light emanating from a nearby street lamp. The man, wearing a hard hat and work clothes bearing the insignia of the Los Angeles Department of Water and Power, glanced over at the trio and then turned away. Mulder also took note of a plain black van parked across the street from Karen's house. His instincts told him this was worth looking into. He broke off from Karen and Rachel and approached the man.

"Hi," he said, breaking out his friendliest smile. "Working late all by yourself, huh? What's going on?"

"Just checking the area," the man murmured, still looking away from Mulder. "Power outage nearby." He took a couple of steps back from the FBI agent.

"That's funny," Mulder replied. "I was just driving around in this area and I didn't see any signs of an outage—every streetlamp was lit." The man mumbled an unintelligible response and moved toward the edge of the sidewalk. Mulder pulled out his FBI badge with one hand and subtly reached for the pistol in his holster with the other.

"FBI," he announced. "Please show me your identification."

The man swiftly yanked off his hard hat and threw it right into Mulder's nose. Mulder struggled to blink away the countless spots now flickering before his eyes. Meanwhile, the other man bolted, heading straight for the van across the street. Trying to ignore the sharp pain in his nose, Mulder took off after him. The man got to the van, swung open the door on the driver's side, and began to climb in. But Mulder caught up to him, grabbed him by the collar of his shirt, yanked him out onto the street, and slugged him in the jaw. The man collapsed to his knees in front of the FBI agent.

"That's for the Marcia Brady moment," Mulder told the man as he handcuffed him.

Karen came running up, alone. "Where's Rachel?" Mulder asked.

"In the house. What's going on?"

"That's what I intend to find out." Mulder grabbed the man and held him up. The light from the nearby street lamp revealed his round, doughy face and curly brown hair. Mulder studied him for a second-and-a-half before recognition kicked in.

"He looks kind of familiar," Karen said.

"He should," Mulder replied. "He's the maintenance worker from the warehouse."

Scully was wrapping up at the coroner's lab—having made no further progress in her investigation—when the call came in from Mulder. Since he had the car, she called a cab to get her over to LAPD headquarters as quickly as possible so she could rejoin her partner. By the time she arrived, Mulder had already begun to question the suspect he had captured. Scully stepped into the dimly lit interrogation room to see Mulder looming over the burly man, who sat at a wooden table slumped in a chair, hands folded on his lap and looking defeated.

"Scully, this is Carl Jones," Mulder began. "Originally from Jupiter, Florida. Seems he's had his eye on Karen Porter—and X-Plicit Entertainment—for a while now."

Mulder glanced over at the sheet of information he had obtained about the man. "Took a maintenance job at the warehouse a couple of months ago—just so you could get close to them, right, Carl?" Jones looked down at his hands, remaining silent.

Mulder continued. "But you were just pretending to be a worker for the Department of Water and Power. Was that so you could spy on Ms. Porter at her home—or was it really just about getting to dress up in the fancy uniform?"

Jones sat up straighter. "I'm a crusader," he declared, looking at Mulder directly.

"For what?" Mulder replied. "Stalkers United?"

"For morality," Jones said firmly. "An end to the disgusting filth that is dragging our society down into the bowels of Hell."

"If you're referring to country music," Mulder said, "I'm with you 100 percent."

Scully barely managed to hold back a chuckle. Jones, however, was having none of it.

"Pornography goes against the will of God," he proclaimed. "It's an addictive scourge that promotes the indulgence of lust and sexual irresponsibility, and destroys healthy, stable, monogamous relationships. It needs to be eradicated!"

Scully spoke up. "And how do you intend to do that?"

"It's already happening," Jones told her. "After this latest production shutdown, how many more do you think there'll be before the authorities finally decide to ban that evil industry for good?"

"You're saying you were directly responsible for the deaths of those two men?" she asked.

"They were necessary sacrifices," Jones stated with no emotion. "Two of the top male stars in the business, both of them paired with the top female star. There would be no way for the slime bags who run the industry to sweep that under the carpet."

"And Karen Porter?" Mulder interjected. "Was she your next intended victim?"

Jones looked horrified at the thought. "Absolutely not," he insisted. "I care about her. I want to save her from that world."

"Yeah, she's bound to see you as her knight in shining armor," Mulder responded coldly.

"What did you do to those two men?" Scully demanded.

Jones took a deep breath. "I tainted their water. With a virus. Completely untraceable."

Scully and Mulder exchanged a glance. Untraceable? That would certainly gibe with their findings. "What is this virus?" she pressed. "Where did you get it?"

"I met someone," he answered. "He works for the government. Has access to stuff at the highest levels. He agrees with what I'm trying to accomplish, and sold it to me." Jones paused for a long moment, then added, "The virus. It's… extraterrestrial in origin."

Scully saw Mulder's eyes widen briefly, and he moved in closer to Jones. "Who sold it to you?" he asked forcefully. Jones did not answer.

"Come on, Carl," Mulder pressed. "Who sold you the virus?" Jones remained tight-lipped.

Scully saw Mulder shoot her a quick glance. He winked at her.

"Never mind," he then told Jones. "I already know. There's only one person it could have been: George E. Hale. It was him, right, Carl?" Jones did not move or utter a sound.

"I *knew* it," Mulder continued, looking over at Scully. "We have to take him down. It's going to be awful for his wife, and those two little kids of theirs, but this… this is a crime of the highest order."

"He'll get the death penalty for sure," Scully responded gravely.

Mulder headed for the door. "Come on, Scully, let's go get him." She moved to follow him.

"Wait," Jones blurted out. Mulder and Scully stopped and turned toward him. "I'm a good person," he insisted. "A righteous person. I can't let an innocent man be punished, face the death penalty…"

Mulder leaned in close to Carl Jones and glared into his eyes. "Then tell us who it is, Carl… or George E. Hale goes to the electric chair. Tell us, damn it!"

Totally unaware that "George E. Hale" was a name Mulder used occasionally as an alias, Jones told them.

Karen had just put Rachel to bed—though "to bed" and "to sleep" were two very different things. It was nearly 10 p.m., but it was also not unheard of for the little girl to still be awake at midnight. But on this night, Karen herself intended to be in a deep slumber well before that.

It had been one hell of a day—a week—a month. But the impromptu dinner with Agent Mulder was a genuine bright spot amid all the gloom. And their conversation had gotten Karen thinking about her life and her future like never before.

She was in her living room, curled up on the couch, drinking a glass of red wine. The Judy Garland version of *A Star Is Born*, which she'd already seen more times than she could count, was playing on the TV. She was determined to finish her drink and then slip into bed and shut down till morning. At which point her focus would be solely on Rachel—getting her ready for school, preparing her lunch, putting her on the school bus. Thinking about her daughter brought a smile to Karen's lips, which she maintained as she took another sip of wine.

Suddenly the phone rang. She looked at the number on the caller ID screen. It was Bob Berkley's direct line, from his office at X-Plicit. Karen, somewhat hesitant, picked up the phone and said, "Hello."

"How are you holding up, sweetheart?" Berkley's voice asked. It sounded sincere, but tinged with an urgency that made Karen think he was not calling solely out of concern for her.

"Okay, under the circumstances." She filled him in on the stalker, and how Agent Mulder had been on hand to apprehend him.

"What do you know, a useful fed," he replied with a short chuckle. Then, as Karen anticipated, Berkley moved on to the *real* reason for his call. "Listen, Kary, I really need your help. No one knows how long this latest shutdown is going to last. If they don't figure out what's causing these deaths, and how to stop it, we may be out of action for quite a while… maybe long enough to put X-Plicit out of business."

"What are you saying, Bob?" She wondered what he thought she could do to stop an industry-wide production shutdown.

"The partners and I have been talking," he told her. "We've got a plan to keep putting out fresh product, which'll keep the money coming in. We'll shoot a bunch of new scenes, in another location. Real quietly, involving as few people as possible. People we can really trust. We'll backdate the production schedules, so it'll look like we already had all these scenes done before the shutdown."

Karen was silent, but she became more and more uncomfortable as Berkley continued.

"All we need is a few weeks," he said, "and we can film enough stuff so that we can keep uploading a new scene onto our paysite twice a month—keep the audience coming back—for a good long while. And then we can take all the scenes and sell them on compilation discs later on, for additional revenue."

Karen now understood where Berkley was going.

"We're gonna need our top star," he continued. "Ashley Ford is the main attraction in this industry right now, and a steady stream of new scenes featuring her will guarantee we hold on to our customers. I know I can count on you, babe."

Karen bit her lower lip, feeling a surge of tension burning within the base of her neck. She closed her eyes and took a deep breath. Finally, she found her voice.

"Bob… I've decided I want to get out. Retire." Suddenly, it was as if a heavy weight had been lifted from her shoulders.

Now it was Berkley's turn to be silent. After a long moment, he spoke again, sounding like a man trying desperately to maintain his composure.

"I hear you, sweetheart," he said. "This crisis has got us all freaked out. I understand why you would see this as the right time to walk away. But I *really* need you right now. And I know you wouldn't want the company to go under—we've been very good for each other, X-Plicit and Ashley Ford."

"I'm sorry, Bob. I just can't do it anymore." Another long pause of silence. Karen was now anxious to get off the phone.

"I get what you're saying, Kary," he said. "How about this—we make this your last hurrah. Just do this next batch of scenes, and then you're out. We'll market it as your big farewell."

Karen vacillated between simply hanging up to make a harsh-but-clean break and letting herself be swayed by Berkley. She desperately wanted to avoid doing either.

"I need time to think about it," she said.

"We don't have a lot of time, kiddo," he replied. "We've got to get started right away, make all the arrangements. We have to get everyone on board— the crew, the other performers—anyone you want to work with, sweetheart."

Karen scowled. He wasn't going to let up. "I'll talk to you tomorrow," she said flatly.

"I know you won't let me down, babe," Berkley responded. With that, Karen hung up the phone.

She sat on the couch, tightly hugging a throw pillow, filled with dread and hopelessness.

Then, suddenly, Karen felt a presence in the room. She turned to see Rachel standing beside the couch, in her pink-and-white Disney Princesses nightgown, with a troubled expression on her face. It looked like it was going to be another late night for the little girl. But this time, Karen didn't mind. She tossed the pillow to the side and took Rachel into her arms, holding her close. Rachel hugged her, patted her on the back, as if to reassure her mother that everything was going to be all right. It was then that Karen's tears started to flow freely.

DOWNTOWN LOS ANGELES, CALIFORNIA
12th MARCH, 1999, 12:10 a.m.

A dark-green, beat-up Honda Accord arrived at a mostly empty parking garage on South Spring Street, not far from LAPD headquarters. The car pulled into a well-lit spot on the third floor, and the door on the driver's side opened. A tall, bald, middle-aged, and overweight African-American man pulled himself out of the vehicle. He wore a red, stretched-out polo shirt and jeans. The man looked around cautiously and, seeing and hearing nothing, leaned against the car and folded his thick arms against his broad chest. After a few moments of whistling and humming, he reached into the right pocket of his jeans and pulled out a test tube with a rubber stopper jammed into the top. He looked at it briefly, slid the tube back into his pocket, and then resumed his whistling and humming.

Mulder took a couple of steps out of the dark corner in which he had been concealing himself. At the sound of the approaching footsteps, the man said, "You call me here on such short notice, Jones, the least you can do is not keep me waiting."

"People can be so inconsiderate," Mulder replied, stepping into the light. The man was visibly taken aback and began to reach behind himself for the car-door handle.

"Sorry, I was supposed to meet someone here," the man said. "But it looks like he's not coming, so I'll just—"

He kept his eyes on Mulder as he grabbed the handle and tried to pull the door open, but to no avail—Scully had snuck up beside him and placed her hand on the door to keep it shut.

"FBI," Mulder announced. "Carl Jones couldn't be here tonight, so Agent Scully and I will gladly accept the test tube on his behalf."

"It's not what you think," the man blurted out.

Mulder shot him a skeptical look. "You go by the name Brett Manning?"

The man nodded nervously.

"Then it's what we think." Mulder pulled his pistol out of his holster and pointed it at the man. "Hand the test tube over to Agent Scully."

The man hissed in exasperation but nonetheless did as he was told. Scully examined the tube closely.

"What is this?" she demanded. "How did you get it? Who are you, really?" The man didn't answer.

"I'll run you through every government database in existence," Mulder told him flatly. "We'll find out who you are soon enough." He pulled out a pair of handcuffs and approached the man. "And then we'll find out what you sold to Carl Jones that killed those two men."

"For crying out loud," the man shouted, "it was all just a scam! A *con*!" Mulder stopped walking.

"What do you mean?" Scully interjected.

"The test tube, there's nothing in it. Just like the other ones I sold Jones. He is one gullible son of a bitch."

"Go on," Mulder prompted.

"Look," the man began. "My real name is Robert Mantle. I met Jones a few months ago and had him pegged as a total mark. He was completely obsessed with stamping out porn and rescuing this one starlet from a life of sin—I can't remember her name."

"We've got that part covered," Mulder told him.

Mantle continued. "So I played him, and he bought it. I told him I was a well-placed government official—that back in the eighties, I'd worked on the Meese Commission report on the harmful effects of pornography. And then I started throwing in the most ridiculous nonsense I could think of, just to see how far I could go with him—I mean, a virus from outer space? Come on!"

Mulder scowled at him.

"But he believed every word," Mantle said. "And he was willing to pay real money. And I was more than willing to take it from him. But that's it. I had nothing to do with any deaths. I may be a con man, but I'm no killer."

Mulder looked at Scully and saw in his partner's face a reflection of his own uncertainty. If Mantle was telling the truth, what the hell caused those deaths? "Let's bring him in for further questioning," he said, but then Scully's phone rang. She answered the call, and Mulder watched her expression turned to shock and disquiet.

"That was our contact at the LAPD," she said without emotion after ending the call. "Bob Berkley was found dead in his office. Apparently... his head exploded."

Mantle's eyes widened. "I swear," he told the two agents solemnly, "there was *nothing* in those test tubes."

It seemed that Bob Berkley did not believe in surrounding himself with luxuries and extravagance in the workplace. The furniture in his office was limited to a brown wooden desk with an executive chair, two smaller chairs for guests, a couch with black fabric upholstery, a bookcase, and two tall metal file cabinets. The few personal touches consisted of several framed photographs showing a smiling Berkley with some of his lead performers, including Ashley Ford, and a handful of trophies from the Adult Video News Awards sitting on top of the bookcase.

And now nearly all of it was splattered with blood, flesh, and bone. Berkley's body—including what was left of his head—was still in the room, slouched in the chair at the desk.

"His wife became worried about him," LAPD Detective Jack Silbert, lead investigator on the case, explained to Mulder and Scully when they arrived. "It was late, he hadn't come home, and he wasn't answering his office phone or his cell. So she came to check on him and found him like this."

"Any idea why he was here so late?" Scully asked. "Or whether anyone was with him?"

"Apparently he was just working," Silbert replied. "There are financial documents all over his desk. And we've spoken to the building's cleaning staff—as far as they know, he was the only one here when they left for the night."

"So this thing is now moving beyond performers," Scully commented. "Beyond movie sets. And we still have no idea what we're dealing with." Her frustration was palpable.

Mulder was equally frustrated, and anxious to examine the office—just him and Scully. He turned to Silbert. "Can you give us the room for a little while?"

The detective looked a little miffed at first, but ultimately acceded to Mulder's request. "Not too long, though," Silbert said. "I've got a job to do here, too." He stepped out of the office.

The two FBI agents focused primarily on the area around Berkley's desk. Mulder took a closer look at the body and noticed a small object on the dead man's lap. It was Berkley's notebook.

"Scully, do you have a pair of rubber gloves?" She pulled a pair out of her shoulder bag and handed them to him. Mulder put on the gloves and picked up the notebook, careful not to move the body. He flipped through the pages.

"Interesting," he murmured.

"What is it?" Scully asked.

"Apparently, Bob Berkley was a compulsive note-taker. He jotted down key details of every meeting, conversation, phone call, bowel movement— just kidding about that last one."

"Does it say what was happening just before he died?" Scully asked. Mulder flipped to the last few pages with writing on them and skimmed quickly.

"Yes. He was here alone, working on a plan to get the company through the production shutdown. And it seems ol' Bob wasn't the most scrupulous guy on the planet, based on what he had in mind. His last phone call was to—" Once Mulder saw the name, and the written comments that followed, everything seemed to fall into place for him.

"Who?" Scully prompted. He looked up from the book and locked eyes with her.

"Let's go. I'll explain on the way."

Karen Porter was bewildered and pissed off. Who the hell was knocking on her front door at 4:30 in the morning, awakening her from a much-needed sleep when she had to be up in an hour and a half to get Rachel ready for school?

She forced herself to get out of bed, threw on a robe, and grabbed a baseball bat from her closet. If this was some kid pulling a prank, or another stalker, she'd make it abundantly clear that she was not to be messed with. As Karen stomped toward the front door, she could hear a female voice coming from outside that sounded familiar, but she couldn't quite place it.

"These abilities you're suggesting," she heard the voice say. "I think you're really pushing it this time."

"I'd be disappointed if you didn't," answered a male voice—one that Karen did recognize. She looked through the peephole and, sure enough, Agents Mulder and Scully were standing outside. Karen was relieved it was them—especially Agent Mulder—but she knew that an unexpected visit at that hour was almost never a good thing. She put the baseball bat down and opened the door.

"Can we come in?" Mulder asked. He seemed ultra-serious, even grim—a sharp contrast to the warm and funny man she and Rachel had dinner with just hours earlier. Karen resisted the apprehension gnawing at the back of her mind, and let them in the house. Mulder got down to business immediately.

"Bob Berkley died a few hours ago," he told her.

She gasped and put a hand to her mouth. "I spoke to him right before I went to sleep… what happened?"

"He died the same way your co-stars did," Scully answered.

"Oh my God." Karen sat down on the sofa. "What is happening?" she exclaimed, her eyes filling with tears.

Mulder approached her. "Miss Porter—Karen—you were directly involved with each man at the time of his death. You told me yourself you didn't really want to shoot the scenes with Jon Longfellow and Tim Gordon. And Bob Berkley—you were the last person to speak with him. We know you told him you were quitting the business, and that he was putting pressure on you to stay."

Karen looked at him incredulously. "You think *I'm* responsible for all this?"

"Not consciously," he assured her, then sat down beside her. "I believe you may possess unique mental abilities, ones you're not even aware of. Some sort of combination of telepathy and telekinesis, that comes into play when you feel trapped or cornered. You use it to lash out psychically, targeting whomever you perceive to be the source of your stress, building up pressure inside that person's head until it bursts."

Karen glared at him with disbelief. "You think I'm some kind of freak? A monster?"

"No," he assured her. "But three men are dead. And if you're responsible, we need to know—and to figure out how to help you get these abilities under control, so nobody else dies."

Karen looked over at Scully, who was standing a few feet away. "You believe this too?"

The female agent looked uncomfortable. "I'd like to think there's a less… *outlandish* explanation," she admitted.

"Well, I'm not responsible," Karen insisted. "I didn't do anything!"

"Mommy?" Everyone turned toward the sound of a little girl's voice. Rachel was now standing in the living room, rubbing her eyes, looking confused and concerned. She walked over to Karen and embraced her.

"It's okay, baby," Karen told her gently.

"They made you upset," Rachel replied. It was not a question.

Mulder managed a small grin as he said, "We're here to help, Rachel."

But the little girl scowled. "Mommy doesn't think so," she declared. "I thought you were nice, but now you're bothering her, like those men who tried to make her do yucky things she didn't want to do."

Karen's eyes widened as she looked at her daughter. Karen had always gone to great lengths to shield Rachel from anything having to do with her work. How did the little girl know?

"I felt it, and saw it in my head," Rachel said, as if the question had been asked out loud. "But I wished really hard, and that made the men stop."

Suddenly Karen felt as if ice water was running through her veins. What Agent Mulder had described—it was *real*? But not coming from her. Coming from…

Karen was overcome with shock and disbelief. She couldn't speak. She could only watch as Mulder scrutinized Rachel closely.

"Rachel," he began with a warm smile. "Can you remember when you first started feeling and seeing these things in your head?"

The little girl thought for a moment. "Spring break. I was off from school. Mrs. Parides was watching me on the days when Mommy worked."

Mulder turned to Karen with a questioning look. She had managed to regain some of her composure. "Mrs. Parides is one of our neighbors," she explained. "That was a little over a month ago."

"Around the time when Jon Harper died," Mulder pointed out. "Karen, we need to talk to Rachel. Both of you need to come with us."

"Just leave us alone," she said, a wave of fear rising within her. "Please."

"We can't do that," he replied gently. "Three people are dead. You knew them. Doesn't that mean anything to you?"

"You're not taking my daughter away from me," she said, her fear turning to anger.

"No one's going to do that," Mulder said firmly.

She hissed derisively. "If the government got their hands on her, they'd lock her away and study her and test her like she was a lab specimen!"

"We won't let that happen," Scully insisted, stepping closer to the sofa.

"Maybe you really mean that," Karen acknowledged, "but how are you going to stop them?"

Mulder got to his feet. "Look, we have to—"

"Leave us alone!" Rachel screamed. She glared furiously at Mulder and Scully, and the two agents suddenly slammed their eyes shut, clutched their heads, and staggered backwards, gasping and crying out in agony. Streams of blood began to flow from their nostrils and their ears as they sank to their knees.

"Rachel!" Karen shouted, kneeling down and grabbing her daughter's shoulders. "Stop! Stop now! Don't—don't 'wish hard' anymore! You're not helping me, baby! Listen to me! No matter what you think I'm feeling, don't do this! This is very bad, Rachel!"

The little girl's expression softened and she let out a deep sigh. Mulder and Scully crumpled to the floor like marionettes whose strings had just been cut. Karen prayed that they weren't dead. She rushed over to them to make sure they were still breathing. They were, thank God.

"Go get dressed, baby," she told Rachel. "We have to go on a trip—right now."

"Where are we going, Mommy?"

"We'll find out when we get there."

─── 𝒳 ───

ALEXANDRIA, VIRGINIA
19th MARCH, 1999, 10:05 p.m.

Returning from Los Angeles, Mulder entered his apartment, dropping his luggage next to the front door and sighing heavily in disappointment. After six days of searching for Karen Porter and Rachel with no success, and no promising leads, he and Scully could not justify remaining in California. Wherever the young woman had ended up, it was a damn good hiding spot. Even in the burgeoning Internet Age, it was still possible to disappear, at least for a while, if you worked at it hard enough.

The phone rang. He picked it up. "Mulder," he said unenthusiastically.

"It's me," Scully replied. "Just want to make sure you're okay—you seemed really down the whole flight back."

"This is one of the few times I'm not happy about proving you wrong on a case," he told her.

"Oh? As I recall, after we got zapped by that little girl, your first words to me upon regaining consciousness were, 'I told you so.'"

Mulder frowned. "Yeah, well, that was before our search for her and her mother turned out to be a bust. I'm keeping an eye out for any reports that could lead us back to them."

"Of course," Scully said. "Until then, there are other cases to work, more X-Files to discover. See you tomorrow, Mulder."

"Thanks for calling, Scully. See you tomorrow." He hung up the phone.

Then Mulder entered his walk-in closet and removed a large brown cardboard box filled with VHS tapes—the Ashley Ford section of his private video library. He carried it to the front door, which he opened. Mulder had decided to take the box down to the nearest garbage dumpster and toss it in. It just didn't feel right to have those videos in his home anymore.

He stepped out into the corridor and headed to the elevator. But then he stopped, turned around, and went back into his apartment. Opening the box and looking over its contents, Mulder began removing some of the videotapes and setting them aside. He figured maybe he didn't have to part with *all* of them…

THE END

The truth is Out There

FOUNDLING

By Tim Waggoner

ECHO HILL, VERMONT
25th APRIL, 1997, 1:14 p.m.

"I'll do it! I swear I will!"

Mulder held his SIG-Sauer P226 tight in both hands, the barrel trained on the middle of the woman's forehead. Sweat dotted her brow, and as he watched, the beads began to slide downward. Her eyes were wide and madness glimmered within, but he saw fear in her gaze, as well, and sorrow.

She gripped her own gun—a .45—but instead of pointing it toward him, she held the muzzle pressed against the temple of a baby. Her baby.

Mary Ann Matthews knelt in a grassy field on the edge of woods. A brown-haired woman in her late twenties, she wore a light blue dress that was stippled with her husband's blood. She clutched her son, Billy Matthews, tight to her chest with her left arm, the .45 held against his head with her right hand. It was a pleasant spring day. Cloudless blue sky, sun shining, gentle breeze blowing. A Native American phrase came to Mulder's mind: *This is a good day to die.* He supposed it was better than some, but as far as he was concerned, it was an even better day to live.

"Take the gun away from Billy's head. Please."

His own weapon didn't waver, and his finger tightened ever so slightly on the trigger.

Billy—who seemed remarkably placid given the fact his mother was prepared to end his life—looked at Mulder with glossy obsidian eyes. As the child breathed, gill-like slits fringed with cilia gently pulsed on the side of his neck. Billy wore only a diaper, and aside from his eyes and neck, he looked like a perfectly ordinary chubby baby.

"You don't understand. He's not right. You can see that, can't you?"

Mary Ann's voice was strained, but Mulder heard the weariness beneath it. Tired people were unpredictable. They teetered on the edge, might go one way or the other. It would only take the slightest nudge to send them over, but you never knew which way they'd land until it happened.

Billy blinked. He had normal eyelids, but he also had a pair of nictitating membranes. Mulder found the child's double-blink oddly beautiful.

"I can see he's special," Mulder said. "But being special doesn't make him dangerous, Mary Ann."

"His father was dangerous. He put this… *this* into me. And sometimes he'd talk to me in the middle of the night. When he was sleeping. Not with words, but with pictures. His dreams were so *loud.* That's why I had to shoot him. I couldn't take another night of his dreams screaming at me." She glanced down at Billy. "This one… when he cries, I see colors. And they're not *normal* colors, either. They're… *wrong.* So very wrong."

After Mulder and Scully had discovered Jeff Matthews dead in his home, they'd searched the house but found it empty. Scully had gone to the elementary school to make sure the Matthews' oldest child, a daughter named Nikki, was safe. Mulder had gone out the back door to check out the small woods behind the Matthews' property. He'd found Mary Ann and Billy on the other side.

"Your husband wasn't a monster, and neither is your son. They're both a result of genetic mutation, a natural part of the evolutionary process."

Even as he spoke these words, Mulder knew they sounded too clinical and detached. And there was an eagerness in his tone that he hated, but he couldn't prevent it. Where Mary Ann saw her husband and son as monsters, he saw them as miracles. Amazing, beautiful accidents of genetics, something to be celebrated and admired instead of condemned and destroyed.

"I know it's been hard, Mary Ann, but if you—"

She pulled the trigger.

Mulder stood there, shocked, unable to move or think. A moment later, tears streaming from her face and cradling her child's dead body, Mary Ann put the .45 to her head and pulled the trigger once more.

AMBERGRIS FALLS, OHIO
13th MAY, 1997, 10:36 a.m.

"Interesting name," Scully said as they drove past the town's welcome sign.

"Ambergris is a substance produced in the digestive system of sperm whales. It was once used as a fixative in perfumes."

"So women used to use material from a whale's bowel to smell better?"

"I guess it's all in the nose of the beholder."

Mulder was driving the rental car they'd picked up at the Cincinnati airport—a silver Ford Mustang. Ambergris Falls was about an hour's drive from the airport, but they'd lost almost twenty minutes at the National Guard checkpoint half a mile back. Despite receiving advance notice that a pair of FBI agents would be arriving, the guard members had taken their time verifying their identities and searching their persons and the rental vehicle for communication and recording equipment. The government had ordered a complete information blackout regarding the situation in Ambergris Falls, and when they said *complete*, it appeared they meant it. In the end, everything checked out, and once Mulder and Scully had surrendered their phones, they were free to continue their journey.

It was mid-May, and the trees were in full bloom. This part of Southern Ohio was hilly, and so there were fewer farmers' fields than Mulder had expected. It was warm out, but not hot. They drove with the air-conditioner off and the windows cracked. The air smelled green, and Mulder thought it would be nice to take a vacation someplace like this, where there were a lot of trees and everything was quiet. He could use a break—especially after what had happened with Billy Matthews. What he had *let* happen.

"Something wrong, Mulder?"

As useful—and, he had to admit, comforting—as it was to have a partner who was able to read his emotions as easily as if they were written in ten-foot-high neon letters, sometimes it could be a real pain in the ass.

"Other than the fact that the guardsman who searched me was a little too free with his hands, I'm fine."

Scully frowned, but she didn't push the issue.

Ambergris Falls was small, and the closest neighboring town was located thirty miles away. Not exactly isolated in this day and age, but it was hardly a bustling metropolis. For this reason, Mulder expected to find the town home to businesses with names like Dew Drop Inn, Cheap Smokes, E-Z Loans (No Payments Due for Thirty Days!), and of course the usual chain fast food restaurants that sprang up in America like mushrooms after a heavy rain. And at the center of it all, a decaying downtown whose best years were long behind it. But Ambergris Falls surprised him. The buildings were old but well maintained, stately rather than shabby. And the colors... instead of conservative browns, grays, blacks, and whites, the good citizens of this town went in for brighter hues. Reds, yellows, blues, purples, oranges, greens, pinks—often combined in ways that should've seemed garish and clashing, but which somehow worked. It was almost as if he and Scully were driving into a storybook town, or maybe a backlot set for a really weird movie.

And the businesses fit with the town's nonconformist aesthetic. Tea and coffee shops, organic grocery stores, yoga and meditation studios, new age bookstores, hemp shops, vegan restaurants, aromatherapy supplies, oxygen bars... there were recycling containers on every corner, bike racks in front of every business. There were signs for the usual professionals—doctors, dentists, and orthodontists—but other less common services were advertised as well: holistic medicine, homeopathic remedies, past-life regression therapy, and personal energy alignment.

Ambergris Falls had quite a few churches, too. All the familiar religions were represented: Christian, Jewish, Muslim, Buddhist, Hindu, and Unitarian, as well as ones Mulder had never heard of, like The Temple of Inner Light and the Third Eye Collective.

It didn't take long for them to reach the center of town, and Mulder parked the Mustang in front of the town government building and turned off the ignition. Ambergris Falls was small enough that the mayor's office, courthouse, police station, fire department, and emergency medical services were all housed in the same surprisingly bland-looking building—a nondescript two-story structure with a gray stone façade and columns in front. Staid and traditional, rather than vibrant and eccentric, like the rest of the town.

"It looks like an older building," Scully said. "Probably built in the late 1800s. The rest of the town looks like it was frozen in the sixties."

Mulder looked at her and grinned. "Are you suggesting we're dealing with some sort of temporal anomaly here?"

She gave him what he thought of as The Look.

"Hardly."

They got out of the car and Scully came around to stand next to Mulder. They stood in silence for a moment while they regarded the area. More new age and alternative shops here, along with a microbrewery that Mulder wouldn't have minded checking out.

"I think we've stumbled onto the legendary Hippies' Graveyard," Mulder said.

As soon as he made the joke, he regretted it. Not the hippie part, but rather the graveyard bit. The streets and sidewalks of Ambergris Falls were empty. They hadn't seen a single person or moving vehicle since they'd arrived. It was, in fact, this absence of residents that they'd come here to investigate.

Less than thirty-six hours ago, a state trooper had driven through town—on his way somewhere else, naturally. It was night, and he immediately noticed there were no lights on anywhere. He tried calling the town police, but when he couldn't get through, he drove to the government building to check it out. He found it empty, just as he found every other building he checked. He reported what appeared to be the total desertion of Ambergris Falls by its residents. A couple hours later, the National Guard arrived and set up roadblocks and checkpoints at every road into town. The CDC received a call soon after and immediately dispatched a team. It found no sign of chemical or biological contamination, and no sign of violence or distress. The CDC contacted the FBI, and Assistant Director Skinner had reached out to his contacts in the military to find out if anyone had been conducting "tests" of any kind in the area. They'd all denied having any knowledge about the situation in Ambergris Falls, but Mulder and Scully knew that didn't mean much.

Their assignment sounded simple enough on the surface. Go to Ambergis Falls and find out what happened. But Mulder knew from long and often frustrating experience that the assignments he and Scully were given were never that simple.

"I have a hard time believing that every man, woman, and child in this town left overnight," Scully said. "What did the welcome-to-town sign say the population was? Over a thousand people?"

"One thousand, one hundred, and twenty-three," Mulder said.

Scully nodded. "No one left any notes saying where they were going or why—at least none that have been discovered so far. And it's not like the entire town's been searched. From the report we received from the Ohio field office, less than half the homes and businesses were checked. Even so, no one found any sign of a mass exodus. People's clothes and important possessions remain in the homes, and their vehicles are still parked in their garages. And if for some strange reason they *did* all leave, someone would know about it. Relatives or friends. After all, they would've had to go *somewhere*."

Not only did the search team not turn up any residents, there were no signs of pets. No dogs or cats… Even the fish tanks were empty.

"Maybe wherever they are, they aren't able to contact anyone," Mulder said.

She scowled at him. "Don't tell me the entire populace was abducted by aliens."

He shrugged. "Maybe they had a really big ship." When her scowl didn't let up, he added, "There've been a number of mysterious—but well-documented—disappearances throughout history. The Lost Colony at Roanoke. The crew of the *Mary Celeste*…"

Scully opened her mouth to reply, but before she could speak, her eyes focused on a point past Mulder and she frowned.

"Turn around," she said.

Her voice was emotionless, and while there was no overt warning in her words or tone, Mulder was instantly on guard. As he turned, he reached inside his jacket to take hold of his gun, but he didn't draw it from its shoulder holster. Not yet.

At first he wasn't sure what Scully wanted him to see. The street and sidewalks remained deserted, without any hint of movement or sound. There wasn't even a breeze. But then he saw… something. Or *things*. They were barely visible, their forms little more than suggestions, blurred shimmerings that only partially existed. He squinted his eyes, and that helped bring them into focus a bit more. There were a lot of them—they filled the street—and they were roughly humanoid, but they lacked any sort of fine detail to distinguish one from the other. Whatever they were, they appeared to be simply standing in the street, watching.

"Do you see them, Mulder?"

He wasn't sure that *see* was the right word, since whatever these beings were, they were only partially visible, but he said, "Yeah."

But before either he or Scully could say anything else, a piercing cry cut through the silence. The sound came from behind them, and they spun around, guns drawn, only to see a small blanket-wrapped bundle lying on the steps leading up to the government building's entrance. Steps that had been empty only a few seconds before.

Scully holstered her weapon and started toward the baby—its cries were unmistakable—but Mulder paused to look back over his shoulder. The not-quite-there creatures—whatever they were—were gone. Or maybe they were still there, watching, and he just couldn't see them at the moment. Not exactly the most comforting thought, but he had a more immediate problem to worry about. Still holding his weapon, he hurried up the steps to join Scully.

She crouched next to the baby, who was wailing at the top of its lungs. While she gave the child an examination to determine its condition, Mulder swept his gaze around the area, searching for any sign of who had left the baby here. But he saw nothing.

"How is he?" Mulder asked.

"*She* appears to be in good health," Scully said. "No outward signs of injury, and she doesn't appear to be malnourished or dehydrated. Her diaper's dry. If I had to guess, I'd say she was hungry."

Her examination complete, Scully picked up the child and stood. As soon as she did so, the baby quieted.

Mulder holstered his gun.

"Looks like someone got left behind," he said.

"You know she wasn't here a moment ago."

"I know nothing of the sort. There are any number of logical reasons why we might not have noticed her even though she was lying here the whole time."

Scully gave him another Look.

"I just wanted you to see what it felt like for a change." He nodded toward the street. "Our semi-visible welcoming committee is gone."

"Whatever's going on here, the first thing we need to do is get this child to a hospital for a full examination. If we still had our phones, we could call the Guard and have them send someone for her."

"But since we don't…"

They returned to the car. Mulder figured they'd drive the girl to the Guard checkpoint and they'd call paramedics from a neighboring town. He and Scully would wait until the EMT's arrived and checked out the girl, and they could return to town and resume their investigation.

They climbed in the Mustang—Scully holding the baby on her lap—and Mulder put the keys in the ignition and turned them.

Nothing happened.

He tried several more times, but without any better result. There wasn't even the clicking sound of the starter engaging.

"Awfully convenient timing, huh?" he said.

He popped the hood, got out, and took a look at the engine. As far as he could tell, everything seemed fine. Then again, he was no mechanic.

He closed the hood. By this point, Scully had gotten out of the car and joined him. She gently bounced the baby in her arms, and the motion seemed to make the child happy. At least it kept her quiet.

For the first time since they'd found the baby, Mulder took a good look at her. He judged her to be six months old, maybe less. She had a surprisingly thick shock of brown hair, and her eyes were a clear, sharp blue. Her cheeks were red, probably from crying so hard, and her eyes were moist, although no tears issued from them at the moment. The child regarded him steadily and without reaction. Her silent scrutiny reminded him of how Billy Matthews had looked at him just before...

"You okay, Mulder?"

"Sure," he said. "Why wouldn't I be? Deserted town, mysterious wraith-like beings that appear and disappear, and an abandoned baby that pops out of thin air. Just another day on the job, right?"

Scully didn't say anything. She didn't have to. Sometimes her silences spoke far louder than words ever could.

"The car dying could be a coincidence," she said.

"Could be the Watchers don't want us leaving town—" he nodded toward the baby—"and taking Scully Junior with us."

Scully didn't respond to that. There had been a time when she would've argued with him, offered a number of possible and, more importantly, plausible alternatives. But they'd seen far too much since then. He'd never admit it to her, but sometimes he missed those days.

"So what now?" he asked.

"We find some formula," Scully said. "And diapers. Who knows? While we're looking for supplies we might run into someone."

"Sounds good." So they were looking for a grocery, a pharmacy, or maybe a convenience store. He glanced up and down the street and saw none. As he was trying to remember where they'd seen one on the way into town, Scully stepped close to him.

"One more thing," she said, and pushed the baby into his arms. Out of reflex, he took hold of the child. "You get to carry *Mulder* Junior."

He wanted to hand the child back to Scully, but she stepped away before he could.

"What kind of name is Mulder for a baby?" he asked.

"What kind of name is Scully?"

"Good point."

They picked a direction and started walking.

The baby kept looking up at Mulder as they walked. It was probably his imagination—God knew he had plenty of that—but he couldn't escape the feeling that the child was scrutinizing him in a deeply intense and extremely disquieting fashion. He wanted to ask Scully to take the girl back, but doing so would give her an opening to ask why he didn't feel comfortable carrying the child, and that was a conversation he wasn't ready to have yet. Maybe ever.

Scully hadn't pushed him to talk about what had happened with the Matthews family, although she had been asking him how he was feeling more often than usual these last few weeks. He knew why she'd insisted he carry Junior, and although he resented her taking this opportunity to play psychologist, he knew she only thought she was helping. And it wasn't as if it was Junior's fault. Still, he hadn't been able to save Billy Matthews. What if he wasn't able to protect Junior, either?

They reached the end of the street and turned the corner. As they approached a lamp pole, Mulder said, "There's another one."

He nodded toward the poster taped to the metal. It was a simple design, obviously made on a home computer and printed out on yellow paper. In large bold capital letters it advertised something called THE GATHERING, and underneath the slogan *Take Yourself to the Next Level!* Below that was a date and time, but no location and no other information to indicate who was gathering and why.

"I've noticed them too," Scully said, "mostly in the windows of businesses we've passed. What about them?"

Mulder had been carrying the baby in his left arm, but it was starting to ache, and he shifted her to his right. The girl continued staring up at him, eyes wide, face impassive.

Stop doing that, kid, he thought. *You're creeping me out.*

"Don't you think it sounds kind of sinister?" he said. "The Gathering…" He spoke these words in a deep voice, enunciating them slowly to make them sound scary.

"Given what we've seen of the town so far, I'd guess it's some kind of new age festival they hold here. A street fair, maybe. That's why there's no location listed. The festival is probably held throughout the town."

"Did you notice the date?" he asked.

She frowned and stepped closer to the poster. She examined it then turned back around to face him.

"It was two days ago."

He nodded. "And the state trooper discovered the town was deserted that night. It *might* be a coincidence…"

"But it might not be," Scully finished. "It certainly doesn't look like any sort of festival or celebration took place here recently."

"Not one with psychic readings and people selling crystals anyway," he said. "Have you seen any more signs of the Watchers?"

"Sometimes I think I detect movement out of the corner of my eyes, but when I turn—"

"Nothing's there."

She nodded.

"Same here."

They looked at each other for a moment, but there really wasn't anything more to say. They needed to take care of Junior, then see if they could find a phone to call someone to come get her. They continued heading down the block, Mulder doing his best to ignore the flickers of motion in his peripheral vision. He knew Scully was doing the same.

On the next street over they found a drugstore, although the hand-carved wooden sign above the door said *Apothecary*. The entrance was unlocked, and as they entered, Mulder said, "Where did these people think they lived? Middle Earth?"

The place smelled of exotic spices and floral incense, but despite this—and its name—inside the business resembled a normal pharmacy—more or less. The display shelves were made of wood instead of metal, and the products lined up on them were primarily natural alternative medicines. But there was a small selection of more common products—analgesics, decongestants, antihistamines, cough suppressants, and the like. Natural remedies were all well and good until you felt *really* crappy, Mulder thought.

There was a phone behind the front counter, next to the register. Mulder lifted the receiver and wasn't at all surprised to discover the line was dead. They managed to find baby formula, although the only kind the "Apothecary" carried was soy-based. No disposable diapers—bad for the environment— but they found a package of cloth ones. Scully found a package containing several glass baby bottles and rubber nipples, and since the shop didn't have a restroom, she used alcohol and cotton swabs to clean her hands along with the supplies before preparing a bottle for Junior. Mulder was afraid Scully would make him feed the child, and he was relieved when she took the baby from him, sat cross-legged on the floor, and attended to the task herself.

He sat down next to her. The lights were off in the store—it seemed electricity wasn't working in the town either, which corroborated the trooper's report—but enough light filtered in from the front windows for them to see.

Mulder expected Junior to suck greedily on the bottle, but she didn't. She took the formula without hesitation or resistance, but she did so without enthusiasm. It seemed to Mulder that she ate almost dutifully, because it was expected of her, not because she wanted or even needed to.

"Do you ever think about it?" he asked.

Scully had been watching Junior's face as she fed, but now she looked up at Mulder. She kept her expression carefully neutral as she spoke.

"You mean about what happened with the Matthews family?"

"*No*," he said, the word more barked than spoken. Then, more softly, "I mean about having kids, maybe adopting."

She looked back down at Junior.

"Sometimes. But given the kind of work we do..." She looked to him once more. "You?"

For a split second, he saw Billy Matthews looking at him with obsidian eyes, cilia-fringed neck slits pulsing, gun muzzle pressed to his temple so hard it puckered the skin around it, turned it white.

"Not anymore."

Before either of them could say anything, there was a soft creaking sound of a door opening. Mulder rose to a crouching position and drew his gun. He motioned for Scully to stay put, and—still crouching—he started making his way down the aisle to the front of the pharmacy, senses alive and alert. He wasn't going to let another innocent child die, no matter what it took.

As he reached the end of the aisle, he straightened, and saw a woman standing near the front counter. Although he could see both her hands were empty, he trained his gun on her and shouted, "FBI! Don't move!"

Startled, the woman raised her hands and froze. She was in her late twenties, tall, trim, with short black hair and understated make-up. High cheekbones and a sharp chin gave her a severe—although not unattractive—look. She wore a light jacket over a white blouse, along with blue jeans tucked into calf-high black boots. No jewelry of any sort.

"Wow, *this* is awkward. I had no idea anyone else…" She broke off, eyes narrowing as she scrutinized him more closely. "Hey, you're Fox Mulder, aren't you?"

In his world, whenever he thought things couldn't get any stranger, that's when they usually did. He almost said, *What took you so long?* Instead, he decided to keep it all business. He also kept his gun trained on her. Just because she didn't appear to be armed didn't mean she wasn't a threat.

"Who are you?" he asked.

Before the woman could answer, Junior started crying for the first time since Mulder and Scully had found her. The woman looked confused at first, but a moment later she broke out into a grin when Scully stood and came over to join Mulder, Junior in one arm, gun gripped in her free hand.

"And Dana Scully! Of course you're together. You're a team, right? Like peanut butter and jelly. Cookies and milk. Death and taxes."

Mulder gave Scully a quick sideways glance.

"Do you recognize her?"

She shook her head.

"I don't suppose you have any ID on you?" she asked the woman.

The woman's stance became more relaxed, but she didn't lower her hands.

"Sure I do. The name on it is Andrea Chapman."

"But that's not your real name," Mulder said.

The woman just smiled.

Scully holstered her weapon, handed Junior to Mulder, and stepped forward to frisk the woman. Mulder held the child in one arm and kept his weapon trained on "Andrea" with the other. Junior had stopped crying, but now she whimpered softly, her blue-eyed gaze locked on the woman. Mulder heard a soft rattling, as if a heavy vehicle was going by outside, the vibrations of its passage causing the products on the store's shelves to shake. But there was no vehicle in the street, and it wasn't as if Ohio was known for its earth tremors.

Scully pulled a 9mm Glock from beneath the woman's jacket, along with a butterfly knife and small leather case. She put the knife and gun in her jacket pocket, and then stepped out of the woman's reach and opened the case.

"Lockpick tools," she said.

She closed the case and slid it into her other jacket pocket. She looked at the woman. "So you're a thief."

"If you like. But I prefer to think of myself as a procurer of rare curiosities."

"More Indiana Jones than Raffles," Mulder said.

She smiled. "Something like that." She turned to Scully. "You've disarmed me. Is it okay if I put my hands down now?"

Scully gave Mulder a questioning look. Over the years, they'd come to rely on each other's instincts as if they were extensions of their own. But it wasn't just the two of them now.

"I don't know," Mulder said. "Junior here doesn't seem to like you, and you know what they say about dogs and small children. They're excellent judges of character."

Still, he gave Scully a nod and lowered his gun, although he didn't holster it. Scully then gave the woman permission to lower her arms.

"So, *Andrea*," Scully said, "what brings you to Ambergris Falls? And how do you know who we are?"

"We're in the same business, after a fashion," she explained. "More competitors than colleagues, though."

"You work for another branch of the government?" Scully asked. "CIA? NSA?"

Mulder thought about how the woman had described herself: a procurer of rare curiosities.

"She works for Easton Rodgers," he said.

The woman's eyes widened in surprise, but she tried to play it cool. She smiled and clapped her hands slowly.

"Bravo, Fox. Maybe you really *are* as good as your reputation."

Scully frowned. "Easton Rodgers, the billionaire? He made his fortune in the hi-tech industry, didn't he?"

Mulder nodded. "Rumor in the paranormal research community is that he reverse-engineered his 'discoveries' from bits and pieces of recovered alien technology."

Andrea's smile widened. "I can neither confirm nor deny any such rumors."

"Are you on his payroll or are you freelance?" he asked.

"Somewhere in between, actually. My name doesn't appear in any HR database, but I've been working for Mr. Rodgers almost exclusively for the last several years."

"So you're here to poke around and see what you can find to take back to your employer," Scully said. "How did you find out what had happened here?"

"Mr. Rodgers has sources in every walk of life, in every industry and branch of government, and some of them hold very prominent positions. I'd bet that Mr. Rodgers knew about this incident before you two did."

"And you know who we are because of Rodgers' 'prominently positioned' sources," Mulder said. "My guess is that she follows us, kind of like a hyena scavenging the leftovers of a lion's kill. Once we're done with a case, she finds out about it and visits the site to see what, if anything, she can recover."

Andrea pursed her lips in irritation. "Don't flatter yourselves. I'm not big on sloppy seconds. That said, you two *have* provided me with some useful leads a few times, and for that, I thank you."

"All part of the service," Mulder said wryly. "How long have you been in town?"

"About four hours. And before you ask, I haven't found anything more exciting than empty homes and businesses without power or phone service." She focused her gaze on Junior. "But it looks like you've found something. Or should I say, someone."

Junior seemed to draw back from the woman's gaze, pushing herself harder against him. Her whimpers became a soft keening, and he once more heard the sound of bottles and jars rattling on the shelves, only this time it was louder than before.

"You didn't see *anything* else?" Scully asked the woman.

Andrea looked away from Junior—almost reluctantly, Mulder thought— and turned to Scully.

"Why? Should I have?"

Scully didn't reply.

Andrea turned back around to face Mulder and Junior. Smiling, eyes locked on the baby, she stepped forward.

"She's beautiful." She reached a hand toward the child's face. "Where did you—"

The woman's fingers were only inches away from Junior when the baby let out an ear-splitting shriek. At the same instant, every item on the Apothecary's shelves tumbled to the floor. Some of the bottles, jars, and metal tins bounced, but a number of glass containers shattered. Mulder turned his head to watch the small-scale destruction, his mind already turning over possibilities. Burst of psychokinetic energy? Some sort of sonic effect induced by Junior's cry? He was distracted only for a few seconds, but that was all Andrea needed.

She rushed forward and jabbed her fingers into a nerve bundle on Mulder's shoulder. Pain flared through his entire arm, and he let go of Junior. Before he could try to catch the baby in his other arm, Andrea snatched her away and darted past him. She ran toward the back of the shop, undoubtedly hoping to find a rear exit.

"Are you all right?" Scully asked him.

"I'm fine. Go after her! I'll take the front!"

Scully nodded, drew her weapon, and ran after Andrea.

Mulder was furious with himself for letting his guard down. Junior may or may not have caused the pharmacy's shelves to empty themselves, but regardless, she was a mystery—exactly the sort of "curiosity" that Easton Rodgers would be interested in acquiring, examining, and quite possibly reverse-engineering—a process which would at best be extremely painful for Junior, at and at worse could prove fatal.

Not this time, he thought.

Arm aching like hell, he headed for the front door.

The Apothecary was bordered by an organic smoothie shop on the right and a pet psychologist on the left. The alleys between the buildings were narrow, but there was plenty of space for a tiny woman carrying a tiny baby. Mulder stepped far enough into the street so he could cover both alleys and drew his gun.

Andrea came running out from between the pharmacy and the smoothie shop. She held Junior tight against her chest, but she was no longer unarmed. In her free hand she gripped a Glock. Had she somehow managed to retrieve her weapon from Scully? If so, did that mean Scully was hurt? He thrust the thought aside. His first responsibility was to Junior. He trained his gun on Andrea, turning sideways to provide greater stability for his one-handed stance.

"Do I need to say it again?"

She froze, gun held at her side.

"I must be losing my touch," she said. "You should still be lying on the pharmacy floor, writhing in agony."

"What can I say? I try to get eight hours of sleep a night, and I do my best to avoid carbs."

Mulder raised the barrel of his gun until he was aiming at Andrea's head. The last thing he wanted to do was risk hurting Junior. He sensed more than saw movement around them, but he didn't take his gaze off Andrea. He didn't need to. He knew they had an audience, visible or not.

Andrea's gaze flicked back and forth, and Mulder guessed she'd detected the Watchers, too. He wondered if she saw them or was simply aware of their presence—hair rising on the back of her neck, stomach muscles tightening… Her eyes focused on him once more, and she raised her gun and pressed the muzzle to the side of Junior's small head.

The baby whimpered.

"I don't suppose you'll lower your gun and walk away," she said.

Panic welled inside Mulder, and he felt cold inside, as if his blood had been replaced with ice water. It was happening again, and just like last time, he was helpless to do anything about it. No, he realized, that wasn't entirely true. There *was* one thing he could do—stall. Slowly, he knelt and lay his Sig Sauer on the ground. Then he straightened and held his hands out before him, palms up.

"Just don't hurt her."

Andrea smiled, but she didn't take her gun away from Junior. "I won't, not as long as I'm able to deliver her to my employer. After that little trick she pulled in the pharmacy, Mr. Rodgers will pay quite a pretty penny for her. Maybe enough that I can retire if I want to. Ah, who am I kidding? I'll never retire. I love my work too much. And you know what I love about it the most?" Her smile widened. "Beating a worthy opponent."

Scully stepped silently out of the alley and pressed her gun to the back of Andrea's head.

"I guess it's not your day then," Scully said.

Andrea's features hardened and her gaze turned cold. Her expression frightened Mulder. She looked like a woman who was determined to win, no matter the cost. Or determined to at least make sure that no one else won if she couldn't.

Scully won't shoot, he told himself. She wouldn't execute the woman in cold blood, even if she did kill Junior, but Andrea didn't know that. Or did she? She knew who they were and what they did. Who knew how much information she had about them? As much as Easton Rodgers could pay for, he supposed, which would be quite a lot.

Mulder was desperately trying to think of a way out of this stand-off—a way that resulted in Junior remaining alive and unharmed—when Junior's face turned red and her eyes glistened with tears. She then opened her mouth and released an ear-splitting shriek.

Andrea's gun hand began to tremble. Her eyes widened in alarm, but then her brow furrowed and she gritted her teeth, as is she were marshalling her concentration. Her effort appeared to be in vain, though. Her hand began to shake furiously, the tremors spreading all the way up her arm. She slowly pulled the gun away from Junior—or, from the look of it, was forced to. Her arm straightened until the Glock pointed skyward.

Mulder stepped forward, intending to take the weapon from Andrea, but before he could reach her, the Glock fell apart. There was nothing spectacular about it. The weapon didn't explode in a soundless burst. It simply disassembled itself and the pieces dropped to the ground.

Mulder continued forward. Enough feeling had returned to his left arm that he could move it, and he took Junior from Andrea. The woman continued holding her arm straight up, her entire body shaking now, an expression of absolute terror on her face. Scully took several steps away from Andrea, keeping her gun trained on her. Junior quieted when Mulder took her, and as she fell silent, the woman's paralysis ended. She let out a gust of air and her arm fell to her side. Scully stepped over to Mulder, keeping her Glock aimed at the woman.

"Sorry it took me so long to get here," Scully said. "She ran to another shop, went inside, and then managed to slip past me and double back."

He looked at Andrea. "You saw Scully and me go into the pharmacy, and you left a back-up weapon in the alley, just in case we disarmed you, right?"

Andrea looked down at the scattered pieces of her Glock lying on the ground.

"For all the good it did me," she said.

Mulder turned to Scully. "Maybe we should start calling our little friend Carrie. She appears to have a knack for psychokinesis."

"She sure does."

Mulder frowned. "What? You're not going to tell me there's no scientific evidence for my claim?"

"I'm a skeptic, Mulder, but I'm not an idiot. I know what I saw."

"So what do we do now?" Mulder asked.

"Let me go?" Andrea suggested.

"Hardly," Skully said. "We need to get Junior out of town, *and* we need to get Ms. Chapman here to a holding cell. And unless you think we can find a working vehicle, we're stuck walking."

"Sounds like a plan. At least the checkpoint isn't too far. If I'd known we were going to spend so much time on foot, I would've brought my hiking boots."

Mulder shifted Junior to his left arm. It was still numb, but it held her okay. "Give me your gun. I'll cover her while you cuff her."

Scully nodded, handed Mulder her weapon, and removed a pair of handcuffs from her jacket pocket. Andrea kept her gaze fastened on Mulder as Scully pulled the woman's arms behind her back and locked the cuffs around her wrists. Mulder returned Scully's gun to her, and then walked over to retrieve his own weapon. He holstered it so he could maintain a solid grip on Junior. He then joined Scully behind Andrea—making sure to give their captive a wide berth—and Scully aimed her weapon at a point between the woman's shoulder blades.

"Start walking," she ordered.

But before any of them could take a single step, a fierce wind erupted in the street, tearing at them with gale force. Mulder couldn't pinpoint which direction it originated from. It seemed to come from all directions at once, but that wasn't possible.

Maybe not with actual wind, he thought. But with psychokinetic force? A force directed at them by any number of semi-invisible Watchers? That seemed entirely possible.

Mulder held tight to Junior with both arms, and Scully stepped close to him and took hold of his arm to steady herself. She still held her gun, but the winds buffeting them were so strong, she couldn't keep it trained on Andrea.

"What's happening?" Scully had to shout to be heard over the wind's roaring.

"I think the Watchers would prefer Junior stay here!" he shouted back.

Junior started crying again, this time letting forth a piercing full-throated wail. As if in response, the wind intensified, and Mulder and Scully huddled closer. The air rippled and distorted with a heat-wave effect Mulder had seen earlier, only increased a hundredfold, making it impossible to see more than a few feet. If Andrea was still close by, he had no way of knowing it.

Mulder heard a voice then. No, not heard. It didn't come to him as words, not exactly. It was more like information was directly implanted into his brain, and he translated the data into words.

Return her to us.

"Scully?"

"I hear it, too!"

The demand was repeated, over and over, louder and faster. Mulder felt pressure building inside his skull, bringing with it a pain so intense that he thought he might black out. And then, just as suddenly as it had come, the wind stopped. It didn't ease down, didn't diminish to a breeze. One instant it was tearing at them like some great savage beast, and then it was gone.

Mulder and Scully were weak and shaky and they leaned upon one another for support. Scully had managed to hold onto her weapon and she gripped it at her side, almost as if she'd forgotten about it. Once the wind stopped, so did Junior. She no longer wailed, but instead sobbed softly to herself. Mulder rocked her gently back and forth, hoping to calm her, at least a little.

Scully glanced up and down the street. "No sign of Andrea. Think she escaped?"

"I doubt it. She threatened to kill Junior. I have a feeling the Watchers took an extremely dim view of that."

"What made them stop?" Scully asked.

Mulder shrugged. "Maybe they realized they were upsetting the baby."

The Watchers slowly appeared around them then, filling the street with their transparent not-quite-there forms.

Scully looked around, eyes wide. "There must be hundreds of them."

"I'd guess one thousand, three hundred, and twenty-three." He looked down at Junior. "Minus one."

"You're saying the Watchers are the citizens of Ambergris Falls?"

"Think about it, Scully. This entire town is dedicated to spiritual, mental, and physical advancement. Churches of all kinds, organic foods and medicines for sale everywhere you look… It's like these people came here to create a kind of spiritual refuge. A place where they could leave behind the rest of the world and focus on what was truly important to them."

Scully realized she still held her gun. She started to raise it, but then, as if thinking better, she holstered it.

"And what would that be?" she asked.

"What have human beings always searched for? The ultimate state of spiritual growth: Enlightenment. Remember all those posters? *The Gathering: Take Yourself to the Next Level.*"

"Are you suggesting that the entire town evolved and somehow moved onto a higher plane of existence at the same time?"

"I think they found what they were looking for, and they went there together. But one of them somehow got left behind." He smiled at Junior. The child gazed up at him with her achingly blue eyes. She no longer sobbed, and she didn't seem as frightened as she had before. She looked uncertain, but maybe a bit hopeful, too.

"So if they won't let us leave with her…"

"Presumably her family is among the Watchers. Parents, siblings, grandparents, aunts, uncles, cousins… And while she might look like an ordinary baby, we've seen her demonstrate high-level psychokinesis. She's still an evolved being. She's just resisting what surely is an enormous—and very scary—change for her."

Scully smiled. "Like a child who's afraid to leave for the first day of school."

Two of the Watchers left the others and came gliding forward, their legs not moving. They proceeded with an eerie but also surprisingly beautiful grace until they stood only a couple feet away from Scully, Mulder, and Junior. Then one of them held out its arms. There was no way of telling whether the figure was male or female, father or mother, but Mulder supposed it didn't matter.

He looked at Junior, and she looked at him. Then she looked at Scully. And finally she turned her head to look at the two Watchers. Then she looked up at Mulder once more. She gave him a tiny smile, giggled, and then vanished. For a second, Mulder could still feel the weight of her in his arms, but then the sensation passed. He looked toward the two Watchers, but they were gone, too, as were their companions. The street was once again empty.

Mulder slowly lowered his arms and looked at Scully.

"They grow up so fast."

As they headed back to the government building and their rental car— which Mulder hoped would be functional now that Junior had been reunited with her family—they came across a pair of handcuffs, still locked, lying in the street. Scully picked them up and slipped them into her jacket pocket without a word.

A few minutes after that, Mulder said, "If it's okay with you, I'd like to talk about Billy Matthews now."

Scully looked at him, smiled gently, and said, "Of course."

Mulder took a deep breath, released it, and began.

THE END

the truth is out there

WHEN THE COWS COME HOME

By David Farland

NEAR GALLUP, NEW MEXICO
11th AUGUST, 2000, 1:00 a.m.

A flash and crack, like a close lightning strike, wrenched Burt Zonderman from sleep. No thunder followed. Instead, the bawling of cattle and an urgent human voice penetrated from the fields outside his home. Burt rose, shoved aside the window curtain, peered out.

Out in the cornfield beyond the farmyard fence, lights swung erratically, casting the summer-withered stalks into swaying, skeletal silhouettes.

"Damn!" he said through his teeth. He reached for his Levis and boots.

"Honaw?" his Hopi wife called from her pillow. The endearment meant "bear," and it fit the burly farmer well.

"Somebody in the cornfield," he said as he dressed. "Could just be kids out joyriding, or maybe illegals trying to rustle cattle."

At the ranch house's back door, he removed his hunting rifle from the gun safe and pocketed a handful of rounds before he grabbed a flashlight and stepped into the chill of the high-desert night. Stars blanketed the sky, enough for Burt to see as he strode across the farmyard.

He kept the light off, not wanting to lose the element of surprise.

A man's voice rose on the night breeze, a sing-song wail that carried above the moos and bellows of agitated cattle. Didn't sound like Spanish or Hopi to Burt. Navajo, maybe? It certainly wasn't English.

He vaulted the rail fence, then paused to load the rifle. "Hey!" he yelled. "Get the hell out of my field! I'm armed, and I'll shoot!"

The wail ebbed, then swelled to a banshee pitch that made the hair rise at the back of Burt's neck. Rifle ready, he set his teeth and shouldered along a row of wind-rattled stalks, moving toward the arcing, blue-white lights.

The corn was so high, he got only glimpses of distant lights, circling, circling.

He slid between the cornstalks, heard distant mooing. The cattle were in the cornfield.

Strange, the moos came in a sing-song pattern—flat and atonal, five notes. The moist air from freshly watered fields filled his nostrils as he slid between the corn.

Burt heard movement just ahead, something big rushing toward him. He pulled his flashlight and clicked it on: Light glinted from the whites of a big black bull's rolling eyes. It lowered its head and charged.

Jump, Burt thought just as the bull's curved horn pierced the center of his chest with the impact of a mule's kick. The bull lifted him, flailing, over its massive shoulder and flipped him in the air.

He landed with a thud, and wondered, *Am I hurt? Am I hurt?*

Burt reached to his chest, felt something hot and sticky, as the stars overhead began to fade to black. In the distance, an engine gunned and the cattle mooed… an unearthly cadence, a haunting melody, a dirge for beasts.

"Here's one for the X-File," Skinner said. "One dead rancher, some missing cattle, and a crop circle that appeared overnight in a cornfield east of Gallup, New Mexico."

Fox Mulder cast a sideways glance at Dana Scully. "Crop circles? We're on our way."

With the FBI helicopter hovering a thousand feet above the cornfield at the Laughing Kokopelli Ranch, Mulder thrust his head through the open hatch. He squinted against the sun's glare and the hot wind that pummeled his face. Even muffled by his headset, the rotors thrummed overhead like a racing heart.

From that altitude, the shape that was crushed into the field didn't resemble any crop circle he'd seen before. The only circular part appeared to be a head crested with wavy tentacles. The head topped a hunchbacked torso with stick-figure arms and legs, except that the hands and feet each ended in four curved claws.

Mulder shifted to make room when Scully joined him at the hatch. She studied the shape for several moments, her mouth pursed, before she shouted through the throbbing rotors, "This doesn't look like any pattern we've investigated in the past. It looks more like the Anasazi petroglyphs you'll find on the canyon walls a few miles north of here. I'm betting some drunk high school kids on dirt bikes or ATVs did this."

"Let's take a closer look," Mulder yelled back. "I want to take a few pictures."

Moments later, the helicopter settled into the ranch yard in a cloud of swirling russet dust. Donning his sunglasses against the bright, high-altitude morning, Mulder jumped down first. He offered Scully a hand, and as she joined him, he turned to survey the farmyard.

Barns, sheds, and what fences Mulder could see from here were well maintained. A cattle truck and a large, green-painted harvester stood under their shelters. Only the County Sheriff's patrol car pulled up before the barn, and the yellow crime-scene tape strung along the fence enclosing the cornfield, appeared out of place. The sheriff stood by his vehicle, waiting for the helicopter's rotors to die down.

"This way," the sheriff called, leading into the field. They ducked under the yellow tape and followed him, between rows of corn heavy with full ears, to a spot where the stalks had been fractured and trampled. Several trails of cloven hoof-prints, one larger than any Mulder had ever seen, tore the sandy soil. The hoof-prints sank deeply in a broad, darkened area, dried but exuding the unmistakable odor of blood.

"This's where Zonderman's ranch hand found him early this morning," the sheriff said. "Gored through the chest and then trampled."

"Gored? You're sure of that?" Scully asked.

"Wasn't a gunshot." The sheriff shook his head. "No exit wound. I saw his body before the coroner took it."

Scully nodded. "Thank you, Sheriff. Did Mr. Zonderman have any enemies that you know of? Anyone who might have reason to damage his crops and set his cattle loose?"

"Nobody I'm aware of." The sheriff shook his head. "Mostly kept to themselves out here, he and his wife. She's local, grew up on the reservation. Their kids are grown and gone; they're pretty much retired."

"We'd like to look around," Mulder said, and the sheriff nodded and moved off.

Mulder and Scully followed the trail of hoof-prints and trampled corn farther into the field, picking their way through soil clods and stubble, until Scully stopped short. "Tire tracks," she said.

They'd been made by a three-wheeled vehicle, with broad outer tires designed for traction and a narrower center tire. The imprints' sharp outlines in the dry soil made it clear that they were no older than the hoof-marks.

"Looks like an ATV," Scully said. "What did I tell you, Mulder? A bunch of high school kids with a little too much beer and free time on a summer night."

They followed the ATV trail until the tracks abruptly doubled back, never quite reaching the figure in the cornfield. There were no signs of footprints, indicating that the kids might have made the crop circle.

Mulder smiled. A familiar, creepy sensation stole over him. There was something more here than what met the eye. "Maybe aliens scared off your drunken kids, Scully."

He pressed on between the corn rows, toward the formation.

Yards later, he stepped into the open. Three or four acres of flattened corn, he guessed, hemmed on all sides by standing stalks. He glanced at his partner. "Here's the torso of your Anasazi witch figure." As Scully stepped up beside him, he scrutinized the ground beneath his feet. "I don't see any tire tracks, just a lot of hoof-prints. It looks like the cattle were stampeded through here. Let's locate the figure's head and extremities."

Mulder had seen crop circles made by college students in the past, so he watched for the tell-tale signs—the freshly raked earth that indicated human movement among the fields, but found only... cattle tracks.

An hour later they stood in a trampled-out claw at the end of one hand. "No tire tracks. Not even human footprints," Scully said. "I don't see any sign that people did this, or that it's a natural effect from the wind."

Mulder pointed out, "You know, in the past, I'd have suspected that college students had trampled this ground. But this crop circle looks as if it was made as a prank... by cows."

He looked up into the sky, wondering, and imagined that strange figure. Some people thought that it represented extraterrestrial life—drawings made by ancient Anasazi who had seen aliens.

Had aliens been here last night?

Scully wondered in that maddening way of hers. "There must be a logical explanation... Maybe a new strain of Mad Cow Disease? One that causes affected cattle to run together in tight herds?"

"But to shape something this enigmatic and complex?" Mulder shook his head. "Only with some external force steering them." He shaded his eyes with a hand and peered between thinning corn tassels. "We're near the fence that faces the desert. I can see a few cattle out there. I think we should check them out."

The cattle beyond the fence, white-faced with rusty-red coats, watched placidly, still chewing their cuds, as Mulder and Scully climbed between the fence rails. As if their arrival were a signal, however, two cows clambered heavily to their feet and began to amble purposefully up a nearby rise.

"Let's see where they're going," Mulder suggested.

Scully rolled her eyes, muttering something about following every cow-path across the desert.

The two cows stopped at the hill's crest, blinking back at Mulder through glazed eyes from beneath white lashes. Their red-brown hides were patchy rather than sleek, but they didn't startle or trot off when Scully approached one of them.

"Healthy animals have bright, clear eyes and shiny coats," she informed Mulder. "These cattle don't look well to me. I'm holding onto my theory of a Mad Cow variant. Perhaps it makes them susceptible to human suggestion."

Mulder chuckled, but a gusty breeze from the desert carried an odor of decaying flesh. Scully grimaced, too. They turned, and peered into the wash below. A carcass lay sprawled under a twisted juniper tree, its belly laid open from just behind its forelegs to where its udder had been.

They made their way gingerly down the loose sandstone slope. Mulder waved away flies as he crouched beside the carcass, and they rose in a buzzing cloud of green and black.

Scully leaned over her partner's shoulder. "Coyotes probably killed it. If she was sick and became separated from the herd, she would've been an easy target."

"She would've been," Mulder replied, "but coyotes don't make a single long, clean incision." He pointed along the hide's raw edge. "And they wouldn't gut it this thoroughly. Even the udder was removed... almost with surgical precision—and a hoof taken." He attempted to shift the uppermost hind leg, which ended abruptly at the dead animal's hock. "This was done with something like a hacksaw."

Scully frowned. "Why would someone kill an animal for its hoof?"

Mulder looked up. "Some people think that aliens that stop by our planet aren't just studying mankind, but all of Earth's flora and fauna. Perhaps they wanted a sample of cattle. I mean, the cells in a hoof would provide enough genetic material to clone tens of millions of cattle."

As he turned to Scully to emphasize his point, a distant, shiny object caught his eye, barely visible above the small hill they'd just come down. "And I think they're coming back," he said, pointing. He shot to his feet and scrambled up the rise, sending loose stone fragments clattering down behind him.

By the time Scully joined him, she had her cell phone in her hand. "I'm checking with NOAA," she said. "It's probably a weather balloon."

Mulder nodded, barely listening to her side of the call. As he squinted after it, the silvery disc slid up behind a cloud.

"Most likely a weather balloon," Scully confirmed as she pocketed her phone. "The NOAA office in Albuquerque says one snapped its tether yesterday." She favored Mulder with an I-told-you-so gaze. "I think we should pay a visit to Mrs. Zonderman."

They found her in the living room of the ranch house, accompanied by a rugged, somber man in work-stained jeans, and a younger woman who was clearly Mrs. Zonderman's daughter. A short but obviously sturdy Native American woman, with once-black hair fading to mouse-gray and dry but downcast eyes, Mrs. Zonderman sat on the sofa, rocking a little and murmuring over and over, "Nukpana... nukpana."

"What is she saying?" Scully asked Mulder under her breath.

"It's the Hopi word for 'evil,'" Mulder replied.

Mrs. Zonderman accepted Scully's murmured condolences graciously and squeezed her hand.

"You should talk to Danny, our ranch hand," Mrs. Zonderman said, and nodded toward the silent man. "He's the one who... found my Burt."

"Thank you," Scully said, and glanced at Mulder.

He beckoned to the ranch hand, who wordlessly joined them on the back patio. Navajo, Mulder guessed, by his round face and long, black hair, tied back at his nape.

"Our sympathies about your boss, Danny," Mulder began. When the Native American only nodded, Mulder said, "The initial report we received suggested that several of Mr. Zonderman's cattle had been stolen. Do you know how many? We found a few head wandering loose outside the cornfield, and a carcass in the wash behind the hill." He watched the ranch hand as he added, "It had been surgically eviscerated, including the udder and a hind hoof."

The man's dark eyes widened, then narrowed, and he clipped his words. "They're not my boss' cattle. After the cops got here, I checked the corral behind the barn." He pointed at it with a thrust of his jaw, a gesture Mulder recognized as distinctly Navajo. "Mr. Zonderman's cattle have the Kokopelli brand, like this." He dropped to his heels and traced the design in the dust with his finger. "All his cattle were there when I counted."

Mulder and Scully exchanged glances over the ranch hand's head. The glassy-eyed cattle and the dead cow had worn no brand.

"Are there any other ranches around here?" Mulder asked.

"Not close enough for cattle to walk here overnight." The man rose and locked stares with Mulder, who only nodded when the ranch hand warned, "You'd better be careful."

"Thanks for your time, Danny." Leaving the house behind them, Mulder addressed Scully. "I got the impression he has suspicions of his own. He had a pretty strong reaction when I mentioned how that cow had been mutilated."

"I saw that," Scully agreed. "The Navajo have some really dark superstitions."

"I think the cattle were transported here," Mulder said. "I'd like to take a stroll around the perimeter of that cornfield." He signaled the helicopter pilot to wait and started down the drive, Scully at his elbow.

Half a mile along the tarred driveway, between the house and the two-lane county road, a metal gate offered entrance into the field. Its top rail lay even with Mulder's shoulders. A two-rut track, the kind worn into soil over time by farm equipment, curved away into the corn inside the gate.

"Too tall for cattle to jump, even in a panic," he said, and examined the heavy latch and padlock. "No signs of forced entry. Either the intruder had a key to the lock, or he didn't bother to use the gate." He bent to slip between the rails.

The tarred spur of the lane ended a yard or so beyond the gate. A fresh gouge near the end caught his attention, and he stooped to probe it with his fingers. "Looks like a loading ramp was dropped here," he told Scully, and scanned the rust-colored soil beyond the ramp. "And yep, here are hoof-prints, heading off down the track. Here's that set of extra-large hooves." He pointed them out. "They all look as fresh as the ones we saw this morning." He faced Scully.

"So someone unloaded a truck full of cattle here?" she wondered.

"Maybe it wasn't a truck," Mulder offered. "There are other kinds of vessels."

Scully rolled her eyes. "Who'd want to transport a bunch of cows in their spaceship? Think about it, Mulder."

As he climbed back through the gate, Scully said, "You know, maybe if we want to know where the cattle came from, we should take a look at where they're going."

"What do you mean?" Mulder asked.

She explained, "Last year my neighbor's little Yorkie got out of her car at a gas station about twenty miles from home. It ran off, and she couldn't catch him. But four days later he was sitting there on her doormat, wagging his tail, when she got home from work. Maybe… the cows are heading home."

"Good idea." Mulder quickly dusted himself off. "Let's take the helicopter."

Scully lowered her binoculars and called over the rotor noise, "They're all on the move now. The two we followed this morning are several miles in the lead, but they're all heading the same direction. I can see… eight, nine, ten… eleven of them."

"Give me the coordinates on their positions," Mulder requested, as he brought up a regional map on the PC in his lap.

Over the next few moments the pilot rattled off lat-and-long sequences, ending with the coordinates for the cattle in the lead.

"Okay, Daisy-Bell, let's see where you're heading," Mulder muttered as he plotted the cattle's course.

A startlingly straight, red line appeared on the PC with a ripple. "Pay dirt!" Mulder shouted to Scully. "There's another ranch about thirty miles up ahead. Why don't we make a little social call?"

The "ranch" in question consisted of a traditional round hogan, built of logs with a domed soil roof, its door facing east. A modern blue port-a-potty stood behind the hogan, along with a couple of ramshackle outbuildings and a sturdy log corral. A wind-and-sun-battered cluster of human construction in the middle of a wire-fenced parcel of desert. About fifty acres, Mulder estimated.

"Set us down in the pasture," he directed the pilot. "We'll walk up to the hogan. There's no need to appear threatening."

He and Scully had almost reached the hogan's closed wooden door, which appeared to have been taken from some other building, when movement in the nearest shed wrenched them around. An old Native American shuffled from its shadows, blinking in the afternoon sun.

Hair faded to silver-gray, secured only by a bandana around his head, hung loose about his shoulders. He wore a threadbare plaid shirt, cinched at his lanky waist by a silver concho-belt studded with large chunks of turquoise. He approached them unperturbed, humming an odd, five-tone tune over and over.

"Elder," Mulder addressed him, then hesitated. "Do you speak English?"

The old man nodded, peering up at Mulder through rheumy eyes, almost lost among folds of weather-crinkled, bronze skin. He continued humming the atonal melody.

"My companion and I," Mulder included Scully in his gesture, "wondered if you've seen any strange, bright lights in the sky during the last few nights."

"Lights in the sky?" the old man asked, and turned his face upward. "Lights would only be strange if they were unusual."

Mulder's pulse quickened. "Do you see lights in the sky often?"

The elderly man returned his gaze to Mulder's, and all bleariness had left them. "It is best not to involve yourself in things that you do not understand," he said.

"But we want to gain understanding," Mulder persisted.

When the man favored him with a fleeting, scant smile, Mulder took it as permission to ask questions. "How often do the lights appear?" he asked. "Have you ever seen ships? Have you ever seen them land?"

The old man smiled, a knowing expression this time, and he shifted nearer. "The lights from the sky visited our grandfathers long before the white men came to our lands," he said, gazing skyward once more. "The Light People gave my grandfathers knowledge of great power."

Mulder's heart-rate skipped up once more. "You've actually seen them? The—the Light People?"

Another sage smile, and the elderly man began again to hum his five-note tune.

As he stepped away, still humming, Mulder glimpsed a handful of objects lying in shadow on a bench in the nearest shed. Three peyote buttons, the paws of a mountain lion and a bear, both apparently mummified, and the severed hoof of a cow.

Recognition froze Mulder for an instant. *He's an ánti'ihnii, a Navajo witch.* He snatched his pistol from its holster.

The old man's smile turned menacing. He made a slight swiping motion with fingers curled like claws. Mulder's pistol spun from his grasp as if torn away, and blood erupted from four deep gashes, as if a big cat's claws had struck the back of his hand.

Seizing his wounded hand, Mulder glanced up. For an instant the ancient Navajo before him, with his curled hand and fierce grin, appeared as a large mountain lion, ears flattened to its skull, teeth bared in a snarl. Mulder reflexively drew back.

He started from the vision at the sharp report of Scully's sidearm somewhere behind him. Saw the old man vanish, a puff of dust on the rising afternoon breeze.

He blinked at a blur of motion at his periphery, and twisted to focus on it. A phantom mountain lion leaped the wire fence enclosing the hogan and galloped into the desert. Each great stride covered a mile at a time. He watched it run, farther than he knew he should be able to see so clearly with unaided eyes, and muttered, "We'll never catch him."

As if in response, the old Native American's grave voice seemed to murmur near his left ear, "I did not mean to harm anyone."

"My cattle strayed through another man's fences," the old voice continued, "and he stole them. I only meant to call them home. I had them make the crop circles as a warning."

"Mulder!" Scully said.

He pivoted, still clutching his torn hand. Blood oozed between his fingers.

Scully had retrieved his pistol. "That's going to need sutures," she said, eyeing his bloodied hand. "It's a good thing we've got the helicopter." She said "Come on" with a toss of her head, and he started after her.

"What was that about?" she questioned as they strode down the dirt path toward the chopper.

"He was an *ánti'ihnii*, a Navajo witch," Mulder said, "probably the kind they call a skinwalker. I saw him take the shape of a mountain lion. He told me he was only trying to retrieve his stolen cattle, he didn't mean to hurt anybody."

Scully puckered her fine brows. "He told you that? How?"

"His spirit voice." Mulder glanced at his hands, one tightly clenched around the other. "This really smarts! There's nothing else for us to do here. No crime was committed. Let's go."

As the sun settled on the ragged horizon, torching the cloud-streaked sky with gold and scarlet, the old Navajo opened the gate of the log corral near his hogan. In a moment, the cattle stepped out from the long, blue shadows, lowing as they ambled toward him, their heads and tails swaying.

"Shimsani," he called the first one to approach, the eldest of the cows, and he stroked her flat forehead. "Mosi, light on your feet… Ooljee, with the shape of the moon on your side…"

He called each cow by its name as it strode through the gate. At last came the bull, a black mountain of a beast, with dried blood caked inky on one horn. "Ya, my Anaba, my warrior," he said, patting the solid flank. He swung the gate closed and chained it.

The cattle followed his movements, his gestures through glazed eyes, all quietly mooing an odd, five-note tune.

THE END

the
Truth
is out
There

AUTHOR BIOS

HANK SCHWAEBLE is a writer and attorney in Houston, Texas. He has won two Bram Stoker Awards, including one for his first novel, *Damnable* (Penguin/Jove 2009). His short fiction has appeared in anthologies such as *Alone on the Darkside*, *Five Strokes to Midnight*, *Death's Realm*, and *V-Wars: Night Terrors*. He has also been nominated for a World Fantasy Award. A collection of his short fiction and novellas, *American Nocturne*, was released in February 2016, and his third novel, *The Angel of the Abyss*, is slated for June 2016. When he's not reading or writing, Hank enjoys playing guitar and flying planes. You can find out more through his website, www.hankschwaeble.com, and he can also be found on Facebook and Twitter, honing the edges of his rapier-like wit and laughing at cat memes.

DAVID SAKMYSTER is the award-winning author of more than a dozen novels, including *Jurassic Dead* and *The Morpheus Initiative*, a series featuring psychic archaeologists (described as "Indiana Jones meets The X-Files"). He also has an epic historical adventure, *Silver and Gold*, the horror novel *Crescent Lake,* and a story collection, *Escape Plans*. His latest is *Final Solstice,* and he has two screenplays optioned for production. www.sakmyster.com

SARAH STEGALL researched and co-wrote the first three volumes of *Official Guide to The X-Files*, which spent fourteen weeks on the *New York Times* best-seller list. She often visited the offices, sets, or locations of *The X-Files*, conducting research. Her interviews with Chris Carter and Mark Snow were featured in the first *X-Files Magazine*, and her *X-Files* trivia contests appeared twice a week on the *TV Guide* website for several years. In addition, she wrote official calendars, desk diaries, and other tie-in projects. She writes science fiction, mystery, and horror; she is the author of the *Phantom Partners* paranormal mystery series. Her next novel, *Outcasts*, is about the writing of *Frankenstein* and will be released in May 2016, in time for the 200th anniversary of the book. Sarah lives in northern California with her family. Her website is at www.munchkyn.com. She can also be found on Twitter.

HANK PHILLIPPI RYAN is the on-air investigative reporter for Boston's NBC affiliate, winning 33 Emmys and dozens more journalism honors. Best-selling author of eight mysteries, Hank has won five Agathas, two Anthonys, two Macavitys, two Daphnes, and the Mary Higgins Clark Award. Reviewers call Ryan "a superb and gifted storyteller." Her *Truth Be Told* is a *Library Journal* Best of 2014 and won the Agatha for Best Mystery. Her newest book is *What You See*, named a *Library Journal* Best of 2015. (Watch for her *Prime Time* and *Say No More* in 2016.) A founder of MWA University, Hank was 2013 president of national Sisters in Crime. www.HankPhillippiRyan.com

KELLEY ARMSTRONG is the author of the *Cainsville* modern gothic series and the *Age of Legends* YA fantasy trilogy. Past works include *Otherworld* urban fantasy series, the *Darkest Powers* and *Darkness Rising* teen paranormal trilogies, and the *Nadia Stafford* suspense trilogy. Armstrong lives in southwestern Ontario with her family. Her website is KelleyArmstrong.com, and she also can be found on Twitter and Facebook.

JON MCGORAN is the author of six novels, including the biotech thrillers *Drift, Deadout*, and their upcoming sequel, *Dust Up* (April 2016, Tor/Forge Books), and the forensic thrillers *Body Trace, Blood Poison*, and *Freezer Burn*, written as D.H. Dublin (Penguin Books). His short fiction includes the novella *After Effects*, from Amazon StoryFront, *Bad Debt*, which received an honorable mention in Best American Mystery Stories, 2014, and stories in a variety of anthologies, including IDW's *Zombies vs. Robots: No Man's Land*, and *G.I. Joe: Tales from the Cobra Wars*. He is a founding member of the Philadelphia Liars Club, a group of published authors dedicated to writers helping writers. Find him on Twitter, on Facebook, or at www.jonmcgoran.com.

KAMI GARCIA is the #1 *New York Times, USA Today* and International best-selling coauthor of the *Beautiful Creatures* Novels, and the author of the instant *New York Times* best-seller *Unbreakable* in *The Legion* Series and the sequel *Unmarked*, which were both nominated for Bram Stoker Awards. Her forthcoming YA contemporary romance *The Lovely Reckless* releases in Fall 2016 (from Imprint). *Beautiful Creatures* has been published in 50 countries and translated in 39 languages, and the film, *Beautiful Creatures*, was released in theaters in 2013, from Warner Brothers. Fascinated by the unexplained, Kami was instantly hooked on *The X-Files*. Find her online at www.kamigarcia.com, or on Twitter, Instagram, and Facebook.

GREG COX is the *New York Times* best-selling author of numerous novels and stories, including the official movie novelizations of *Godzilla, Man of Steel, The Dark Knight Rises, Ghost Rider, Daredevil, Death Defying Acts*, and the first three *Underworld* movies, as well as books and stories based on such popular series as *Alias, Buffy the Vampire Slayer, CSI: Crime Scene Investigation, Farscape, The 4400, Leverage, Riese: Kingdom Falling, Roswell, Star Trek, Terminator, Warehouse 13*, and *Xena: Warrior Princess*. Visit him at www.gregcox-author.com.

BEV VINCENT is the award-winning author of several books—including *The Stephen King Illustrated Companion* and *The Dark Tower Companion*—over seventy short stories, and hundreds of essays, interviews, and book reviews. His work has been nominated for the Bram Stoker Award (twice), the Edgar Award, and the ITW Thriller Award. His short fiction has appeared in anthologies and magazines such as *Doctor Who: Destination Prague*, *The Blue Religion*, *Ice Cold*, *When the Night Comes Down*, *Ellery Queen's Mystery Magazine*, *Apex Digest,* and several *Shivers* anthologies. He is a contributing editor with *Cemetery Dance*, where he writes the column Stephen King: News from the Dead Zone for each issue of the magazine and is writing historical context essays for the Stephen King Revisited project. He can be found lurking in various corners of the internet, including at bevvincent.com, at his book review blog OnyxReviews.com, and on Facebook and Twitter.

KENDARE BLAKE binge-watches *The X-Files* every couple of years. Her favorite episode is the one where the virtual reality game starts to really kill people, because she likes to hear Scully say that Mulder is getting his ya-yas out. She's also the author of six novels, including *Anna Dressed in Blood*, *Antigoddess*, and *Ungodly*. Find her online at kendareblake.com.

DAVID LISS is the author of nine novels, most recently *The Day of Atonement* and *Randoms,* his first book for younger readers. His previous best-selling books include *The Coffee Trader* and *The Ethical Assassin*, both of which are being developed as films, and *A Conspiracy of Paper*, which is now being developed for television. Liss is the author of numerous comics, including *Mystery Men*, *Sherlock Holmes: Moriarty Lives,* and *Angelica Tomorrow*. Liss can be followed on Twitter and Facebook.

RACHEL CAINE is the *New York Times* and *USA Today* best-selling author of nearly 50 novels, including the 15-book *Morganville Vampires* series, the 9-book *Weather Warden* series, the critically acclaimed and award-winning *Great Library* series, and many others in fantasy, SF, horror, and suspense. She's been a proud, die-hard *X-Files* fan from the original airing of Episode 1. Her website is rachelcaine.com, and she can also be followed on Twitter and Facebook.

GLENN GREENBERG is an award-winning editor and writer whose work has appeared in such publications as *TIME Magazine For Kids*, *Scholastic News*, *Time Out New York*, *Back Issue*, and *Smoke*. He has also worked for Marvel Comics and DC Comics on such world-famous franchises as *Spider-Man, the Hulk, the Silver Surfer, Thor, Iron Man, Dracula*, and *Star Trek*, and Web-based tie-in projects for the film *Superman Returns* and the weekly comic-book series *52*. Glenn has also written several works of *Star Trek* fiction for Simon and Schuster. He avidly covers all aspects of popular culture on his blog, "Glenn Greenberg's Grumblings" (http://glenngreenbergsgrumblings.blogspot.com), and welcomes anyone and everyone to check it out.

TIM WAGGONER has published over thirty novels and three short story collections of dark fiction. He teaches creative writing at Sinclair Community College and in Seton Hill University's MFA in Writing Popular Fiction program. You can find him on the web at www.timwaggoner.com.

DAVID FARLAND is an award-winning, best-selling author with over 50 novels in print. He has won the Philip K. Dick Memorial Special Award for his science fiction novel *On My Way to Paradise* and over seven awards for his fantasy novel *Nightingale*. He is best known for his *New York Times* best-selling series *The Runelords*. Farland has written for major franchises such as *Star Wars* and *The Mummy*. He has worked in Hollywood greenlighting movies and doctoring scripts. He has been a movie producer, and he has even lived in China working as a screenwriter for a major fantasy film franchise. Find him on Facebook or Twitter or on his website http://davidfarland.com.

JONATHAN MABERRY is a *New York Times* best-selling author, five-time Bram Stoker Award winner, comic book writer, and anthology editor. He writes the *Joe Ledger* thrillers, the *Rot & Ruin* series, the *Nightsiders* series, the *Dead of Night* series, as well as standalone novels in multiple genres. His comic book works include, *Captain America, Bad Blood, Rot & Ruin, V-Wars* and others. He is the editor of many anthologies including *The X-Files, Scary Out There, Out of Tune,* and *V-Wars.* His books *Extinction Machine* and *V-Wars* are in development for TV, and *Rot & Ruin* is in development as a series of feature films. A board game version of *V-Wars* will be released this year. He is the founder of the Writers Coffeehouse, and the co-founder of The Liars Club. Prior to becoming a full-time novelist, Jonathan spent twenty-five years as a magazine feature writer, martial arts instructor, and playwright. He was a featured expert on the History Channel documentary *Zombies: A Living History* and a regular expert on the TV series *True Monsters.* Jonathan lives in Del Mar, California, with his wife, Sara Jo. www.jonathanmaberry.com

ON THE RUN, FOX MULDER
WILL NEED ALL THE HELP
HE CAN GET TO KEEP AHEAD
OF A MYSTERIOUS NEW
VILLAIN WHO HAS HIS SIGHTS
SET ON THE U.S. GOVERNMENT.

THE X FILES™
SEASON 11

THE NEW SEASON BEGINS HERE!

JOE HARRIS
MATTHEW DOW SMITH
JORDIE BELLAIRE
MENTON3